THE BINGO KILLER

Copyright © 2024 By Travis Knight

All rights reserved. No part of this book may be used or reproduced in any form whatsoever without written permission except in the case of brief quotations in critical articles or reviews.

This book is a work of fiction. Names, characters, businesses, organizations, places, events and incidents either are the product of the author's imagination or are used fictitiously. Any resemblance to actual persons, living or dead, events, or locales is entirely coincidental.

For more information, or to book an event, contact: knighttravis280@gmail.com

Book design by Travis Knight
Cover design by Travis Knight

Dear Reader:

Thank you for taking the time to read my debut novel, **The Bingo Killer**. This story is the first book in a series of four action-packed adventures of Detectives Sam Riley and Kate Barker. This series has been nothing short of three years of exploring my creative side, numerous rewrites and edits and ultimately, parting with dear friends as I set my detectives out into the world for readers to enjoy.

- **Travis**

Prologue

April 17th

1:54 p.m.

Franklin Fawcett laid comfortably in his bed at the Golden Years Retirement Home where he chose to spend his remaining years. His days were mostly confined by an oxygen mask a few times a day and a special diet. He had the capacity to walk up and down the hallways as exercise. His nurse, Cynthia, came into his room to check his vitals.

Franklin jolted awake when he heard her voice so loud and close to him. He looked around the room in a slight confusion. "Cynthia, call my daughter for me. I need to speak to her. It's majorly important."

"Right after I check your vitals, Mr. Franklin. Give you your afternoon meds, okay?"

"Oh, thank you so much, Cynthia. You're an angel! A real sweetheart."

"I'll straighten out your pillow for you too. Looks like it's causing you some problems."

Cynthia refilled his water, threw away old tissues and finished checking on her patient before she left

THE BINGO KILLER

his room. Cynthia was one of the better nurses at the Home.

Franklin resumed his attention to reruns of older shows from the 70's and 80's.

Cynthia made her way to the nurses station and called Robin Mills. Robin had asked Cynthia to call her if her dad needed her or if he needed medical attention.

On the second ring, Robin answered her cell phone.

"Miss Robin, your father asked me to call you and see if you had any free time this afternoon to come see him. He said it's very important."

"What did he want?" She loved her father more nowadays, having overcome a lot of the issues of their past. It's safe to say this is one of the reasons she chose her career in psychology. Helping herself by helping others.

"He didn't say what exactly, only he wants to speak with you, Ms. Robin."

"Thank you, Cynthia, I'll come down there as soon as I can. Probably after work."

"Alright, Ms. Robin. We'll see you then. Bye now!"

Robin came to see her father after hours. Her office wasn't too far from the Home and at least she could avoid rush hour traffic.

Cynthia was checking on her patient again when Robin knocked softly on his door.

"Hi dad," she said as she came in all smiles.

"Her smile can light up any room she walks into. I feel better already." Franklin held out his arms and warmly smiled at his daughter. "Come in, come on, my dear Robin. Give your dad a hug."

Robin leaped over to hug her dad tight. She patted his shoulders hard enough to be sincere but not hurt the man. "How are you today?"

"Better now that you're here," Franklin said with a smile. He pointed at Cynthia. "She keeps running off and leaving me high and dry." Franklin laughed. "She pops in like a little bird looking for twigs to build a nest.

"Now, Mr. Franklin, you know I have other residents to care for. Besides, I can only handle you in small doses."

Franklin laughed. "That's the way I like it, darlin'."

Robin laughed. "Be nice, Dad."

He held Robin's hand.

"I'll let you two visit while I go make my rounds," Cynthia said.

"Thank you, Cynthia," Robin said.

Cynthia quickly left Franklin's room.

Franklin dropped his cute old man act. "Close the door, Robin. I don't want anyone hearing our conversation. We got a lotta shit to yap about."

Robin closed the door. "What's on your mind, Dad?"

"You tell me, Robin? What is on my mind?"

Robin sat confused at her dad's sudden request. "What do you mean?"

Franklin took a deep breath and sighed, like he was annoyed at having to explain himself. "Listen to me, Robin. You know my past and the questionable things I've done over the years.

"Yes I do, but let's not talk about that right now."

Franklin gave his daughter a concerning look. "We have to talk about it, Robin. I have unfinished business and you're going to finish it for me. I don't trust anyone else but you. Your brothers and sisters don't want anything to do with me. You're my only child who can carry on the legacy."

"I'm not sure what you're talking about. Are you feeling okay, Dad?"

"I'm fine, dammit! Look, I don't know how much time I have left and I have some scores to settle with certain individuals who tried to stop me years ago."

"What do you mean scores to settle? I don't understand what you're saying."

Franklin gazed forward and focused on his feet.

Robin waited for him to speak and tensed up when she heard his voice in her mind. "Did you just speak without speaking, Dad?"

Franklin nodded. His eyes were glazed over, like he was in a haze or fog.

"Dad, you're freaking me out. Stop this!" Robin said in a panic. She grabbed his hand and shook his arm about to snap him out of his self-induced trance.

Relax, Robin. I have a special trick that has served me well over the years.

"Easy for you to say," she said softly. "Why are you telling me this now?"

"You have this gift too, Robin. You got it from me."

KNIGHT

"How do you know I have this gift?" Robin asked.

"Robin, I made sure you had it before I decided to say something to you."

"How so?"

"I've been testing you during your visits the past few months and you didn't even know it."

Robin wasn't sure what exactly her father was spouting off about. But she felt used. Mistreated and violated in so many ways. "Dad, tell me what you mean by testing me, dammit!"

Franklin laughed at his daughters' curse. "That mouth of yours, girl! I see what's on the horizon and we have to get our shit together to tie up loose ends and get our money back," Franklin asserted.

"And if I say no, Dad?"

"We don't have a choice, Robin. It's time for you to step up and take my place as a Believer. Maybe you'll be more ruthless than I was and finish things right this time."

"I knew it! I fucking knew it!!" *God, how could I have been so dumb and blind to think he had something important to actually tell me?* "Just a matter of time before you start with your Believer bullshit."

Franklin kept silent and looked at Robin.

She shook her head in disgust. "No, Dad! You don't say things like that to me."

"Prove your worth to me. It's not like you have to kill anyone. We have people out there who will do that for you."

"Who's we?" Robin inquired.

"Pawns in the game, Robin."

"I'm not killing anyone for you or anyone. That's a deal breaker," Robin said.

"You don't have to. I've already taken care of that for you."

"How fucking convenient!"

"You have no idea, Robin."

"I don't want any part of this," Robin declared. "I have a good life and a good job. I help people. I don't want the life you led. I have my own and I'm not risking it for you, no matter how much money is involved."

"Millions, Robin. MILLIONS!" Franklin said loudly.

Robin looked at her dad with contempt. "Millions? Why not let someone else get it? Why me?"

Franklin glared up at the television.

"Yes, I remember him and the trial."

"What about him, Dad?"

Franklin told Robin his plan. "George Nettles stole ten million dollars from us."

"I don't believe you, dad. This is all some sick game I'm not interested in playing."

"Wanna bet?" Franklin said, laughing.

"What?" Robin asked.

"Come in!"

"There's no one—" Robin jumped at the loud knocking at the door. Robin had a shocked look on her face. "Cynthia, right on time—" Robin looked back at the door and saw a middle aged man, with a mustache, walking into the room.

"Naw, I'm not Cynthia," the man said.

Robin looked back at her father. "Who is this man, Dad?"

"Brother Pete. Welcome back, my boy!" Franklin smiled. "I've missed you."

"Not anymore. I'm Al Dockson now. I'm a changed man now but I have the same soul."

Franklin shook Al's hand wildly. "Good to see you after all these years. You're lookin' good for your age, sonny boy!"

"Thank you, sir. It's great to be back in The Masters' graces again."

"Yeah, I hate to break up this little reunion we got going here but can either of you tell me what the hell is going on? Why am I here?" Robin asked.

"He was my right hand man back in the old days. There's nothing he couldn't do. He's the James Bond of criminals—this guy!" Franklin poked his finger at his old associate. "He's here to smooth things over for me."

Robin looked at Al. "Why the name change? Do you need an alias?"

Yeah, he dresses the part. He looks like he's from a 70's disco club in New York.

Franklin focused back on his daughter. "I heard that Robin. Show some respect to our guest."

"What are you talking about—you heard what I was thinking. Of course you did!" Robin threw her

THE BINGO KILLER

hands up and slapped her knees. "I forgot. My dad's one of the X-Men. The bald guy in the wheelchair."

Al glanced over at Robin and spoke in a low tone. "That wasn't a nice thing to say about our leader, young lady."

Robin looked back at Al with an annoyed look on her face. "Do you know what a joke is?"

"I do."

"I don't think you do. I don't need your permission to joke around with my father. While I'm down this rabbit hole, I don't give two shits why you're here. I have no use for you or this cockamamie plan."

"Now, hold on there. You don't know that for sure. I'm more involved than you think."

Franklin smiled at seeing his daughter and Al go back and forth like barking chihuahuas after the doorbell went off.

"Still dont give a shit." Robin looked at her dad and sighed. "Well if this guy is working for you, then I think I have to as well, so he doesn't fuck up and derail the entire plan. I don't particularly care to hear what business of yours is unfinished but I also don't trust honky-tonk Travis Bickle over here."

"Are you in, Robin? Make me proud!"

Robin sat in her thoughts for a few seconds as she stared out the window. *Fuck, I'm going to regret this but the money is enticing. Everyone has a price I guess. I already regret this. That's my dilemma and it will be for years to come. I wonder how far I can take these psychic powers. I'd be a fool not to take advantage of my powers. I can do all sorts of experiments on people. It's worth exploring for the benefit of science. I can test the boundaries of ethics and dance on the other side of the law.*

Franklin spoke to his daughter through his gift. *Robin, my favorite daughter, it's your time to take my place. I want you to take my place within the Believers. Take care of loose ends and get the money back from Nettles.*

Only if I'm in charge. I CALL THE FUCKING SHOTS!

Franklin stared at Robin.

I want your word, Dad. You and I are mentally linked now. I'm going to work on my powers and take them to a new level. I have no choice. That's what will keep us safe.

People like us, we're never safe.

Robin looked at her dad. "Danger is a matter of perspective. I think it's being creative."

"See boss, she gets it. Finally!" Al winked at Robin.

Franklin smiled. "She's my daughter."

"Fuck you! Stand over there by the door and shut up!" Robin pointed at the door with an angry vigor.

Al crossed his arms and leaned against the wall in defiance of Robin Mills.

Franklin glanced at Al. *So far so good. She just needed a little motivation. Just ignore her for now.*

Al nodded. "What's our assignment?"

"Assignment? Are you in the 3rd grade?" Robin asked.

Franklin demanded Robin drop her brashness.

"Not while he's here." She pointed at Al.

"He's here because I asked him to be here. He's very much needed, like you wouldn't know. Al's a professional."

"Professional loser?" Robin asked, looking Al up and down.

"You're wasting my time. Robin, you're The Master now. You're in charge."

"Fine! What do you want us to do?" Robin asked.

Franklin coughed and struggled to take a deep breath. "Guide Al as he makes his way East to Illinois to meet up with Sister Lily. She doesn't know he's coming yet. Robin, your powers go far and wide."

"What's so special about Illinois?" Robin asked.

"Loose ends that can send us all to prison. One stuck a knife in my side and took Sister Lily away from us. Another one who was bad with our numbers but good at hiding them."

"I'll take care of them." Al looked at Robin with a smirk. "Besides, my bride is there."

"Your bride?" Robin asked with a quick laugh. "Sister Lily?"

"That's right. The love of my life."

"Lucky you! If she's anything like you, we're so, so blessed." Robin said with an eyeroll that could make the seasons change.

"Your sarcasm is cute, Robin, but unnecessary. You're the Master now. Act like it," Franklin demanded.

"Fine. I'll cut him a break." Robin looked at Al. "You better prove yourself to me. I wanna see just how loyal you really are. Just because you have history with my father, doesn't mean shit to me."

Al laughed. "You're a real firecracker, aren't you?"

Robin stood up and took a few steps towards Al. She stopped a foot in front of him. She practiced her new psychic powers by communicating with him.

Al wasn't sure what Robin was trying to tell him. Her powers weren't that strong as of that moment. All Al could do was laugh and take a quick bow before Robin. "At your service, ma'am!" Al raised and pointed his finger at Robin. "WHOO!!" Al glanced at Franklin. "I'll see you, boss. Nice meeting you, Robin. We'll be in touch." Al strutted out of the room.

"Asshhole!" Robin turned back to her dad. "What the hell was that?"

Franklin smiled. "My insurance policy. It'll take you some time to get your powers at a decent, helpful level."

"He needs a psych evaluation. Not by me. He doesn't stand a fair chance. I know something's wrong with that man."

Franklin laughed. "You're the Captain flying the plane, Robin! You make sure passengers are in the right headspace."

"Don't think I owe you or him anything. I didn't want any of this but you pushed it into my lap."

"Take the money, Robin. I'll die happy knowing you get it instead of your opponent."

"Opponent?"

"Yes, one just like you!"

THE BINGO KILLER

"Great! More good news! One just like me! PERFECT!!!" Robin declared. "Another Master?"

"Another psychic. Level up your powers, Robin. Make them fear you. Respect you."

"How do I do that?" she asked.

"Use your imagination. You're a smart woman and now a dangerous one. And you can make him think it's his own damn fault. That's the fun."

Robin got up and looked out the window.

Chapter 1

Monday, Sept. 1st.

5:30 a.m.

"Fuck, if it isn't Monday. That damn alarm clock waking me up so damn early," I said as I rubbed the grit out of my eyes. Like most people, I laid in bed for a few more minutes, wondering why I wasn't CEO of my own company where the rules didn't apply to me as much. I looked over to my right and saw an empty space where my ex-girlfriend used to sleep. Savannah Rose had been gone for a few months now. *I hope you're happy now, Savannah. I wanted to be the one waiting at the end of the aisle for you. But you had other plans with another guy.*

"Time to go to work," I belted out to myself. I guess I developed the habit of talking to myself in an empty house. *Officer Sam Riley reporting for duty on my last day as a patrol officer. Tomorrow, I'll be a homicide detective. Hopefully!* A quick shower and ten minutes later, I'm in full uniform, heading to my kitchen for two bowls of Raisin Bran and a glass of orange juice. I grabbed my utility belt and headed to the police station for the morning roll call on A-shift. I loved the peace and quiet of living in a small, one story, three-bedroom house on the outskirts of Bloomfield.

6:20 a.m.

Walking into a half-empty squad room at the BPD had become second nature to me and like my second home. I had sat in every seat in this room over the years but still didn't have a favorite. The squad room was filled with older, sturdy tables with scratched surfaces, blue carpet and cream-colored walls. A wooden podium towered in front of the room, near the windows with lowered white blinds. Two large dry-erase boards hung behind the podium for important police information: patrol assignments and the donut flavor of the week. Information vital to our job.

"How's everybody this morning?" I asked my fellow officers.

"Another day, another dollar," said Officer Rick Pickens. "Rick Pick" as we called him. Pickens was about 6'4", with a mustache just as thick as his country accent. Pickens was the no-nonsense, just the facts and by-the-book type of officer.

"Good morning, Riley," Davis said, between bites of his bacon and egg breakfast sandwich. Davis, with his short height of 5'2", as well as a rounder belly that made him a good candidate for a mall-Santa Claus in his retirement years. Davis' attitude was passive but he can get serious when he needs to. He's a good cop but not someone I'd want to be partnered with. We wouldn't last more than a day or two before I just drove off and left him somewhere and patrolled Bloomfield by myself.

"I see you're off to a good start this morning. Better than my sugar breakfast," I said.

"Fruity Pebbles?" Davis asked.

"Two bowls of Raisin Bran."

"I should have known you were the cereal type. I prefer a more healthy breakfast," Davis said.

"Sugar versus cholesterol. Take your pick, Davis."

My unofficial partner, Officer John Sloan, walked into the room and took a seat behind me. Sloan was born and raised in Bloomfield. Same as me. We went to school together—a grade apart but we've been friends ever since. I liked having Sloan as a partner, more than the other officers. We've worked well together over the years. Sloan's good with the forensics side of law enforcement and was often eager to assist with various crimes, even if he wasn't directly involved in covering those crimes.

"Hey John, how's it going?" I turned to ask Sloan.

"Tired as hell, man! I haven't had my coffee yet. That's my first priority this morning. What about you?"

"Can't complain. How was your weekend?"

"Me and my girls went fishing down at the river. I caught a few but threw most of them back. The girls fished for a few minutes but started playing. After a while, the girls said they wanted pizza so we went into town for dinner," Sloan said with a smile. "I'm always outnumbered when it comes to family dinners."

"Yes, you are, Sloan. I haven't been fishing in so long,"

"We'll have to go sometime," Sloan said.

"Yeah, before it gets too cold, as long as we stand on the bank. No boat. You know that, Sloan. I still have nightmares of almost drowning while saving that kid in that damn Arkansas lake."

Sloan nodded, "I imagine so, Riley."

The thought of falling overboard into the lake and drowning scares me to my core.

A few other officers walked in the room and sat down in empty chairs.

Patrol Sergeant J.D. Whine strolled in like he was a war hero—smooth, calm and cool. Whine was a good sergeant and I respected the man.

"Good morning, day shift. Let's make this short and quick. First, roll call." Whine pulled the attendance sheet out and counted the room. "It's Monday and you know what that means."

"Anderson?"
"Sleeping!"
"Davis?"
"At the buffet."
"Riley?"
"Meditating!"
"Sloan?"
"Gone fishing."
"Sparks?"

"Hawaii–"

"Crisp?"

"Caribbean cruise–"

"Prater?"

"Flying to Vegas."

"Pickens?"

"On vacation."

"O'Malley?"

"Getting laid."

"Brown?"

"Chicago Bears game."

"Carson?"

"Cruisin!'"

"Harris?"

"Here!"

The officers pointed and smiled at Harris during roll call. "That poor sucker said "here," and according to our long-standing tradition, that officer has to buy lunch for their partner that Monday. We only do it on a Monday, mainly to see who's paying attention. I haven't said "here" in a year.

Whine smiled and pointed at Harris. "Took you all long enough. Harris has to buy lunch today."

"Shit, not a good way to start the day. This is gonna cost me in more ways than one. Please don't give me Davis, sarge," Harris said.

Davis laughed hysterically as he looked over at Harris. "Come on Sarge, me and Harris haven't partnered in a while."

THE BINGO KILLER

"No, hell no! I'm not putting you two together today. I don't want this town to run out of food." Sergeant Whine said. "Chief Williams will kick my ass."

Laughter filled the room as Davis shook his head.

Whine grabbed his glasses and shuffled his papers. "Okay, today's partner assignments are as follows so listen carefully. Anderson and Davis will patrol the south end of town. Riley and Sloan are heading North to catch the Northside Burglar. Crisp and Brown—Downtown! Sparks and Prater are headed to the wild, wild west side of Bloomfield. Pickens and O'Malley—the east side of town. Carson and Harris, you two are backup support, floaters. Respond as needed," Whine said. Whine continued with the briefing and reminded them of the dangers we face. "As some of you may have heard, Don's Donuts was broken into early this morning around three o'clock this morning and it looks like the work of the Northside Burglar. I can't tell you how important it is that we catch this guy."

"What is that, like the fifth break-in?" I asked. "I wonder if the seven cars that have been vandalized since May are related?"

"Yeah, something like that," Whine said. "Two homes and three businesses up there also."

"We'll do our best to keep an eye out for him," I said. Today, more than previous days, felt different in our pursuit of The Northside Burglar. Maybe we have new evidence that leads us to this guy?

"Carson, you are thinking about what you want for lunch. Don't let Harris off cheap, now. You get that combo plate, ya hear! Take a picture of it and send it to me so I know it's going down," Whine said, with a laugh.

"Taco Heaven has a good combo plate," David said. "That's where me and Anderson are going for lunch."

Anderson looked at Davis. "That's all you think about. Food! Food! Food! What's good to eat!"

"No, I don't." Davis said, confused.

"Yeah, you do. You talk about food more than anything else. This is what I have to listen to for the next twelve hours. But you know what's good in this town and all the good deals," Anderson said. "Mr. Menu, over here."

Davis looked up proudly, smiled and whispered, "Yeah, I do."

"Also, Chief Williams will announce who's made the detective position that came open recently, with Tucker's retirement. So good luck to all those who applied. Riley, Sloan, Carson and Harris, stick around for a few minutes. I want to talk to you guys. Okay, that's all I've got today. Anybody have anything else?" asked Whine.

"No?" He paused. "Be safe out there. Get to it!"

I stayed behind with Sloan, Carson and Harris while the other officers grabbed their papers, gear, and filed out of the squad room to their assigned areas.

THE BINGO KILLER

"Okay, you guys, Chief wants this guy caught. Riley and Sloan have the northside this morning. Carson and Harris, I want you guys to stick close to the north end as well, in case backup is needed. You two can swoop right in to assist Riley and Sloan. Do your thing. Ask the witnesses and keep your eyes open. He'll slip up and when he does, we'll nail him. Stay in touch and work together. Get at it, gentlemen!"

"Yes, sir!" I said with a smile. "We'll check things out at Dan's Donuts. Get Sloan his gallon of coffee."

"Good idea, Sam. Keep your eyes open," Whine said. "Dismissed gentlemen."

Sloan and I headed to our cruiser and Sloan drove us to the north end of town.

"These 12-hour shifts are always the roughest after having weekends off," Sloan said.

"Yeah, it feels weird having two days off during the week and then starting your week, when most jobs are Monday through Friday. But I don't make the schedule. I just work it," I responded.

"Hard to get going this morning, even with coffee," Sloan replied. "But at least I don't have to spring for lunch today." Sloan had a good sense of humor, especially with two daughters at home. One thing I admired about him over the years.

"What if I left my wallet at home, Sloan?"

"Maybe you'll be mowing my lawn on your day off, Riley?"

I shook my head. "No, thanks."

Hopefully the Chief will choose me as the new detective.

Chapter 2

7:30 a.m.

Officers Sloan and I arrived at Dan's Donuts to interview the witnesses.

"Dispatch, come in?" I asked.

"Go ahead, Unit 07," said Haley Phillips, the dispatcher at the BPD.

"Yeah, Officers Riley and Sloan are en route to Dan's Donut's to follow up on the break-in this morning."

"10-04, Unit 07."

"Let's go talk to these folks."

"Let's do it," Sloan replied.

Sloan and I noticed the damage to the door handle when we approached the front door. I snapped a few pictures of the door for evidence. The lock was busted all to hell and the door didn't shut all the way. Sloan walked up to the counter and asked Molly, the cashier, to speak to the manager.

"Let me guess, the break-in?" asked Molly.

"Correct," Sloan said.

"I'll go get the manager," Molly said.

Sloan and I stood by the counter looking at all the different donuts and pastries.

THE BINGO KILLER

"Damn, those look good," I said.

"Careful Riley, you sound like Davis just then. Except he'd arrest every donut, tag and bag them as his own evidence."

I laughed. "Yeah, he would."

Dan Donner came around the corner. "What can I help you officers with today?"

"Officers Sloan and Riley. We're following up on the break-in this morning," I said. "Do you have surveillance cameras?"

"Yeah, we do in the back. Care for a donut or cinnamon roll first?"

"Oh no! If I have one, I'll eat them all," I stated.

Donner laughed and agreed. "That's why I got into this business."

"Bless you," Sloan said softly before looking at me. "Uh…I'll get a large coffee to go."

"Come on back guys. I'll show you what I showed the other officers earlier this morning when I got here." Donner pointed to the tables. "Say Molly, can you wipe off some of the tables? Just because we got hit doesn't mean we can have things dirty."

"Yes sir!" Molly grabbed a rag from a side counter.

Sloan and I followed Donner to his back office. "I kept the tape at the time the burglar broke in. Easier that way in case I have to show it again," Donner said.

We stood around the tv monitor in his office as Donner pushed play on the control box. The video showed the burglar tearing up the front door lock with a crowbar, coming into the store and going straight for the cash register and then the back office, from a different camera, looking for a safe.

"Just as I suspected, he's wearing all black with a ski-mask. Gloves. Can't make out a positive description, except height. He's about six feet tall. Probably has a toolbelt that he can put his tools on to get in so quick and easily. He's clever but not that smart," I stated.

"Did the burglar take anything? Money? Anything of value?" Sloan asked.

"No, I took my deposit to the bank after we close every day," Donner explained.

"That's a good move, Dan," Sloan said. "Were there any witnesses that you know of?"

"No, he hit before we opened this morning. We opened at five a.m., so he hit before that. In and out," Donner said.

I handed Donner my card. "We'll keep looking and patrolling the area. If you have any questions or remember anything, give us a call."

"I appreciate it, Officer Riley. Don't forget your coffee on the way out."

"No sir!" Sloan quipped.

Molly poured Sloan his cup of coffee before we made our way out to our cruiser.

Sloan dropped two dollars on the counter and turned towards me. "What do you think, Sam?" he asked.

THE BINGO KILLER

I looked back at Dan's Donuts, walking to the cruiser. "Looks like a random hit! Couldn't have been any other business." *Why a donut shop though?*

"Dispatch, we are 10-24 here," I said as I got into our cruiser.

"10-04. Unit 07, we just received a call about a suspicious person loitering around the nail salon in the Pine Point Shopping Center. Caller said the driver is driving a red, two-door truck and taking pictures of their store. Customers are a little worried. Can you swing by and check this out?" Haley asked.

"10-04, dispatch. We are 10-76, en route." I replied.

*****

The sounds of my favorite music echoed through my apartment. You'd think I'd have my own music in rotation in my playlist but no Jill Sanders music allowed. Tickets were available for those songs. I stared at my charging phone by my purse on the kitchen table as the call from my mother went to voicemail. I had just woken up and wasn't ready to interact with the outside world just yet. The puppy calendar near my refrigerator read September 1st. I couldn't believe it was already September. I stood in the middle of my kitchen, deciding my next move--Coffee or a shower? That's when I heard a knock on my front door. *Who in blue blazes has the gaul to visit me so early on my days off? This better be good.* I strolled over to open my door and somewhere near my recliner I heard keys rattling from the outside. A few seconds later, in pops Connie Sanders--My mother, who I affectionately and jokingly dubbed, "Hurricane Connie." Her habit of barging in was a nuisance but I appreciated her. Typical mom-daughter stuff. I didn't get a "hey mom," out before she took off around my apartment like a boomerang thrown in the Australian outback.

"Jill! Jill! Where are you, girl? It's mom," She said loudly as she looked in my kitchen.

"Mom, I'm right here. Hello?" I waved right in her face to get her attention. Nothing! *Oh My God! She's lost it!* I thought to myself.

She then flew into my spare room I used as my music room. Then my bathroom. "Jill! Where are you? It's mom!"

I said from my living room, "Oh my God!! Do you not hear me, Mom? What's wrong with you? Why are you ignoring me? HELLO!!!" The nerve of this woman to ignore me. *Calm down, Jill. Relax and listen. Breathe. Just like you do before you go on stage.* I looked at my mother in tears and couldn't help but freak out. My calming technique wasn't working.

She opened my bedroom door and rushed inside. She screamed my name before she ran back out and collapsed on my couch. Hysterical and in tears.

I frantically walked over to where my mom lay draped across the couch. I grabbed her hand and I squeezed for dear life. How my mom couldn't feel my hand or hear my voice left me in a state of confusion

I've never experienced. Of course, no one could tell because I didn't feel anything, which made it all a thousand times worse. No sweat! I didn't even feel my heartbeat! Was this some sick prank? Was I on one of those reality prank shows? Time's up! What gives? Next thing I knew I'm surrounded by complete darkness. Void of my mothers' voice. Void of the outside world and reality. That's where I was—THE VOID!!

7:55 a.m.

"Good morning, Detective Barker," Sergeant Whine said as we crossed paths in the hallway.

"Morning, JD. How's it going so far?"

Sgt. Whine cringed his face and wobbled his head. "Same shit, different day."

"I'd call that normal, JD. And it's not even eight yet," I replied.

"You're right about that, baby! Bring on the chaos!" Sergeant Whine laughed. Whine always knew how to make me laugh. He got a kick out of seeing me in smiles when he said funny things.

"Duty calls, JD. I'll talk to you later." I grabbed my time card and wrote down 8 a.m. in the starting time square and returned it to the slot. *Detective Kate Barker reporting for duty.* I sat my coffee in its own spot on my desk so it wouldn't spill all over my desk. It's safe to say I'm a bit of an organized nerd. Sue me! I can proudly say no criminal I've ever charged with crimes has been acquitted due to faulty police procedures and paperwork. There is no such thing in my world. I pride myself on being on top of my police work to keep Bloomfield safe. And the Northside Burglar case is no exception. I noticed a police report in my inbox about the break-in of Dan's Donuts a few hours earlier.

I grabbed my coffee and embarked on a quick one minute walk down the cross hall towards the dispatch side of the building. "Good morning, Haley," I said, approaching the dispatch booth.

"Good morning, Detective Barker," Haley replied.

Betsy Riddle, the blonde-haired, blue eyed, 5'8" janitor working the BPD, had just clocked in and stopped at the dispatch desk. "Good morning, ladies."

"Morning, Betsy," I said. "Busy day?"

"Yeah, everyday is busy around here," Betsy said. "That's how I like it."

"Yeah, me too. Makes the time go faster," I quipped.

"Morning, Haley!" Betsy said.

"Hey Betsy! Don't work too hard." Haley said.

"You ladies work harder than me. Guess I better get started." Betsy walked towards the custodian's closet a few feet away, around the corner, from dispatch to get her cleaning cart ready.

"Later Betsy!" Haley said. Haley graduated from the University of Illinois a few years ago with a double Bachelor's degree in communications and psychology. She moved back to be closer to her family until something better came along, although she had good job security working the day shift dispatch, from 7 a.m. to 3 p.m. Haley was a great asset to our department.

"What can I do for you, Detective Barker?"

I replied, "Please, call me Ms. Barker. I insist." I took a sip of coffee.

"Sure, Ms. Barker. As long as I'm not breaking any rules?"

"No, of course not, Haley." I smiled. "See, I call you Haley and I'm not breaking any rules," I said.

Haley laughed. "You kind of make the rules around here, Ms. Barker."

I nodded. "I think you're doing an amazing job. I need to know everything about the break-in from Don's Donuts."

"Absolutely. I can give you my call log in sheets from last night. I'll pull the officer's reports as well."

"You are a saint," I said. "I appreciate the fast cooperation. You have a good grasp on records and paperwork."

"Thanks. Years of practice in action." Haley retrieved the reports from a small mountain of paperwork on the other side of her desk, from the "to-be processed" tray and made copies. I took another sip as Phillips presented me with what I asked for. "Okay. I have an incident report, property destruction report and a copy of the 911 call sheet. There you go."

"Alright. That should help me out a lot this morning. I appreciate it, Haley, as always."

"Anytime, Ms. Barker. Glad I can help."

"You know, Haley, I was thinking, we should grab lunch one day this week."

"Sure. I usually take my lunch around noon but I can go anytime that's good for you," Haley said.

"Absolutely. I know where to find you." I felt my cell phone vibrate and quickly answered the call. I grabbed the papers and waved goodbye to Phillips. "Detective Barker speaking."

Officer O'Malley informed me of the 911 call he just received about a woman finding her daughter dead in her bedroom apartment.

"Damn, that's horrible. Where's the apartment?" I asked.

"Eaglewood Apartments. Apt. Four, near the main office."

"Got it. I'll be there shortly. Thanks for calling, O'Malley."

"Sure thing, Detective Barker."

I hung up the phone and scurried back to my desk to grab my report binder. God forbid I leave without my coffee. Two minutes later, I'm out the door, on my way to the Eaglewood Apartment Complex on the east side of town.

8:30 a.m.

THE BINGO KILLER

Sloan and I arrived at the Pine Point parking lot with minimal traffic on a Monday morning. "Dispatch, we are 10-20 on scene, driving to the location now. Stand by for a moment," I radioed back to dispatch.

"10-04."

"Dispatch, negative on that 10-37. We didn't see any red truck at this location that fits the description," I said. "10-12 for a moment while we talk to the witnesses."

"10-04, Unit 07."

Sloan and I walked into Nia's Nail Salon and spoke to Tara Brown, the receptionist and cashier. "Good morning. I'm Officer Sloan and this is Officer Riley. We got a call about a suspicious vehicle driving by the salon a few minutes ago."

"Yeah, umm, it was a red two-door truck. He just stopped out front and took pictures of the front of the store. It's all glass windows. Same as all the other businesses here," said Brown.

"Did you happen to get a good look at the guy? Was he wearing anything that stood out?" I asked.

Brown said she thought the man wore a black ski mask and a green coat. "I thought that was odd because it's not quite sweater weather yet. It's still 80 degrees in the afternoon here."

I wrote down the details Brown gave us. "Did you get a license plate by any chance?"

"I stepped over to the window to write the license plate number down but didn't see one," Brown said.

"It must have been on the front of his truck if he had one at all."

"Do you have cameras out front or just inside?"

"Just inside here," Brown said. She pointed to the one in the corner behind her, overlooking the entire salon and another one in the back corner, giving the opposite view.

"Can we speak to your manager, please?" Sloan asked.

"Absholutely." Brown called her manager to the front to speak with us.

"Hi, I'm Jen Jenkins. Can I help you officers?" Jenkins was an older woman, with short styled, blonde hair. She had on a black top and blue-gray pants. She fit the part of salon owner.

"Can we see the security footage of your salon from the past twenty minutes, please. We're inquiring about the suspicious truck that drove by earlier," I asked politely.

"Sure. Follow me to the back." Jenkins said, smiling at me.

Sloan wobbled his head at me, then at Jenkins.

We followed Jenkins to the manager's office and took a seat as she pulled up the footage from earlier.

"There's the truck. It's slowing down. I see the camera. Can't make out a face. Truck drove off. No plate in the back," Sloan said.

"Nothing," I said. "Looks like he's done this before. And there he goes driving off." *This guy must*

THE BINGO KILLER

have a good time frame for each burglary—something he's perfected the past few months, I thought to myself.

"Thank you so much for your time," Sloan said. "We'll keep an eye on the roads for the rest of our shift.

"If you see the truck driving by again anytime, give us a call immediately and try to look for a license plate if you can." I handed Jenkins my card. *Worth a shot!*

"We will for sure. Thank you for coming," Jenkins said.

"This may be the guy," I said, walking back to the cruiser. "Dispatch, this is Unit 07, we're done here at the salon. The manager showed us the security footage of a red truck but negative on any plate or positive ID."

"10-04, Unit 07."

"Dispatch, 10-76, back downtown for a while," I said. "10-77 is ten minutes."

"Copy that, Unit 07."

Chapter 3

8:30 a.m.

I parked next to the cruiser in front of the main office. A slight breeze blew through the air, causing my hair to dance freely around me. I paused to collect and fix my hair before walking inside apartment 4B.

"Morning, Detective Barker."

"Morning, O'Malley. Do we know who the victim is?"

O'Malley told me the victim was 30-year-old Jill Sanders, an up-and-coming singer and musician. Her popularity grew over the past five years since she started singing publicly.

"I've heard of her," I replied as I put my gloves on.

Sanders' apartment was decorated with different works of art and pictures of dancers, performers and concert hall stages and old records hung about as art. Sanders' apartment was simple and damn near spotless, although my guess is she didn't spend much time there.

"Wow, this place is really clean," I exclaimed. "Better than my place."

"It was that way when we got here," O'Malley said. "Impressive to say the least."

I noticed two older women sitting on the couch in the living room. I turned to O'Malley and whispered, "Is that the victim's mother?"

O'Malley nodded. "Yeah, her name's Connie Sanders. She's been here since she called 911. I assume the mother called her friend, Mary Owens, after her 911 call. They were both here when we arrived."

Connie Sanders, sat on the couch in the living room, comforted by her friend, Mary. Connie didn't say anything but cried harder when she looked up and saw me.

"I'll talk to them shortly. Is the coroner on the way?" I looked at the hallway leading to the bedroom and bathroom.

"Yes, I called them after I called you."

"Forensics?" I asked.

"On their way as well," O'Malley said.

"Thanks for doing that. Good work, O'Malley."

"I'll take a look at the body first, then talk to Connie Sanders."

"She's in the bedroom. On the right, over there," O'Malley said.

"Thank you."

I slowly walked into Jill's room and saw her lying in bed, neatly tucked in, undisturbed, peaceful. I glanced around the room for blood or anything out of place.

KNIGHT

Nothing looks out of place. It's harder to see something out of place in a clean home than a dirty house. The closet door is closed. A glass of water on the nightstand, next to the antique glass lamp. No dirty footsteps on the white carpet. House shoes placed neatly beside her bed. "Seems too clean for a single woman," I said to myself. I opened the closet door, looked under both sides of the bed and around the nightstand. Nothing but dust. I went to the kitchen and saw Jill's purse and phone on the kitchen table. "Connie, can you show me Jill's phone?"

Connie slowly got up off the couch and walked over to the table. I gave her the phone and she showed me Jill's calls–both in and outgoing. I scrolled through her calls but didn't find anything of concern. All of her calls were accounted for including the many calls from Connie herself. Connie then dug through Jill's purse but nothing suspicious was found. The purse fell over on its side and an empty, torn, white tea packet stuck to the underside caught my eye. I asked Connie about the small packet but she had no idea where it could have come from. *Probably nothing but why risk it?*

Ten-year veteran Coroner Ernie Smalls walked through the door with his exam bag. Mr. Smalls reminded me of one of the characters in *The Sandlot*—the one they called "Smalls." Somewhere during our time working together I started calling him by his last name, which was a throwback to one of the popular movies of my childhood.

"Morning, Ern," O'Malley yelped out.

Connie and Mary looked at Smalls.

"Morning, O'Malley?"

O'Malley nodded.

Smalls looked at the two ladies sitting on the couch. "Parents?"

"Yeah!" O'Malley said sparingly.

Smalls walked over to me standing in the kitchen. "Good morning, Detective Barker."

"Morning, Smalls. And no, it's really not a good morning," I said. "Follow me through here, Smalls."

I stood by the bedroom door and pointed inside. Smalls sat his bag down on the foot of the bed and walked over to Jill's side of the bed. "Subject appears to be resting nicely in the covers I see."

"Yeah, my guess is she died right there, in her sleep. Natural causes probably. I didn't see any blood on her head or neck. None on the sheets. No red marks around her neck."

"No, I don't see any from this side." Smalls walked around to the other side of the bed and looked at Jill's body. "None from this side that I see either. Now we can remove the covers slowly down to the feet. I'll need your help, Detective."

"You're killing me, Smalls," I quipped.

Smalls laughed. "I get that a lot, Detective. I don't mind at all." Smalls looked in his bag and grabbed a pair of blue gloves for himself and a par for me. We both slowly pulled the covers back to Jills' feet. She wore a vintage, black Rolling Stones t-shirt and gray sweatpants. No socks. "No signs of blood on her clothes or feet. None on her arms, wrists or hands. Might be natural causes?"

"Doesn't look like any signs of forced entry or anything. Nothing's out of place. There's no dishes in the sink or cups left out. Nothing to indicate someone else was here the past few days, besides just her," I replied. "Fresh bag in the trash can."

"We'll get her back to the coroner's office, do our autopsy, tox screen and see what we come up with. Excuse me for a moment while I go get the stretcher." Smalls grabbed his bag and left the apartment.

I stayed in the room with Sanders. The silence in the whole apartment was interrupted by a soft whimpering from the living room. I sighed and took a deep breath as I knew I would have to face the toughest part of my job: talking with a grieving parent. But I still had a job to do.

"Excuse me, Mr. O'Malley," Smalls said as he finessed the stretcher into Jill's apartment.

O'Malley quickly jumped out of the way, cleaning a path. "Sorry, sorry!"

Smalls tried his best to maintain his tough, no bullshit exterior demeanor, even avoiding eye contact with Connie Sanders as he pushed the stretcher back to the bedroom. He opened the door as wide as he could and rolled the stretcher in with ease, as he had done this a thousand times before. He lowered the stretcher to floor level to be as gentle with Jill as possible. "Okay, Detective Barker. I'll need your help if you don't mind. If you would please, come to the end of the bed, grab her feet while I stand by the nightstand and grab her shoulders. I'll swing her out over the stretcher and we can gently set her down."

"I'm grabbing her feet?"

"Yes. Go on three. One. Two. Three." We sat Jill down peacefully on the stretcher. Smalls got a white sheet out of his bag, covered her body and tucked the sheet under her feet and back. He then clamped and pulled the straps to hold her body down tight in place.

I stood by as Smalls raised the stretcher.

"Okay, she's ready for transport back to the morgue."

"Hang on, Smalls. Don't go anywhere yet," I demanded.

"Why? What's up, Detective Barker?"

I quickly stepped into the living room. "Officer O'Malley, would you join us for a minute here please?"

O'Malley came into the room without hesitation, walking past Connie Sanders and her friend.

"Close the door, please O'Malley," I asked. I spoke in a low tone so as not to give too much out in case they were listening at the door. "Okay, here's what we're going to do. O'Malley, you go outside and wait by the door. I'll take Connie Sanders and the other woman to the manager's office, across the parking lot and use their conference room to ask them some questions. When I get over there, give Smalls a signal and only then, can he take Jill's body out to the transport vehicle and head back to the morgue. I'm trying to save that poor woman as much grief as I can. Sound like a plan, guys?"

"Yes, it sure does," O'Malley said.

"I'll follow your lead Detective Barker," Smalls said.

"O'Malley, you go first and keep watch by the door," I ordered before opening the door and walking out. I went straight to where Connie sat. "Connie Sanders, I'm Detective Kate Barker with the Bloomfield Police Department. First and foremost, let me offer my deepest sympathies for your loss. I can't imagine what you're going through."

Connie sat on the couch, covered in tears. She held Mary's hand for comfort. Connie gave me her scarce attention. I felt her sorrow.

"Thank you," Connie whimpered, barely shaking her head, followed by more tears.

"Connie, I know this isn't a good time but I need to ask you a few questions if you feel up to it. We can go to the manager's office across the way to talk."

"I could use some fresh air," Connie said. "I need to get out of here for a while."

"Sure. There's plenty of fresh air between here and there," I said. We stood up and moved towards the door.

Chapter 4

9:30 a.m.

Connie and Mary entered the main office before I did. I spoke to the receptionist, "Good morning, I need to speak to these two women alone, in a conference room or some place private."

"I'm sorry. We only reserve our hospitality room for actual residents and I don't remember seeing you here before, so NO!" Monroe said rudely, rolling her eyes, as she went back to reading her magazine.

I laughed at the attitude this young lady threw in my face. "Oh, really? Is that so?" I said as I looked at her name plate on the desk. "Tiffany, is it? Guess what, girl? I'm not asking for your permission."

Tiffany looked up at me and again, rolled her eyes hard enough to shift the poles a few degrees.

I grabbed my badge and glared at Tiffany. "My partner here says I can use any goddamn room in this place I want. I'll take them to your house and ask my questions in your living room if I damn well please. Do you understand me, Ms. Monroe?"

Tiffany slowly looked up at me and spoke softly. "Yes ma'am!"

"Good! I DON'T think you want to see my backup," I quipped, pulling my jacket behind my sidearm.

She shook her head and looked down to avoid eye contact with me. "No, ma'am!"

"I think we understand each other here. Thank you, Tiffany."

"I'll show you to our hospitality room," Tiffany said, as she stood up.

"Thank you so much! Ironic how you finally show some hospitality instead of going to jail for obstruction of a police investigation, TIFFANY!!" I had no intention of following through on what I said to Tiffany. I just wanted to give her a lesson in customer service. And I think she got the message.

Tess Taylor, Property Manager at the Eaglewood Apartment complex, flew out around the corner, from her office. "What is going on out here?" She saw Tiffany standing by the edge of her desk. Tess looked at her receptionist with disdain. "Tiffany, how do we treat our guests?"

"Sorry, Ms. Taylor."

"You should be. I'm so sorry you ladies had to see all this." Tess smiled and gave me her undivided attention. "How can I help you?"

I extended my hand out to greet Tess. "Detective Kate Barker of the Bloomfield Police Department."

"Is everything alright?"

I informed Tess that Jill Sanders was found dead in her apartment about thirty minutes ago.

THE BINGO KILLER

Tess gasped and held her face with both hands. "Oh my god, I'm sorry to hear that. Jill was a lovely girl and a great person."

"That she was. I need a place to talk with Jill's mother, Connie."

"Of course. Absolutely. Follow me, please!" Tess led us to a safe, secluded space further into the main office. "Let me know I can get your ladies anything."

Mary and Connie found a comfortable seat on the couch. I sat in a chair at the end of the couch next to Connie. Tess closed the door behind us.

"I have to apologize for my brashness a few seconds ago. I'm normally not that hot-tempered but she pushed the wrong button this morning."

"It's quite alright—"

"No, Connie. She was very rude to us. You didn't deserve that."

"I have a feeling about you, Detective Barker. I have good reason to believe you'll find out what happened to my daughter and who did this," Connie said.

"Thank you! That means a lot to me, Connie. Thank you for agreeing to speak with me this morning despite your tragedy and heartbreak to say the least. This is the hardest part of my job and it never gets any easier. The day it becomes easier is the day I QUIT!" I said loudly, hammering my point home. *When it's acceptable to tell parents their children are dead, that's when humanity is lost and I want no part of it.*

Connie and Mary smiled.

I thanked Mary for comforting Connie. "I appreciate you being here Mary. More than you know. It's good to know Connie has your love and support through all this."

"Thank you!" Mary said, holding Connie's hands. "Anything for my best friend."

I looked at Connie. "Can you tell me exactly what happened before you found Jill in her bed?"

"Well, I called several times trying to get a hold of her last night and a few this morning. I sent several texts too. It wasn't like her to not answer my calls or texts. I knew immediately something was wrong. So, I came right over first thing this morning and found her in her bed," Connie explained.

"I saw on her phone that she had four missed calls from you," I said. I read Connie's phone number out loud from my notes.

"Yeah, that's my number," Connie said.

"And then what did you do?"

"I did the only thing I could think of, which was drive over here as quick as I could and check on Jill. I came inside, called her name but she didn't answer. I hurried to her room and tried to wake her up but she didn't move at all. I kissed her forehead and left a lot of tears, as you can imagine. My world shattered before my eyes. After a few minutes, I gathered the strength to get my phone from my purse and I called 911."

I reached for Connie's hands and squeezed tightly. "Again, Connie, I'm sorry for your loss."

THE BINGO KILLER

"Thank you!" Connie started to cry again.

"And what about you, Mrs. Owens?"

"After Connie got off the phone with 911, she called me and I rushed right over here to be with her," Owens replied.

"Then Officer O'Malley showed up. Then you came, detective," Connie said. "And here we are."

"Did you have a key to Jill's apartment or did someone from the office let you in?"

"No, Jill gave me a spare key if I needed to use her apartment or come check on something," Connie explained.

"I see. I appreciate you telling me this. You didn't see anyone suspicious around her apartment or know of anything out of the ordinary she may have told you about recently?" I asked. "Any threatening letters in the mail? Emails? Obscene phone calls?"

"No, not that I can remember. Jill never mentioned anything like that to me. I suppose I'll have to check her mail today or tomorrow. Jill was a singer/performer. She traveled all through the South, up the East Coast playing in clubs and theaters. She wasn't home much but when she was home, she wanted her peace and quiet."

"I don't blame her one bit. I've heard a few of her songs. She has the voice of an angel."

"Yes, she did," Conne declared. "I like to think she got it from me." Connie smiled through her tears.

"What did you two talk about the last time you spoke to Jill?"

KNIGHT

"It was a week ago or so. We talked about her schedule and how she was looking forward to some time off in a few weeks."

"Did she say anything about her health or anything? Any headache or chest pains?" I asked.

"No. Nothing. She said she felt fine. She was eating well. Exercising. Plenty of sleep. She didn't smoke or drink. I can tell you that."

"No boyfriend or anyone she was seeing that you knew of?"

"No. She didn't have time for a boyfriend. She told me she was focused on her music, performing and touring."

"I see. And what about Jill's dad? I need to speak with him as well."

"Oscar Tidwell. He lives here in Bloomfield," Connie said. She put her phone on the coffee table for me to write down his cell phone number.

I jotted down his number. "Connie, I appreciate you taking the time to answer my questions. You've been a big help. More than you know," I declared.

Connie reached for my hands and looked right into my eyes. Her pain and anguish was clear as sunlight. "Please catch my daughter's killer, Detective Barker. I say that with my heart knowing she was murdered. It's broken and will never fully heal as long as I live. I don't know if you have a daughter of your own but I pray you never feel the pain I feel right now."

THE BINGO KILLER

"I can say I'm not sure this is a homicide. This could be a death by natural causes. We'll know when the toxicology report comes back in a few days. But if this is a homicide, I promise you, I'll find who's responsible."

"Thank you from the bottom of my heart," Connie said through a waterfall of tears.

"It's the least I can do. Here's my card if you need to speak with me or remember anything. I insist, so please don't hesitate to give me a call. I'm also at the BPD if you need to see me in person."

"Thank you, Detective Barker. I feel a little better," Connie said.

I asked Mary if she could take Connie back to her house for today and take care of her.

"She's going to come stay with me and my husband for a few days. I'm not going to leave my best friend alone," Mary said eagerly.

"No, Mary, I'll be fine."

Mary looked at Connie. "Like hell you will! You're staying with me and that's that. Now let's go get your purse from your car and go to my house," Mary said. "We can come back to get your car tomorrow and check Jill's mail." Mary and Connie hugged each other.

Connie nodded. "Okay!"

"That's a good idea and thank you for taking care of Connie. She really needs you right now," I said. "Thank you ladies for your time. I'll walk you to your car."

We exited the living space and headed back to the front lobby.

"Bye Tiffany. Be good to your guests," I said as we walked past Tiffany's desk and out to Mary's blue car. Connie got in the passenger's side while Mary and I talked.

"Mary, we're going to lock up the apartment for a few days after forensics has gone through Jill's apartment. Shouldn't take long but we'll have someone from the office lock the door. If it's a homicide, which it very well may be, we'll be back to search Jill's apartment again. If Connie needs anything out of Jill's apartment, don't hesitate to give me a call. I insist."

"Thank you. Take care, Detective. We'll be in touch I'm sure." Mary said.

I walked back towards O'Malley standing by the front door. Smalls had already left and returned to the morgue. I stepped inside the apartment to talk with Troy Prater, a five-year crime scene technician.

"Hey Troy, how's it going?" I asked.

"Always a pleasure to see you, Detective Barker," Prater said.

I walked over to the table where Jill's purse was tipped over. "Take a look at this. I wanted to show you this sugar packet under her purse. Let's get this to the lab for examination. Might not be anything but let's double check," I ordered.

"Absolutely. Good call, Detective," Prater said. "I'll tag and bag it for you."

THE BINGO KILLER

"I appreciate it very much. I didn't find anything else but that doesn't mean much, which is why we rely on you, Smalls. Also, Mr. O'Malley will be outside until you finish your work. Let me know what you find out about the torn packet paper under her purse. You've got my number."

"I do. Have I ever let you down Detective?"

"Fair point! The answer is no," I responded.

I stood in the living room and wrote down notes about the apartment, what I found, the evidence, what I did to help Smalls, and my interview with Connie Sanders. Like a good fiction novel, details matter. Before I left Jill's apartment, I made sure O'Malley had his standing orders. One of the perks of being a detective is outsourcing orders to patrol officers. Those orders from then-detective Gerald Riley, during my patrol years, made me feel useful. "Officer O'Malley, can you get someone from the office to come lock this apartment after forensics leaves?"

"Absolutely. I'll make sure the door is locked," O'Malley stated.

"Please do. Not much more I can do here. I'm heading back to the station to talk to Chief Williams about all this. I'll put in a good word for you."

"Have a good day, Detective Barker "

I paid Tess another visit to talk about Jill's apartment before I left.

"Yes, how may I help you again?" Tess said with a somber, relaxed tone.

KNIGHT

"Listen, we're going to lock up Jill's apartment for a few days. Consider it a crime scene and tell anyone as such if anyone asks. No one goes in or out without my permission."

"Of course. As you wish, Detective Barker."

"Thank you. We'll be in touch."

Tess and I both exchanged business cards before I returned to the BPD. I put my shades on and walked back to my cruiser.

THE BINGO KILLER

Chapter 5

After a ten minute drive downtown, Sloan pulled into a vacant lot overlooking North Avenue and parked the cruiser inside the lot entrance.

"Dispatch, we are 10-77 at the vacant lot on North Avenue in front of the parking garage."

"10-04, Unit 07."

Twenty minutes went by as we watched traffic from both directions. The lot spot was a good area to get speeders but no drivers had a lead foot that Monday morning. A few multi-colored triangle flag ropes were strung up across the back of the lot.

I spent the next hour filling out reports from Dan's Donuts and from Nia's Nail Salon, while Sloan kept his eye out for speeders. Sloan noticed a man in a green jacket loitering on the sidewalk across the street from the vacant lot where they were parked. "Hey Sam, this guy on the corner over there across the street, he has on a green jacket like the one that was reported at the nail salon earlier."

I looked up from his paperwork and saw the man standing by the no-parking sign on the other side of the street. "Yeah, that could be him. Let's go ask him," I said.

"We'll pull up next to the street where he's standing and ask him what he's doing there."

"Alright," I said.

"Dispatch, this is Unit 07," I said. Sloan gave me the moniker "Radio Riley," because I always worked the radio, back and forth with dispatch. Sloan always took the wheel.

"Go ahead, Unit 07."

"We have a visual on that possible suspect from the nail salon reported earlier. We're going to talk to him and ask him some questions. 10-12," I said.

"10-04."

We pulled up beside the suspect and stopped our cruiser near the sidewalk. I took my seatbelt off and stepped out of the car. Our suspect saw me walking towards him, hesitated a few seconds and then ran South, past a two-story parking garage on North Avenue.

"Ahh shit—he's running," Sloan yelled out. "Dispatch, Unit-07, we are 10-80, in pursuit of a suspect on foot, running South on Pine Street."

"Stay where you are. Stop running from me!!" I shouted, over my feet stomping the pavement as I chased my suspect up the street. Luckily, no civilians were walking on the sidewalk during our little foot race. I heard the sirens wailing as Sloan sped down the street past me to cut off the suspect at the end of the street. Instead, my suspect crossed the street after Sloan passed and ran back up towards North Avenue, away from Sloan and I.

"Dispatch, suspect is now running North on Pine Street, back towards North Avenue," Sloan declared.

"10-4, Unit-07."

I chased the suspect as fast as I could while Sloan did a u-turn in the middle of Pine Street, barely missing the front left bumper of a parked car.

"What are you doing, Sam? Get in!"

I ignored Sloan's request and chased the suspect around the corner of Pine and North Avenue, running east, past the parking lots of different small businesses. He gasped for air, as his energy was depleting fast, slowing down at the end of North Avenue but he quickly turned south on Maple street. I caught up with and tackled him to the ground. I wrestled with him until I was able to slap my cuffs on him.

Sloan pulled up, parked the cruiser and ran over to assist me in arresting our suspect. "I got him, Sam. Let's get him to his feet and in the back of the cruiser."

"Yeah, I'll feel better," I replied.

Sloan and I helped the man to his feet.

"You're under arrest for fleeing an officer, loitering, and suspicious activity," I said, as I secured the cuffs on the suspect. Officers Carson and Harris quickly arrived to assist Sloan and I.

"Dispatch, Unit-03 here, we are 10-23 here on scene with Unit-07," Carson stated.

"10-04, Unit-03."

I introduced myself and the officers to our suspect. "These three officers are Sloan, Carson and Harris of the Bloomfield Police Department. I am Officer Riley, the one chasing your ass from two blocks away. Once again, you are under arrest for fleeing an officer, loitering and suspicious activity." I took the lead in arresting my suspect, having chased him down. I read him his legal Miranda rights. "Do you understand these rights as I've explained them to you just now?"

"Yes I do. I'm not saying another word until I get a lawyer," my suspect yelled.

I explained to him why I approached the suspect before he ran away.

"I want my goddamn lawyer," my suspect declared.

"Okay. Dispatch, 10-95. Suspect is in custody and has been read his Miranda rights. 10-12," I radioed in to dispatch.

"Anything in your pockets we should know about before I search you," I asked. "Any drugs, needles, guns, knives or anything dangerous on your person, right now?"

"Stick your hand in there and find out, cop," our suspect said.

I gave him my go-to-hell look just as he was giving me his look. I frisked and searched his pockets. "Phone, keys, lighter, a few coins, altoids." I took the suspects' wallet and held on to it.

Silence from our suspect.

"What's your name?" Sloan asked.

"Save your breath, pig. I'm not talking until I get my lawyer," our suspect said.

THE BINGO KILLER

"Okay, that's your right. But you're under arrest for the crimes that Officer Riley listed earlier. Maybe more, after we do some investigating here," Sloan said sternly.

"Do you need our assistance with anything?" asked Officer Carson.

"No, I think we got it for the most part. He's all lawyered up now. He matches the description of the guy seen on camera, driving back and forth in front of the nail salon at the Pine Point Shopping Center, taking pictures of the building and front doors," I said. "Probably for a hit in the coming weeks."

"Do you think he's the Northside Bandit?" Officer Harris asked curiously.

"We won't be sure until he talks with his lawyer here soon," Sloan said.

I opened the suspect's wallet and saw his driver's license. I grabbed my radio, "Dispatch, this is Unit-07, that suspect's name is Terry Wayne Duckett. We're bringing him to the station for booking shortly after we do our investigation," I said.

"10-04, Unit 07."

"Last chance to talk. Why did you run?" Sloan asked.

"I want my lawyer," Duckett said. Mr. Duckett had a green army jacket on that reeked of cigarette smoke. Peach fuzz on his chin and cheeks in a ripe peach color ironically. However, not much hair on his head. Duckett wore blue jeans, a red t-shirt and white sneakers.

"That's okay. You'll get your lawyer when we take you in to formally charge you with the crimes we told you earlier. Just sit tight," I replied.

Sloan put Duckett in the back of Unit-07 and shut the door.

"Thanks Sloan!"

Sloan walked back over to me as I fixed my uniform.

All four officers huddled around the cruiser that Duckett was held in.

"Well that was exciting, Sam. Not to mention a bit crazy. What were you thinking? Running that far that fast? You could have just got in the car and saved your energy," Sloan asked me with frustration.

"What can I say, Sloan? I learn the hard way," I said.

"You don't learn at all, Sam," Sloan said. "That's your problem."

"What are you talking about, Sloan? I got him though," I stated. "He won't run from me again."

"Yeah, you did, John Wayne," Sloan quipped.

"John Wayne? More like Keanu Reeves!" I said.

Sloan shook his head. "Enough chit chat, let's get him back to the station."

I looked across the street by chance. "Hey Sloan, see that red truck parked across Maple street?"

Sloan looked over to his right. "Yeah, what about it?"

"Might be the one we saw in the video earlier. Let's go check it out," I suggested. "Carson, Harris, you keep an eye on him for a few minutes."

"Sure. Good work catching this guy, Riley. I know I couldn't have run him down like you did," Harris said. "I'm not Superman."

"Thanks, Harris. We'll be back shortly."

Sloan and I walked across maple street to the red truck.

"Dispatch, Unit-07 here. We're 10-37 with a red truck fitting the description in the video from the nail salon reported earlier."

"10-4, Unit-07."

We saw the license plate as we approached the truck from the front. "This has to be where he was running to. This is the red truck that matches the description on the nail salon security video. I remember seeing all those stickers on the back window," I said, pointing to the back windshield. Various obnoxious statements and political and social slogans on the stickers. The kind that makes other drivers shake their heads in disbelief that the driver has a license.

"Dispatch, can you get a 10-28, on an Illinois license plate "AJY 408" on this vehicle right quick?" Riley asked.

"10-04, Unit 07. 10-12."

I wrote down the plate number so I could include it in my reports. And believe me, there would be many reports. The passenger side window was down and a pile of black clothes was balled up on the passenger's side floor. Sloan peaked inside and saw part of a hammer and a pry bar on the floorboard beneath the clothes. We searched the truck and found several cups, soda bottles, napkins and fast food bags full of burger wrappers and straw covers littered all over the passenger side floor board. The drivers' side was covered in dirt and dust. The ashtray was full of old cigarette butts. A pine scented air freshener hung from the mirror. We also found a small digital camera in the glove box. Sloan turned the camera on and went through the pictures. Photos of Nia's Nail Salon and Dan's Donuts and various other businesses showed up on the tiny screen. "What a find, Sam. All the evidence we need is right here."

"Yeap, Score one for Sloan, Good find, man!" I said.

"These black clothes match the ones shown in the break-in video at Dan's Donuts. It also fits the description from the witnesses from the other break-ins. I think Duckett's the Northside Burglar," I replied. I grabbed the clothes and tools and bundled them up. I expected a firearm to fall out of the clothes but to my relief, nothing fell out.

"Unit-07, That vehicle is registered to Terry Wayne Duckett, of Bloomfield."

"10-04, dispatch," I said. "He has to be our guy. The Northside Burglar"

"Whole new set of charges are coming his way," Sloan said. "Let's tow it back to the impound lot. Forensics can do their work there."

THE BINGO KILLER

"10-04, dispatch. Can you call a tow truck to have this vehicle towed to the impound lot?" I asked.

"10-04, Unit-07. 10-12."

"10-4, dispatch!"

I rolled up the passenger's side window to keep potential evidence secure during transport back to the impound lot.

"Unit 07, the tow truck is on its way to your 10-20. CSI has been notified to meet the vehicle at the impound lot. They have the license plate number."

"10-04, dispatch. Thanks for the help this morning," I said.

"10-04."

"Dispatch, Unit-07, we are 10-76 back to base to interrogate the suspect," I said.

"10-04."

Sloan and I returned to our cruiser and took custody of Duckett. I put the clothes in a big paper bag and put it in the trunk. Sloan asked Officers Carson and Harris to stay with the suspect's truck until the tow truck arrived. Carson and Harris drove over to the red truck and parked behind it until the tow truck arrived ten minutes later.

Chapter 6

10:00 a.m.

I arrived back at the BPD and headed to Chief Williams' office with two coffee cups. He leaned back in his leather chair, reading out of a manila folder when I knocked. The Chiefs' office had blue carpet and a red couch near the glass windows. Two wooden chairs in front of his desk. A big poster of John Wayne hung on the wall behind him. *Not my choice but to each his own. I admired the Chief's John Wayne approach when it was necessary. I must admit.*

"Kate, come in," Chief said. "Are one of those mine or are you that thirsty?"

"Chief, I got you a peppermint hot chocolate." Most in the department called him Chief WIlliams but I resorted to simply calling him Chief.

"Thank you, Kate. Please have a seat. I appreciate the drink. Always a nice treat," Chief said happily. "Damn, that's good," Chief said, taking a sip. "How's yours, Kate?"

"Delicious."

"Good."

"Excuse me, Chief Williams," said Maureen Downs, the Chief's secretary.

THE BINGO KILLER

"Yes, Maureen."

"Officers Sloan and Riley just brought in the suspect they caught a few minutes ago. They believe they caught the Northside Burglar. They're in the interrogation room."

"I guess my wish came true," I said, looking at the Chief.

Chief raised his eyebrow and looked at me with eagerness. "Yeah, mine too. Thank you, Maureen. Excuse me, Kate. I'll be right back in a few minutes. Sit tight!"

I sat patiently, drinking my cappuccino. I thought about the case and couldn't wait to interrogate the suspect.

******

Riddle asked Riley if she could clean the interrogation room. "Not now, Betsy. We have a suspect in there. Maybe sometime after lunch."

"Okay. I'll go clean the conference room instead."

Chief walked to the interrogation room and saw Riley about to close the door.

"Sam!"

I waited for Chief WIlliams. "Yes, Chief?"

We talked outside, where Duckett could hear our every word, not that I cared.

"Good job catching this guy, Sam. That was tough I'm sure."

"Thanks, Chief. Not too bad!" Two blocks is enough for me. One more block was about all I could do before I would have hopped into the cruiser.

"What's the deal with this clown?"

"Terry Wayne Duckett, of Bloomfield, isn't talking without a lawyer.. I noticed the green jacket he wore while loitering on the corner of North Avenue and Pine street. It wasn't the loitering that caught my attention as much as it was the green jacket. He ran towards a red truck matching the description of the same red truck seen at Nia's Nail Salon earlier this morning. We searched the truck and found a hammer, prybar and black clothes that we believe were used in the break-in at Dan's Donuts."

Chief asked about the red truck.

"I noticed the same stickers on the back glass from the security footage from the nail salon. It's been impounded so forensics could retrieve physical evidence," I said.

"Is all of this in your report?" Chief asked.

"It will be, yes sir!"

"Excellent work. Please make me a copy of your report and give it to my secretary. She'll see that I get it. Oh, and an extra copy for Det. Barker. She's working on the Northside Burglar case."

"Yes sir, as soon as I get them done," I said.

"Have Sloan, Carson and Harris do the same," Chief asked.

"Yes sir!"

THE BINGO KILLER

"I'll have one of the desk officers come and watch him until his lawyer gets here. Stick around and get those reports done quickly." Chief said. "Come find me around 11:45. We're going to lunch and discuss some good business."

"Will do, Chief!"

Chief walked back to his office and informed his secretary to make copies of the reports from Officers Sloan, Riley, Carson and Harris and give one each to himself and Detective Barker.

I radioed to my fellow officers about the Chiefs' request.

"10-04. Working on that now, Sam," Sloan said.

"10-04. We're on our way back to drop our reports off," Carson said.

"10-04," I replied. I waited by the interrogation room for about three minutes until Sgt. Whine came to guard Duckett. I found an empty desk in another part of the station to finish my reports. I took the reports from my fellow officers as I got them.

11 a.m.

Five minutes passed until the Chief came back to his office. "That was a doozie. He's not saying shit until his lawyer gets here. Sloan, Carson and Harris should bring their reports to me soon. I asked Officer Riley to do a separate report since he caught Duckett on foot no less. I'll make sure you get copies, Kate, since you're working the case after all. I'll let you have first crack at him until his lawyer gets here. Maybe he'll talk to you. He'll definitely talk to me but I'm not good with a first aid kit."

"I'll pretend I didn't hear that last thing you said," I said.

"Because I didn't. Kate, I want you to look over these reports and try to get a warrant to search Duckett's house."

"I will, Chief!"

"Now tell me about the Sanders' crime scene. What did you see?"

"Well, when I got there, Officer O'Malley was guarding the apartment. The victim was thirty-year old Jill Sanders, a local singer/performer. She was found in her bed by her mother, Connie Sanders, after her phone calls and texts went unanswered. Connie called 911, then she called her friend Mary Owens, who then came to the apartment and waited with Connie until we showed up," I said.

"Okay. Then what, Kate?" Chief said.

"When I arrived, I didn't say anything to Connie right away. I immediately went to the bedroom to check on the body but didn't find any blood stains on her face or neck or anything out of the ordinary. She was under the covers when Connie and I found her. Her apartment was exceptionally clean for a single woman. Not even a cup or plate in the sink," I said.

"Did you find anything?" Chief asked.

THE BINGO KILLER

"I did a sweep of her bedroom, under the bed, in the closet and the rest of the apartment but didn't find anything until I came into the kitchen and saw her purse on the table. I didn't find anything important in her purse. I saw the calls and text messages from Connie on Jill's phone. I moved her purse and found a small, ripped sugar packet stuck to the bottom of her purse. I let forensics know before I left," I said.

"It's weird the sugar packet is all we have to go on. But maybe that's all we need," Chief declared. "Gotta start somewhere. I've discovered more from less."

"What about the coroner? What did he say?"

"Smalls said he didn't see any unusual marks on her arms, legs, neck, head, that he could see. He took the body to the morgue and they should be performing her autopsy and a tox report. I helped him put Sanders' body on the stretcher," I said.

"Looks like natural causes to me. No wounds or anything. Has to be a medical reason, and probably not anything crime related, but we'll see. We'll wait until both reports are available in a few days," Chief instructed. "What about the mother? What did she say?"

"We talked over in the clubhouse while Smalls took the body out. I didn't want Connie to see her daughter taken out on the stretcher. She didn't give anything worth pursuing. She told me that Sanders didn't have any health problems. She took care of herself. Didn't drink or smoke. Exercised and ate healthy," I said.

"Could be a heart or brain-related cause of death! I'm not a doctor, obviously but if I had to guess, that would be it," Chief said.

"I agree. Definitely not what I was expecting but whichever it is, I'm glad she passed peacefully in her sleep," I said. "That doesn't make it any better, nor do I feel any better.

Chief nodded his head.

"I told O'Malley to stay behind until forensics worked Jill's apartment. Forensics showed up as I left to take the two women to the clubhouse for interviews. I gave them my card and told them to call me if they remembered anything. We put caution tape across the door and had someone from the manager's office lock the door in case it becomes a crime scene in a few days," I stated.

"Good work there, Kate. A crime scene can only tell us what we are open to seeing and hearing. Always keep your eyes open, Kate."

"I will, Chief! I promise," I said.

"The details of this womans' death has me hunching there's more to this than we see. Stay on top of this like you're walking on thin ice, Kate," Chief said.

"Absolutely. I promised Connie I'd find the truth about her daughter. I don't think this is all some weird coincidence—the way she died, I mean."

THE BINGO KILLER

Chief pointed in my direction. "That's why you're a damn good detective, Kate."

"Thank you, Chief. I appreciate that very much." *One thing I admired about our chief is he knew how to lift my spirits and believe me, my spirits needed lifting.*

Chief sighed and looked around his desk. "But I find myself at those same crossroads today." Chief grabbed a folder from his right drawer and leaned back in his chair. He quickly glanced over the folder. "Another thing I wanted to get your opinion on, Kate."

"Anything, Chief."

"Officer Riley applied for the open detective position a few weeks ago. Scored high on the tests. Same as last time. Him catching that burglar today sure helped propel him to the top of the list. Before I make my final decision, what's your opinion of him?"

"I've known Sam since I've been with this department, Chief. We went to college together–we took a few classes together. We attended the academy together. I've worked with his dad on a few cases before Gerald retired. I enjoyed working with Mr. Riley. He taught me so much about what it means to be a detective and I'm sure he taught Sam even more."

Chief nodded. "Gerald Riley was one of the best law enforcement officers I've ever worked with. Flawless record. Professional."

"I agree. I try to live up to his example every day," I said.

"Do you think Sam will make a good detective? I need to know if you can trust him and be comfortable with him as your partner?"

"Sam's in a good position to be a detective and switch over from patrol to the detective division. I'm sure he has the experience and training to be a great detective in time. I'd be happy to acclimate him to the way I do things and take him under my wing."

Chief laughed. "Under your wing. You would, would you? Good one, Kate."

"We were the two choices last time and honestly, Chief, you could have chosen him and you still be in just as good hands as you are with me. Although I don't think Sam would have brought you as many drinks as I have over the years," I said.

"That's true, he wouldn't. Plus I don't like ass-kissers but I do love a good cup of hot chocolate, so we're even." Chief said with a smile.

I smiled at the Chief's subtle hint. "I don't kiss ass, Chief."

Chief bobbed his head up and down with sarcasm. "Sure, Kate. Do you see that elephant in the back corner behind you?"

"But to answer your question, I think Sam will be a great detective. I think he wants to have the same career as his dad. I think Sam and I will be great partners together," I said. "I'd be honored to show him the ropes for a few weeks."

THE BINGO KILLER

"I get that feeling from Sam also which makes things a little easier. He could use some guidance from you. He'll need it."

"I can whip Sam into shape in a week or two."

Chief smiled. "Right! I also don't want to make a mistake and lose Sam to another department. I don't want him thinking he has no future here and leave for something better," Chief said, looking out his office windows.

I nodded. "I agree. "Sam deserves a chance at least."

"Do you have any plans for lunch?"

"Not today I don't."

"Good. You're coming with me and Sam out for lunch at 11:30.

"Sure. I'd love to. I'll come back around that time. In the meantime, I'll go talk to our suspect and see if I can get him to sing," Barker said.

"Good luck. He's lawyered up pretty tight. Won't say a damn word," Chief said.

"I'll try my best," I said.

"Give him his phone call and get his lawyer down here, would you please? They can talk while we're at lunch."

"Yes sir! Not a problem," I said, before walking to the interrogation room.

"Morning, JD!"

"Morning Detective Barker."

"I'll just pop in for a few minutes—try and make this bird sing."

"Do your thing, baby," Sgt. Whine said as he walked back to his desk.

I took a seat on the opposite side of where Duckett sat. "Okay, Mr. Duckett. I'm Detective Kate Barker. You've been keeping the Bloomfield Police Department busy for the past few months. Allow me to return the favor by giving you one last chance to answer my questions. Yes or no?"

Duckett glared at me through his thick glasses. "NO! I'll talk when my lawyer gets here and only then. I'll wait as long as it takes. You can sit there pretty and confident or you can give me my phone call."

"Fine. Do you have a specific lawyer you want or should I call the public defender's office and they send over some ambulance chaser?"

"Send me the damn ambulance chaser," Duckett said. "Speaking of chasers, how's your cop buddy? Did he catch his breath yet? I didn't think he'd stay on my ass as long as he did."

"Very well Mr. Duckett! That can be arranged. Officer Riley is better than ever. He's filing charges on you as we speak and believe me, there are a lot of them," I said. "Excuse me while I make a phone call." I stepped outside to call the local public defender's office to tell them Duckett was in custody for suspected burglary crimes and needed counsel. *Give this scumbag his lawyer.*

I returned a few minutes later. "Good news Mr. Duckett, your lawyer should be here by noon."

THE BINGO KILLER

"About time you fucking pigs did something right."Duckett huffed.

"Yeah, we caught you real easy, didn't we? Sounds like we did the right thing."

Duckett scoffed at my reply.

"Scoff all you want. You're in cuffs and not going anywhere for a while."

"Fuck off, cop!"

"As you wish, Mr. Duckett. You had your chance. I'll get started on that search warrant for your house. What do you think we'll find, Mr. Duckett?"

"You'll find me waiting here for my lawyer. It's not hard to understand."

I left the room but couldn't help thinking to myself, *Well, isn't he a charmer?* I walked back to my desk to gather the reports and other paperwork to officially charge Duckett with a host of various crimes, including a string of summer burglaries and fleeing an officer.

Phillips brought me the 911 call log and dispatch traffic from this morning. "I heard you were back in the building so I thought I'd bring you these updates in case you needed them. Today's been hectic for sure."

I looked at Phillips and smiled. "You don't know the half of it. Crime scenes, police chases, break-ins," I said. "It's not even noon yet. That asshole they brought in—Duckett, he's not talking. I hope he doesn't take the chickenshit way out and sign a plea-deal," I said.

"Will you be okay if he does? I know the DA has a say in formally charging him but you've worked your ass off with this case for months now," Phillips asked.

"It's ultimately up to the prosecutor's office. I just want him to see years of jail time but we'll see," I responded. "I'm just killing time until lunch. How's your morning so far?"

"Busy but it slowed down in the past 30 minutes. I better get back so I don't miss anything. You know where to find me if you need me," Phillips said.

"On the beach with cute, hot guys?" I asked with a smile. *I'd rather be in Vegas myself. I remember that spring break trip all too well.*

Phillips laughed. "Maybe next summer," Phillips said, before walking back to her dispatch station.

I started what paperwork I could, which was difficult not knowing what Duckett was going to do. Hopefully things will be clearer after lunch. I called Oscar Tidwell to tell him about Jill Sanders' passing but he didn't answer. I left a voicemail for him to return my call at his earliest convenience. *I wouldn't be surprised if Tidwell didn't call me back. I can't blame him either. But I still had a job to do. It never gets any easier.*

Chapter 7

11:20 a.m.

I handed our reports to the chief's secretary. "All done, Mrs Downs."

"Thank you, Officer Riley," Downs said. "Chief Williams should be happy."

Chief motioned me into his office as he hung up the phone. "Ahh, right on time, Sam. Hope you're hungry."

I stood in the center of the room, behind the two chairs in front of the Chiefs desk. "Yes, I am. A good cheeseburger with fries sounds good."

Chief glanced up at me like I insulted him. "Cheeseburger? Oh no, Sam. We're going to La Buena Casa, my favorite Mexican restaurant. The food is bueno, amigo!" Chief said merrily.

"Oh! Well, that sounds even better, Chief. My lucky day!" Riley said. "I'll bring my pepto tablets and toilet paper."

Chief looked at Riley with suspicion. "Sarcasm, Sam!!!"

"Maybe just a little. I don't like to eat spicy foods during work hours."

"Right. You prefer greasy cheeseburgers and deep-fried cholesterol," Chief Williams said.

I laughed and smiled. "Yes sir. I'd say that's right. Guilty as ordered."

"That's okay, Sam. Nothing wrong with a good burger. Just don't order it at a Mexican restaurant. That's kind of weird in my opinion. You don't see Italian restaurants serving burgers. Well, maybe on the kids menu?" Chief declared.

"Good point. I'm picky about my food but I'll give La Buena Casa a try."

"Yes, The Good House! Damn good enchiladas."

That's when Detective Barker walked into the Chief's office. "Good morning, Gentlemen."

I have to admit Ms. Barker looked mighty fine in her suit, walking in the way she did. I looked at her and smiled.

She smiled back at me. "Impressive work this morning in catching Duckett. You made my job so much easier, Sam."

Chief slowly and sarcastically clapped his hands as she joined us for lunch. "And not on time, Detective Kate Barker."

"What? I'm two minutes late," Kate said.

"It's Monday. Which is why you're buying us lunch at La Buena Casa," Chief said.

"Awesome. I love that place. I go there once a week," Kate quipped.

"Good, let's go. Sam, you're driving." Chief walked to his door and turned the lights off. "Say Maureen, we're going to lunch. We'll be back around 1

THE BINGO KILLER

or 1:30. Duckett's attorney should show up shortly. Can you make sure his lawyer finds Duckett in the interrogation room? They can talk as long as they need to. We'll get to them when we get back. Call me if you need me," Chief said.

"Yes, Chief. Not a problem. Enjoy your lunches," Downs said as she continued working.

"Let's go y'all," Chief said. "Hasta pronto!"

The officers and detectives, alike, were always amused at our Chief showing off and being so funny, confident and set in his ways. We respected Chief Williams for many reasons. We walked through the doors of La Buena Casa about fifteen minutes later. And right on cue, like switching on and off a robot, Chief walked in first and instantly went into politician mode—working the room—shaking hands with the waiters, waitresses and the owners like they were family. Kate and I stood by the cashier stand, watching the Chief work the room. He eventually came back to speak to the hostess. "Chief really does like this place," I said.

"Yeah, he's not this friendly at the station," Barker replied.

"Hola, ¿cómo estás señorita?" Chief Williams asked politely, as we waited for a table.

"Hola, Señor Williams," said Lisa, the hostess.

"Quiero una mesa para tres personas, por favor?" Chief asked.

"Si, señor! A table for three, right this way," Lisa said as she led us to our table in the center of the restaurant. The chief and Kate sat on the side of the table facing the windows, while I sat on the other side, facing the drink station and the register.

"This is where me and Vivian sit when we come here."

The tables had a clear epoxy coating on top of different designs carved into the table. Each had different rich and vibrant colors in the designs. Banners with the Mexican flag stretched the ceiling from one side of the restaurant to the other in all directions. The walls were painted bright yellow. The plates were blue. The chairs were all green. Red tiled floor. Perfect for a Simon Says-themed restaurant, I thought.

"Good afternoon, Chief Williams. How are you today?" asked Rhonda, our waitress. She sat the menus down in front of us.

"Bueno, bueno!"

"Si, si. What can I get you to drink?"

"Sweet tea for me," Chief said.

"Same for me," Barker said.

"Same," I said.

"Trés tes," Chief said happily. "What can I say, they take after their beloved Chief." Chief smiled at us.

Kate and I both smirked. She took after the Chief more than I did.

Chief was in such a good mood that afternoon. Although I didn't quite know it just yet at the time, he was delighted in the fact he was about to, again, have two great, well qualified detectives in his department.

THE BINGO KILLER

I respected Chief Williams. I wasn't as chummy with him as Kate was but I thought highly of the man.

Another waitress was right behind her with three bowls of salsa and bowls of made in-house tortilla chips.

"Gracias," Chief said.

"I can't help judging a restaurant by their salsa and chips, even if it's just a little bit. Ya know?" Kate commented as she dipped a chip into the salsa. "It's the first thing they offer customers so why not put the best on the table."

"True. I think their white queso is a good indicator of food quality. This place has excellent queso."

"Fresh guacamole?" Kate asked.

Chief grabbed a chip and dipped in the salsa. "Nah, I don't care for guacamole. Reminds me of turtle shit. Always has."

Kate and I burst out laughing.

Chief smiled. "Don't tell them that, though. You'll be cleaning cruisers for a week."

"Never heard that one before but yeah, now that you mention it," I said.

Rhonda brought our drinks back to our table. "Three teas."

"Ahh our teas," Chief Williams said. He took his first sip, then smiled. "My kind of sweet."

"Are we ready to order?" asked Rhonda.

"Si, señorita. I'll have the Pollo Monterrey lunch plate, with extra rice instead of beans. Absolutely no beans. I'll have the guacamole, sour cream and Pico de Gallo set up on a side plate," Chief said. "Extra cheese."

"You want the onions, peppers and mushrooms also?

"Si."

"And for you ma'am?"

"I want the three cheese enchilada combo plate with beans and rice. White queso on top."

"Excellent choice. That's our lunch special. It's a dollar off," Rhonda said.

Kate nodded. "Awesome."

"And for you, sir?"

I hesitated for a minute. "Uhhhh—"

"Come on now, Sam! Don't flake out on us. Order the spice!" Chief winked at Rhonda and nodded in my direction.

"I guess I'll have the taco plate with rice only."

"Beef or chicken?" Rhonda asked.

"Chicken, please."

"Kid's taco plate. Okay. I'll get these in and have them out as soon as I can," Rhonda said.

"I didn't say the kid's taco plate!" I said.

Rhonda bolted back to the order station, ignoring me completely.

Chief rolled his eyes. "He guesses? I would have called your mother, Sam, and told her if you ordered the cheeseburger and fries at a Mexican restaurant."

Kate laughed as she looked at me. "That's what you get—the kid's plate."

THE BINGO KILLER

I shrugged it off as a little light hazing for a rookie.

"This guy can chase down a suspect for three blocks but can't try spice foods?" Chief said.

"I play it safe for a reason. Long way back to the station before I can get to the bathroom," I said.

"What he lacks in good food, he makes up for in stupid pranks," Kate said with a straight face.

"So I've heard, here and there," Chief said.

I crinkled my face in frustration. *I can't catch a break with these two*. I said the only thing I could think to say, relevant to the conversation. "So why did you ask me to lunch, Chief?" I asked. I had a feeling it was about the open detective position but I didn't want to assume anything too soon.

"What difference does it make? I'm buying today," Kate said with a smile.

"None, I guess. And thank you, by the way, Kate," I said. But I went with my second theory. "I figured it was the Chief's way of congratulating me for catching the Northside Burglar this morning."

"You're most welcome, Sam," Kate said, without missing a beat. "And it's Detective Barker."

The brief, tense silence was interrupted by a loud crunch, as Chief ate a chip while enjoying the conversation. Kate and I stared at each other.

"If you become a detective one day, you can call me Kate."

"Okay, then! Apologies, Detective Barker." *Did I just blow my chance at becoming the BPD's new detective? Maybe I'll be stuck in a patrol car for God knows how many more years. Probably until I retire in 15 years.* I took a sip of my tea until a loud slurp rang out. I raised my glass to get Rhonda's attention for a refill.

"I'm sure Sam didn't mean any disrespect, Kate. But I did in fact want to show my appreciation for catching the Northside Burglar this morning. That was not easy," Chief said.

"Thanks, Chief," I said.

"Be back in a few," Chief said.

A few awkward, tension-filled moments eventually passed as Detective Barker and I sat quietly, eating chips and drinking tea.

He came back a few seconds before Rhonda sat a big tray of food on a nearby table.

"Pollo Monterrey for the Chief. Careful, that plate's hot," Rhonda said quickly.

"Delicioso."

"Enchilada plate for you ma'am. Enjoy those enchiladas."

"Gracias," Kate said.

She looked at me and smiled. "And a kid's taco plate with rice only for you."

"Kid's taco plate? I wanted the regular taco plate," I said, confused.

"I know. That's the regular taco plate. I was just kidding you. You're handsome in that uniform," Rhonda said, smiling.

"Oh, okay. Ha! Thanks. Looks great," I said, before I glanced over at Kate and smiled. "She thinks I'm cute."

THE BINGO KILLER

Kate rolled her eyes.

"Thank you Rhonda," I said.

"What do you enjoy doing outside work, Sam?" Kate asked.

I didn't think my answers mattered anymore and, for some reason, I resorted to sarcasm. "I collect spores, molds and fungus," I quipped and waited for Kate to laugh—silence.

Chief laughed and looked at me. "Good one, Sam."

"This ain't Star Wars or Lord of the Rings," Kate said assertively.

I looked at Kate in confusion. "What? Tell me I didn't hear what I think you just said?"

Chief looked at Kate. "Kate, you gotta learn more about movies, famous quotes and characters. That was kind of embarrassing."

"I know fine dining. I read books on history, science. I exercise. I go out and do things when I'm not working. I'm not that kind of nerd like Sam is. I don't read comics, collect toys, play nerdy games, binge watch superhero movies in costumes or pajamas."

I took a long sip of tea. "What makes you think I do any of that?" I asked.

"Most men do those things nowadays."

"I can't believe someone who claims to be versed in fine dining doesn't know great lines from the classic films. They go hand in hand. How can you enjoy great food and not know lines from classic movies?" I added.

KNIGHT

Kate knew she was losing ground but continued eating her enchiladas.

"I like it when my detectives can jab back at each other and not let each other get too high and mighty and bossy. I expect them to be honest and know they're not pushovers. I need to know they can do this job and not take any shit," Chief said.

"I didn't let the Northside Burglar get past me," I said. "Barker didn't know one of the most popular lines from one of the most popular 80's comedies."

"We get it, Sam. You can stop now," Kate said.

Chief looked at me and asked a few questions. "Why do you want to be a detective, Sam? If it's because your dad was one and you want to follow in his footsteps, that's not a good enough reason for me. I need something better."

"I--," *Fuck it, just go with the first thing that comes to mind,* I thought.

"Quick, Sam, quick," Chief demanded.

"Well, I believe it's my purpose in life, Chief. I've wanted this since the first day I put on my uniform over ten years ago. My attention to detail and service record speaks for itself. I'm capable of going beyond the call of duty not only to apprehend suspects but save lives, at great risk to my own safety. I've proven this every day since," I proudly proclaimed.

"Well said, Sam! But you forgot one thing," Chief said.

"Yeah, what's that Chief?"

THE BINGO KILLER

Chief looked at Kate with a raised eyebrow. "School Kate over here about the beauty, splendor and wisdom of the timeless 80's classic, nostalgic films. She needs to know what Howard The Duck stood for, how to solve the Labyrinth, who ya gonna call?"

"Anytime, Chief. That I can do. She'll be trivia-team ready in no time." I assured the Chief.

"I know good movies, alright, Sam," Kate declared.

Chief raised his eyebrow, as he looked at Kate.

I asked her a quick question I had in mind. "Oh, yeah? Who's James T. Kirk?"

"He's in Star Wars, right?" Kate said.

Chief sighed in disappointment. "Come on, Kate."

I looked over to my right as Rhonda came over to our table. "Rhonda, who's James T. Kirk?"

"James Tiberius Kirk was Captain of the U.S.S Enterprise," Rhonda said. "How are we doing over here?"

I smiled and pointed at our waitress.

"See! That's how you do it, Barker," Chief said.

"I love you," I whispered to Rhonda.

Rhonda laughed.

Kate scrunched her face. "Okay. I get it. You've proven your point, Sam."

"You're definitely buying our lunch today, Kate," Chief said.

"We're doing just fine except for Gene Siskel over there," I said, looking at Rhonda.

"Let me know if you need anything," Rhonda said.

"I can't win for shit right now," Kate said.

"That was…fun," Chief said.

"You learn something new everyday," I said.

"Whatever. It's wrong to judge me on what I don't know," Kate declared.

I laughed at Kate's comment.

Chief paused for a few seconds.

I was curious what the Chief had to say. There was a reason why we were having lunch. Having Kate with us was no coincidence.

"Alright, both of you listen. Here comes the serious part of our gathering here today." Chief Williams looked at Detective Barker. "Four years ago, I chose Kate to be the new Sergeant/Detective in our department. I have no doubt I made the right choice but it was very tough though. I'm not gonna lie. Four years later, I don't have any regrets. You've gone above & beyond what I expected from you as a detective, Kate," Chief said.

"Thank you, Chief." Kate said.

"Sam has done the same in catching the Northside Burglar this morning. You're the frontrunner this time and this time, it's not even close. I think having both of you as detectives and working together will be a winning move for the department and Bloomfield."

I felt a lot better about my chances after the Chief spoke. I sat quietly and finished my lunch.

THE BINGO KILLER

Chief rubbed his hands together and took another swig of his sweet tea. "Okay. Detectives Sam Riley and Kate Barker. Sergeants. Homicides, burglaries, break-ins and thefts—It's all up to you two now. I know you'll do well both separately on smaller cases and together on bigger cases. Agreed?"

Both Kate and I looked at our Chief.

"Absolutely," I said.

"I agree," Kate said. "You can call me Kate, by the way."

I nodded. "Call me Sam."

"Good. Listen Sam, we have a possible homicide on our hands from this morning. Kate went to the crime scene this morning before you caught the burglar. She has all the details and can fill you in. I want both of you working together to solve Jill Sanders' death as soon as possible. I have all the faith in you two," Chief said.

"Congratulations, Sam. You've earned it. I look forward to working with you," Kate said, offering to shake my hand from across the table.

I quickly shook my partner's hand. "Thank you, Kate. I appreciate that. Likewise. I look forward to trivia night. I'll go easy on you."

Kate tilted her head and smirked. "Yeah, whatever. Don't push it, Sam!"

Chief finished his meal, put his silverware on the plate and draped a napkin over it, like an important meal ritual. "My grandfather did this every time he finished a meal. Guess I got it from him."

KNIGHT

Kate and I finished our lunches. I couldn't help but enjoy the rest of the day with my good news.

Rhonda came back to the table and took our empty plates away. "Does anyone want a sweet tea to go?" She asked kindly.

"I'll have one. Thanks, Rhonda."

"Coming right up, Chief."

"Well, this has been quite the day," I stated.

"Seems like it will never end," Kate said before sipping the last few drops of her tea.

"What do you mean Kate?" I asked.

"If only you could read my mind, Sam."

I shrugged my shoulders. *I had a feeling I didn't want to read Kate's mind. Well, not at that exact moment.*

Rhonda brought a to-go cup to the Chief. She also brought the check and sat it down between myself and the Chief. "You can pay at the register when you get ready," Rhonda said.

Chief took a sip of sweet tea and nonchalantly slid the receipt over to Kate.

"Oh, you weren't kidding?" Kate asked.

"Neither were you about Kirk being in Star Wars. You'll pay for that one way or the other, Kate," Chief declared.

"Fine. Guess I'm buying." She grabbed the receipt, her purse and walked to the register to pay. Chief and I both left a five-dollar tip for Rhonda.

Kate also left a five-dollar tip with her payment.

"Let's head back to the station." Chief said his goodbyes and followed us detectives out to the car.

Chapter 8

Chief sent text messages to other officers in the BPD on the way back to our station. I returned around 1:20 p.m. to a wonderful surprise.

Sergeant J.D Whine was the first to congratulate me as we walked inside the BPD. "Detective Riley! I never thought I'd live to see the day," said Whine, as we shook hands and hugged.

"Thanks, Sergeant Whine. Finally!"

"Look forward to working with you, Detective Riley." Whine was happier for me than I was, not that I minded in the slightest. I welcomed his support and belief in me. I had the same sentiment in working with him as well. Whine was a great officer in many ways. His wisdom was comical but comforting.

"Likewise. It'll take some getting used to being called Detective," I said.

"Naw, it's all good, man! They still give you a free donut or two," Whine said, lightening the mood with a laugh. "You'll get used to it in a day or two."

"How ya doing, Jerry Don?" Kate asked.

"I'm making it, baby! Making it! How about yourself?"

Kate pointed at me. "We'll see with this one, huh!"

KNIGHT

Whine looked at me and laughed. "I know that's right, baby!"

Kate laughed with Whine. "Well—you know."

I nodded and smiled. "Go ahead and get it over with. Get your laughs in," I said. *All part of the rookie initiation.*

Kate excused herself to the bathroom while Whine and I talked. I took a chance and asked Whine about Kate. "Any advice on working with Detective Barker?"

"She's a firecracker, Sam. I'm telling you, man. Stay on your toes," Whine said with a chuckle. "She's a good detective but good luck with her."

I nodded. "Good to know. Thanks! "

Chief came back from the bathroom and walked over to where his three sergeants were standing. "Kate, Sam, go look into the Sanders murder this morning. And check up on Duckett while you're at it. Hopefully his attorney came while we were gone."

"I'm on it, Chief!"

"I'll let you guys get back to work and so will I," Whine said.

"Sam," Kate called out from near the briefing room. "Follow me!"

Kate and I went to our work space to discuss our cases from earlier that morning.

"Welcome to the pit, Sam. I named it a few years ago. I was going through a somewhat tough time and it just popped into my head. I've referred to this side of the building as the pit ever since."

THE BINGO KILLER

"Great name for our workspace, Kate. I like it."

Kate sat down at her desk and finished the paperwork from the Northside Burglar case.

I stood still near my dad's old, empty desk, admiring it before I sat down. *Funny how Kate didn't get this desk. Must have been saving it for me*, I thought. *Either way, it's mine now.* I sat behind my desk on the left side of the room. Windows lined my side which gave me a good view of the street and buildings around the BPD. I decided to play a quick prank on Kate to break the ice. I looked at my desk. "Oh man! I need some pens and office supplies if I'm going to do this job right," I said calmly. I opened and closed my desk drawers looking for anything I could find. The desk was totally empty. I got up and went over to Barker's desk and grabbed her pens, Post-It notes, paper clips, etc., like they were my own.

"Excuse me, what the hell do you think you're doing?" Kate looked at me with a mix of anger and confusion, as I opened her top left drawer.

I smiled at Kate. "Shopping, of course."

"You can't just go through my space freely without my permission." Kate swirled her arms around her desk area, like a karate kid move. "This is Kate's space. You got that, Sam!" She pointed towards the front of the pit. "Supply closet is down the hall near the janitor's closet. Get your own supplies."

I laughed and ignored her. I reached for her pens and paper clips as she held on for dear life.

KNIGHT

"Go! Get, Sam! Leave my shit alone. This is Kate's space. You have your desk over there."

I looked at Kate with a smile. "Oh, I'm sorry, were these things yours?"

Kate's anger intensified in her face like she was about to explode like dynamite.

"God, I'm so, so sorry! I thought we were sharing." I paused for her reaction.

"Not funny, Sam. I'm not big on pranks during work hours, unless they happen to you."

Kate shot her serious look at me, which I found cute.

I glanced behind her and saw her boxes of Cheez-Its. "Oh look, snacks!"

Kate swirled her chair around as I lunged for her snacks. "NOOOO, Sam!!! Those are mine. Leave my crackers alone," she ordered.

I sat her things down and laughed at her intensity surrounding her snacks. "Oh come on, Kate, I was just kidding you. Trying to lighten the mood. A little ice breaker never hurt anyone." I went to the supply closet and came back with a box lid full of items I needed. "Chief Williams said we should work on the burglar and murder case from this morning. What do you have Kate?"

I slid my chair to her side of the room, near the edge of her desk and curiously waited.

Kate looked up at me again with a straight face. "My period! Come closer, Sam!"

THE BINGO KILLER

"Yeap, okay! Going back to my side now," as I pointed. I wrinkled my face and slowly scooted back to my desk, never breaking eye contact with my partner.

Kate giggled. "Too easy, Sam! Too easy!" Kate proved she could hold her own in the sarcasm department and wasn't afraid of showing it. Something I hoped would reveal itself. It wasn't a requirement for being my partner but it sure as hell helped.

"What I got is a burglar and a dead woman who I suspect was murdered instead of natural causes,"

"Yes, we do. I caught the bastard," I said proudly.

Kate looked at me with a smug smile. "That was awesome how you chased after Duckett for two blocks."

"Yeah! The cardio worked out in my favor," I said. I reclined in my leather chair.

"Comfortable?" Barker asked.

"Just getting a feel for it. I'm the second Riley who sat in this chair." *Dad kept it warm for me.*

Chief hobbled around the corner and stopped in front of our desks. "Hola, amigos! Here's the deal. I talked to Duckett's attorney and he's willing to make a plea deal for a reduced sentence. Full confession to the burglaries."

Kate crossed her arms and leaned back in her chair. "What does he want?"

"Three years and early release for good behavior. after two."

"Not sure the DA will go for that deal," Kate said.

KNIGHT

"I just got off the phone with Kathy Hopper and she said she'd consider it. I'm supposed to call her back after I talk it over with you two," Chief said.

"I think it's a shitty deal. Seriously, who the fuck is this guy to dictate anything to us? He deserves at least five years, to be honest," Kate said.

Chief looked at me. "What do you think, Sam?"

"I didn't run him down for a two-year sentence. Five to 10! But it's the DA's call."

Chief looked at me and sighed with hesitation. "Okay. I'll let them know. Be looking for my email, Kate."

"Sure thing, Chief!"

"Did Kate help you settle in, Sam?" Chief asked.

I looked at Kate. "Not exactly, Chief. She's on her period, though. Go figure!"

"Why do you think I paired you two up today of all days?"

Kate and the Chief both laughed.

"Sam, you have a lot to learn about us," Chief said.

Kate laughed and continued her paperwork on Duckett.

I sat behind his desk, stewing in my slight embarrassment, staring at my partner. *Good job, Sam! Way to make a first impression.* "Payback for lunch, huh?"

Kate nodded.

Chief pulled out an old wallet with a detective's badge inside and handed it to me. "I've been waiting for so long to give you this. It means more to you than it does me. Congratulations, Detective Sam Riley."

I held the badge in my hands and looked it over like a long lost treasure. "I've seen this many times before as a kid. Seeing it on my dad's belt before we parted ways in the morning. And now it's mine. Thank you, Chief! I appreciate this!" *It's finally mine!*

"Call your Dad and tell him. He'll be glad to hear your good news."

I nodded, as Chief left the pit. I grabbed my phone and called my dad and told him the good news. "Hey dad, what are you doing right now?"

"Nothing really. Just standing here at the mall. Your mom's trying on dresses. Boy, she still looks as pretty as the day we met," dad proclaimed.

"That's great, dad. Look, I'm calling to tell you I made detective. Chief Williams just gave me my badge a few minutes ago and told me to call you."

"You made detective? Wow, Congratulations, Sam! That's great news."

"Thanks, Dad. Finally made it. Another Detective Riley." I didn't know my dad already knew I caught the Northside Burglar. The chief called his good friend earlier that morning to talk about my good deed and promotion. Of course, in true Dad fashion, he asked me what happened.

"Well, I noticed Terry Wayne Duckett loitering on North Parkway, in front of the parking garage, across the street from the empty lot. We drove over and I got out of the car to question him and he took off. I caught him two blocks over," I explained.

"That's good work, Sam. You did it. I'm proud of you and happy for you, son," my dad said.

"Thanks, Dad. Be sure to tell Mom. I'll talk to you later. I've got a lot of work to do right now to get caught up."

"Yes, you do! Alright, Sam. Talk to you later."

I hung up and got back to work. "Sorry about that. Had to deliver some good news."

Kate overheard my conversation with my dad. Although Kate found it cute, she wasn't about to relinquish any ground to me that I didn't earn on his own. She looked at me and laughed. "You wanna call my dad and tell him I'm on my period? I'm sure he'd love to hear that," Kate asked.

I perked up and smiled. "Sure, Kate. Dial the number! I have some questions to ask him, too. Like, what's stuck up your butt? What turns you on?"

Kate shook her head and kept writing. "No, no, no!"

"I can't wait to meet your parents one day." I brushed it off and looked at Kate.

"Ehh, that's not happening!" Kate declared.

"We'll see."

Kate shot a dirty look my way with her piercing eyes.

"So what about the woman who was killed?" I asked.

THE BINGO KILLER

Kate put her pen down and turned towards me. "Jill Sanders. Well, her mother, Connie Sanders, went to Jill's apartment after she didn't answer her phone calls. Connie called 911 the next morning after she found Jill. Officer O'Malley showed up first. I went over there and the place was spotless. No signs of forced entry. We got one piece of potential evidence but we'll just have to see what the toxicology report says in a few days," Kate said.

"That's not a coincidence, her apartment being that clean–I mean. She didn't have a maid or house cleaner?"

"No, Connie was the only one who had a spare key," Kate said. "Jill traveled a lot for work. She was a singer and a musician. Easy to have a clean house when you're hardly there.

Maureen Downs came around the corner and handed me some tax forms and insurance papers for me to fill out for my new position. "Chief Williams wants you to fill these out and get them to me by the end of the day," Downs said calmly.

"Thanks Maureen. You got it!"

Downs went back to her desk and Kate continued with her rundown.

"The whole thing doesn't make sense. It's too cut and dry to be a coincidence! Clean apartment. She passed peacefully. Healthy. She didn't drink or smoke. Ate good food," Kate said.

"Seems odd for someone in good health. Well, the good news is the plea deal will free up our time for

Jill's murder investigation, if that's what you think her death was." I responded.

"I'm not sure just yet. We'll see what the evidence says. As much as it was a bullshit cop-out, I agree. It's a blessing in disguise," Kate declared.

"Think Hopper will go for it?" I asked.

"I don't know. She's pretty tough on crime. But then again, it's not every day someone requests a plea deal that includes a full confession. We know how hard those are to get from suspects," Kate said.

Kate heard a ping sound from her laptop and noticed an email from the Chief. She told me that Hopper accepted Duckett's plea deal.

"Okay, Duckett should still be in the interrogation room," I said. "Let's go pay him a visit."

Kate sat down on Duckett's right side while I sat on the left side of the table.

"Where's my plea deal?" Duckett asked.

"Mr. Duckett, again, I'm Detective Kate Barker and thanks to your game of freeze tag this morning, this is Detective Sam Riley."

"Well, well! I'd say that makes us even, Detective Riley. I ran, you caught me, you got a promotion and so did I," Duckett said mockingly.

"Sure you did, Duckett," Kate quipped.

"You think I owe you something? You think I'm in your debt because you ran from me and I had to chase you down? You couldn't be more full of shit if you tried, Duckett," I declared.

THE BINGO KILLER

Duckett scoffed at my comments. "Piss off, you fucking pig!"

"Before we go any further, why did you run?" I asked.

Duckett asked, "Where's my deal?"

"Hang on Terry, for what it's worth, I was going to let you off with a warning and send you on your way but you're dumb ass had to run. That's when you fucked up," I said. I didn't want this scumbag thinking he has some inside dirt on me or I owed him any favors in case he had plans to cash in while in the county lockup. Or like some criminals, use it against me as a get out of jail free card.

"Did I fuck up? You wouldn't be a detective if it wasn't for me running," Duckett exclaimed. "You owe me a favor."

I looked at Duckett. "I don't owe you shit, Duckett."

Duckett smiled. "We'll see!" As guilty as Duckett was for his crimes, he was partially right in his assertion of the morning's actions.

"Okay, Mr. Duckett. Enough with the bullshit," Kate said sternly.

Duckett smiled. "Anything for you, babydoll!"

"Don't call me babydoll," Kate declared. She took a deep breath before she acted on her impulse and perhaps might have gotten a few charges herself. *Lord give me strength!*

"Oh, now princess, I'm just having a little fun. Too bad you caught me, Mr. Riley. I sure would love

KNIGHT

to have you, Detective Barker, frisk and strip search me." Duckett said.

"You'll have better luck in prison, Mr. Duckett," Kate said.

Duckett laughed. "You're a bottle rocket instead of a Roman candle, lady. That's all you got! No wonder you haven't gotten any good dick in a while," Duckett said as he looked at me. "Right, Riley?" Duckett tried his best to bring out the bad cop in at least one of us. Duckett wasn't ready for either of us. I give Kate credit for keeping her composure.

"Excuse me? Watch your fucking mouth, Duckett."

"Oh, someone's wound up, now." Duckett laughed.

Kate knew his game all too well. "Mr. Duckett, the prosecuting attorney's office has agreed to your plea deal for a full confession to the Northside burglaries, in exchange for a three-year prison sentence with early release after two years for good behavior," Kate explained. "Personally, I think you should do at least five years for the burglaries and break-ins alone. Another year for making my partner chase you this morning. But it's out of my hands, sadly."

Duckett put his elbows on the table. He pointed with his two fingers forward and looked at Kate. "Oh, that's good sweetheart! I like that. I say jump, you ask how high?" Duckett said with a smile. "That's

THE BINGO KILLER

precious!" Duckett saw the confused look on Riley's face.

I didn't move a muscle as I stared at Duckett. "Enough stalling, Mr. Duckett. Do you accept the plea deal or go to trial, be convicted and receive 5-10 years in prison?" I asked. "Entirely up to you?"

Duckett scrunched up his nose. "Sure! I'll play along. It's my party after all. And I get my cake and eat it too."

Kate slid over a legal pad and a pen she brought with her. "Alright, Mr. Duckett, write your confession on that paper and you get your deal. It's literally that easy."

Duckett wrote his confession out in about seven minutes or so. He took his time to be thorough and include each crime he confessed to, including where and when. He gave the pen and pad back to my partner.

Kate quickly looked over the confession and passed it to me. "That's quite the detailed confession. This will do. I'll give it to the DA. Just so we're clear, we're charging you with five breaking and entering charges, five burglaries, theft of property, property damage, fleeing an officer and loitering. Lots of serious crimes."

"Sure, doll. Whatever keeps me on your mind," Duckett said.

I read his confession as Kate spoke.

"Alright. That should do it. Stay here until an officer comes to get you to transport your ass to the county lockup," Kate demanded.

KNIGHT

Duckett remained silent until we got up to leave the room. "Bye boss lady! I'll see you again!"

We immediately went to the Chief's office and gave him the confession. The Chief told us to have a seat while he read the confession. "Okay. Good work, detectives. Slam dunk case we have here."

Chief then called Kathy Hopper. "Kathy, Chief Williams here. Good news. We got our confession from Mr. Duckett for all of the Northside burglaries and a few other crimes from his arrest this morning. One of my officers chased him down for two blocks. I promoted him to detective," Chief Williams said.

"Amazing work, Chief. Have one of your officers send over the confession and paperwork and we'll be in touch," Hopper asked. Chief Williams told her that Duckett was going to the county lockup that afternoon.

"Good. I'm so glad you guys caught him and he'll be spending a few years in jail."

"Thank you, Kathy!" Chief said.

"Bye, Chief!"

"We got him! Good work. The credit belongs to both of you. Hell of a start for you two going into the murder investigation. Which I hope will go just as quickly and smoothly," Chief proclaimed. "Kate, Sam, have all the paperwork done by three."

"Absolutely, Chief."

"You know where to find us if you need us," Kate said.

"Si, senorita!"

THE BINGO KILLER

Kate and I went back to the pit to help each other with our separate reports.

Kate sat in her chair with a box of Cheez-Its on her lap.

"That's your favorite snack?" I asked.

"Cheez-Its? Absolutely. I'd kill for a box. Fair warning, don't be surprised if I call you and ask you to bring a box or two back to me. I'm not afraid to pull rank for my cheesy treasures," Kate said, before popping a few into her mouth.

I smirked. "Cheez-Its, it is. Cheesy Kate! I'm fond of green apple licorice."

Kate looked at me. "That's disgusting, Sam. All licorice is disgusting,"

I shook his head in disbelief. "What? You're crazy. Green apple licorice is the best licorice on this planet."

"Yeah, I'm not buying any of that for you. I wouldn't buy that for a starving orphan in Africa," Kate declared.

"Oh no, no, no!" I said. I shook my head feverishly. "I wouldn't expect that, seeing as you're this big food connoisseur and all."

Kate grabbed a few more crackers. "I am. The sooner you accept that, the better off we'll be."

Before I could respond, the vibrating ring tone of Kate's phone caught her off guard. Kate wiped her hands off on a napkin on her desk. Crumbs went flying all over her lap and some landed on the floor. "Detective Kate Barker, speaking!"

"Is this Detective Kate Barker?" Tidwell asked.

"Yes, this is Kate."

"Hi, this is Oscar Tidwell."

"Mr. Tidwell, how are you today?"

"Oh, I've had better days. If this is about Jill's passing, Connie already called me and told the horrible news. I just can't talk to anyone for a few days. I'm sure you understand."

"Absolutely, Mr. Tidwell. I completely understand and I think it was better coming from her than me. That being said, Mr. Tidwell, I need to ask you a few questions about Jill's death."

"Sure, we can talk about Jill in two or three days. I don't feel like answering questions today. My daughter just died."

"I understand, Mr. Tidwell!"

"Thank you, Detective," Tidwell said as he hung up.

Kate received an email from the Chief saying the BPD would send out a press release confirming the death of Jill Sanders and another announcing the arrest of the Northside Burglar. Kate was asked to send a short statement for both press releases to Sergeant Whine. I also got an email asking for a brief statement on my promotion to detective.

THE BINGO KILLER

Chapter 9

9:01 p.m.

The moon rose quietly in the star-filled, Illinois night as I settled down on the patio in my backyard, to do some meditating and reflecting on one of the toughest and most rewarding days of being a law enforcement officer. I put down two towels on the concrete. I closed my eyes and immersed myself in the peaceful sounds of the country, with a calming stillness. *Mind, body and spirit! Mind, body and spirit!* I took a few slow, deep breaths which helped me tune into my own energy. *Focus, focus, focus!* I suddenly had a flashback of all the sad, embarrassing and painful moments throughout his life, all at once, like a short movie on a loop. A single tear fell freely from but I let it fall. My memories then shifted to the positive and happy memories. I kept breathing and feeling my body for a few more minutes. I wondered if I had truly earned my promotion to detective. *I know I did everything to get it but did I really deserve it? Sure, I want it more than anyone but am I ready for it? Do I have what it takes? I sure could use some guidance.*

The moon shined down on me through the pine tree near the corner edge of the fence. Little thin shadows of pine needles and cones danced all around me on the patio and against the side of the house. I heard some faint clanging noises coming from the chair next to him. I looked over at the chair and saw it move slightly. I thought it was the wind but didn't think much more of it.. I closed my eyes and let my thoughts flow but was interrupted by a faint voice that got louder and clearer every time I heard it. The sounds of bugs and other critters off in the distance blended together with the words I heard.

When I opened my eyes, I saw moonlight highlighting the silhouette of a figure sitting in the chair to my right. I crawled away back towards the glass door behind me as the sudden, clear sight of this mysterious figure. "Who are you and what are you doing here?" I shouted. Not that anyone could hear or help me if I needed help. My sidearm was in my bedroom. I didn't think I'd make it in time to retrieve my service weapon if I were attacked. I kept my eyes on this thing sitting a few feet from me.

"It's me, Mystery! Capital M! That's what you can call me from now on."

"Mystery? That's your name? How convenient!" I replied. "Are you the figure from my dream this morning?"

"No! What dream? I don't show up in dreams. In person only!"

Well, aren't you a real charmer? "I see that."

"I'll show you how charming I can be. Don't look at me, mister! Finish that yoga shit you're doing so we

THE BINGO KILLER

can get down to business," Mystery said in an angry tone.

I looked at Mystery, not sure what to say. *Okay, let's get one thing straight, Mystery. I'm Detective Sam Riley, so don't give me any of your shit. Do you understand me? Drop your attitude!* I took a deep breath to calm myself down after being scared half to death by Mystery.

"Damn dude, chill!" Mystery said.

"Wait, how did you hear my thoughts?" *How did Mystery hear my thoughts? What is going on? How is this possible? I honestly didn't expect my thoughts to be read so easily. Who does?*

"How the hell should I know? I just do. I'm confused as hell as to where I am and why I'm here."

"You're in my home, on my property. Remember that!" I reminded Mystery as I looked in his direction. "Now, how did you get here?"

"I've followed you since this morning when I first heard your voice. I don't hear much. It's quiet in my world. I stayed invisible out of fear it wasn't safe for either of us. I didn't know what else to do."

I asked where Mystery followed me from.

"I walked by the red truck this morning and saw you arrest that guy."

"You've been with me all day? Even at work?"

Mystery nodded yes.

I took a deep breath instead of reacting and losing the moment. *What do you want with me, Mystery?*

"I think I was murdered in St. Louis."

What I had feared just came to pass. I figured this Mystery guy wanted something that I wasn't really able to deliver or help with: solving his murder. Yes, that's my job but St. Louis was a hundred miles away. On the other hand, what would Mystery do if I didn't help him?

"What's the last thing you remember doing?" I asked.

"I was walking my dog. I turned a corner, saw a pair of headlights coming towards me quickly. I ran to get out of the way and here I am. That's all I remember. *I'm more worried about what happened to my dog than what happened to me.*

I see. Well, Mystery, hate to break it to you but you're dead. That's the only way we can talk to each other. I'm speaking to you with my mind right now. I leaned over and reached for Mystery's legs but my hand went through the thin air. *Did you feel that?* I leaned back up straight and refocused.

"Shit, I must really be dead. I didn't feel a fuckin' thing."

"Some people don't when they die," I said. *Do you feel like you're sitting in that chair or floating?*

Mystery looked around his chair and saw his body sink down into the chair an inch or two. "Oh shit!" Mystery jumped up and took a few steps away from the table and patio until he stood in the grass. "What's happening, man? Why was I floating like that?"

"I don't know. Maybe your energy isn't strong enough or maybe it's the chair."

I stood perfectly still, with my energy focused on Mystery. *Relax, Mystery. Everything's okay. I know that's*

THE BINGO KILLER

not what you want to hear but trust me, it's all okay. Again, saying the only thing I could think of to say. I didn't know if Mystery was a ghost or an angel or some mythical folklore creature.

"Trust you? How is it going to be okay? I'm a ghost, man!"

You can't die twice, genius. First time was so quick, you didn't know what happened.

"Screw you, Sam! You try dying and be perfectly happy with it. I swear man, everyday feels like death."

I almost died a year ago trying to save a little girl from drowning while on vacation in Arkansas.

"Oh, no shit, man. I didn't know that."

Most people don't. I don't talk about it much. If it means anything, your reaction just now was perfectly normal. I expected you to freak out.

"Not really."

"Yes, really. It's normal to freak out about your death, I imagine. You have my permission if it helps you out, Mystery." *I'm just here to hear what you have to say. So make it worth my time.*

"You think I'm here for you? I don't need you to listen to me. I'm fine on my own."

Then why are you here? Why aren't you talking to someone else? I don't see anyone else lining up to listen to you.

We paused in silence.

Mystery thought about my questions and slowly realized death was a new, permanent reality. Mystery calmed down upon realizing I could shut off communication instantly and would have to wait longer for answers. Nothing Mystery could do about it either. I'm running this supernatural show!

"I don't know why I'm here. I don't even know where I am."

Bloomfield, Illinois. Just across the border. You're safe here as long as you behave like Casper and not like Beetlejuice.

"Deal, Mr. Riley! I'll be your friendly ghost, blah, blah, blah!"

Good. Not like you had a choice but I like your enthusiasm.

"This should be a lot of fun," Mystery said.

"For one of us, at least."

"You asked for guidance earlier, Sam. Maybe I'm that guidance?"

I didn't believe Mystery's hot take on him trying to make sense of our social meet and greet. I'm not that lucky and the universe has bigger wishes to grant or prayers to answer to give me the guidance I selfishly asked for. "Why you, Mystery?" I asked.

"Now we're getting somewhere, Sam," Mystery said. "Time will tell."

"I looked up at the moonlight and paused to take it in before I went inside."

Okay, I'm calling it a night. That's enough practice for tonight. We'll talk again I'm sure.

"What am I supposed to do? There's no ghost hotel around here for me to check into?"

Go sleep on the couch. Just don't be standing over me when I wake up in the morning.

THE BINGO KILLER

I slowly took a deep breath but didn't see Mystery. I stood up and grabbed the towels and walked inside. I noticed an owl perched on one of the fence posts, looking right at me, as I shut the patio door. I stood looking at the owl for a few seconds.

"DON'T THINK I'M GONE YET, FOOL!!" Mystery belted out next to my ear.

I damn near jumped 10 feet high and immediately turned around. "Jesus, you scared me!" It took me a good minute to catch my breath and calm down from Mystery's jump scare.

"HA! We're even now, punk!" Mystery said.

"No one's keeping score," I said. I rubbed my forehead and yawned. "Goodnight, Mystery!"

"Get some sleep, Sam. You're going to need it tomorrow."

I locked the doors in my house before I went to bed. Who could blame me for not trusting Mystery to behave like a model houseguest and leave me alone for a few hours? I locked my bedroom door for the first time in years. I didn't quite trust Mystery—ghost or no ghost. When I woke up the next morning, Mystery was gone. I soon realized how unpredictable spirits truly were. Showing up at the worst times and to hell with the consequences of their complete disregard for time.

Chapter 10

Tuesday, Sept. 2nd.

10 a.m.

Connie Sanders opened Jill's mailbox and retrieved her mail, before turning in the extra key to the main office. Connie had forwarded Jill's mail to Connie's home. Connie flipped through a barrage of junk mail, different letters from businesses concerning her music and such, a few letters from close friends and one letter she knew nothing about. Connie saw a suspicious letter and walked over to Mary's car to show her the envelope.

"Mary, look at who this one's addressed to," Connie said. Connie handed the letter to her friend as she put the bulk of Jill's mail in her purse to read later on.

"That's not something you can ignore, Connie. Better call those detectives," Mary replied.

Connie got her phone and called Detective Barker.

"Good morning, Detective Kate Barker speaking."

THE BINGO KILLER

"Hi, Detective Barker. This is Connie Sanders. I hope I'm not bothering you this morning, am I?"

"No, ma'am, you're not. Now can I help you?"

"I came to Jill's apartment to check her mail one last time and I found a letter in her mailbox with Detective Riley written on the front. I don't know why anyone in the world would send anything to him here," Connie stated.

"Are you still at Jill's apartment?" Kate asked.

"Yes, we're parked in front of the main office, near the mailboxes."

"Okay, great. We're on our way. We'll be there in less than 10 minutes," Kate said.

"Yes, ma'am! We're in the blue, four-door Corolla. You can't miss us."

"Okay, thank you!" Kate said.

Kate grabbed her purse and leather binder. "Saddle up, Sam! We gotta make a run to Jill Sanders' apartment. Her mom found a letter in her mailbox that has your name on it."

"What? Are you serious, Kate? That's weird," I responded.

"You're driving, Sam," Kate declared.

"Let's take my truck."

Someone has to be playing with me or this is one of the Top 10 List of letters sent to the wrong addresses with dire consequences. I grabbed my blazer and car keys. *Why would someone send me a letter at that address?* I asked myself that two or three times on the way to Jill's apartment.

KNIGHT

I pulled up next to the blue Corolla and rolled down my window. Connie got out as I took off my sunglasses. The aroma of pina colada and coconut hit Connie hard.

"Wow, it smells like Hawaii in here," Connie proclaimed.

"Yeah, new air fresheners," I said.

"You have something for me, Connie?" I asked.

"Yeah, here's the letter, Detective Riley."

"Thank you so much. We really appreciate it," I said.

"Thanks for taking my call," Connie said.

"No, thank you for calling me, Connie," Kate said.

I put my sunglasses on the dashboard. I saw my name and Jill's address on the front of the letter. I pulled out a piece of paper with several dice and numbers on it. I showed it to Connie Sanders and then to Kate. *What the hell is this shit?* "It's some kind of coded message. I guess we're doing encrypted messages now, like some damn spy ring. Great, now we're hunting the goddamn Zodiac. Fantastic!"

"What?" Kate asked. "Let me see."

I handed the paper to my partner. "What do you think, Kate?

Kate drew a blank. "It's a cipher we'll have to solve. More than likely, it has something to do with Jill's murder. Otherwise why send it here, to us here?"

THE BINGO KILLER

I tilted my head in agreement as I put the cipher back into the envelope. "I'll take my time looking at it closer when we get back to the station."

"Good luck, Mr. Riley," Connie said.

"Thank you, Connie! I appreciate that. We need all the luck we can get these days," I said.

Kate shook her head in agreement.

"While I'm talking to you two, Jill's funeral is next Monday at 10 a.m. at Candlewood Cemetery. I'd like it if you two can both come. It'll give me comfort in knowing you guys know how important solving her murder is to me," Connie said.

I looked at Connie with reassurance. "I'll be there for sure." This would be my first funeral I attended as a homicide detective. People in my line of work don't usually attend funerals so as not to get emotionally involved with the victims but I never understood that. Maybe some detectives and officers should attend more funerals to be reminded of who we work for. But a promise is a promise. I had this overwhelming feeling I needed to be there. I couldn't explain it and I didn't think Kate would understand if I tried to tell her.

"We'll see. I don't like to commit to something a week ahead and let people down if I don't show up," Kate said. "I prefer to play things by ear. I promise to do all I can to solve Jill's murder either way."

"We both promise," I said as I looked at Kate and back at Connie.

KNIGHT

Connie reached for my hand and a tear fell from her eye. I squeezed her hand and held it for a few seconds. "Bless you, Mr. Riley. Bless you both."

"That's our job, Ms. Sanders," I said. "If you need anything Connie, please feel free to call me. You have my number."

Connie nodded and patted my hand. "I'll let you go and get back to work."

"Yeah, we better go figure this out," I said.

Connie said goodbye to us and got back in the car.

I looked over at Kate. "Well, that was interesting." I put the letter in the middle console between me and Kate. I hesitated for a few minutes. Buying some time.

"What are we waiting for Sam?" Kate asked.

I gathered up small items of trash and fidgeted with things in my truck. I looked in the rearview mirror as Mary and Connie drove out of the parking lot. "Let's go!" I unbuckled my seat belt.

Kate got out and joined me in front of my truck.

"I'm going inside to ask them in the office some questions about this letter. Meet me over at Jill's apartment, Kate. I want to take a quick look inside," I said.

Kate walked over and waited for me to join her.

I walked through the office front door and flashed my badge to Tiffany Monroe. "Detective Sam Riley, Bloomfield PD. I have a few questions for you

THE BINGO KILLER

and your supervisor. Can you bring him or her out here, please?"

"Yes, I can go check and see if she's available," Tiffany said, in a soft spoken voice.

"Please do!" I said, before looking around the office.

Tiffany returned a minute later. "She's finishing up a call and will be with you momentarily."

"Great!" I stood in front of Tiffany's desk.

Her boss came out of her office and saw me standing in the doorway area, facing the other side of the room. She looked at Tiffany and looked at me. *He's hot!*

Tiffany smiled and looked at me.

"Thanks," I said.

"I'm sorry?" she said, taken aback by my compliment.

"I–um…I said thanks for seeing me on such short notice," I replied quickly. I realized I could hear what she was thinking without saying a word. Just like last night with Mystery. With anyone else I'd freak the fuck out but Tiffany's boss was gorgeous.

She gained her composure and introduced herself. "I'm Tess Taylor, Property Manager here at Eaglewood Apartments. Can I offer you a tour of one of our apartments or an application at least?"

I thought Tess was stunning in her office attire. Professional indeed. Well, my definition at least. I walked over to Tess and shook her hand. Her tan, mocha skin and long, flowing hair caught my attention. She wore a black dress with a single, white

KNIGHT

stripe down the left side. I got a strong sense that Tess had a first date that went bad recently. I wanted to make a good first impression. "Well hello, Tess Taylor," I said.

Tess raised her hand. "Ms. Taylor. No ring yet?"

Lucky me, I said to myself. "Guess I won't have to arrest someone for stealing you off the market."

Tess laughed and smiled. "I feel protected already," Tess said. *He can serve me all night.*

"I've done my job then. I own my own home but for you, I just might consider living here. You know, just to keep an eye on you. Are all the property managers as stunning as you are?" I asked. I sat down on the edge of Tiffany's desk and faced Tess.

"Can't hurt a girl to ask. Besides, you'd make a great tenant for sure, detective."

I rubbed my beard as Tess smiled. "Yes, I certainly would. I'd give up my cosplay lightsaber fights after 9 p.m. to live here," I said as I handed Tess my card. "Riley. Detective Sam Riley."

Tess laughed at my nerdy Star Wars joke. "What can I help you with Mr. Riley?"

"I have a few questions about Jill Sanders that I'd like to ask the both of you."

"Absolutely."

I looked at Tess. "Don't worry, you're not under arrest. Unless you want to be?"

Tess smiled and looked away towards her office. "No, I'm fine out of handcuffs."

THE BINGO KILLER

I rubbed his beard. "I see that. I mean, you're a hard working woman trying to survive."

Tess smiled again. "Guilty as seen, detective."

"Unfortunately, this isn't a social visit. I do have police business," I said. *I can flirt with Tess some other time.*

"Business, Mr. Riley," Tess said with a smirk.

I nodded at Tess. "Have either of you had any strange people hanging around the office or gotten any weird phone calls the past week, asking for Jill's address?"

"No, I don't believe so. I haven't seen anyone. Then again, I spend most of my time in my office when I'm not giving tours or checking on the maintenance men," Tess said.

"I see. I know where to find you if I need you." I looked at Tiffany. "What about you? Did you see anyone enter Jill's apartment by any chance, the past few weeks? Any weird letters to any of the tenants here?"

"No. I would have been the first person to hear of such things but I haven't," Tess said.

Tiffany looked at me. "No, I didn't. Jill only came by to pay her rent every month. She was friendly but still kept to herself."

"The reason I'm asking is because I got a letter with my name on it and her address. We had to come and get it from her mom, a few minutes ago." I said.

Tiffany told me that Connie gave her the mailbox key about 15 minutes before I arrived.

"It's a shame what happened to her. Jill was one of our best residents and a great person to be around," Tess said. "I'm going to miss her around here."

"I promised Connie I'd do all I can to find out what happened to Jill," I replied. "Tess, you call me if you remember anything. I insist," I said.

Tess smiled at Riley. "Absolutely, Detective Riley!"

"Well, I better go before my partner comes in here with guns blazing and wondering what the hell happened to me."

Tess laughed. "You're safe here."

"Say Tess, can you walk with me and unlock Jill's apartment? I want to see inside. My partner was here yesterday but it's my turn today."

"Of course. Let me get her key."

Tess and I walked over to Jill's apartment.

"Good morning, Detective Barker. How are you?" Tess asked.

"Hello! I'm good, thanks!"

Tess unlocked the door and told me I can lock the door from inside when I'm done.

"Darn, I won't get to see you before I leave. You're killing me, Tess."

Tess smiled, "You know where to find me, Detective Riley."

I thanked Tess for her time before she retreated to her office.

THE BINGO KILLER

"My pleasure, Mr. Riley." Tess sighed as she walked away. *Damn, he looks so good in his suit and beard. I may have to call him and have him jog my memory.*

Kate cleared her throat to get my attention and stop my disastrous flirting. "You done, Sam? Tick tock! We're on the clock."

"Right!"

I opened the door to Jill Sanders apartment and strolled in like I had been there plenty of times. Kate wasn't lying about how clean and organized Jill's place was. "Show me around, Kate. What happened yesterday?" I asked as she closed the door.

"Well, I got here and noticed Connie and Mary Owens sitting on the couch. I went to the bedroom and saw Jill in her bed. I searched her room but didn't find anything. Until I came into the kitchen and found Jill's purse on the table. I noticed the calls from Connie to Jill's phone and voicemail messages."

"That's when you found the piece of evidence?"

"The white packet." Kate nodded. "I turned it over to forensics."

I looked around the corner and into the bedroom. I felt a sharp pain in my head and my vision got very bright and started to spin. Not that it mattered because all I saw was Jill lying in her bed. Must have been around midnight. My guess was the vision I saw showed Jill already deceased. *What the hell am I seeing? I know Jill's not here.* My vision lasted for about fifteen seconds but seemed like an hour. Just as it came, the sudden flash-up of Jill left my head and my headache left. I struggled to catch my breath as I wiped sweat

KNIGHT

from my forehead. I felt fine after that, even though it was hot as hell in Jill's apartment. Someone had shut off the air conditioner but not the electricity. I immediately left the bedroom and made my way over to the purse on the kitchen table. It was still laying on its side, minus the white packet that was taken in by our forensics unit. Part of me wanted another vision of the white packet so I could maybe get a headstart in his investigation. I got nothing except a blank stare at the bottom of her purse. One of those brown, leather purses.

"Sam, what's wrong? You okay?" Kate asked as she walked over to me.

I glanced back at my partner with a smirk. I didn't want to alarm Kate and think I can't do my job. "Nothing, Kate. I'm just doing my job." I was put in a precarious position with the things that had happened since last night. I'm walking a fine line between my detective work and these things that allowed me to do the unthinkable. One false move and everything crashes down. I had to put this puzzle together, one piece at a time and not force a piece into a place where it doesn't belong.

"Fair enough. I hope you're doing your job instead of wasting time."

Believe me, what I've seen today isn't a waste of time at all. Even though I have no idea what was happening to me since nine o'clock last night.

"Thank you, Kate. Nothing I do from now on is a waste of time."

THE BINGO KILLER

"Sure, Sam." Kate said. She looked at me with inquisitive eyes. "Anything, Sam?"

"No, I guess not. I trust you did your work very well yesterday and we'll just have to wait."

"Of course I did, Sam. I'm good at my job."

I looked at my partner and patted her head like a new puppy. She didn't return the smile.

"Let's wrap this up and get back to the pit so we can solve this cipher."

"Alright. I'm done here. I can come back if I need to."

I locked the door from the inside and shut the door after Kate walked out. We made it back to my truck. "I had to ask a few questions about Jill Sanders." I said as I buckled my seatbelt and drove back to the BPD.

"It's okay. You're doing your job," Kate said.

I saw a good opportunity to tease my partner a little bit. "Good call coming out to get the letter, Kate. That property manager lady was flirting with me," I said.

Kate looked at me with curiosity. "Really? Did she now?"

"She wanted to give me a tour of the apartments and fill out an application. She said I could serve and protect her anytime."

"You don't say, Sam," Kate said sarcastically. *Spare me! That shit has nothing to do with me.*

"I told her I had to leave before you came in with guns drawn, looking for me," I replied.

"Sam Riley! You did not!" Kate smiled.

KNIGHT

I smiled at my partner and laughed. "What did you mean when you said you don't like to commit to things ahead of time?"

"Funerals aren't my thing. I just don't like dealing with all that sadness and getting emotionally involved with the victims. I know what my job is without having to go to funerals or talk with grieving families," Kate explained. Say what you will about Kate Barker. She had essentially mastered the ability to shut off her emotions when it was necessary. She desperately avoided moments that would easily bring down her walls.

"I was just wondering, Kate. I didn't mean to step on a landmine there."

"I know how that looks. That I'm mean or cruel-hearted or I don't care but at the end of the day, we're the ones who have to find the bad guys and arrest them," Kate said sternly. "We have to be strong for the people we work for. What are people going to think if they see us as emotional wrecks for victims?"

At the risk of having bad blood between me and my partner, I took her words as guidance to not get too attached. Kate was partly right though. We had a job to do and couldn't let our distractions get to us. I nodded and looked at Kate. "Yeah, I get what you're saying for sure. I'm not judging you Kate, if that's what you're wondering."

Kate stared out her window. "I didn't think you were, Sam. And I wouldn't care if you were."

"Not even a little?"

THE BINGO KILLER

Kate glanced over at me. "No, Sam. Let's just get back to the station."

"You wanna stop and get some Cheez-Its while we're out?"

"You know what rookie—actually, yeah, that sounds good. I'm down to my last box and need to restock for the week," Kate said.

Sam Riley with the assist. "Do you want me to go get them—yeah, I'll get them," I said.

I went inside our Walgreens and bought three boxes for $10 on sale. "I'm going to send you a bill at the end of the month for all these boxes of Cheez-Its," I said as I hopped back into my truck. I put the receipt in the middle console. "Tax write-off, Kate."

"Good thing I make more money than you," Kate said.

"Yeah, no kidding."

We arrived back at the station about 10:45 that morning. "We need to show Chief Williams the letter," Kate insisted. She walked to the Chief's office and knocked on his door.

Chief Williams motioned for us to come in and have a seat.

We stopped in front of his desk. "Chief, we have something to show you regarding Jill Sanders' death," Kate declared.

"Alright, let's see it."

I handed him the envelope and we waited.

Chief Williams pulled out the cipher paper and looked at it for a few seconds. "What is this?"

KNIGHT

"Kate and I got a call from Connie Sanders earlier this morning. Connie said she found that letter with my name on it in Jill's mailbox and called us immediately. We went over there and I asked the property manager and the receptionist some questions about Jill Sanders but they hadn't seen or heard anything out of the ordinary. We took a second look at Jill's apartment. Needless to say, this letter led us to look again. We thought maybe someone else broke in and left evidence behind.

Chief Williams looked at us. "I see. Well, Sam, you have an admirer of some kind." I then looked at the envelope. "It says here it's postmarked from Chicago."

"Really? All I saw was my name, as if I thought this thing was a sick prank by some attention-seeking jerk. Maybe a deranged fan of Jill's that took some of her lyrics too seriously?"

I didn't notice that detail, although the letters were skewered by a partial postmarked stamp, as it was easy to miss. Chicago, the Windy City. Somehow the wind blew that letter all the way down here to Southern Illinois. Why Chicago? Why not St. Louis or Nashville? Someone's luring me out or is covering their tracks. I won't know until I have one of those visions flashes I had at Jills' apartment, if I'm lucky. I hoped one would come to me by now. Maybe it's a one-time thing? Maybe it'll happen when I'm eating dinner and the thought of the letter runs through my mind?

THE BINGO KILLER

Chief Williams looked at me. "Someone's either playing a sick joke or else it's a game of cat and mouse and this is your piece of cheese, Sam. I don't like it any more than you and it's the last thing any of us need. But here it is."

"That's true, Sir!" I said. "I hope it's nothing."

"Let's hope this-is-nothing is right. Make me a copy and go figure this out. Kate, help Sam where you can. Keep me informed." Chief Williams noticed Kate was carrying a bag of Cheez-Its boxes. "Hey Kate, bring me a bowl of those cheesy cracker things when you can."

"Sure, Chief!" Kate went to the pit to grab a foam bowl and poured some crackers for Chief Williams. She was interrupted by a phone call. *God, what now?* "Detective Kate Barker."

"Hi, this is Brad Sessle with *The Bloomfield Times*. I'm calling to confirm and to get a statement about the death of Jill Sanders."

Kate looked at me.

I could tell she was annoyed with whoever she was speaking with. "I can confirm the death of Jill Sanders but the investigation is on-going and we don't comment beyond that. We sent out an official statement yesterday afternoon to the press. You should check that."

"Okay, that's what I'm looking for. We're doing a tribute piece to her for tomorrow's paper," Sessle explained.

"Great. I'll be looking for it. Have a good day, Mr. Sessle."

"Thank you, Det. Barker."

Reporters! Kate brought Chief Williams his afternoon snack.

Chapter 11

Wednesday, Sept. 3rd.

8:30 a.m.

I walked around the corner and found Betsy mopping one of the hallways, as I made my way to the pit. "Morning, Betsy!" I said, as I jumped to one side to avoid falling on my ass.

"Congratulations Detective Riley," Betsy said. Betsy often wore the same clothes to work two or three days in a row a week. Either her pants or her shirts, depending on the day. Maybe she didn't have a washer and dryer? I didn't mind really. Betsy did one hell of a job as a janitor and she was fun to be around.

"Thank you, Betsy. Don't work too hard, now!"

Betsy nodded. "Not a chance!"

Kate's lonely days in the pit were over as I settled at my desk and noticed an email from Dr. Bert Kline, our departments' part time, in-house psychologist. Kline made himself available every Wednesday.

"Hey Kate, I'm going to talk to Dr. Kline for a few minutes. Introduce myself and get his advice about how to cope with your addiction to Cheez-Its."

KNIGHT

Kate nodded. "Okay, Sam!" I could tell she was trying with all her might not to acknowledge my joke. But I saw that I was getting through her defenses and making an impression I'm sure. Which one will be revealed in time. I seem to have that effect on people eventually.

While Detective Riley spoke to Dr. Kline, I stepped into the conference room to call Mr. Tidwell. "Mr. Tidwell, how are you today, sir?" I leaned on the back of one of the chairs.

"Oh, hello! Detective Parker, right?"

"Barker. B as in boy. Barker."

"Barker, Barker. My apologies. I haven't been up to par since Jillybear's passing, as you can imagine. I've been an absolute mess to be honest."

"It's totally fine, Mr. Tidwell. I'm incredibly sorry for your loss and I'm sorry to bother you this morning."

"Thank you, Detective Barker. I appreciate that." I heard Mr. Tidwell's voice cracking. "You're not bothering me. It's good to talk to someone."

That struck me as odd. Surely Mr. Tidwell spoke with Connie Sanders about Jill's death? Unless their relationship was almost non-existent? Not that uncommon nowadays. I felt terrible for the man. "I have some questions about Jill. When was the last time you spoke to Jill?"

"I spoke to her Sunday afternoon, well into the evening. She visited me at my house for a few hours. She talked about her singing and performing all over.

THE BINGO KILLER

We talked about memories and life in general. Things we usually talk about when we were together. I would go further Detective Barker but I want to remember our conversations as they happened in Jill's memory."

"I completely understand, Mr. Tidwell. I just have a few more questions. Did she say anything unusual, someone following her or any trouble she might have been having?"

"No, she didn't say anything like that. She didn't even have a boyfriend."

"She told you that?" I inquired.

"Detective Barker, I'm a retired private investigator. You and I have access to information most people don't. Jill didn't have a boyfriend," Tidwell declared.

I believed him. *Just a dad protecting his daughter.* "I see. No problems with her manager or anyone that worked with her?"

"No, not that I recall. Things were good with Jill," Tidwell stated. "That says a lot about who she was as a person. Everyone liked Jill."

"I see. Jill didn't seem sad or depressed?"

"Absolutely not. She was the same Jill. Happy and upbeat. Smiling. That's how I'll always remember her, as she was the last time I saw her. That gives me some comfort in all this pain I have. She didn't deserve to be murdered the way she was."

"I completely understand. Why do you believe she was murdered, Mr. Tidwell?"

"Detective Barker, I know my daughter. She was happy and healthy and all of the sudden she's gone.

That's not a coincidence. My gut tells me she was murdered." Part of me wanted to believe he was correct but I still had a paper trail to follow—the autopsy and tox reports. They always lead me to where I need to go. "Mr. Tidwell. One last question, did Jill have to eat or drink at your house?"

"She had cranberry juice. She brought a jug of the stuff and went straight to my kitchen to get a glass when she first arrived," Tidwell declared. "Jill said it was good for her kidneys. She was kind of a health nut. At least that's the impression I got from our conversations. My guess is she wanted to care for her voice and her stage presence. She said she was working on her nervousness and anxiety."

"Did Jill have anything that required sugar? Did she have any tea?" I asked. The white packet was all I had to go on.

Tidwell paused for a moment. "Uh, yeah, yeah. Come to think of it, we had a few glasses of tea before she left. That was one of our traditions. When Jill was a young girl, we used to have little tea parties in her room," Tidwell said with a heavy sigh. Over the years, Jill and her dad moved from bedroom tea parties to the kitchen table or living room.

"That's good to know, Mr. Tidwell. I can tell you that our investigation is on-going and if I have any more questions, I'll be sure to give you a call."

"I expect you will. Call anytime. Please find my daughter's killer, Detective Barker."

THE BINGO KILLER

I heard the desperation in his voice as plain as day. I stared at the conference table and thought about how he felt. Mr. Tidwell more than likely felt so damn lost, like an asteroid floating in space with no known trajectory—waiting to crash into some planet or moon, knowing he couldn't do a thing to solve his daughters' supposed murder. *Would Mr. Tidwell crash?* I asked myself. Not if I could help it! "I'm doing my best. Thank you for your time, Mr. Tidwell." I paused to gather my thoughts about Jill's death before I made my way back to the pit.

******

Dr. Kline gave me the number of a local psychic he had known for years.

After our forty-five minute session, I went back to the pit and had a few minutes to call Lydia Tate before Kate returned. I dialed her number and heard Lydia's voice on the third ring. "May I speak to Lydia Tate, please?" I put the card in my top drawer to hide it. Of course, all Kate had to do was open my drawer and my cover was blown.

"This is Lydia. May I ask who's calling?"

"Hi Lydia. This is Detective Sam Riley of the Bloomfield Police Department. How are you this morning?"

"I'm doing very well. Thanks for asking. What do I owe the pleasure of your call, Mr. Riley?"

KNIGHT

"I got your number from Dr. Bert Kline. I spoke with him earlier this morning. He suggested I give you a call. I have an urgent, personal matter to discuss with you. Today if possible?" I asked kindly.

"He did, did he? How is that old fart?"

"Yes he did. He's good. He's enjoying the classics. I'll say that."

"Kline is a classic—which one is up to him," Lydia said with a laugh. "Well, what kind of personal matters are we talking about here, Mr. Riley?"

I paused before I answered her question. I lowered my voice and held the phone closer to my ear. "The kind we both share," I said.

"I see. I'll give you one hour of my time. How about two o'clock this afternoon? Candlewood Cemetery. Will that work?" Lydia asked.

"Yes, absolutely! That works great for me. Thank you so much, Mrs. Tate."

"See you then. Mr. Riley."

I hung up as Kate rounded the corner and walked to her desk.

"So who were you on the phone with? Hot date or a colonoscopy appointment? It's okay, Sam. I won't tell…..everybody."

"Oh really?" I nodded. "I'm sure you won't Kate. I'm taking my mother shopping at two o'clock. Big sale on groceries. Meats and….things."

He can't even lie well enough to be taken seriously.
"Meats and things? Sure, Sam! Have fun shopping. Bring me back a big box of White Cheddar Cheez-Its.

THE BINGO KILLER

I'll keep your secret as long as you bring me what I asked for. It's not a bribe either. It's an order!" Kate smiled at me.

"Adding Cheez-Its to the list. Got it," I said. "Done!"

Kate paused and swerved to her right, crossed her arms and gawked at me. "Shopping? That's the best you can do? You know Sam, there can't be any secrets between us. Middle of the afternoon isn't very subtle."

"Yeah, well, Kate, I'm going to try to figure out this cipher." I looked at my partner with a straight face.

Kate nodded. "Okay!"

I gave her a comforting look. *Damn, she's good. Maybe Kate should have these psychic powers? Then I'd be out on patrol again. I'll keep them as long as they keep me in the pit.*

I looked up different ciphers on the Internet. At first I found the ones relating to the Zodiac killer out in California in the late 60's. I eventually found a dice cipher that included 26 dice symbols with an assigned number to it—one for each letter. I printed off the guide and matched up letter by letter, dice by dice, until I spelled out some semblance of words.

"Kate, come check this out right quick," I asked my partner.

"What now, Sam?" Kate said as she meandered over to my desk.

"Save the Last Dance, I'm closer than you think," I said. "This has to refer to Jill Sanders." *Save the Last Dance. She was a musician after all.*

KNIGHT

"I'm closer than you think," I repeated. *This has to be the one who sent the cipher letter.*

"What do you make of it, Kate?"

Kate said the message could have something to do with Jill Sanders. "These ciphers usually come in pairs. More might come in so we don't have the entire message, Sam. We have to take it with a grain of salt."

"Or sugar," I said. "We need to make a copy of this and get it over to forensics right away."

Kate nodded.

I went to make a few copies of the cipher and returned to the pit.

She took one of the copies of the cipher from me and taped the copy to one of the windows near my desk. "There! That's our evidence board."

"Let's go show Chief Williams what we have so far," I suggested.

"After you, Detective Riley!"

THE BINGO KILLER

Chapter 12

1:45 p.m.

"Don't be late for your shopping appointment, Sam. And bring me back my Cheez-Its," Kate said.

"For sure, Kate." I nodded and smiled as I left the pit. I drove to the cemetery and parked my truck near the flagpole, towards the back of the cemetery where the roads meet. The city had recently paved the roads of Candlewood Cemetery with asphalt. A big pile of dirt had been dumped by the edge of the woods, yards from the flagpole. The pile had footprints all around it. Probably from neighborhood kids with nothing better to do all summer?

I got out and looked around. I noticed an older woman sitting on a small bench and walked over to introduce myself. *This must be Lydia Tate. But where's her car? Did someone drop her off? Does she need a ride back to her house?*

"Hi, Lydia. I'm Sam Riley. I appreciate you meeting me this afternoon." I felt a sudden chill up my left arm that stood my hairs up like an army platoon standing at attention. I ignored it and figured it was the wind doing its job.

"Hello, Mr. Riley," she said.

"How are you, Mrs. Tate?" I asked.

"Do you come here often, Detective?"

"No, I don't. I don't have any family or anyone I know buried here. Not yet, anyway."

"You will soon, Mr. Riley." She focused her gaze straight ahead on the headstones in front of us, across the road.

"Okay. Thanks for the warning," I said, with a confused look.

"You're welcome! It's peaceful here this time of day."

"Yes, it sure is."

Slight breeze and sunshine. The American flag flapping in the breeze. She didn't say anything. She nodded and gave me a menacing look disguised as a smile—one of those sinister smiles that you can tell some evil shit's about to go down.

And I walked into this trap! Good job, Sam! Kate knows you're shopping with your mother instead of playing hide and seek with the ghosties. I quickly looked away like it never happened and saw the parked cars. "So Ms. Tate, I know it sounds crazy,"—CARS!!! *I didn't see a second car when I got out.* I looked to my left and saw a blank space where the woman I talked to, sat. I stood up and looked all around me trying to find the woman. I took a deep breath. *Son of a bitch! That's the second ghost I've seen this week,* I thought to myself. I saw Lydia getting out of her car and waving at me from a distance.

THE BINGO KILLER

"Detective Riley, how are you?" Lydia said, walking towards me.

I raised my hand at Lydia before I looked down and saw a square, gray stone with an "S" engraved on it. "I'm….fine." I muttered. I don't know if Lydia heard me or not but I was far from fine.

"Sam Riley. Nice to finally meet you." I shook her hand.

"Hi, Sam! I'm Lydia Tate." Lydia wore a thin, white sweater and jeans.

"Thank you for seeing me today. I hope I wasn't keeping you from anything important."

"Not at all. You caught me on one of my good days. Were you talking to someone just now, Mr. Riley? I could have swore I heard you talking to someone?"

I nodded. "I thought it was you sitting besides me but I was mistaken. The woman who sat beside me just up and vanished when I saw you get out of your car," I said.

"Really? There's no other cars here besides ours. She couldn't have gone far."

I combed the area around the bench again. "I don't see anyone else out here besides us."

Lydia looked around and pointed off to her right. "I do. She's over there by the Smith headstone." Lydia said the woman had an older blue dress on with tiny red roses on it. Her gray hair was up in a bunn. The woman I saw gave me the impression she lived in the 1930's, if I had to put her in history. I looked at Lydia. "That's why I'm here. Cat's out of the bag, or should I say spirit's out of the body?" I didn't know how she would take my small dose of sarcasm.

"That's a new one. Fair enough," Lydia smiled. "Let's take a walk. It's a nice, sunny day."

"Sure. I could use the exercise." I patted my stomach and smiled. I wasn't sure I could or would make a good impression on Lydia with my gifts but I had my humor. I was shooting for mixed results.

Lydia led us down the road away from the vehicles. "So Mr. Riley, you said it's a personal matter. Care to elaborate?"

Let me start from the beginning. I had this wicked dream early Monday morning. I caught someone who didn't have a face. In my dream, Bullseye–that's his name. He said, "he's coming and will kill again." I told Lydia the same thing about my dream as I described to Dr. Kline, when I saw him a few days ago. The flashbacks of my dreams became engraved in my brain like my favorite movie.

A strong gust of wind blew through the cemetery. "That's weird. Sounds like a warning. Foreshadowing. Maybe even Karma. I hope it's just a dream but I've been wrong before. Being a psychic isn't an exact science. It's more hearsay, hunches and lucky guesses," Lydia declared.

"Dr. Kline said the same thing, which is what I'm afraid of. Hearsay and hunches and hope that my guesses are lucky. All the things I can't use in an investigation," I said.

THE BINGO KILLER

Lydia stopped and looked at me. "I understand. There's a lot at stake in your line of work. And you're right to be skeptical. It's not something you get used to overnight, or even in a few days. It took me a year or two to adjust to my psychic powers."

"A few years huh? Terrific! I don't have a year. Hell, I don't have a week. I'm glad you understand. If anyone could help, Kline said you could, Lydia. I need to get a hold on whatever this is as soon as possible."

"Patience, Mr. Riley. Make friends with it," Lydia said. "I know a few things."

I nodded. "I believe you, Lydia."

"Now Sam, I have a few questions to ask you. This is important in understanding and working your psychic powers or abilities."

"Sure. That's why I'm here," I said. Well, half of me was there. I was there to find the other half.

"What have you experienced since Monday?" Lydia asked.

"I've seen one spirit that calls itself Mystery, at my house Monday. He heard my thoughts and heard my voice during an arrest Monday morning. Mystery apparently followed me home," I said.

"Clairaudience. It comes in waves. It's annoying to have one voice speaking to you at the same time as a living voice, let alone twenty voices at the same time," Lydia said.

"Yes, it's like shouting at thin air and being called crazy," I said. I guessed that part. I didn't have the slightest idea about anything in Lydia's world.

Lydia smiled and nodded. "Wanna hear something kind of sad?"

I nodded. "Yeah!" *Couldn't be any more sad than a thirty-year old man seeing ghosts and trying to make sense of it all?*

"I didn't have anyone to help me or talk me through it. Growing up was tough for me. My parents thought I was having some sort of mental breakdown," Lydia said. Lydia had it rough in school, growing up with trouble she got herself into. The taunting and teasing and rumors from the other kids. Especially in her teen years. She heard "Looney Lydia" whispered among the kids, snickering at her high school during the class changes. She trained herself to walk straight to her locker and to her next class.

"I'm sorry you had to go through all that. I can't even imagine what that was like for you," I said. *I guess there is something more sad than my situation.*

"I appreciate that, Sam. I've made peace with my past and my parents. I forgave them for what they didn't know how to do," Lydia replied. She overcame a lot of childhood trauma—with the help of Dr. Kline, to finally forgive her parents. *Not that they deserved my forgiveness. THEY DIDN'T LISTEN! It's not my fault!*

"That's really decent of you to do," I said. "Was it hard?"

THE BINGO KILLER

"It took some work but eventually I did. But we're here to talk about you, Sam." Lydia shook her head out of her trance.

I had things a little different, as the timing was very unusual.

"Your job and people's lives are on the line," Lydia said.

I nodded, "Yeah, tell me about it. How do I control it?"

"You may not know this or haven't noticed but spirits are drawn to your energy. You have a high energy level, Sam. That's what helped you catch the Northside Burglar the other day," Lydia explained.

I stopped walking and stood in silence. "How did you know it was me? That little detail wasn't on the news," I asked.

"Oh come on, Sam. I've been reading you since you stepped out of your truck. I sensed your energy like that gust of wind a few minutes ago."

"Just checking, Lydia." It never occurred to me to do the same to her. I'm still that guy who doesn't know what he's doing.

Lydia threw out her own surprise for me. "Oh yeah? Check your phone!"

I pulled his phone out of my pocket to prove Lydia wrong. "My phone's not ring—." My phone vibrated. I tapped the answer button. "Well speak of the devil, if it isn't my partner, Kate Barker."

Lydia smiled.

"Not yet I'm not, but we'll have words if you don't bring me my Cheez-Its, Sam. Since you're, you know, shopping with your mom." Kate said.

"I promise I'll bring them when I get back to the station. Priority one!" I said.

I hung up. "Sorry Lydia, that was my partner. She wants Cheez-Its for some strange reason. Anything to keep her happy," I said. *Orders from the side.*

"That was interesting," Lydia smiled. "I get a sense of her being really comfortable with you. I think she's really glad you two are partners."

I wasn't too sure about Lydia's assessment of mine and Kate's partnership. *I'll take it. Couldn't hurt anything.* "No, she's just pulling rank and I'm trying to keep the peace," I said.

"Yeah, Sam. That's how it starts," Lydia explained. "Good luck with that!"

"No, no, we're just partners. How did you know she—"

"How did I know she was going to call you?"

I nodded. "Yeah! What's up with that?"

"I'm telepathic also. One of several levels of psychic abilities," Lydia said.

I shook my head in disbelief. "Here we go! You don't say?"

"I do say, Sam!" Lydia winked at me.

I laughed. "Okay, okay! You said spirits are attracted to my energy. How so?"

THE BINGO KILLER

"They see it as help, more than anything. They see the white light around you and gravitate towards you like flies on horseshit. Pardon my language!"

I didn't mind Lydia's language. Her honesty is what I needed to hear. "Do you see a white light around me?" I asked.

"I sure do, Sam. It's bright and pure. Calming and reassuring. I get the sense of safety and comfort around you. That's the vibe you give off, whether or not you mean to. That's what I feel," Lydia said.

"That's good to know I guess." That caught me off guard. *I ain't gonna lie.*

"Of course it is, Sam. Take it as a confidence booster. But you have to be open to your true self to fully know your energy. That's when the spirit's voices become clear and loud enough to hear them legibly," Lydia said. "Spirits will know if you're in tune with your energy or not. They see it as an open or closed sign, basically."

"Yeah, that makes sense, I guess," I said.

"Sam, it's entirely up to you in how you use your gift. Will you help those spirits seeking your help? Or will you use it to randomly read other people's energies and risk doing more harm than good? Those are the questions you have to ask yourself." Lydia said.

Who has a suitable answer for such a question? "No doubt I'm at a crossroads, Lydia. But it's my choice. I think I can do both if I have strong enough evidence," I said. Evidence—the definition of that word changed for me as I knew it in a single moment.

KNIGHT

In a flash, it no no longer included the physical. It now included the meta-physical. The evidence beyond the evidence. The kind that you had to see with your eyes wide shut. The corner of your eye-kind. The hair-raising kind.

"Yes, it is your choice, Sam. But you're walking down a path under cloudy and dark skies."

"I've done that once this week." *Can't you tell, Lydia?* With a confused look on my face, I asked, "You think I'm going to make a mistake?"

With great power comes great responsibility, kept popping into my head over and over again, even though I tried to ignore this expression. Not much was pushed out of my mind the past few days, no matter how hard I tried. I looked all around Lydia and myself. "You're right, Lydia. With great power comes great responsibility. I heard you loud and clear."

"What are you talking about, Sam? I never said those words to you. I wasn't thinking that," Lydia said as she looked at me.

"You didn't just say that to me a few seconds ago?" I asked

"No, dear. I didn't. Must be someone else here with us." Lydia looked around but didn't see anything or anyone.

We stood in the middle of the cemetery. I looked around in all directions but didn't see anyone. "I don't see anyone, Lydia. I think I need more practice."

THE BINGO KILLER

"Yes, you do Sam. What just happened is called Clairvoyance. It's when you see people or know things you wouldn't otherwise see or know."

"Great! Put that on my gift list," I said.

Lydia looked at me for a moment and gave me a little honest perspective. "I don't see any Star Wars/dark side of the Force or Sith powers at work here. Okay, Sam?" How she could tell would remain a secret.

"Good to know," I said. "I mean I understand your reference."

"I've talked with many detectives over the years. I've always told them, and other mediums like us, that our gifts are not meant for us to read someone's energy with a false or negative intent. Even if they committed a crime and you can clearly see it, you have no physical evidence. Just a memory in someone's head—a passing thought, Sam. You'd probably get fired for something like that for violating their rights. Memories are not probable cause just because you can see them. I can't stress that enough. I tell that to everyone I speak to regarding our common interests."

Lydia had a great point that really hit home for me. I might get around legal issues and be covered if I can ask the right questions relevant to the conversation. "Lydia, what about seeing spirits?"

"I will warn you—speaking from experience—they'll sneak up on you, out of nowhere, and scare the ever-loving shit out of you. The scariest one for me was when I woke up early one morning from a dream of an old woman telling me to get out of her house. I woke up and that same woman was standing over me, yelling at me to get out of her bed."

"I'd piss my pants if that happened to me," I said.

Lydia laughed and nodded. "That's what they do sometimes. Some of them are angry or confused." I considered these spirits' emotions or even their anger.

"So I've heard. Well, this has been very interesting and most helpful, but the one thing I still don't understand—and I'm sure you get this a lot—but why me? I didn't ask for this."

"No one does when they're born. But there are lots of reasons, Sam. Near-death experiences, your gifts passed down through your family. You've had your gifts but they were dormant until they showed up with that dream and they took over. Lifestyle change. Mental transformation. Spiritual awakening. Take your pick," Lydia said.

"Maybe. I don't believe I'm the chosen one or any of that bullshit. I just don't see it. I'm just an average guy, nothing special."

"Maybe? Maybe not, Sam. Your world has changed drastically. How you cope and deal with this change is entirely up to you? You have to trust your instincts and go with what your heart and mind tell you."

"That's what I hoped you'd say," I declared.

"I want you to treat and use your gifts as such. Good faith, Sam! Good faith!"

"Good faith!" *Good faith!*

THE BINGO KILLER

"I feel like I'm riding a roller coaster, blindfolded, in the dark. How do I control it or get in sync with my energy?" I felt like a kid in some high school psychology class the way I asked her these questions. And Lydia's lecture was college-level.

"Meditation is the best way. Clear your mind of everything. Feel your body and spirit. That loud voice, different from your conscience, you know the one, will get quieter and quieter. You can tune out these spirits the more you practice."

"Is it really that easy?" I asked.

"That depends on how comfortable you are with the person you are. Do you like and enjoy the hobbies you have? The shows you watch? Are you overall happy with your life and direction? The company you keep? Is your energy peaceful and positive? Those kinds of things."

"I see. I'm willing to do the work, Lydia." It's not so much of a question of whether or not I have to, but I want to do the work. The stakes of ignoring my gifts are just as high as my gift interfering with my job.

"I think you'll do well, Sam, with a little effort. Do you know how many people would kill for your gift?" Lydia asked.

"No, but I know you know, Lydia."

"Out of close to 8 billion people on the planet, I'd say about a few million, Sam. And not all of them for good either."

That's what scares me—the ones with negative intentions. I tell myself I'm one of the good guys. What's the difference between the good guys and them, one might ask? I have the

KNIGHT

U.S. Constitution on my side. State and federal laws. The Federal Rules of Evidence. And so do the bad people. "Wow, I had no idea," I said. "But that makes sense." None of it makes much sense. How could it? This whole world is new to me. I'm going on day two and Lydia's practically a legend in her field as far as I'm concerned. Lydia took me to school.

"No one ever thinks it's that high. Give them a little power and they're a different person." Lydia shook her head at me. "Don't become one of those people!"

I nodded. "I won't. I'll try to play fair until I can't anymore." *I can't blur the lines between work and play.*

"I understand, Sam. I know you have a job to do."

We finally made it around the loop and back to our vehicles. "Well, Lydia, this has been a very interesting conversation this afternoon. I've had my eyes widened and my mind blown. Thank you for your time and wonderful insight. I really appreciate it very much."

"You're most welcome, Sam. Glad I could help another great detective," Lydia said.

"That you did. Unfortunately I have to go now. I have to stop at the store for those damn Cheez-Its," I said with a smirk. *Orders from the side.*

Lydia smiled and gave him a hug. "If you need me, call me. We'll meet again. I promise. Goodbye, Sam."

"Alright. I'll see you later, Lydia." I walked back to my truck and drove away.

THE BINGO KILLER

Lydia slowly walked over to her car. She opened her door but quickly turned around.

She looked out at the headstones scattered about. *No, follow him. Watch him. If you two talk, report back to me everything he says and does.*

"And if he crosses the line?"

Lydia shut her door and rolled down her window. "We'll save him from himself," she replied. Lydia drove out of the cemetery back to her next appointment. *Whatever it takes!*

Chapter 13

Thursday, September 4th.

10 a.m.

Kate stood in the shade of a pine tree outside the BPD. "We'll head over there right now." She came back to the pit and stopped at the edge of her desk, next to a stack of files. Pictures of her family graced the other side of her laptop computer. Kate was an only child—just her and her parents. "Sam, I just got a call from the medical examiner. We need to head over to the morgue. Let's go." Kate grabbed her keys. "We can take my car. I promise I won't scare you too badly. Besides, if you can survive my driving, you can survive anything," Kate said with a smile.

    I stood up as my chair slid back towards the wall. "This should be fun. Nothing like the rookie's first time going to the morgue." I grabbed my cell phone and followed my partner to her car. I was hit with the overwhelming aroma of vanilla car scent when I got into her car. She drove us to the Moss County Morgue. "Do you think you have enough vanilla scented fresheners, Kate?" I asked. "Smells like a vanilla ice cream cone in here."

THE BINGO KILLER

Kate looked at me. "No, I need some more for the backseat, now that you mention it, Sam."

"Sure. Good to know what kind of detective you are," I said.

"And what kind of detective am I, Sam?" Kate asked. She glanced at me for a few seconds and then back on the road, curious about my answer.

"Don't take it personally."

"No, not at all, Sam. Vanilla is my favorite car scent."

"I meant it as a compliment, if anything," I said.

"You were saying?"

"What?" I asked. The vanilla scent took my concentration away for a split second.

"What kind of detective am I?" Kate asked.

"Uh—you're more order than chaos, like some people. It's a good thing. I'm impressed how well you take care of your car. I'm the same way," I explained. I didn't want to get on my partner's bad side. *She might shoot me if I say she's driving too fast or to look out for that car up ahead.* I didn't dare say a word about her driving, not that I had anything to complain about. Barker had never gotten a speeding ticket since she was old enough to drive.

"So Kate, did the doctor say anything else about the report or her autopsy?" I asked.

"He just said come to the morgue. That's all!" Kate said. "Let me do most of the talking, Sam."

"Sure. I don't have anything to say to a dead body." *A ghost, yeah, probably.*

Kate quickly glanced at me. "I hope not, Sam. Otherwise, you have a bit of a problem," She said with a smirk.

Yeah, I'll say.

Kate parked in the first open visitors' spot to the right of the handicapped sign. Kate greeted Patty Stewart, the secretary, as she and I walked into the morgue lobby, which let off a cool and peaceful atmosphere inside the building, with its blue walls and white floor tiles.

"Hi Patty, how are you doing?"

"Good, Ms. Barker. And you?"

"Oh, you know, I make a living off the dead, drunk and desperate," Kate said hesitantly.

"Don't we all," Patty said. She looked at me. "Who's this tall drink of sweet tea?"

I welcomed the compliment with a smile. "I'm Detective Riley. How are you, Patty?"

"I'm alive," Patty moaned.

"Would you two please sign in? It's a formality. I couldn't care less who comes and goes but as long as it's not the dead who sign out, I'm good."

"Or signing in for that matter," I said sarcastically.

"No shit!" Patty said.

Kate and I signed in.

"We're here to see Dr. Willow about a case we're investigating. He's expecting us," Kate said.

"Of course," Patty said. "Down the hall. He's back there somewhere with a body on the table. Big windows. Can't miss him."

THE BINGO KILLER

"Later Patty," Kate said.

"Later doll face," Patty said.

"Thanks," Riley said.

We walked into the well-lit autopsy room and stopped near the entrance. Dr. Willow wore his blue scrubs and a white coat. He stood at the sink vanity near the back wall of the room. He washed his hands before introducing himself. I like ME's and coroners with clean hands.

"Dr. Willow, how are you today?" Kate asked.

"Ah, Detective Barker! Glad you could come on such short notice."

Willow grabbed his clipboard and walked over to greet his guests.

"Yeah, that's our job. Always good to see a colleague I admire," Kate said.

Dr. Willow stuck his hand out to shake my hand. "And you are?"

"Detective Sam Riley. I'm new so take it easy on me."

"Nice to meet you, Detective.

"Thanks for washing your hands, doctor."

Dr. Willow laughed. "I'll try but it doesn't always go that way in my line of work."

"Sure it does, doc!" I replied. "Soap. Hands. Water. All clean!" I smiled.

Dr. Willow laughed. "Thanks for the tip, detective. I like your partner's sense of humor, Kate."

"Glad someone does," Kate retorted as she glared at me.

KNIGHT

I shook my head. I couldn't hide my squeamish feeling being in the same room with a dead body. Granted, I've seen my fair share of homicides and car accidents over the years but I didn't have to spend time with them in the morgue. *Gotta play the role, Sam! Might skip lunch today also!*

Kate slightly turned toward Dr. Willow. "Doctor Willow, what did you find about Jill Sanders?"

Dr. Willed flexed his eyes and tilted his head to the right. "Let's go look at her personal belongings right quick. It might help you in your investigation. Right this way, Kate." Dr. Willow led my partner out of the room.

"Be back in a moment, Sam." Kate pointed. "Keep an eye on Jill Sanders. Make sure she doesn't go anywhere okay!" Kate smiled at me.

"Sometimes they go to the bathroom and come back. It's really weird at first but I appreciate the courtesy of not having to clean them up," Dr. Willow said, looking at me. "One of the perks of the job." Dr. Willow smiled.

"Sure, get it all out. Have your laughs, Kate. Dr. Funny!"

Kate and Dr. Willow stepped out of the room and walked down the hallway.

I slowly turned around and exhaled. I don't know what in the hell compelled me to do what I just did next. *Not my finest moment!* I walked over to the exam table and lifted up the sheet over the victim, exposing only Jill's head. I paused for a second and sighed. Two

THE BINGO KILLER

seconds later, Jill's eyes popped open and looked directly at me. "JESUS!!!" I screamed, as I jumped back. I felt my soul leave my body for a split second. My heart skipped a beat. I bumped into the table behind me. The table buckled with enough force to move it a few inches. I quickly grabbed the table with both hands to prop myself up. I stood against the table, leaned back as I tried to catch my breath. I looked over at Jill's body and saw her eyes closed. I looked around the room before composing myself and walking over to the table. *I saw…her eyes open. She sure as shit opened her eyes. I saw them.*

"BOOOOOO!!!" Jill Sanders' ghost yelled into my right ear.

I let out a quick yell as I turned to my right.

She stood behind me. She ducked down under the table just as quickly as I turned around. I backed away from the exam table with Jill's body on it. I gawked at her body like I expected it to move on its own.

Jerry Teeks, an older, hefty security guard with a thick mustache reminiscent of the wild west, walked by and heard my little fright fest. He immediately came into the room. "You okay, mister?"

I looked at Teeks in confusion. "What? Yeah…yeah…I'm fine. I just got startled. I thought I felt something touch my shoulder." I pointed at Jill's body and the room. *Not the place you want someone to touch you without your permission.*

Teeks curiously looked at me. "Ain't nothing to be afraid of, son. Hell, it's just a dead body. It's the live ones you have to worry about."

KNIGHT

Yeah, until they sneak up on you. "Yeah...that's...good call." I nodded. I looked back at Jill's body. I looked at Jerry.

"That's right. Watch out for the living," Jill said. She stood back up from underneath the table.

I looked back at Jill. "Right, right. Good advice," I said. "I'll keep that in mind. Thank you!" I turned back to look at Teeks.

Teeks shook his head. "You take it easy, son. You hear?"

I nodded. "Sure. Absolutely. Thank you!" I waved Teeks goodbye.

Teeks walked out of the room with his hands on his belt and down the hallway towards the lobby.

"Holy fuck! What just happened," I asked as I took a deep breath. I walked over to the glass wall and looked in both directions. Teeks was out of earshot of the autopsy room. I turned around and saw Jill's ghost standing on the left side of the table, looking at me intently. "Who the hell are you and what are you doing here?" That table was all that separated me and her ghost. *Too close for comfort*.

She looked down at her body. "Isn't it obvious?" Jill hinted. A tear rolled over her left cheek and hit the white sheet covering her body. She looked up at me with tears in her eyes.

"You can hear and see me?" Jill asked.

"Bet your ass I can. Did you think whispering in my ear, in a morgue, would somehow make me happy? You scared the shit out of me, Jill."

THE BINGO KILLER

Jill looked at me with fear in her eyes. "Yeah, you're scared? Try seeing your body on this table and then you can be scared." Jill took a few moments for herself.

Get a grip, Sam. She can't hurt you. She's just scared and confused.

Sanders walked to the front of the exam table, leaned over and kissed her forehead. More tears streamed down her face and evaporated before reaching her skin. *What kind of fucked up world doesn't let a ghost's tears touch her own face when mourning over her own body? I deserve that at least.* "I can't believe what I'm seeing right now. Me, dead! How do you make peace with that? This is the only life I had and now it's gone. All because some selfish asshole decided I shouldn't live anymore. How do you let that go?"

"Relax, your funeral is next week," I said. "You can cross over or whatever you do in the afterlife. Have fun!" I didn't realize just how insensitive and rude my comment was until it was too late.

Jill shot me an angry look that I clearly deserved. "Relax? What am I supposed to do until then? Coffee and scones at Starbucks? I'm a ghost. What do I know about being a ghost? Who does? There's no class on how to be a ghost," Jill said, looking at me with frustration.

"You're free to haunt anyone besides me Jill. I have a job to do." It didn't include dealing with ghosts and babysitting them. Or maybe it did and I didn't care.

KNIGHT

Jill looked at me with anger all over her face. "You work for me, Detective. I hired you when I was killed, remember? Or do you need reminding?"

As much as she terrified me with her solid black eyes, she was right. I do work for her. Hell of a way to remind me, not that I needed reminding.

I countered with a little pushback. "You don't have to lecture me about doing my job. It's my first week but I don't need any help from a ghost."

Jill laughed. "Are you sure about that? Kind of looks like you do, if you're the only one that can see and hear me. I beg to differ, Sam."

"Detective Riley!" I said sternly. I turned around to give his answer. "I'm quite positive. Thank you very much. Besides, what can you offer me? Any clues about why you're on the meat slab over there?" I said, pointing to the table.

Jill looked at me but paused before she spoke her truth. "You insensitive prick! Who's ass did you have to kiss to become a detective?"

"Excuse me?" I walked back over to the exam table. "I don't think you can afford to insult the people solving your murder. If you were murdered?"

"I was murdered," Jill said assertively.

"You don't expect me to believe the word of a ghost, do you? You could be protecting someone or her twin? Protecting your sister? I shouldn't be talking to a dead person. I don't know how any of this is possible. I don't believe in ghosts or the paranormal or anything like that," I said.

THE BINGO KILLER

"I don't know either but it's my first time being dead."

"Fair point," I said. "Why are we talking?"

"Well, I'm now a ghost and my body is right here. You can hear and see me. It's really simple. The sooner you realize the reality of the moment, the better off we are."

Kate walked back into the examination room, followed by Dr. Willow. "Who are you talking to, Sam?" Kate and Dr. Willow stopped at the foot of the table, close to Jill's toe tag, which was mostly hidden inside the sheet.

I looked at Kate. "Nothing! You wouldn't believe me if I told you." I looked at Jill's body. Her ghost was gone or hiding.

"You can tell me later," Kate said.

"No, I can't." I don't think I will either.

"Speaking of strange, the toxicology report showed a sudden intake of a high amount of caffeine. Very potent stuff. It could be in a pill or a powder of some kind. Same shit they put in those damn energy drinks, well if you drink enough of them at once. Three-dollar heart attack in a can," Dr. Willow said.

"So, it's a caffeine overdose?" I asked.

"Yes, the overdose sped up her heart rate to an astronomical level, so fast that it caused her heart to overwork itself and eventually stop. She died in her sleep so she didn't feel any pain. It was quick," Dr. Willow explained.

"No, no, that's not right. I hardly ever drank soda. Where did the caffeine come from? How did it get into my system?" Jill said.

"That is what we have to find out," I said, looking at Jill.

"Who are you talking to Sam? You okay?" Kate said, as she and Dr. Willow looked at each other in confusion.

I looked around the room for Jill.

"You okay there, Detective Riley? You looked bug-eyed for a moment," Dr. Willow inquired.

"What do we have to find out?" Kate asked.

"Why did she have so much caffeine in her system if she didn't drink such drinks or even sodas," I asked.

"How do you know she didn't drink energy drinks or sodas?" Kate asked.

"Only thing I drank before I died was tea at my dad's house," Jill said quietly.

I looked down at Jill's body. "What I mean is I don't want to miss anything," I said. "I'm speculating here." *Questions, Sam! Ask them!*

I looked at my partner and Dr. Willow. "We'll start with her dad. Maybe he knows something about the tea they drank," I declared.

"How did you know they had tea, Sam?"

"You tell me Kate?" We're partners. No secrets, remember?"

"I agree but I don't think I told you that yet."

THE BINGO KILLER

"You did. Must have slipped out. Besides, how many other drinks are there that have caffeine and need sugar?"

"Right!" Kate said.

Dr. Willow walked over to Jill's table. "Right! Well, we don't have any signs of blunt force trauma, no stab wounds, no red marks around her neck. Not sure if this is even a homicide."

"She could have accidently ingested the caffeine somehow? Maybe she got some medicines mixed up?" I asked.

"There were no other drugs in her system. No alcohol or any other recreational drugs. Everything else came back normal, in fact, for a healthy 30-year-old woman," Dr. Willow interjected. "Except for the caffeine overdose. And that's putting it mildly."

"Happy now, detective? That proves I was murdered. Someone killed me!!" Jill said.

"What time did she pass away?" Kate asked.

"Between 11 and 11:15 Sunday night," Dr. Willow estimated.

"So why the sudden caffeine overdose if there wasn't anything else traceable in her system? Did she just up and one day decide to take that much caffeine for the fun of it? Something doesn't add up," I said.

"No, I didn't. Why is no one listening to me?"

"That's for you two to figure out. I just tell you what I find when I find it," Dr. Willow said.

Jill appeared right next to me. I felt her presence. "Get to it quick, Mr. Riley," Jill said.

"Well, we know what killed her and how. Who and why remains to be seen," Kate said.

"Hopefully the crime scene evidence will tell us something," I said.

"Anything else, Dr. Willow? Kate said.

"No, but if I find anything I'll let you know."

"Please do. Always a pleasure, Doctor," Kate said.

"Bye Patty," Kate said as we walked out of the lobby after signing out.

"Bye dear. Stay safe out there," Patty replied. "Only come back here alive, dear!"

I waved as I pushed the door open with my back. We walked back towards the parking lot to return back to the station. I was weary of my partner asking me about what happened in the autopsy room and who I was talking to. But I wanted to make a good impression with Kate and keep the peace, especially on his first day.

"Well that was awkward. Wouldn't you say, Sam?" Kate asked. "What was that about?"

"I'll tell you later. I'm still trying to figure it out," I said as I buckled my seatbelt.

"Go ahead, Sam. Tell her about me," Jill said, from the backseat behind Kate.

Kate turned around quickly and looked in the backseat. "I swear it felt like someone kicked the back of my seat." *There's nothing back there.*

I glanced at the backseat where Jill sat. "Nope! Nothing's back there."

THE BINGO KILLER

"That was weird," Kate said. *Talk about the heebee jeebies.*

Chapter 14

Monday, Sept. 8th.

10 a.m.

I parked a little way in front of the hurst, on the loop inside Candlewood Cemetery. I walked up to Jill Sanders' grave site. The Brown, Golden, Magruder, Cobb and Pierce gravesites formed an arch around Jill's, to the edge of the road. Her family and friends had gathered and were seated before the service started. Connie Sanders noticed me standing off to the side. She sat next to Oscar Tidwell, Jill's father. Tidwell stared at Jill's casket the whole time from what I could tell. I didn't get too close but I was there.

Connie got up and walked over to have a quick chat with me. "Thanks for coming, Detective Riley. I appreciate it very much."

I gave Connie a quick hug. "It's my pleasure, Ms. Sanders. It's the least I can do. I read the write-ups about Jill in the papers the past few days. I'm sorry I didn't get to meet her before she passed. She was an incredible woman with a promising career and future," I said. A week later and I still hadn't forgotten what happened at the morgue.

THE BINGO KILLER

"Yes, she was. She was not only my daughter. She was my best friend. That bond will never be broken between mother and daughter. Not even in the afterlife." Tears fell from Connie's eyes as she looked down at my blue tie. "I'm sorry I'm such a mess as you can imagine."

"It's perfectly okay. Nothing to be sorry about Ms. Sanders. I am truly sorry for your loss." I gave Connie another hug.

"Thank you! Forgive me for asking but have you any news about Jill's passing? Please, Mr. Riley, I really need to know."

"Yes there is but we can talk about that after her service. I promise you," I said.

Connie smiled for a brief second which seemed like ten minutes to her I'm sure. That was probably the most she's smiled in the past week.

Jill's ghost popped up from behind me and walked around me to speak with her mother.

Connie turned around and went back to her seat in the tent.

"Mom!! It's okay, Mom! I'm here. It's okay." Jill's ghost wore a white sun dress and black boots. Her hair was in a ponytail. Jill paused for a moment. "Mom, can you hear me? Detective Riley, why can't she hear me?"

She looked back at me with a frustrated look and shouted, "You can! Why can't she?"

I looked at her with a straight face. *Because most of the living can't hear the dead. They don't want to either. It's either scary or annoying or both.* I communicated to Jill.

"How am I any of those?" Jill asked.

"Are you serious, Jill?" *You scared the shit out of me when I saw you open your eyes at the morgue.*

"Wonderful thing to say to a ghost at her funeral. Beautiful graveside manner, Mr. Riley. I'm impressed! Did they teach you that at the police academy?"

I ignored Jill's comment. I knew she didn't mean it. I stood in silence waiting for the service to begin.

"Why aren't you speaking to me even though I can clearly hear you in my head?"

I realized that Jill was used to getting what she wanted. I picked up on the fact she thought she was entitled to other people's time. *Something new I'm trying. And it's working. I can't draw attention to myself with all these people around. This is the best way for us to communicate, trust me.*

"Men! Such great communicators."

I slowly nodded my head. Jill's comment made me smile.

Jill rolled her eyes at me in frustration and stormed away in her true southern fashion. She walked over to sit next to Connie but Mary Owens sat down first. "Mary, move!! I want to sit next to my mother." Jill paused but Mary hugged Connie and held her hand. "Mary, move so I can sit next to my mother!"

Connie continued her mourning. She reached for Tidwell's hand.

He comforted Connie's hand and looked at her with tears in his eyes. They didn't fall until he felt

THE BINGO KILLER

Connie's hand merge with his. It felt like the first time he fell in love with Connie. Connie saw the loneliness in his eyes with each tear.

"Our baby girl is gone, Oscar. She's gone. Jill's gone!"

Oscar hugged his ex-wife.

"WELL FUCK!! A girl can't even get a front row seat at her own funeral. I'll just stand over here by my casket. Anyone know how that feels?" Jill yelled out as she looked at her family and friends.

Preacher Nathan Perry began his service with a prayer and offered a short sermon on life and love. He found no comfort in promising Jill that he would recite her favorite Bible verse at her funeral. Instead, he found comfort in knowing her favorite verse was his as well. "Jill and I had many conversations about life, love and experiencing life on the road. It wasn't easy but she loved it. She felt it was her calling to uplift her audience's spirits. She once told me it made her feel closer to God. Being on that stage, bringing joy and happiness to their lives. I promised her, if this day ever came, I would say her favorite Bible verse and build her sermon around that verse. First Corinthians, Chapter thirteen, verses four through eight. Love is patient and kind; love does not envy or boast; it is not arrogant or rude. It does not insist on its own way; it is not irritable or resentful; it does not rejoice at wrongdoing, but rejoices with the truth," Perry said confidently. "This is how she tried to live her life. Spreading love and joy through her musical performances, wherever she could. We honor Jill

KNIGHT

Sanders by being here today. We honor her by spreading love and goodwill to our family, friends, neighbors and even complete strangers who need to know someone cares about them. That's her true legacy. Not just her music and performing."

By the time Perry was done with his sermon, I moved closer to the tent to hear his sermon.

Jill looked at her gray, glossy casket. "Every word the preacher said was beautiful. I know my life is over but I wasn't ready. No one ever is I don't think. I've tried to live the best life I can. Give people hope through my music. And this is my reward?" Jill said, as her words became one with the wind.

I was the only one who heard her. She was right! I work for her now. Why did my first murder case have to be Jill Sanders?

After her service concluded, Mary went to start the car for Connie, who stayed behind for a few minutes. Jill sat down next to her, on her right. She grabbed her mom's hand and put her head on her right shoulder. "Finally a good seat. I'm sorry mom I hurt you by leaving so soon. It's not fair you outlived me. I can scream about unfairness all day long but that doesn't matter when I see you in so much pain and heartache. Given the life I've lived. Singing on those stages. Making people happy for a while. Having you as a mom. You raised me to become who I was. I'd say my life is more than fair. I got to live out my dreams, if only for a few years. I'm sorry I put my career first instead of having a family and giving you a

THE BINGO KILLER

grandchild. That's my one regret. You would have been a great nana," Jill said.

Connie stared at the gray casket. "Goodbye Jill. I love you, my baby girl." *My world is beyond shattered. I feel like there's no air around me and I'm expected to breathe. How do I heal from such heartbreak?*

Jill squeezed her mom's hand as crocodile tears fell like rain. "I'm always with you, Mom and you'll always be with me."

I heard every word Jill spoke to her mother. Connie hugged Oscar one last time.

Oscar Tidwell sat in his chair looking at Jill's casket.

Connie eventually got up and placed three roses on her daughters' casket. She turned and walked back to Mary's car. Jill held Connie's hand as they walked to the car. Jill knew she couldn't leave with her mother. Jill saw me as she passed me. Jill returned to her casket and spoke softly. "That's it. My life ends in a hole in the ground." She paused for a minute and thought about her life in flashbacks from her childhood to the night she went to bed before she passed. Jill's tears fell again. "Nothing more I can do here." Jill took one last look around and walked over to me. "Tell my story, Mr. Riley. Tell it to everyone you know."

I'll make sure my children know about you someday, Jill Sanders.

"Thank you, Mr. Riley! It's nice to be remembered as anything more than a murder victim."

Should I call you Jill's ghost or Ms. Sanders?

KNIGHT

"My ghost. My body. I'm one in the same, Mr. Riley. I'm Jill Sanders through and through."

I didn't say anything out loud until after the funeral was over and the chairs were put away for transport back to the funeral home. A loud thud suddenly echoed around her gravesite. She and I both looked back over to the grave and saw a cloud of dirt rising up and settling back down again. "Well, it's over for sure when the dead lady can't sing anymore." Jill looked at me with fire in her eyes.

I sensed her frustration. "You okay, Jill?"

"I'll never be okay again. Let's get to work, Mr. Riley." Jill demanded.

I nodded. "Okay."

Let's take a walk so we can get far enough away from here that I can actually speak.

Jill joined me for a walk. "Might as well," she sighed.

We walked around the loop until we came up on a smaller, dirt road that curved around two giant oak trees, down and up a hill that connected with a paved road that led to the older part of the cemetery—The 1800's graves—and out to Candlewood drive.

"We're good now," I said.

"What's so important, Mr. Riley, that you have me strolling alongside a handsome man on a beautiful, sunny day?"

"Did you just call me handsome?" I asked. "Maybe I was wrong about you, Jill? I didn't really know you."

THE BINGO KILLER

"What were you wrong about, Mr. Riley?"

"I see a different side of you, Jill. That's all."

"I hadn't noticed, Mr. Riley. I was busy consoling my mother at my funeral. I was a bit distracted."

"I understand. I think we can help each other, Ms. Sanders. We didn't get to finish our conversation at the morgue the other day."

"We were rudely interrupted by Detective Barker, as I recall. She didn't mean to, I don't think."

"No, she didn't. Plus, you were afraid, scared and confused. Can't say I don't blame you. I was too."

Jill nodded. "Perhaps you had better tell her soon, Mr. Riley. You don't want her holding a grudge or doubting your worth as a partner. Although she suspects something about you, I'm sure."

"When the time is right. I don't want to freak her out. All Kate knows is I'm a bit weird and that would have to do for now." I didn't want her knowing about my gifts until I fully knew myself.

"What questions do you have for me? I do have the afterlife but I don't have all day, Detective."

"Right, my apologies, Jill. What was the last thing you remember from Sunday, August 31st? I asked.

"I visited my father, Oscar Tidwell, at his home for a few hours. I returned home, showered and watched television for a while until I felt tired all of a sudden. Must have been the tea I drank. I brought some home from Dad's house. I poured it in the sink and threw the cup away in the trash can. I shut everything off and got in bed. It was about 9:45 or so."

KNIGHT

I wrote down most of what Jill said in my little black notebook. I wrote in short spurts so I didn't miss anything. Often phrases or single words. I had a great enough memory to fill in the clues and details surrounding my scribblings. "I see. That's pretty accurate," I said. It made sense to me—the one person who it should make sense to. *Enough to go on.*

"Funny how I remember that and not much about my childhood and early singing career," Jill said.

"I hope not. What you just told me might solve your murder," I declared.

"Let's hope so." *Fingers crossed this detective knows what he's doing?*

"Jill, has anyone sent you any bad or threatening messages? Phone calls? Have you received any strange letters or packages to your apartment?"

"No, not that I can think of. I never really gave out my address and only a few people knew where I lived. I tried not to do anything that would attract stalkers or mean and threatening messages, especially on Instagram and every other place you can think of."

"You haven't received any gifts or anything from someone you don't know, have you?" I asked.

"No. I didn't take gifts from people I didn't know. Fans of mine," Jill said abruptly.

"Interesting. A perfectly healthy woman doesn't just pass away in her sleep without a specific reason," I said. "A caffeine overdose doesn't exactly spell out natural causes."

"The doctor who examined my body? What did he say?" Jill asked.

"Dr. Willow? Yeah, I made a great impression on him. He probably thinks I'm nuts," I said.

"That makes three of us." Jill smiled. "What did he say?"

"He found a large amount of caffeine in your system. My guess is the caffeine came from those little white packets. The amount of caffeine you ingested was equal to drinking several cups of coffee or a few energy drinks at one time. He thinks that's what killed you, Jill."

Jill paused for a moment. "So that's how they did it? That's how they took my life. Those fucking bastards! That's something out of a spy movie. A silent end to a loud personality. Still doesn't make it right and whoever did this, I truly hope they pay for it. Damn cowards. That's what they are. Cowards! What do you think, Detective Riley?"

"I think we should keep walking."

We walked past the barbed wire fence that led to an open field with only two graves. I gave Jill my honest opinion. "It seems like someone murdered you. It could be a mix-up somewhere and caffeine packets got mixed up with sugar packets or salt packets. I don't think you would purposely kill yourself and more so, not that way. Someone did it and I'm going to find out who."

"Well if that doesn't put wind in my sails on the Louisiana bayou, I don't know what will," Jill said. "Of course I didn't kill myself. I loved my life. I had

KNIGHT

so much more to do. I wanted to be a wife and a mother someday. Have a hit record or two? Sell out a few arena's on a world tour?"

I wanted all of that for her. I stopped in the middle of the road and saw the pavement at eye level a few yards ahead. "So what will you do now, Jill? I'm just curious."

"You sly around and have no control over where you go!" She said with a smile.

I stopped for a second and thought about what Jill said. *Sly around? What does that mean? Did she mean slay around? Slay, as in being killed? Having no control over where you go, that must be what it's like being a ghost? You end up where you are seen or heard, totally out of your control. Then why did she pick me and not anyone else?* I never heard that before. Makes sense I guess.

A gust of wind came through and blew the oak tree leaves about twenty yards away, near the fence separating the cemetery from the forest the city owned. I turned to Jill but found myself alone in the cemetery.

"And she's gone again." *Must be awesome to just disappear in certain moments when you want to.*

Jills' grave was filled in when I returned to my truck. "They don't waste any time, do they?" I looked at her gravesite and paid my respects one last time. "Goodbye, Jill." I drove out of the cemetery and stopped for Kate's Cheez-Its. I arrived back at the pit around around 11:15.

THE BINGO KILLER

Kate took the sack of Cheez-Its and sat them down on her desk. "Thanks for the Cheez-Its, Sam. I guess you can teach an old dog new tricks."

I smiled and nodded in agreement, before I got back to work. "Eat your cheesy crackers and let me work in peace.

"How was the funeral?" I asked.

"Her funeral was something else. I haven't been to one in a while but hers was one I'll never forget."

Kate spun her chair towards me. "Yeah, how so?"

"Well, there were more people there than I thought. People she worked with. Lots of fans. Just goes to show Jill was a rising star who passed before her time," I said. "We have to find out what happened to Jill Sanders. We have to keep our promise to Connie Sanders. *Otherwise, why do we have these badges*?

"We will, Sam! While you were gone, I got a call from the crime lab about that torn sugar packet piece I found under Sanders' purse last week. Turns out it was from a caffeine packet disguised as a sugar packet. Stuff you can get on the dark web, undercover, where ninety percent of known Internet users don't go or even know about." Kate said.

How the packets found their way to Jill Sanders is the question? Maybe her dad can tell us the answer.

I nodded. "Shit from the dark web doesn't have a paper trail for a reason, which keeps us guessing, like we are now. They won't tell us anything. We don't have jurisdiction in foreign countries," I exclaimed as I shrugged his shoulders. "Beyond that, it's a needle in a sugar stack."

Chapter 15

Wednesday, Sept. 10.

9:45 a.m.

Tess Taylor sat at her desk, finishing up some paperwork on a potential tenant to move into Jill Sanders' apartment. She saw my business card underneath the glass on top of her desk. Tess wasn't one to make the first move but felt she and I had a connection when they met over a week ago. Who was I to argue the connection a woman as beautiful as Tess felt she had with me.

I grabbed my buzzing phone, leaned back and put my feet up on my desk. "Detective Sam Riley, speaking."

"Hi, Sam. It's Tess Taylor. How are you this morning?"

I sighed and grinned a smile as big as Texas. "Good morning, Tess. What a surprise, indeed. I'm doing pretty well. How about you?"

"I'm doing well, thanks for asking. I'll cut right to the chase. Are you free for dinner one night this week?" Tess kindly asked.

THE BINGO KILLER

"Yeah, I'm free for dinner every night. I don't have a curfew. What did you have in mind, Tess Taylor?"

Tess laughed. "Tonight. Seven o'clock? Here at the apartment complex clubhouse. How's that sound?"

"Sounds wonderful. I'll see you tonight, Tess."

"Yes you will. Lovely!! Until tonight, Detective Riley."

"Have a wonderful day, Tess."

"You too, Mr. Riley."

I hung up just as Kate came into the pit and sat down at her desk.

"Anything important, Sam?" Kate asked.

"Nothing important. Just a friend asking to have dinner tonight. That's all."

"Did you tell them it's okay to have dinner every night?" Kate asked with a smile.

"Good one, Kate. Your sarcasm makes my day," I replied. "But yes, I did. More or less."

Kate smiled.

I left the station around 5:30, headed home to shower and change my work clothes. I left my house around 6:30 and arrived at the Clubhouse twenty minutes later. I parked in front and saw a light on in the back of the building, through the open window. *I hope she's cooking something good in there.*

Tess welcomed me in as after she heard my knocks on the door.

"Good evening Tess," I said.

KNIGHT

Tess wore a low cut turquoise dress that caught his attention. I reached for her hand and twirled her around enthusiastically. "Wow, let me get a good look at you, Tess. You look absolutely dynamite tonight."

Tess smiled as I pulled her closer. "Thank you, Mr. Riley. You look handsome yourself."

"Thanks but I just threw on something much more comfortable than my work clothes."

"Don't be so modest, Mr. Riley," Tess said with a smile. "Right this way." We walked over to the big table near the kitchen. Her lasagna was still baking when we walked into the kitchen together. Tess went all out with the candles, fancy plates and banquet glasses.

I appreciated the hell out of Tess's efforts that evening. I sat at the end of the table near the oven. "Quite the set up here, Tess. I'm impressed. No one's ever made me feel so welcome for dinner."

"Is that so? First time for everything, Mr. Riley." Tess smiled.

"Yeah, so far so good, Tess."

"Wine, Mr. Riley?" Tess asked.

"No, I've had a great day so far. Thanks for asking."

Tess laughed. "No, I mean, would you care for some wine?"

"Oh wine! I don't drink. Bad for my heart. I'll take a coke, pepsi or tea if you have it."

"Coming right up, Mr. Riley," Tess smiled.

Tess brought me over a pepsi in an ice cold mug.

THE BINGO KILLER

Classy move if I say so myself. God's she good. Double points for the mug. "Smooth move with the mug, Tess."

"You don't mind if I have some wine, do you Sam?"

"Absolutely not. In fact, bottoms up, Tess! I figured it was okay for you to call me Sam instead of Mr. Riley when you poured the wine. Besides, my dad's not here."

Tess laughed as the wine gurgled into her glass.

I looked at Tess. She had a sparkle in her eye and a glow about her.

"So Tess, would you say this is a date? Not that I'm complaining or anything. I figured it was just two—."

Tess looked at me and played it off as a slip of the tongue. "Oops, you let the D-word slip out. How dare you?" Tess said, followed by laughter. "It's still early and we haven't had dinner yet."

I laughed at Tess' joke. It caught me off guard but I liked her sense of humor. *We'll see about that*, I thought. I paused and smiled for a few seconds. I took a sip of pepsi. "The mug makes it better. "I was surprised to hear from you this morning. Your invitation was thoughtful, especially with good company," I explained.

Tess caressed my shoulder and smiled. "Thank you, Sam."

"Most welcome, Tess. I just meant I don't get asked out to dinner much and I don't ask either."

Tess looked at me in wonderment. *Is that so? Well it's a good thing I asked you.*

"That's hard to believe but I'd like to know more, if I'm not intruding. I don't want to make this weird."

I nodded and took another sip of Pepsi. "It's the truth," I said.

Tess nodded in agreement. "Nothing wrong with that, especially in your line of work. I imagine you can't be distracted too much. Playing it safe with a dangerous job."

"Oh, the irony! It's enough to make Shakespeare ask what the fuck?"

Tess almost spat out her wine from laughing at my joke.

"Speaking of playing it safe, may I use your bathroom before dinner is ready?"

"Absolutely," she said as she pointed down the hallway behind her. Tess couldn't stop smiling.

"Be back soon!" I stood in front of the mirror for a minute, trying to little intel on Tess. All I needed was a little something to get an edge. *Things were going great, sure but—Sam, just use your charm. Turn on the charm. Turn on the charm. Charm. Charm.*

I made my way back to the table, as Tess smiled.

"Started to think you got lost. I didn't know who to call," Tess said.

I laughed. "I haven't heard that in a while."

Tess nodded.

"So what do I owe tonight's rendez-vous to? Anything with my case or did the universe give me a break and bring us together tonight?" I asked.

THE BINGO KILLER

Tess laughed after setting her glass down. "I'd definitely say the universe gave us both a break, Mr. Riley."

"Well, just checking," I said calmly. "Please, call me Sam."

"I'm sorry. Slipped my mind for a second. I like your name, Sam."

"Thanks. Tess is a good name too. Classy, yet humble. It's one you don't hear often but I think it suits you. Your parents named you well," I said.

"Actually, it was my grandmother who named me. I was raised by my grandmother in California. It's a long story from my childhood so I'll stop there and spare you the details." Tess frowned and looked at her glass of wine.

"No, Tess, please continue. I'm curious. Can't start something and not finish it," I said, holding Tess' hand. I took a sip of my drink.

"Are you sure? I don't want to ruin our date with my tragedy." Tess asked politely.

"I'm curious, Tess. You have nothing to be ashamed of."

"Well, my mom died in a car wreck about a week after I was born. I didn't have a name for a few weeks. My grandmother told me my mother called me "baby" until my grandmother named me Tess. My mom was undecided between Tess and Marie and unfortunately didn't pick one. So my grandmother named me Tess. I think it was a simple flip of a coin type of thing. My dad was in the U.S. Navy and obviously couldn't have a kid on a battleship. So I lived with my grandmother. I saw my dad every now and then growing up."

I apologized for her loss. "That's a bittersweet story, Tess."

"No, it's okay. I'm just proud of my name and story behind it. I tell it more than I should," Tess stated.

"As you should be, Tess. I like that about you."

She caressed my shoulder and smiled at me. "Thank you, Sam."

I raised my mug, which had defrosted enough so I could raise it normally. "A toast to each other and our good health?"

"To us," Tess quipped.

I told Tess how wonderful the food smelled. "What are we having?"

"My grandmother's recipe," Tess said.

"Can't wait to try it, Ms. Taylor."

"Absolutely. Excuse me, Sam." Tess checked on the lasagna, which was done.

Good timing, Tess.

Tess brought me a plate of lasagna. "Dinner is served, Sam."

More points for her. I told Tess I was impressed with her choice for dinner tonight. "Can't go wrong with lasagna."

"No, you can't. It's a family recipe, believe it or not," Tess said as she sat down with her plate.

"I do believe it," I said, taking his first bite. "Lucky me! I think it's great when I get to try

THE BINGO KILLER

someone's family recipe. It reveals a lot of good things about those families."

We began our lasagna and spilled little, random facts about ourselves.

"One more thing about my name," Tess interjected.

I put his fork down and looked at Tess. I was amazed at how elegant she looked in the glow of the faint candlelight around the room. *She's sparkling.*

"I'm so sorry, Tess. That was me taking you in just now. Please continue," I said.

"No, it's okay. I'm just proud of my name and the story behind it."

"I like that about you," I said. "That's really special."

"What else do you like, Sam?" Tess sipped her wine again.

I smiled at Tess. "I need to know more about you to know what I like about you." I said sparingly.

"Fair enough." Tess said.

"If we dare to take this exit off the highway."

Tess smiled at his reply. "I do, indeed."

"You don't have any skeletons in your closet or homicidal tendencies, do you?" I asked before taking another sip.

"No, I don't. I haven't had any skeletons in a while." Tess declared.

"Just checking, Tess. Neither do I."

Tess found it nearly miraculous how my jokes were funny enough so she could open herself up to me. "Tell me about yourself, Sam."

KNIGHT

I told Tess my work took up a lot of my time, especially trying to solve Sanders' murder, but I didn't really discuss the case or go into too much detail about my work.

"What about you Tess Tylor?" I eagerly asked.

"Well, I'm Plain Jane to be honest. Single girl. Semi-satisfying job. A few friends. I'm not a fan of reality TV shows. They try too hard. I can't take them seriously. Well, some are okay but most aren't," Tess explained herself.

I nodded. "Good answer. Much better than mine." I wouldn't know to be honest. I don't watch a lot of television anyway. I go to the movies more than anything" I stated.

"I love binge watching shows more than going to the movies." Tess differed.

I nodded and inquired about her job as property manager. "I get the feeling you don't like it here, Tess."

"I don't like finding junk left in vacated apartments that we have to clean out without collecting a penalty fee. You'd be surprised how much we have to do. It's ridiculous. I don't mind the paperwork. It gives me a chance to work in peace. And I'm not fond of having to do the same pitch presentation to new tenants but at least my rent is free. All I pay is bills," Tess proclaimed.

"Wow, not too bad, all things considered," I replied. "Lucky you!"

THE BINGO KILLER

I was almost done with my lasagna when I asked Tess if she had any hobbies. As much as I wanted to use my gift, I had to learn when not to use it. So I relied on simple conversation topics instead of telepathic intrusion into Tess' mind.

"You may find this strange but hobbies are for those who have little or no sense of adventure and don't take risks outside their comfort zone. They play it safe. Coin collectors. Stamp collectors. I have a bucket list of goals I want to do in life before I'm forty and some after I'm forty. Best way to avoid a midlife crisis, in my opinion." Tess explained.

"Really? Name two goals," I asked curiously. I was more of a hobby guy than an adventure man.

Tess laughed but answered sincerely. "Out of town adventures, Sam."

I shifted towards Tess as she looked me in the eyes. "We could've had dinner out of town. That's an adventure," I said with a smirk.

Tess laughed as she took our plates away and refilled their drinks.

"Is dinner-with-a-detective on your list?" I asked.

Tess laughed and nodded as she sat back down. "Actually yeah. I'm having a great time. So why not?"

"Fair point, Tess."

"But I'm talking about the kind where you get your feet wet, Sam. I'll be partaking in them around Christmas, in fact," Tess answered. "I'm doing something around Halloween but I'm not sure what exactly."

I liked her sense of adventure. "And here I thought I was a brave go-getter," I replied. "I'm glad you're having a great time tonight, Tess"

"What about your list, Sam?"

I took a sip of Pepsi. "Mine's not as active as yours. I'm more of a movie nerd. I wouldn't mind building a Lego community in my house. Shopping for vintage toys. Cosplaying certain characters from movies. Browsing antique shops for old books, vintage and nostalgic items. Rock hunting. Things like that."

"Good to know," Tess said.

"May I ask you something, Tess?"

"Of course. I'm an open book," she said.

"Are you happy?" I asked.

Tess took a sip of wine and paused, never breaking eye contact with me. I'd have to say yes. Things are great for me right now. It's a blessing don't get me wrong but I often wonder when it will come crashing down. You know? That's what I think of every now and then but I know I'm too strong willed and independent to let it get me distracted," Tess explained.

I was mysteriously drawn to how she viewed things. "That's a valid thing to be concerned with."

"Is Sam Riley happy?"

"Yeah. It feels good to know—I mean I've worked hard to get where I am in my career," I said as I looked at my watch. "Well Tess, this has been a fun evening."

THE BINGO KILLER

"Yes, it has. I'm glad you accepted my invitation for dinner," Tess said.

"Most fun I've had in a long time and on a date no less. I've enjoyed getting to know you, Tess. I kind of forgot how fun this is, " I said. "Thanks for reminding me how fun dates are."

Tess looked at me with curiosity, as she bit her bottom lip. "Likewise. Any room for dessert, Mr. Riley?"

I looked at Tess. "What did you have in mind, Ms. Taylor?"

Tess informed me that she had apple pie and ice cream at her place. "It's only a few steps away, Sam. I promise it's worth it." *If you care to indulge your sweet tooth?*

"Sounds delicious, Tess. I'd love some dessert."

Tess smiled.

"Would you like for me to help you clean up?" I asked Tess. The least I could do for such an incredible effort.

"If you want to, I won't mind the help. But it's okay. I can do it tomorrow morning," Tess said. "It's no problem. I keep things tidy around my place."

I put the Pepsi and wine in the refrigerator.

Tess put the dishes in the sink, covered the leftover lasagna and put it in the refrigerator.

I quickly wiped the table and threw the rag in the sink.

"We're good here." Tess said. "Okay, time for dessert, Sam."

I nodded. "Can't wait!"

KNIGHT

Tess turned the lights off as we left the clubhouse.

I waited as Tess locked the main door to the front office.

"So where is your apartment?"

Tess pointed to the other side of the property, opposite Jill Sanders' former apartment. "This way, bottom floor. No one lives above me. It's a show-apartment."

"Awesome. No neighbors above."

We walked slowly towards her apartment, enjoying the breeze.

"You've really got it made, Tess."

"Yeah, I can't complain. I mean, they could pay me a little more," Tess said.

"Yeah, they should. You do a lot around here."

Tess welcomed me into her place. "This is my little slice of heaven." She flipped on her living room lights.

I eagerly looked around her apartment and noticed her artwork on the walls. "Nice paintings. Very creative."

"Thanks. I did them myself," Tess said. "I was in my art phase I guess and I just let my creativity go free and on the wall they went."

"I need some of your artwork on my wall. Amazing job, Tess. Nice use of color and subject matter," I said as I looked into her eyes. "You seem different from most women around here."

"Ehh, you know. I just paint parts of my soul and collect the rent.

THE BINGO KILLER

"They look amazing and so do you, Tess."

Tess put her hand on my shoulder and looked into my eyes.

"I'm sorry. Sam. You wanted dessert."

"Yes I did," I whispered as I gently pulled Tess closer for a kiss.

Tess closed her eyes as I kissed her passionately, before leading me to her bedroom. She turned on the light and the lamp on her nightstand as I joined her. I spun her around, unzipped her dress and slid her dress off gently. She felt my hands caress her back as I kissed her neck. Her dress fell at her feet as she slowly turned around and looked at me with storm-raged eyes. "Dessert is served, Sam," Tess whispered, holding her breath. I closed the door and turned the lights off. We woke up in each other's arms the next morning. I parted ways with Tess but told her to keep in touch. The dinner and dessert were nice but the show was absolutely amazing. But I still had a job to do—solve Jills' murder and keep Tess safe at the same time.

Chapter 16

Friday, Sept. 12th

9 p.m.

I drove through Bloomfield but wasn't ready to go home just yet. I had Saturday off and I figured what would it hurt if I stayed up past my self-imposed curfew. I dropped Kate off at her apartment after dinner at my parent's house.

Although I didn't drink, I needed one that night. I drove to one of the better spots in Bloomfield—a place I hadn't been to in a few years. I walked into *Liquor Lonnie's Bar & Grill* and went straight to the bar. *Lonnie's* was characterized as a hidden gem among the mediocre bar scene in Bloomfield by the local independent weekly papers. A few other patrons occupied seats around the bar, chatting and drinking their beers and shots. The sound of pool balls breaking and voices echoed throughout the bar. Waitresses ran food to diners and refilled sodas and sweet tea. The friday night atmosphere was more on the celebratory side. The building was an older one with a modern vibe to it. The rustic decor included random items on the walls from the early 1920's

THE BINGO KILLER

through the present—washboard and tub, paddle oars and old soda bottles. Cedar tables with a strong and smooth, glossy polyurethane finish lined up the dining area.

I honestly forgot what *Lonnie's* looked like and was a little surprised when I walked back inside. I found a lonely spot and cozied up on a comfortable barstool. *I just want to sit here, enjoy a drink and no one bother me. That's not too much to ask.*

Drew, the bartender, washed off pint glasses when I sat down. "What can I get you?"

I looked at Drew with eagerness. "Whiskey on the rocks."

"You got it, Boss," Drew said. Drew brought my drink over to him less than a minute later.

"Thanks."

"Can I get you anything else?" Drew asked.

"No. I'm fine. It's been a long day."

Drew went back to cleaning the bar. "Yeah, sure thing partner."

I felt the grain of the bar top. It was a little rough in spots where the finish had slightly eroded from glasses and bottles slinging and sliding around. The long mirror behind the bar gave me a good view of the pool tables and the dining area. Several things ran through my mind while I slowly sipped my drink. The case, dinner at his parents that night and eventually these damn psychic powers. I took a drink and felt the whiskey slide down my throat. *Ooh, that's got a punch.* My elbows were perched on the bar like birds on a wire as I rubbed my face. I tried to escape the noise in

KNIGHT

my head more than anything. Noise from the outside world is a sweet tune from a music box, compared to the noise inside my own head. *Ahh, finally, peace and quiet for a few minutes.*

Silence suddenly set in all around me. I put my hands down on the bar and felt the whole building's atmosphere and mood morphing back in time to the 1930's—from bustling and thriving to quiet and laid back in a few seconds, like something out of a horror movie. I turned around and saw a few tables at the back corner of the dining area. There were six guys, in their mid-20's to early 30's, wearing suits, sitting around a table, drinking and playing poker. I barely saw them through the cloud of cigarette smoke surrounding the men. Their cursing conversation and laughing made it easy for me to get closer without being seen or heard. True, I was observing--I think—but I knew these guys were out of place. No one else in *Lonnie's* had suits on and the place was smoke-free.

I slowly walked towards their table while keeping my eyes on them in case they saw me. I heard my footsteps but nothing else. Not the music from the Jukebox, nor the waitresses taking orders and delivering orders. I suddenly stopped when I saw one man sitting with his back to the wall, staring a hole through me. I realized the man was looking past me in fact. The hairs on my arms stood on end the more the man stared at me. I started to sweat a little when I slowly saw all six men looking through me.

THE BINGO KILLER

I turned around and saw Kenny "Dead Eyes" Packard, a 1930's-era gangster from Chicago, standing about seven feet away from me. Packard pointed a tommy gun right at the men at the table. I quickly climbed the stairs a few feet away and turned around. I was out of the line of fire. "Put the gun down. No one has to get hurt here, today," I said calmly.

Packard ignored me and slowly moved closer.

I realized I was just a bystander caught in the middle of a vision of an impending massacre.

Packard never broke eye contact with the men at the table in front of him.

I stood at the top of the three stairs as I watched Packard walk slowly past me. "Don't any of you guys move or I'll fill you with lead," Packard ordered. His voice never waivered or cracked, yet commanded respect.

Sweat dripped from my forehead and upper lip from the tension. Six men with handguns, most likely, versus one man with a tommy gun. I let out a sigh but tried to keep as quiet as I could. I didn't want to be the seventh man.

Each of Packard's steps forward were louder than the last. Packard then ordered all six men to line up against the white wall with their hands above their heads on the wall.

Packard raised his gun up to their heads and hearts and opened fire, killing the six men within seconds.

I looked straight ahead and to my left a little ways as I knew what was about to happen. And there was nothing I could do about it. Seeing those murders would definitely be worse than the nightmare I had the other morning. The thought crossed my mind to stop Packard but I feared I'd look foolish by jumping at something that wasn't there and end up knocking over someone's table and taking food home with me on my clothes.

Bright red blood splashed and dripped down the wall with small pieces of brain tissue scattered all over the wall, complemented with bullet holes. Packard walked through the haze of gunsmoke as he looked at their bodies slumped together in a pile. Blood oozed out and turned the black and white squared tile red and dark red.

I coughed when I smelled the strong odor of gunfire. Packard put his gun in the center of the table. Packard stood with his back to the wall with a clear view of me staring at him. "All in a day's work, gentlemen!" He laughed and poured himself a drink of whiskey on the table. "Jesus, I'm thirsty." He whirled his whiskey around in the glass before he took a drink. He saw a few drops of blood on his left fingers from the bottle. "Hum, how clumsy of me." He reached down and wiped the blood on the clothes of one of the guys he just slaughtered.

I walked backwards towards the bar, not taking my eyes off of Packard. I moved as quietly as I could.

"I don't know who's blood this is but I'm giving it back to you. No hard feelings," Packard said, as he finished his drink. "Better luck next time, fellas." He

THE BINGO KILLER

grabbed his gun and walked up the stairs and proceeded towards the bar.

Oh, shit he's coming my way, I said to myself. I made it a few feet from the bar when Packard stopped and looked right at me. *Why is he looking at me? Can he see me in my vision?*

I looked over at Drew but he was busy talking to other customers like nothing happened.

A row of tables were all that separated the two of us.

Packard's eyes—full of murderous intent and rage—pierced my soul. He matched me step for step as we got closer to the bar, although I was closer.

I suddenly felt light on my feet and more attentive than I had ever been. In other words, I felt truly afraid of my psychic powers. *The dark side!*

"What are you going to do, little boy?" Packard asked in a deep, raspy voice.

Is he talking to me? Can he see me? I asked myself again. I waved my hand in front of his face but he didn't bat an eyelash. I glanced over at my seat at the bar, expecting to see myself but instead, I saw an old-timey barkeep. I didn't catch his name but he was a short, older, bald-headed gentleman with glasses, wearing a black vest, a silk bow tie and a white dress shirt. He had a thick mustache and light peach fuzz on his chin and cheeks.

I turned back to Packard.

Packard's face was consumed with anger that the barkeep ignored him.

KNIGHT

I thought it was brave but foolish to ignore someone with a moniker like *Dead Eyes*.

The barkeep moved away and started cleaning his bar like nothing happened. Maybe it was better he put his head down and cleaned his bar?

I heard footsteps as Packard walked out the back as the sirens got louder and closer.

I stood there in amazement after seeing the murder of six men in cold blood, some 60 or so years before I was even born. My vision suddenly dissipated and I found myself facing the bar. I pretended I went to the bathroom. That was the only excuse I could think of in case anyone else saw me do anything weird. *Sorry! Don't mind me acting out a psychic vision over here. How's your food?* I thought to myself. I sat back down at the bar in awe of what just transpired before my eyes. I tried to rationalize it the best I could but it took a while before anything came to me. Maybe it was the whiskey? Maybe it was me ignoring that part of myself?

The Penguin Lounge Massacre. Holy shit!!! This must be where it happened all those years ago. My powers showed me its darker side. I really wasn't expecting that, I thought to myself as I looked around the room towards what is now the bathrooms. I heard about the massacre in stories his dad and grandfather used to tell him as a kid but I never bothered to look up old newspaper articles to get the full story.

"Are you okay, Sir?" Drew asked again, "Excuse me, are you okay?"

THE BINGO KILLER

I came out of my semi-meditation calmly as I looked at Drew. "Yeah, I'm fine. Long day. I've got to use the bathroom. I'll be back in a minute." I walked over to the bathrooms and stopped for a moment to admire the decor and pictures on the wood-paneled wall. I didn't pick up any energy or voices. I went into the bathroom and washed my hands as Mystery appeared behind him suddenly.

"What did you think of the little show you just saw, Mr. Riley?" Mystery asked.

I turned around and looked at Mystery with piercing eyes. *Horrible!* I said. I returned to the bar as Drew walked back over to my seat.

My eyes met his. "I'm sorry about that. I was lost in thought for a minute or two."

Drew brushed it off as normal.

I quickly took another shot to avoid giving anything away to anyone. I finished the last drop of my drink and ordered one more.

Drew came back over with another whiskey.

"Say Drew," I said. Maybe Drew had the answer.

"Yeah, boss!"

"Do you know the history of the place?"

"No, not really. I've only been here a week. No one's told me anything really," Drew said.

"I was just curious, that's all," I said.

Drew told me that the owner might know the history.

"Is the owner here?"

"Lonnie," Drew said as he motioned her to come over to the bar.

Why does that name sound familiar?

Lonnie walked over to the bar to a wonderful surprise. "Whatcha' need, baby?"

Drew pointed to me and said I wanted to know the history of this place.

She looked at me and smiled. "Sam Riley! Is that you?" Lonnie asked.

I looked at Lonnie. I knew I had seen Lonnie before but I didn't recognize her.

"Yeah it's me. Sam Riley. Detective Sam Riley! "

Lonnie gave me a hug."Oh my gosh, how the hell are you?"

"I'm okay. Making it," I said.

"I knew your mother, Denise, for years. We lived a few doors down from your parents, many years ago."

I shook his head. "Yeah, yeah, I remember now. You were at mom and dad's a lot when I was growing up. You had two daughters, right? Sarah and Julie?"

"Yeah I did. Sara's finishing school and Julie is married with a good career," Lonnie said proudly.

"That's great. I'm happy for you all. Looks like you got an awesome place here. I haven't been here that much but I was curious about the history here?"

Lonnie looked at me and asked me to follow her around. "I want to show you something interesting."

I felt more anxious with every step I took as I followed Lonnie. I was afraid she would show me memorabilia of the massacre.

She stopped by the bathrooms.

THE BINGO KILLER

"Right where you're standing, Sam, is where the Penguin Lounge Massacre happened back in the 30's," Lonnie stated.

I felt relieved that what I had just seen really happened and I wasn't going crazy. It felt like a rollercoaster of mind games in the darker sense. "Really? The Penguin Massacre? Right over there!!" I asked in sarcastic surprise. "Who would have imagined?" Not me, that's for sure. I would have gone somewhere else."

"Yeah, six men from the Penguin Club, in their tuxedos, met every weekend at the-then Old Shoreline Club. It was a speakeasy back in the day," Lonnie said.

"This is where they all died by gunfire. Lots of theories about who killed them and why they were killed. Some say revenge of a scorned lover? Some say bad business dealings with prohibition? The mob?"

I didn't dare say a word about the vision I had moments ago, partly because I didn't understand it myself. *Would I ever be able to control it and not be derailed by my powers.*

"So I've heard. I was just curious. I like to know things like this about the places I visit. Makes the whole experience here that much more lively," I said. *Too lively for my own good.*

"I know. The one thing I know about you, Sam, from growing up, is that you were always curious. And it paid off for you, Detective Riley."

I smiled and shrugged my shoulders. "True I guess. Thanks for showing me that, Lonnie."

KNIGHT

"Well, that's all for history class today," Lonnie said. "Perhaps some other time I can tell you more."

I smiled and agreed with Lonnie. "Absolutely." I gave Lonnie a hug and thanked her for her hospitality.

"It was good seeing you again, Sam. Come back anytime, we have a delicious rack of ribs that we smoke in-house overnight," Lonnie asserted.

"Ribs, huh? You said the magic word there, Lonnie. I'll be back for sure and I'll bring my partner Kate Barker. I like the name of your place here, it's catchy," I said. "Liquor Lonnie's!"

"Thanks. My girls named it a few years ago," Lonnie said.

"I like that. Tell them I said hello," I asked. "I better be going now. It's been a long and busy day."

"Always a pleasure, Sam!"

I shook Lonnie's hand and reached for my wallet. I walked back to the bar and plopped down a $20 bill.

"Keep the change, Drew."

"Thanks, boss!"

Chapter 17

Monday, Sept. 15th.

1:45 p.m.

Haley Phillips walked up to Kate's desk to inform her of a 911 call she just received about a body found on the floor. Haley gave Kate the address.

I stopped his paperwork and focused on Haley's important tip she brought us.

"Who made the call to 911?" Kate asked Haley as her phone rang.

"Hold that thought, Haley." Kate answered her phone. "Ms. Sanders, what can I do for you?"

"Detective Barker, I called 911 a few minutes ago when I found Oscar's body on the floor in his kitchen. I called you since you are working on Jill's murder case."

"Yes, we have officers on the way to Oscar's address. Stay there until I get there and we can talk then." *First Jill Sanders. Now her father? This can't be a coincidence.*

Connie agreed to wait outside Tidwell's house.

Kate hung up the phone and got her things together.

KNIGHT

"Connie Sanders. That's who it was." Haley said she sent Officers Prater and Pickins to the Tidwell residence.

"What's going on with Connie Sanders?" I asked. I was a little afraid something bad happened to Connie Sanders.

"Okay. Thanks Haley. We'll take it from here," Kate said.

Haley nodded her head and walked back to her dispatch station.

"Let's go, Sam."

"After you, Kate."

The ride over to the crime scene was a somber one. "I hope Connie's okay," I said.

Kate informed me that Connie Sanders was okay.

Her ex-husband, Oscar Tidwell, was found dead in his house.

We arrived at the address Haley provided to Kate about ten minutes after the 911 call came in to dispatch. Officers Prater and Pickins stood in front of the house with tape across the front door.

I walked towards the house. "Afternoon, gentlemen. Where is it?"

Officer Prater told us that Tidwell was on the kitchen floor with a head wound and blood on the tile floor. "Connie Sanders went to her car to wait for you, Detective Barker," Prater said.

"Okay, thanks. I'll talk to her in a few minutes. Can you call the tech squad and get them out here?" Kate asked.

THE BINGO KILLER

"I'm on it," Officer Pickins said.

I walked into the house and saw a few envelopes on the hall table a few feet away from the door. "Oscar Tidwell," I said, as I walked away to the kitchen.

Tidwell's house was in a decent shape—somewhere between hoarder and his late daughter's apartment. Tidwell had pictures of Jill Sanders all over his wall. A mini-shrine of sorts dedicated to his daughter. I imagine he stared at these walls for days after her funeral.

Kate followed me as she called the coroner to come out for Tidwell's body.

The pop of latex gloves on my hands echoed throughout the room as we began investigating.

Kate took notes while I got up close and personal with Tidwell.

I reached into Tidwell's back pocket and found his wallet to confirm his identity. "Driver's license says he's Oscar Tidwell." I put the wallet on the countertop. "I remember this guy from Jill's funeral. It's him alright."

Kate looked at Tidwell's body. "Tidwell was Sanders' father. That changes the investigation without question. We either have a one-in-a-million coincidence or a serial killer on our hands."

"I don't have the luxury of coincidences, Kate. We're not that lucky," I replied.

Officer Prater told Detective Barker the crime scene investigators were on their way and went back to guarding the house.

"Thank you Officer Prater."

I knelt down to get a closer look at Tidwell. His body was facing up with visible bloodstains on the left side of his head. "Bloodstains stop at about two inches from the head, on the left. None on the right that I can see but maybe there are stains under his body. We'll know more when the coroner gets here. No wounds on the arms that I can see. None on his face or neck," I said to my partner. We looked around the kitchen and saw some blood on the corner edge of the countertop, facing the living room. I pointed at the center of the kitchen. "I'm thinking that Oscar, here, stumbled back from between the sink and refrigerator, hit his head on the corner over there and fell down on the floor."

I took pictures of Tidwell's body, the countertop blood stains and the kitchen.

"What about that box of sugar packets on the counter?" Kate asked as she opened the box. "These sugar packets look similar to the ones I found at Jill's apartment. Again, I don't think this is a coincidence."

"We'll show them to CSI when they get here," I said. I told Kate I was going to look around the house. "You take the kitchen and living room. I'll be back in a few minutes."

Kate nodded and looked around the living room a few minutes before she went outside to talk with Connie Sanders. Kate searched through the living room but didn't see anything out of the ordinary. The

THE BINGO KILLER

kitchen table had a few dishes on it but didn't have any clues either.

Connie Sanders told Kate that she came over to talk about Jill's belongings and if he wanted any of it. "I had a spare key in case of emergencies—his idea. When he didn't answer, I walked inside and found him dead. I immediately called you, Detective Barker." Connie didn't seem as upset as she was with Jill's passing. Given their history, it's understandable but doesn't help our case.

Neither Kate or myself considered Connie a suspect in the murders at this point. Although she had plenty of opportunity and a wicked motive for money. Could she have done it? Tidwell was a taller man and Connie was a shorter woman.

"You did the right thing, Ms. Sanders. Again, I'm sorry for your loss. You can stay to lock up when we're done here if you want to."

"Thank you, Detective Barker."

Kate walked back inside to finish the crime scene tour.

I checked the guest room and bathroom but found nothing important. No blood stains or anything knocked over. I walked down the hallway to the spare bedroom and eventually the master bedroom. I saw the closet light on and slowly opened the door.

Mystery stood inside the closet. Although startled by Mystery's sudden and unexpected appearance, I stepped back and stood in front of the closet. I looked back at the bedroom door to see if Kate was coming down the hallway but I didn't hear her in the house.

Mystery pulled the light string down and turned the light off. "Boo motherfucker!!" Mystery belted out. "I see you and you see me."

I communicated my thoughts with Mystery so I wouldn't draw my partner's attention in case she came looking for me. *What the fuck are you doing here, Mystery?*

"Someone has to watch over you. You're not exactly Sherlock Holmes," Mystery said.

And why are you following me?

"I have my reasons, Sam. Maybe we can help each other," Mystery said.

Really? Have you now?

Mystery nodded.

Oh, now you want to help me? What if I say I don't want to help you and that I'm perfectly capable of doing my job?

"Just hear me out and you decide," Mystery said.

What's the catch? I asked.

"Let me finish, Sam."

Stop calling me Sam. I didn't give you permission—"

I looked at Mystery. *Fine. What have I got to lose? Enlighten me!* I stood in front of the closet trying to get a sense of who Mystery was. Maybe that was Mystery's plan all along? To remain anonymous as long as possible. Needless to say, I was highly suspicious of Mystery.

"Search the body. However you have to. In the lab. On the slab," Mystery said.

THE BINGO KILLER

Nice rhyme scheme, Dr. Seuss, but that doesn't tell me anything. I need more, so unless you have more and tell me in the next 10 seconds, I'm saying goodbye and shutting this door.

Kate made her way to the rest of the house when I hadn't come back to the kitchen. She walked into the bedroom and saw me standing in front of the closet.

Hold that thought for a second Mystery.

"Sam!" Kate said.

I ignored my partner.

"Earth to Sam! Come in Sam," Kate said as she walked towards the closet.

Go ahead! You were saying? I waited for a response from Mystery.

Kate grabbed my right arm. "Sam, you okay? What do you see?" She looked inside the closet and flipped on the light. All we saw were Tidwell's clothes and several shoe boxes on the upper shelves. She turned the lights off.

"It can wait. Go do your job, Sam! We'll meet again," Mystery said.

Kate stepped in front of me and shook my arm again. "SAM!!!"

I looked at my partner. "I'm fine, Kate," I said, a little annoyed at her persistence. I closed the door and joined my partner in our search of the house

"Did you see something in the closet?" She asked.

"No, I was just looking," I said. *Last thing I want to do is worry Kate and have people questioning my ability to do this job. Somehow I think I'm losing this battle of keeping Kate in the dark.*

KNIGHT

"Let's finish our walk-through and wait for the coroner and crime scene tech's to get here."

Kate agreed and shut the door as I walked to the kitchen again to take one last look at Tidwell's body.

A few minutes later, Ernie Smalls walked in the house and saw Kate and I discussing the crime scene.

"Afternoon friends! Sorry we have to meet on such sad occasions," Smalls said.

"Yeah, no kidding," I said. "How's it going Smalls?"

"I've been better." Smalls said.

"Ernie, we didn't find much evidence besides the tea bags we're going to have tested. We think he fell back and hit his head on the edge of the countertop and fell down where he did. That's where he died. We don't know if the head wound killed him or something else," Kate said.

"Thank you for bringing that to my attention, Detective Barker. I'll take some pictures right quick before I finish my paperwork. I won't be long," Smalls said.

Kate told him she didn't mean to rush him.

"It's all good." Smalls wandered into the kitchen and saw Tidwell's body. "I'd have to agree with your assessment, Detective. I see the blood on the floor. I'll have to take a close look at his head wound when I get back," Smalls said. He told Kate and I to give him a few days. "All we can do is wait for the autopsy and tox reports to come back in a few days. WeI'll give you a call later in the week."

THE BINGO KILLER

"Thanks Mr. Smalls," I said. I watched and waited patiently as Smalls did his evaluation of Tidwell before putting him on the stretcher.

"I might need your help to lift him up, Mr. Riley," Smalls inquired.

Kate patted me on the back. "Your turn, Sam. I helped Smalls with Sanders last week."

Thanks, Kate. Appreciate it! One of Kate's pranks or a rite of passage? "Yeah, sure. No problem. Not the strangest thing that's happened to me today," I said.

"Oh yeah? What's that, Mr. Riley?"

I smirked at Smalls. "You wouldn't believe me if I told you." *I saw Casper the unfriendly ghost.*

Smalls laughed. "Oh, okay!"

Kara Carlson, an eight-year crime scene technician from St. Louis, came inside and spoke to Detective Barker. Carlson transferred to a smaller town to focus on her work and to put her skills to a much better use.

"You got here just in time. We were about to go back to the station. There's only so much we can do with a crime scene without tampering it, accidentally of course," Kate said.

"I apologize about that. I'm still trying to figure out Bloomfield. I just moved here from St. Louis two weeks ago. They had me on office duty and today they let me out into the wild," Carlson said.

"That's quite alright. Welcome aboard and I look forward to working with you," Kate said.

"Thank you so much," Carlson replied.

Kate pointed at me and looked at Carlson. "That's my partner, Detective Riley. I'm sure you know Mr. Smalls over there."

Carlson acknowledged us both. "Hello, gentlemen."

"Welcome to the party," I said to Carlson.

"Kara, our ongoing investigation limits me to what I can discuss with you as you know but not what you can discuss with me, as the evidence relates to our cases, which you obviously know. So you know this is confidential and time sensitive," Kate stated.

"Absolutely, Detective Barker. I served in the Navy for four years prior to my forensics career, so I know all about the Hush and Hussle," Carlson said.

Kate was surprised to hear about Carlson's service record. "Oh, okay then. That's impressive. Good to know. Well, that being said, follow me if you will." Kate walked towards the kitchen but stopped short of Tidwell's body.

Carlson looked at Tidwell's body and then looked around the kitchen. "Let me guess, this gentleman fell back and hit his head?"

"That's my theory. One important thing Kara—-see that box of sugar packets? Can you have that analyzed? I don't think that's sugar at all."

"What is it, Detective Barker?" Carlson asked.

Kate sighed. "I think that's pure caffeine disguised as sugar. Very potent stuff," Kate said. "I found one of those packets at Jill's apartment last

THE BINGO KILLER

week. Not a coincidence as to where it came from either"

Carlson nodded and said she'd put a rush on the packets and let Kate know as soon as possible.

Kate handed Carlson her card. "Call me as soon as the results are ready. Nice to meet you, Kara."

I helped Smalls put Tidwell on the stretcher and covered him up.

"Appreciate your help, Detective Riley," Smalls said.

I took my gloves off and threw them into a plastic bag and placed it on the table.. "Anytime, Mr. Smalls. Well, we're pretty much done here I guess." I took one last look around the kitchen to double check if I missed anything. I expected to see a vision of what happened to Mr. Tidwell but no such luck. *I was a little disappointed but maybe my visions come at the most important of times instead of convenience?*

"Let's get back to the station so we can do our paperwork," Kate suggested.

"That's code for more Cheez-Its," I mumbled as I walked out into the living room.

"Kara, there's two officers outside, keeping watch until you get done here," Kate said.

"Thanks for letting me know. I shouldn't be too long."

"Take your time, Kara. No rush!"

"Thank you, Detective Barker."

Smalls rolled the gurney out to his van for transport back to the Moss County Morgue.

KNIGHT

Kate and I left the same time Smalls did. *Back to the pit!*

Chapter 18

Tuesday, Sept. 16th.

1:55 p.m.

Kara Carlson had a free moment from processing the evidence she collected at the Tidwell crime scene. Carlson called Detective Barker to see if she had a free moment.

"Good afternoon Detective Barker, this is Kara Carlson."

"Kara, what's up? How can I help you?" Kate asked.

"Are you free right now?" Carlson asked.

"Absolutely. Come on over to the pit," Kate said.

"Okay, I'm on my way." Carlson walked into the pit a little intimidated and handed Kate a receipt she found in a plastic bag that fell out of another plastic bag.

Tidwell was somewhere between a hoarder and someone who recycled.

Kate looked at the receipt from Percy's Grocery Store. "Percy's is near Tidwell's house." Kate looked up at Carlson. "How did you find this, Kara?"

KNIGHT

"I was collecting blood samples off the edge of the counter when, from across the room in the pantry, a plastic bag fell from another open bag. I noticed something white inside the bag so I opened it and saw the receipt. Tidwell bought a box of tea bags on August 27th, along with other items, as you can see."

"That's a good find, Kara."

"Thanks. I remembered you mentioned tea and sugar so I thought I'd bring it to you. Might be something or just a coincidence."

Kate didn't believe in coincidences at all.

Me, Mr. Sam Riley, wasn't quite where my partner was.

"Interesting. Definitely worth looking into," Kate said.

"I have plenty to do, so if you need me, I'll be in the basement. You have a pit, I have a dungeon," Carlson said.

Kate laughed. "Yeah, that's true. Have fun down there. I'll see you around, Kara."

I waited until Carlson left the pit before I stood up and put my coat on. "Let's go shopping, I guess. Shopping for evidence. I mean, Cheez-Its!"

Kate got her things and we left the pit in a hurry.

Fifteen minutes later, Kate and I walked into Percy's Grocery Store. We went straight to the business office. I asked Melanie, the clerk, to summon the store manager.

"What is this in regards to?" Melanie asked.

THE BINGO KILLER

"I have a couple questions about a murder victim that did some shopping here recently," I told Melanie.

"Oh! Mr. Swanson's not going to like this," Melanie said, with a sigh. She stood and hesitated before calling him to the front office.

"We just have a few questions. Nothing serious."

"Okay. I'll page him."

A few minutes later, Ted Swanson, Manager of Percy's Grocery Store, came barreling around the corner from the produce side, as if the store were on fire. His dad-bod floundered about as he made his way to the booth. He stopped short a foot away from me.

I smelled the strong aroma from the breath mint he just popped. The mint flavor arrived before he did. I appreciated the courtesy, don't get me wrong.

Swanson held his clipboard in his left arm pit. "Can I help ya, Sir?" Swanson asked, as he adjusted his red-framed glasses. Swanson's typical work attire included khakis, a white dress shirt and either a blue or red tie. His mix of black and gray hair was slicked back and complimented his mustache.

I took a step back from Swanson.

His eyes were deadlocked with mine, as to ask me why I was bothering him this time of day.

I looked at his name tag. "Yes, you can Mr. Swanson. I'm Detective Riley and this is Detective Barker. We're with the Bloomfield PD. Mr. Swanson, we need to see your security footage for August 27th."

KNIGHT

"God, this is all I need right now. How long is this going to take?" Swanson asked.

"As long as it takes. We're investigating two murders," Kate declared. She looked at me and unleashed her silent fury. "I swear to God, I'm so fucking sick of people giving us shit and stepping in our way when we're out here doing our work." Kate then glanced back at Swanson.

"Plenty of room in our jail for them too," I said.

Swanson sighed and shook his head. "Fine. Sure, as you wish. Anything for you boys and girls in blue. Follow me to the security office in the back." Swanson said.

"Thank you for your cooperation," Kate blurted out as Swanson led the way.

Customers and cashiers looked in our direction before we walked down the canned fruits and vegetables aisle.

We made our way to the aluminum, swinging doors leading to the back storage area.

Swanson plopped down in front of the monitors, causing the seat to buckle under his weight. Kate and I stood behind him.

Swanson fiddled the mouse over to the security feed. A double tap later and a screen with each live camera feed popped up before our eyes.

"Here we go! It's working good today for some strange reason," Swanson said.

"Let's hope it stays that way until we get what we're looking for," I said.

THE BINGO KILLER

"What time are you looking for exactly, Mr. Riley?"

"What time did the receipt have stamped on it, Detective Barker?"

Kate told Swanson we needed footage for August 27th, around 10:15 a.m.

"Alright, let me get that up and running on the screen here." Swanson pecked his keyboard.

"Thank you, Mr. Swanson," Kate said.

"May I ask what it is you're looking for?" Swanson asked.

"Well let you know when we find it," I said.

"Okey dokey!" Swanson said with a sigh. Swanson searched for the requested footage on the company's security database. "We keep about three months worth of footage at any given time due to the size of our hard drive. The system automatically deletes footage three months old every single day," Swanson said.

"Good thing we came today, then!" Kate said.

"Only if we find what we're looking for," I declared.

"You betcha! The sooner the better I always say," Swanson quipped.

Kate rolled her eyes. *There's always one with some unnecessary comments.*

"Okay, here's the time and date you requested to see," Swanson said, as he pushed play.

Kate and I leaned in and watched intently to find Tidwell.

KNIGHT

"There he is. This guy, right here!" I pointed to Oscar Tidwell on the screen. Can you pull up that camera on the main screen?" I asked.

The video showed Tidwell pushing his buggy out of the cereal aisle and walking up to register one. He placed his items on the counter and pushed his buggy forward to the end of the register to reload the cart with his bags. He seemed happy and chipper and briefly talked to the cashier.

"Nothing out of the ordinary. Nothing suspicious. Can you zoom in on his items right quick?" I said.

"Absolutely," Swanson said.

I noticed his items on the check-out counter. "Is that a box of sugar packets, by any chance, Mr. Swanson?" I asked.

Swanson said it looked like sugar packets to him. "Probably some off brand. We do carry a few of those."

"You would know better than us, Mr. Swanson. Can you show us where they are in the store?"

"Sure, after we're done here," Swanson replied.

"Did you ever speak to Mr. Tidwell that day or before that you can remember?" Kate asked.

"I do remember that day now that I think about it, seeing him on our footage. I spoke with him as he entered the store and got his shopping cart. We said hello and he started shopping," Swanson said.

"Did he seem nervous or anything?" I asked.

"No. He seemed happy in fact. It was a quick hello."

THE BINGO KILLER

"Can you show us the footage of him actually shopping? I want to see him in the store," I asked. "Where he goes specifically! The things he buys. If he talks to someone in the store. All of it."

Swanson switched over to the camera angle, above, to see the whole aisle. The footage showed him walking past the sugar packets and stopping at the spices.

"He didn't get any sugar from that aisle. But the receipt showed he purchased it," Kate said.

Kate asked Swanson if he could show all of the footage of Tidwell shopping, all angles. "Do you remember seeing anyone suspicious in the store at that time, Mr. Swanson?"

"I didn't. I just came from the back to the front at the time Tidwell came inside. I was checking on the front end and the cashiers to make sure things were good. I went to the back to count the inventory to put out on the sales floor."

We watched Tidwell's shopping trip like it was a documentary.

"Did you see that, Kate?"

"No, I was watching Tidwell," she replied.

I asked Swanson to replay the last minute of footage.

"What did you see, Mr. Riley?"

"Look closely at the woman," I said.

"Oh yeah, I see it now," Kate said.

"Excuse me. Stay here, Kate." I said, "I have to use the bathroom right quick." I knew I'd be okay for a few minutes while Swanson and my partner looked at old footage and wasn't scoping me out on live footage. *At least I had some cover this time.*

Kate watched the rest of the footage and saw what transpired between Tidwell and the mysterious woman.

I exited the security office and went to the meat section. I stood there for a few seconds and had a vision of Tidwell shopping. How I saw this vision and not the others when I wanted to baffled me beyond belief. But lucky me! I saw Tidwell coming towards the meat section on the back wall of the store, off the side, around from produce.

This vision was more important to our case than the ones at Lonnie's a few nights ago. I knew I had to pay extra attention.

"Let's see what they got here," Tidwell said to himself as he made his way down the meat displays. Tidwell was lost in looking at the lean cuts of meat to notice he was being followed.

A mysterious woman wearing sunglasses, dressed in all black with long, straight, black hair quietly and slowly pushed her cart right up next to Tidwell's cart.

I saw the woman approaching Tidwell. I stepped in front of them but stepped back a foot or two to get a clear view of them both.

"Excuse me, handsome man," the woman said.

Tidwell suddenly looked back and smiled at the woman. "Who's handsome? Not me! I'm wearing shorts and a regular shirt," Tidwell said, looking around.

THE BINGO KILLER

"Yes, you! Can you be a dear and hand me a good quality steak for my husband?" said the woman as she smiled and pointed at the meat.

"Sure. Any kind you want?" Tidwell asked.

"Something that will put him to sleep shortly after dinner," the woman said with a laugh.

"That I can do. What a lucky man!" Tidwell grabbed a T-bone steak and handed it to the woman.

"Oh no, I'm afraid that won't do. How about a nice, thick sirloin?"

Tidwell put the T-bone back and grabbed the freshest sirloin he could find.

The woman stepped forward and slipped a small item into his card without him noticing.

"Even better choice. He'll enjoy this one. I like mine slathered in butter as they cook."

I looked at the woman but her face was completely blurred and couldn't make a positive identification of the woman. She reminded me of Bullseye in my dream. Why I could see what she did and not who she was caught my attention more than what she put in his shopping cart. I couldn't help but wonder if Kate saw the same thing I was seeing. What more proof do we need to know this was now a homicide investigation?

"Oh yes! Edward will love this one."

"Must be a special occasion!" Tidwell said, as he handed the woman a sirloin steak package.

"Glad I could help. Have a great dinner, ma'am," Tidwell said.

KNIGHT

"Thank you so much," the woman said as she quickly walked away to the front of the store.

I should have followed her but I had to keep my eyes on Tidwell but the cameras took over where I couldn't.

Tidwell looked back at the woman as he casually walked further down the meat section. He picked out a few packages of pork chops and chicken wings but didn't notice the extra item in her cart.

My vision eventually faded as Tidwell walked away. It's unfair how I couldn't do anything to save Tidwell's life just now. What's done is done. I couldn't even see her face. "Nothing more I can do here," I said to myself before I joined my partner and Swanson in the security office. "Sorry all! I had to use the bathroom." I said as I joined them.

Kate told me she saw the woman place the bag of sugar packets in Tidwell's cart.

"Interesting. Let's see who she is. Mr. Swanson, can you show us another angle of the woman so we can see her from the front? Seeing the back of their heads doesn't show us shit," I asked.

Swanson switched to the meat camera angle.

"Yeah, she wrapped up a box in the sales ad and then put something in his cart without him noticing. No fingerprints on the box besides his. Very clever but we see you," Kate said.

Swanson said those kinds of boxes are wrapped in plastic. Any fingerprints are gone as the plastic is put in the trash.

THE BINGO KILLER

"Can you fast forward to her checking out and going outside to her car?" I asked.

Swanson switched back to the cash registers and fast forwarded five minutes. They watched for a few more minutes until she finally walked up to register two.

"Yeah, right there. Can you zoom in a bit?" I asked.

The woman in black paid in cash and was wearing white gloves before leaving three minutes later. The cameras didn't give us a positive identification of the woman, only what she was wearing.

"What about the parking lot cameras?" Kate asked.

"Coming right up. Cameras one, two and three," Swanson said.

We watched for a minute until the woman in black exited the store and walked down the sidewalk towards the produce side of the store. There was a small road where vehicles could drive around to the back of the store. She turned the corner and disappeared from the two main cameras in the parking lot. Camera three gave a good view of the woman walking past a dumpster.

"She got into the passenger side of a gray sedan with no license plate on the back and the car sped away," Kate said. "She had an accomplice."

"Well, I'll be damned if this wasn't your average shopping trip," I said. *Finally we're getting somewhere.*

Kate asked Swanson for a copy of all of the footage of Tidwell and the woman in black.

KNIGHT

"Absolutely. It'll take me a day to record it all, if you care to come back tomorrow to get the burned copy on CD," Swanson declared.

"That's probably our killer right there," I said.

"Mr. Tidwell is dead?" Swanson asked, as he looked at us.

"Afraid so. We found his body at his home. We're investigating this as a homicide & this footage is the biggest break we've had so far," Kate said.

"Yes, serial killers shop for groceries like the rest of us," Swanson said.

"Yeah, no shit!" I stated. "You probably had one in your store on that day."

"Mr. Swanson, let's keep this confidential. I don't think we need to tell you how important this is. Go ahead and make your reports to your corporate office. Do what you have to do but pretend we were never here if any of your employees ask," I commanded.

"If anyone asks, tell them Perry's sent us to conduct a surprise inspection and you guys almost failed," Kate said.

"I completely understand. Consider our business confidential," Swanson stated.

"Have a great day, Mr. Swanson," Kate said.

I told Swanson that we'll be back in a day or two to get the security footage, before we walked out of the security office towards the front.

"Are you going to get your Cheez-Its while you're here, Kate?"

"No, I've got enough to last me until Friday."

THE BINGO KILLER

"My God, crisis averted!" I said, with excitement.

Kate gave me a dirty look and turned around to go to the chip aisle.

I waited for a few minutes and finally Kate darted around the corner and brought over five boxes of Cheez-Its. "You're buying, Sam!"

"I'm buying?" I asked as I looked at my partner.

"Yes, you're buying." Kate looked at the cashier. "He's buying!"

"Shit, I'm buying!"

Chapter 19

Thursday, Sept 18th.

9 a.m.

I removed my bacon and egg biscuit from the brown bag and sat it on my desk. I settled into my chair and with no less than three bites later, Maureen handed a few letters to Kate and one letter to me. "Thanks Maureen," I said as I looked over the letter. "Wait, this isn't—I hope it's not another one of those damn ciphers."

"I don't know. It came in today's mail and now it's yours," Maureen said softly.

I glanced over at Kate. "Hey Maureen, if you get any more of these, can you bring them to me right away?" I asked. "They're evidence."

"Sure, Sam."

"Thanks, Maureen. You're the best!"

I looked down at the envelope and hesitated to open it. I knew what was inside it without opening it. The timing was not some random stroke of fate either. This was quickly becoming a wicked pattern I could seriously do without. I now had two letters in my possession. They were mine and mine to solve. *Mine!*

I flubbed my finger inside the back flap and opened the envelope slowly. I looked inside and saw what I expected. I took a deep breath and unfolded the paper. "Great! Another cipher!"

I looked back at Kate.

"Yeah, same as before but it's a different message I'm sure. No surprise we get this a few days after Tidwell's murder."

"No, it's not." I said. "There's a pattern here."

"There always is. That's the one consistency with those damn things," Kate stated.

"I'll make a copy and send it to forensics. Try and solve this damn thing. Play the killers' damn game."

I returned a few minutes later after giving a copy of the second cipher to Chief Williams and the original copy to forensics. I handed a copy to Kate and grabbed the cipher key I saved in a separate file in my desk. For the next few minutes, I wrote out the letter for each corresponding dice, according to the key. "Father knows best. Life's too sweet," I said. *Save the last dance. I'm closer than you think. Father knows best. Life's too sweet.* I admit the ciphers were easy to solve. I was glad for that small break at least. "I think each cipher message is referring to each victim," I said.

Kate agreed. "Save the last dance is Jill Sanders. She was a singer/performer. You could dance while she sang I guess," Kate added.

KNIGHT

"Father knows best. Tidwell was Jill's dad. Life's too sweet. Two victims. Sweet must mean the sugar packets disguised as caffeine," I said.

"That makes sense," Kate declared.

But why the empty bingo card? Assuming numbers go on the card, which ones and where? Why these victims? What did Jill and Oscar have to do with a damn bingo card? Whatever the reason, they were more than one of 24 numbers on some damn piece of paper.

Chief Williams came into the pit and grabbed a chair near the wall. He sat down in between our desks and faced Kate and I. Chief had our attention.

"Okay, what do you got? Let's have it," Chief asked.

"Well Chief, the second cipher says, "Father knows best. Life's too sweet," I replied.

Chief looked at Kate, then at me. "Correct me if I'm wrong, but the first one said something about dancing and being watched?"

"Save the last dance. I'm closer than you think," Kate said.

Chief Williams sat back and thought to himself for a minute. *I'm closer than you think? Shit, that can be anyone. Someone who knew the victims or someone we know? Figure that out, we find your killer more than likely.*

"These ciphers are word/clue based, so going forward, I assume we'll get a cipher with every victim we come across. I expected it to be much harder, unless we're totally missing something and completely wrong. It's possible we're using the wrong system

THE BINGO KILLER

here. We'll find out either way I guess. Sam, go backwards also. It's never this easy," Chief declared. "Unless the killer wants it to be easy? Well this round at least."

"What do you mean go backwards, Chief?"

Chief Williams explained how many ways there are to write such ciphers, drawing from his experience in the Navy. "A is one. B is two and so on. Well, maybe Z is one and Y is two,"

"Gotcha, Chief. That's clever," I said.

"Start with that and if you get anything that makes sense, come see me. We'll figure it out," Chief said.

"I certainly will, Chief."

Chief Williams went back to his office.

Kate wrote out the alphabet and placed numbers above and below each letter both forwards and backwards. She rolled over to my desk and handed me her legal pad. "Here Sam. This might help."

"Thanks, Kate. This looks like an extreme game of Hangman."

I added the letters that matched the dice again, both ways. "What I got going backwards just gives us gibberish. It doesn't make any sense. Going forward I get the same thing as I did before."

"Then that's what we'll go with," Kate said before her phone rang. "Kate Barker, speaking!"

"Detective Barker, Dr. Willow here. I've got some news for you and Mr. Riley if you two care to take a ride down here to the morgue and chat with me for a few minutes."

KNIGHT

"Yeah, we're on our way! Thanks Dr. Willow." Kate looked at me. "To the morgue, Sam."

I raised an eyebrow when I heard Kate say morgue. "Do I have to go? Seems like something only one of us can handle? I trust you, Kate." Part of me wanted to stay and work on the cipher instead of being scared out of my mind by another ghost.

"You're not afraid of a dead body, are you Sam? Afraid it's going to come alive and get you?"

"No, I was going to stay here and figure these ciphers out but something tells me I have to go with you to the morgue?"

"Yeah, you do, Sam!"

I set the cipher aside and grabbed my coat. "Fine. Let's go, Kate."

Fifteen minutes later, we said hello to Patty and walked back to the autopsy room. I felt a little afraid and out of place. I knew I couldn't let my fear be seen by my partner.

Dr. Willow stood by Tidwell's body. "Hello Detective Barker! Nice to see you again."

"Likewise. Well, alive anyway," Kate said.

Yeah, no shit! I thought to myself.

"Detective Riley, how are you sir?"

I glanced at Dr. Willow. "I'm good. You?"

"Another day in paradise."

"Sure." I shook my head. *More like purgatory.*

"Alright, join me at the slab," Dr. Willow asked kindly." They've already been stabbed." Dr. Willow grinned as his joke apparently fell flat with Kate and I.

"Not a good joke, Doctor Willow," I said. My anxiety got stronger with each step towards the autopsy table. *I sincerely hope Jill doesn't join her father in tag-team terror.*

Dr. Willow and Kate put on gloves and stood on both sides of Tidwell's body. I stood about two feet away from Tidwell's body, near his feet.

I looked around nervously. "Alright, let's have it, Doc. We have other things to do and other places to be." I said in my anxious panic.

"Easy, Sam. This isn't a horror movie. They're not going to get up and come after you," Kate said.

I looked at Kate with an annoyed look on my face. "Are you so sure about that?"

"Pretty positive," Kate said, with sarcasm.

"Yeah, okay. Sure Kate! That's how horror movies start…just like this."

Dr. Willow assured us that Tidwell was deceased.

"Dead, dead?" I asked. "Not going to open his eyes and move around, dead?"

"If he does Mr. Riley, I'll clean your house for a year."

I desperately wanted to take Dr. Willow up on his offer but I knew I'd risk giving away my little secret. Instead, I casually walked over to Kate and Dr. Willow. "Okay. We'll see."

"Thanks for joining us, Sam," Kate quipped. She looked at Dr. Willow. "Please proceed, Doctor."

"I'll make it quick for Mr. Riley's sake. I'll start with the head wound. The indented wound was consistent with a corner edge of a countertop. Had a slight L-shape to it."

"We figured that," I said.

"That's what killed him. Brain hemorrhage caused by the impact of the countertop. And of course, the bleeding."

Kate wrote down every word Dr. Willow said during our meeting.

"I found a larger amount of caffeine in Mr. Tidwell's system than I did in Jill's system two weeks ago. I'm not sure if their murders have a connection but it would seem so. Father and daughter. Two different victims with the same component in their bloodstream, two weeks apart. That's not a coincidence in my opinion. And no other bodies have come through here since Jill's."

"Jill Sanders," I said as I looked around the room and back at Tidwell's body. "He must have drank it right before he fell or a few minutes before at least."

"We're still waiting on forensics to get back to us on that box of sugar packets," Kate said.

"The caffeine was taking effect, he got dizzy and lightheaded and then fell down. The brain hemorrhage is what killed him."

"Sugar—the spice that isn't nice," I said.

"Tidwell didn't have a history of heart disease, nor did Sanders. Which is all the more strange. His heart started to pump harder, although one of his arteries

THE BINGO KILLER

was half clogged due to elevated cholesterol. That made him dizzy, lightheaded, maybe anxious, and he died where he fell. Consistent with Mr. Smalls' report," Dr. Willow declared.

"Either way, it's still a crime to give someone food or drink laced with a harmful agent—poison, drugs, etc." Kate stated.

"No argument here. It's clear Mr. Tidwell and Ms. Sanders were murdered," Dr. Willow said. "I've never seen toxicology reports with such high caffeine numbers. Even sodas don't have that much caffeine. You'd have to drink several gallons at one time to get that much caffeine in your system."

"So why Jill Sanders before her father? Two weeks no less," I asked.

"She visited him the day before her body was found. She must have had some tea at his house. I found a sugar packet under her purse on the table. She must have added the sugar to her tea, not knowing it was caffeine," Kate said.

"Tidwell didn't drink any that day. Or he had a small glass without any caffeine from the fake sugar packets? Sanders must have had a few more glasses of tea," I suggested. "She just didn't know it was a strong dose of caffeine. Neither did Tidwell.

"When I interviewed Mr. Tidwell a few days after Jill's death, he told me she drank cranberry juice and had one cup of tea. Maybe he got their drink counts mixed up? That very well may be what happened." Kate walked back to the foot of the autopsy table, near the door and waited for me.

KNIGHT

"How he got the box of caffeine disguised as sugar packets is your department," Dr. Willow said as he covered Tidwell back up with the white sheet.

"Dr. Willow, I've always wondered why these body sheets are always white. Why not blue for men or pink for women? Tie-dyed for free-spirited hippies or custom-colored sheets for sports fans? Maybe some blood-soaked sheets for horror movie fans?"

Dr. Willow shook his head. "Are you serious, Mr. Riley?"

"Dead serious. That's your department, Dr. Willow."

Kate sighed and scoffed, as her arms fell to her side. "Oh my God!! Come on, Sam!" *It's like living with a ten-year old.*

Dr. Willow joined Kate by the door.

I noticed I was the only one standing by the body. "Okay, we're done here."

"Kate, I also wanted to mention his funeral is scheduled for next Tuesday. The funeral home folks called yesterday and told me when they needed him there. He leaves tomorrow."

"Thank you again, Dr. Willow," Kate said.

"Thanks Doc. This was interesting to say the least. Let me know about those sheets."

Dr. Willow gave a fake smile as I walked back into the hallway.

Dr. Willow stood in the doorway. "God help you, Kate."

Kate shook her head. "Yeah!"

THE BINGO KILLER

The ride back to the station was quite entertaining.

"What was that in there? Kate asked.

I gave my partner a confused look. "What? Which part?"

Kate kept silent for a few seconds, waiting for my answer as I maneuvered through traffic. "All of it! Seriously, what's up with you, Sam? Is the stress or sight of gross things getting to you?"

"No, Kate! Don't be ridiculous. I was just being cautious, that's all. Best I can do right now, Kate, is say that I'll explain everything later on, after we catch our killer." I don't know why I said I'd wait to tell her my little mystery secret. Kate would have to accept it for now.

"Explain it to me now, Sam!"

"I can't explain something to you that I don't understand myself," I stated.

"How do you honestly expect me to trust you with my life if you don't tell me what's going on?" Kate asked. "There can't be any secrets between us."

"Best I can do, Kate. Take it or leave it." I said, as I pulled into Percy's parking lot. "Be right back!"

"Fine!" Kate said, super frustrated.

I power-walked inside the store and picked a few more boxes of Cheez-Its for my partner. Nothing more than a simple peace offering. I made my way back to the car a few minutes later, with a sack full of cheddar addiction for my partner. "You're welcome. Consider it a gift."

KNIGHT

Kate smirked. "Not bad, Sam. You're learning. But you have quite the ways to go. And don't think you can bribe me with Cheez-Its everytime I ask you something about our investigation."

"Good trip, Kate," I said as I drove back to the BPD.

"Sure, Sam!" Kate said.

Once back at the BPD, Kate walked towards her desk and sat the Cheez-Its in one of the desk corners. She started working on her paperwork for Tidwell's crime scene. Five minutes into putting pen to paper, Kate got a call from Savannah Rose, the local crime reporter at the Bloomfield Times. The call could have gone to me but Maureen Downs knew that wasn't a good idea. Savannah was my ex-girlfriend and let's just say our breakup wasn't exactly forgettable either.

"Detective Kate Barker speaking?"

"Good afternoon Detective Barker, I'm Savannah Rose, crime reporter with the Bloomfield Times." Rose spoke lightly, although her apprehension showed in her voice as she spoke with Kate.

"Yes, what can I do for you Ms. Rose?" Kate tapped her pen on her desk.

"Well this may sound crazy, but I got an anonymous call that one of the detectives working these double murders is psychic. I don't believe it but I have to ask just in case. Would you care to comment?"

Kate leaned back and looked at me. She smiled and laughed. "Let me get this straight, you think one of us detectives is psychic and trying to find a serial killer?" Kate asked.

"Yes," Rose said. "I know it sounds crazy but it's a strange world we——"

Kate laughed again. "You're right, Rose. That does sound crazy. Let me ask my partner if he's psychic. Hang on a second," Kate said as she put her phone on speaker.

I watched with dread as she dragged me into her conversation. I waved my arms back and forth. "NO!!!" I whispered. And wouldn't you know it, Kate ignored me without missing a beat.

"Hey Detective Sam Riley, I've got Savannah Rose on the phone."

I scrunched up my face. "Ahh shit, what the hell does she want?"

"Hello to you too, Sam," Rose said, sarcastically.

"Now, Sam, she's just doing her job," Kate said. "She wants to know if either of us are psychic?"

"Yeah, I've got my six winning numbers already picked out and I ain't sharin' shit!!" I rolled my eyes and cringed. *She should know better than to ask a dumb question.*

"If you win, Sam. Lord knows you lost me much easier," Rose said.

My jaw dropped at such a disrespectful comment. *I didn't lose her. She found other guys.*

"You're right. Yeah, she figured out my deep, dark secret. She got me, Kate! I'm busted! Can't keep much from her now can we? Including other men, right Savannah?" I asked.

"Nice to talk to you too, Sam," Rose said.

"Wish I could say the same," I stated.

Kate's jaw dropped as I'm sure she felt extremely embarrassed at what she just heard. But did I care? Hell no!!

"Sam, this is not the time and place for such talk. I apologize, Ms. Rose. Pay him no mind."

I quickly dismissed Kate's response with a wave of my hand and offered the typical, unofficial, official run around excuse. "Our official position is no comment. We don't comment on open investigations. She should know that. She'll get what we give her when we give it to her," I said.

I quickly wrote down a question on a sheet of paper and held it up for Kate to ask Savannah Rose.

Kate nodded and tried a different approach to find out who tipped Rose off with this bogus rumor I didn't want anyone actually knowing. "Nevermind him, Ms. Rose. I can confirm there have been two victims found deceased in the past three weeks," Kate said. "But as far as the psychic thing, absolutely not. We don't believe in that stuff around here."

"Can you give me their names?" Rose asked.

Kate told Rose the victims were in fact Oscar Tidell and Jill Sanders. "Now who's your source?"

"You want my source, Detective Barker?" Rose asked.

"Yes, I certainly do, Ms. Rose. Someone is spreading false rumors.. I mean, psychic cops? That sounds insane. Surely you don't believe that?"

THE BINGO KILLER

"Well no, I—" Rose said.

"Good. I didn't think so. If you did, you should be doing a story on why you believe in psychics and Casper the Friendly Ghost."

"I never said I did." Rose declared.

Kate played a familiar hand on this type of press poker. "Have you considered your source may be the killer? I mean, it's been my experience that the ones spreading such rumors are more than likely involved in the case."

"I don't think that's the case, Detective Barker." Rose said.

"I do think that's the case. Surely you wouldn't be purposely protecting a killer, now would you, Ms. Rose?" Kate asked. "That would not be a good idea. I mean, if you didn't believe your anonymous tip as you say you don't, then you shouldn't have a problem with giving up your source for the public good."

"Of course she would. She's good at lying and keeping secrets," I yelled loud enough for her to hear me from five feet away.

Kate snapped her fingers and pointed at me.

"Good journalists don't give away their sources. Best I can do is say I don't know. Which can be interpreted as a lie or as me really not knowing. Take your pick," Rose said.

"Fair enough, Ms. Rose. If there's another murder, I'm paying you a visit in the newspaper office. We'll have a nice chat. Anything else, Ms. Rose?" Kate asked.

"No, I don't have any more questions. Thank you for your time Detective Barker," Rose said as she hung up without hearing Kate's goodbye.

Kate hung up the phone "Did she really cheat on you, Sam?"

"Yeah, she did. We were out to dinner one night, two years ago and she couldn't stop texting some guy named Brian."

"That doesn't necessarily mean she cheated on you," Kate said.

"You're right, it doesn't. But the reflection of her screen in the mirror behind her told me everything I needed to know."

Kate shook her head.

I didn't say anything as I looked at my partner. I wasn't going to let Rose push my buttons. I didn't expect her to come back into my life, at least not like this. *How the fuck did she get a tip that I was psychic? Why would Savannah even believe that? Most people don't care to know. Damn sensationalistic journalism! Ain't good for shit. Who was her source? Lydia Tate? Surely Kline didn't tell anyone? They wouldn't do that to me. Would they? I might have to get close to Savannah Rose to see if I can sense who her source is.*

Chapter 20

Friday, September 19th.

6:30 p.m.

I pulled up in front of his parents' house to pick my mother up for a night out at the bingo hall. Kate and I walked inside and we saw my dad sitting in his chair watching television. "Hey Dad, whatcha watching?"

Dad looked up at his son. "Dammit boy, have you ever heard of knocking? Sneaking up on an old man will get you sucker punched, Sam!"

Kate laughed. "I'd love to see that, Mr. Riley."

"What? I knocked as I came in. Not my fault if you didn't hear me because the TV is too loud."

"Glad to see you too, Sam." Dad got up from his chair and welcomed Kate and I.

"Must be time for Bingo. Your mom has been talking about it all day. Bingo this and bingo that. Please take her—"

"Take who where, Gerald?" Mom said as she came into the living room.

"No one, where, honey! You're beautiful and I'll miss you terribly while you are gone for the next three hours while I sit in utter despair until my queen returns," Dad declared.

"That's what I thought you said," Mom said as she put her earrings in.

"I just love how you two go back and forth," Kate said.

Dad flipped through the channels. "Ain't shit on TV worth watching."

"Hi, Sam. Hi Kate," Mom said.

"Hi, Denise. How are you?" Kate asked.

"Hope you've been keeping Sam out of trouble, Kate," Dad said.

Kate looked at me with a straight face. "I don't get paid enough to keep him out of trouble."

I shook my head.

"None of us do, Kate," Mom said.

"Oh come on, I'm not that bad," I said.

"If you say so, Sam!" Kate said.

"Don't let them double-team you, Sam! Stand strong!" Dad ordered.

"Gerald, your dinner is in the fridge. Put it between two slices of bread. Chips are on the counter. Love you!"

"I have my own car and money," Dad responded. "I'll eat what I want!"

"Sure, Gerald. Put some mustard on it." Mom looked at me.. "Are we ready?"

"Yeah, I guess so. Bye, Dad! I gotta get these ladies to Bingo on time."

"Don't let your mom win twice. Then it's taxable!"

THE BINGO KILLER

"I'm playing to win myself," I said.

"Let's not be late and miss getting a good seat next to the stage," Mom said, as she grabbed her turquoise bingo bag full of ink daubers from a table next to the door.

"This should be fun," I said as we walked to my truck.

"I know. It's going to be great. You know I've been looking forward to this all week. So how was your week, Sam?"

I told my mom my week was crazy to say the least. "But tonight is all about having some fun and hopefully winning." *One win is all I'm asking for, if that's even possible for someone like me.*

"Well said! Don't get too upset when I win and you don't, Sam!"

"If you win, mother," I said.

"Now Kate, back there. That's a different story. They might have to double check her card."

I looked at Kate in the mirror, as she pushed her sunglasses up with her middle finger. I laughed at Kate's subtly.

"Stop it, Sam! You be nice to Kate. She's your boss, ya know. She's got a few years on you," Mom warned.

"That is correct, Mrs. Riley—a fact that he forgets sometimes," Kate said.

"I am nice to her, mom. I buy her Cheez-Its all the time. At least three boxes a week. I don't ask or expect anything in return," I said, looking at my mother. "In fact, if I win any money tonight, it goes into the Cheez-Its fund for next week. Some cheddar for some cheddar," I declared.

"Oh, whatever! You're just talking nonsense, Sam," Mom said.

"Thank you, Mrs. Riley. I couldn't have said it better."

"You're welcome, Kate."

A few minutes later I found a spot near the building. "We're here and it's time to win some money."

An older woman named Sue was selling the bingo card sheets and packets when we walked inside the Bloomfield Elks Lodge. The Elks Lodge was host to bingo games on Friday and Saturday nights.

"What do we want to get, Mom?" I asked as we approached Sue's table.

"I always get two six-packs of sheets, Sam."

"Kate?"

"I'll try one and hope I can keep up," Kate said.

"It's just numbers. Nothing to be afraid of Kate."

Kate raised her eyebrows at me.

My mom turned around and gave me a dirty look. "Sam!"

"I'm just trying to make sure everybody gets what they want," I retorted. "Gez, y'all!"

I told Sue we wanted four packets of bingo cards. Six separate bingo cards per sheet for each of the three games before the 30-minute intermission. Kate and I each bought one six-pack of bingo cards. Sue handed me the cards and my change from $100. I

THE BINGO KILLER

knew I'd come back to buy packets during the break for the second half games.

"Yeah, I don't know how this is going to go tonight," I said.

"It gets crazy around here. Especially after the break. Lots of cutthroats in there. They go from sweethearts to real assholes in seconds once they shut the doors," Sue said.

"Good thing we showed up to play tonight." I pointed at myself and my partner. "We're BPD detectives."

Sue looked up at me. "That won't help you. You're outnumbered. Ain't nothing scarier than a bunch of pissed off senior citizens losing a bingo game."

I laughed and said, "We'll see."

"Good luck is all I can tell you," Sue said as she looked away in seriousness through her thick glasses.

Tables and chairs lined up the huge room, enough for 300 people, sitting side by side. There were two sections of 25 tables each. A snack bar was open at the back to serve drinks and snacks. We followed my mom as she led the way to her favorite table and spot, before the games started at 7:01 p.m. Mom put her two bingo sheets beside each other. Kate grabbed a sheet and I put mine in front of me.

I grabbed the blue dauber bottle. Mom chose the red bottle and Kate picked the yellow ink. Kate sat to my right, facing the hallway. Mom sat across from me.

"Anyone want something from the snack bar?" I asked.

KNIGHT

"I'm fine, Sam."

Kate asked for a coke. "You know I brought my own snacks." She pulled out the big bag full of Cheez-Its from her purse.

I shook my head. "I should have known," I said. "You know you could use those Cheez-its to cover your numbers, Kate. Save some ink."

Kate looked at me. "No! Go get my coke, Sam."

A silent glance from Kate as I walked away.

"Okay, be right back."

Players took their seats throughout the room, with their cards lined up in front of them.

I made it back to our table just in time to start.

"Thanks, Sam."

"Good evening players," said Don, the announcer on the stage at the front of the room. He sat next to a huge 75-inch television rigged to show each number to players for around 30 seconds. "Welcome to bingo night at the Elks Lodge. Please refrain from talking on cell phones during the game. Please put all phones on silent. If you have to take a call, please exit into the hallway to take all calls. If you get a bingo, please raise your sheet in the air until one of our staff checks it for you. The first three games will be a single bingo. Are you ready players? Let's play B-I-N-G-O!!!"

Players grabbed their ink bottles and stared at the TV screens lined up along the walls for the players in the back of the room. I looked around at the intensity of these players' eyes and I admit I was a bit

THE BINGO KILLER

intimidated by them. I knew they played for keeps and I didn't need my psychic powers to tell me that.

"Our first game is one bingo," Don told the crowd. The first two games went by with minimal hostility. A few curse words and echoes of paper being ripped apart in unison from the losers. During the third game, I noticed two women come in and sit down at the last table, in the middle of the first section of tables. I had a good view of the ladies at the end of their row of tables. I watched the ladies settle in for a minute or two.

Kate and mom were deep into the game.

"Hey Kate!" I whispered softly.

Kate looked up and saw me nodding in the direction of the two women at the other end of the room.

I muttered to my partner quietly so I didn't distract my mother from her game. "Look over there. That woman with the black hair, sitting at the end down there, who does she remind you of?"

Kate glanced down at the end and back at me. "I don't know. Who? " Kate asked as she kept playing.

"O-70," Don announced.

"I needed O-72," Mom said. "Shit!!"

"She's been grocery shopping, Kate," I said assertively.

Kate looked up and stared at the woman for a few seconds. "It could be her but I don't know for sure. We need to get closer to find out for sure. But after this game."

I looked at my sheet. "I'll have to question her in private." I kept my eye on the woman and my bingo card, not that I expected to win. I was just here to spend time with mom in a low-key way. The older lady sitting one table behind Kate and I yelled out "bingo." A collective sigh filled the air before the echo of ink dauber bottles hitting the table in frustration.

"Shit," said one bingo player a few tables away.

"Cheater!" said another player.

One of the floor girls called out the numbers and Don agreed the woman won that round. The first three games had a prize of $100. Things turned chaotic, during intermission, like an emotional atomic bomb going off. Other players mumbled profanities, insults and the like while they bought their packets for the second half, Frito chili pies and nachos with chili.

Wow, Sue wasn't kidding. This place does get a bit mean when they don't win. I handed my mom $60. "Mom, go and get more cards for us for the next round."

"What do you think so far, Kate?" I asked.

"It's been fun so far, Sam!"

Mom came back five minutes later with three packets.

"I'll be right back, Kate. I'll wave if I need you."

"Sure thing, Sam."

"What's going on? Is everything okay?" Mom asked.

I was a few steps away and didn't hear my mom's question.

THE BINGO KILLER

"Oh yeah, Sam just went to say hello to someone," Kate said.

My mom looked in my direction.

I discreetly pulled one of the floor girls over to an empty table so I wouldn't be overheard and cause a panic of sorts. "Sam Riley, BPD Detective."

"What's your name?"

"Mary."

"Beautiful name!"

Mary was caught off guard by me talking to her. "Can I help you, Detective?"

"I need to use a spare room to talk to someone here, in private and away from everyone. I don't want to cause a scene," I explained. "Just pretend I'm not here."

"Absolutely. There's a small room down the hallway there," Mary said. She pointed to the hallway outside by Sue's table.

"Thank you so much, Mary. I appreciate it!"

I casually walked over to where the black-haired woman sat. I introduced myself as I slumped over her with my hand on the table. "Hi, I'm Detective Sam Riley with the BPD."

"Lisa Wilkins!"

I nodded. "Ms. Wilkins, I need to ask you a few questions about a police matter. Would you please come with me?"

Lisa scoffed in disbelief as she looked at her mother, Jennifer, sitting across from her. "The games are about to start. Are you kidding me?"

"No. This is important," I replied.

"Lisa, what's going on? Who is this?" asked Jennifer.

"It's okay, mom! I'll be back in a minute. This shouldn't take too long!" *It better not take too long.*

I pointed at Lisa as I walked past Kate and my mother.

Kate nodded and watched me escort Lisa out of the main hall. We walked down the hall to an open room. I kept the door open.

"Okay, Mr. Detective, what is this all about?" Lisa asked with a tone.

"Relax, I didn't say you were under arrest. I just said I have a few questions."

Lisa crossed her arms and looked at me angrily. "Hurry up, I don't want to miss my games."

"Do you remember where you were on August 27th? Did you go shopping at Percy's Grocery Store that day?"

"That's what this is about? My shopping habits? Jesus, you guys need to focus on the real criminals—the thieves, abusers, rapists and the murderers." Lisa shook her head and looked away in disgust.

"That's exactly what I'm doing. I'm investigating a double homicide and our prime suspect looks exactly like you," I said as I pointed to Lisa.

Lisa shook her head with a sassy attitude. "Really? I look like your suspect? That's fucking crazy," she stated with a sarcastic laugh. "I don't believe this bullshit."

THE BINGO KILLER

That's when my senses kicked in without me even trying. I sensed a weird vibe when I read Lisa's energy aura. I took a step across the line that I knew I shouldn't, which I knew wasn't enough to arrest her. Definitely not probable cause.

"You're not answering my questions truthfully. Have you even spoken to Jill Sanders or Oscar Tidwell?"

"Jill Sanders, the singer?" Lisa asked seriously.

"Yes," I stated.

"No. What makes you think I spoke with her?"

"You haven't listened to her music recently?" I asked.

"What the fuck does that have to do with anything? Listening to her music doesn't mean I killed her or anyone. What are you, some kind of mind-reading freak?" Lisa asked. She thought back a few weeks when she had, in fact, listened to a few of Sanders' songs. *How the hell did he know what I did a few weeks ago? Doesn't matter. It's not a crime.*

I disregarded the fact this was entirely a coincidence. "Don't call me a freak!" I declared.

"Oh my God! You are one of those psychic types," Lisa said.

"I didn't say I was. You assumed I was, Lisa."

"And you assumed I was guilty of murder," Lisa declared.

"Being a psychic is not a crime but murder is. We're talking about two different things."

Lisa threw up her hands in frustration. "Whatever man. I'm not saying another word until I speak to my lawyer. So you can either arrest me now or we can talk again on Monday with my attorney?"

"That's your right But you're a suspect in the murders of Jill Sanders and Oscar Tidwell. Turn around please." I put Lisa Wilkins in handcuffs as I read her rights to her.

"I understand you doing your job but you have no idea how much you just fucked up, detective," Lisa said.

"Don't leave this room." I barked at Lisa.

"Where the hell am I going?" Lisa rolled her eyes and sighed.

I walked out and saw Kate walking towards me.

"There you are, Sam! I came to see if you needed any assistance," Kate said.

"Glad you're here, Kate. I arrested her for Sanders' and Tidwell's murder."

"Does she match the suspect in the footage?" Kate asked.

"She wouldn't say anything. She lawyered up. She thinks I'm a psychic and arrested her for reading her mind."

Kate went inside and glanced at Lisa.

"Who are you, lady?"

Kate flashed her badge at Lisa.

"Oh, I see what the fuck this is. Some stupid good cop, bad cop act?" Lisa said.

"Maybe it is, maybe it isn't? But just be glad Detective Riley was the one who questioned you," Kate said.

THE BINGO KILLER

Kate and I spoke in the hallway. "Okay. You better be right, Sam. I wasn't here when you questioned her so I can't back you up if the shit hits the fan," Kate stated clearly. "Which means I'll get my ass chewed out myself."

"I'm not asking you to back me up, lie for me or cover for me. I've got a good hunch, intuition that she's our killer. I know I'm right about her, Kate." A hunch is all I had to go on. Maybe I was trying to overcompensate for wanting to make a good impression of my partner and Chief Williams?

"For your sake, I hope you're right, Sam." Kate walked back to the table to continue her games.

Me too!

I called dispatch to have two officers come to the Elks Lodge to take Lisa Wlkins back to the BPD.

Kate told my mother that I would be back in a few minutes. I knew I would have a lot of explaining to do either with her or Chief Williams.

Officers Crisp and Harris arrived a short time later and saw me waiting in the hallway.

"Evening Mr. Riley, you have someone we need to transport for questioning?" Officer Harris asked.

"Thanks for coming guys," I said. I went inside and led her back out to the officers. "Lisa Wilkins. She's a suspect in the double murders."

"Have her stay in the interrogation room until I get there after I leave here. Maybe an hour or so," I said.

Officer Crisp nodded and agreed. "As you wish, Detective Riley."

KNIGHT

I looked at Lisa. "Anything you want me to tell the other lady in there?"

"Tell my mom to come bail me out of jail since I'm now a murder suspect for listening to music," Lisa said.

"I'll tell her. I'll see you in an hour or so."

"Oh, I'll be waiting, Mr. Riley," Lisa said.

The officers led Lisa to their squad car.

I went back to the main hall and straight to Lisa's table. "Excuse me, are you Lisa's mother?"

"Yes, I'm Jennifer Wilkins, Lisa's mother."

I sat down, showed her my badge and explained to Jennifer that Lisa had been arrested a few minutes before. "She's a suspect in a double homicide??"

Jennifer looked at me in horror. "WHAT? WHY? HOW?" She screamed. "Where did you take my daughter?"

I noticed several other players turned and looked at me as I told Jennifer about Lisa's arrest.

I raised my badge around the room. "Go back to playing bingo. This is police business." I stated as I looked back at Jennifer. "She told me to tell you to come bail her out of jail as soon as possible. She's on her way to the Bloomfield Police Department."

"This is bullshit. I know Lisa didn't do a damn thing to no one. You'll be hearing from our lawyer." Jennifer gathered up her things, Lisa's purse, her bingo cards with her and sprinted to her car.

I got up and joined my mother and Kate to finish the second half of the games.

THE BINGO KILLER

"What was that about Sam?" My mom asked. No way I could have kept her from hearing the scene I had a hand in causing.

"I found a suspect in the murders," I said.

"Really? Do we need to go so you can interrogate them?" Mom asked me.

"No, we're good! I told the officers I'd be there in an hour or so.

Kate told me I needed to call Chief Williams and let him know I arrested a suspect in the murders.

"Stop cheating, Kate. Just because I'm not playing doesn't give you a winning edge."

"What?" Kate said as she smirked. "Get off your ass and go call Chief Williams."

"Fine, Kate. Be right back. If you win, we're splitting it 50/50." I walked back to the spare room and called my Chief. "Hey Chief, sorry to bother you."

"Sam, what's crackin' tonight?"

"The double murder case is cracking. I arrested a suspect tonight at the Elks Lodge. Kate and I were playing bingo with my mom. I saw a woman that resembles the woman we saw in the security footage at Percy's Grocery Story where Tidwell bought the box of caffeine packets disguised as sugar packets."

"Oh, really? You don't say. What's her name?"

"Lisa Wilkins."

"Lisa Wilkins?" Chief asked.

"Okay. Tell me what happened, Sam."

"Lisa Wilkins came in with her mom, Jennifer, and sat a few tables down from us. Chief, I had a hunch she's the one in the security footage. She wasn't answering my questions and gave me shit."

"Let me get this straight, Sam, and feel free to correct me if I'm wrong, but you arrested her on a hunch? No evidence? Tell me you're joking," Chief demanded.

"No, of course not. I have video evidence that puts Lisa Wilkins and Oscar Tidwell at the grocery store at the same time on August 27th," I explained. "She looks like the woman in the security tape."

"You have security footage and didn't tell me about it, Sam?"

I apologized for not telling Chief Williams about it. "I was keeping a tight lid on things close to our investigation. I'm starting to believe we have a leak in the department."

"That's no excuse, Sam. I doubt we have a squealer among us. I want a full briefing on Monday morning," Chief demanded.

"First thing Monday morning, Chief. She's in our interrogation room and will probably be bailed out by her mom later tonight," I said.

"That's fine. We'll talk about it Monday," Chief Williams said.

I told Chief Williams that Kate and I would head to the station after we left the bingo hall.

"Okay, Sam. Call me if you need me."

"Yes, Chief!"

I hung up and returned to my seat.

THE BINGO KILLER

Chief Williams called Sergeant Pilgrim and told him to let Lisa Wilkins go once she got there.

"Everything okay?" Kate asked.

I nodded. I noticed my mom only needed two numbers to win the third game. Nevermind my own cards. I knew I wasn't going to win. Kate didn't play my cards, which I wasn't expecting her to anyway.

"G-48," Don said as the number appeared on the big screen.

"Oooh, one more number. Come on O-67."

Kate and I smiled at each other. As fate would have it, O-67 showed up on the screen.

Mom screamed, "BINGO!" and held up her card.

"What!! No you didn't," I declared, looking at mom's sheet and the screen.

Mom insisted she did as one of the floor girls came over and checked the numbers.

"That is one good blackout bingo," Don declared. Hollars, sighs and yells of other players sounded out through the hall as paper was ripped from the cards and crumbled up.

Mom won $750 for getting a blackout.

"That's amazing," Kate said.

I took a picture of mom and her winning bingo sheet. "Good job, mom. Glad I could see you win tonight."

"Thanks, Sam!"

The other players sighing and moaning under their breath sounded like air escaping tires. Players grabbed their bags and purses and made for their cars.

KNIGHT

"That's some bullshit," one player said, as she walked out the door. "I can't ever win. I get two or three numbers away and someone else wins."

"It's all rigged," another player said from a few tables away.

The bingo hall wasn't short on sore losers. I found it hilarious how the players were so serious about a simple game of bingo but apparently, this was a way of life for them. Great! Mom collected her winnings and we left to take her home and go back to the station.

Mom was ecstatic the entire ride home. I haven't seen her that happy in a few years and her win made my night.

"I'm so tickled that I won. I've never won there."

"So what are you going to do with your winnings, mom?"

"I'm not going to tell your father. That's what I'm going to do, so don't you say anything about it," my mom ordered. That struck me as odd but I agreed. I was outnumbered anyway.

Kate laughed. "Sounds like a plan! That's smart, actually."

"Point of order! That won't work with me, Kate," I declared.

"Yes, it will," Both mom and Kate said at the same time and laughed.

I shook his head in disbelief. "I can't win with you two."

"We know," Kate quipped.

THE BINGO KILLER

"Sorry Kate! No Cheez-Its next week because I didn't win," I said assertively as I looked at Kate in the rearview mirror.

"I gotcha girl," mom said. "I'll get you a few boxes and have Sam bring them to you on Monday."

Kate declined Denise's offer and thanked her for her kindness.

"Are you sure dear? You braved the lion's den to see me win. You're my good luck charm, Kate."

"Yes, Mrs. Riley. I'm positive."

"Cheesy-Kate, that's my new nickname for her," I declared as I looked at my mom.

"No, Sam! You can do better by calling her Kate or Lucky Kate."

"I'm kidding, mother!"

I pulled up to his parents house. "Goodnight, Mom. I love you. Glad we went to bingo tonight."

"Love you too, Sam. I enjoyed tonight. Maybe we can do it again sometime," Mom said. "Who knows? I think I overstayed my welcome tonight, more or less."

Seven hundred and fifty reasons you overstayed your welcome.

"Goodnight, Mrs. Riley," Kate said.

"Goodnight, Kate. Thanks for joining us."

Mom turned the porch light off and back on again to let me know she got inside.

"Okay, I'm going back to the station for a few minutes to check on our suspect," Kate said.

"Good. I'm coming with you, Sam." Kate got out of my backseat and jumped in the front.

"I had fun with your mom tonight. She's fun."

KNIGHT

"I looked at Kate, stunned she pointed that out. "Are we talking about the same Denise Riley here?"

"Yes, Sam. We are." Kate rolled her eyes.

"Just checking. I'm the fun one in the family in case you haven't noticed."

"Sure, Sam. Your mom winning tonight proves you're the coolest in your family."

"And let that be a lesson to you, Kate," I said with a slight smile. I'm glad Kate was keeping my mind off of what I had waiting for me back at the station—a royal ass chewing or I caught a serial killer? A few minutes later as we drove through town, I pulled into the BPD parking lot. Kate and I walked into the BPD and saw B-shift Sergeant, Fred Pilgrim, sitting at one of the desks near the Chiefs office. A few other officers and one staff person were on duty that night.

"Sergeant Pilgrim." I said.

"Detective Riley. Didn't expect you to see you here," Pilgrim said, looking up from his paperwork.

"Yeah, we didn't expect to arrest anyone tonight but here we are," Kate said.

"Where is our suspect?" I asked Sgt. Pilgrim.

Sgt. Pilgrim paused and looked at Kate and I. "Your suspect isn't here. Chief Williams let her go without bail twenty minutes ago. But she did ask me to give you this," Sgt. Pilgrim said, as he handed me the note. Pilgrim continued with his paperwork.

I read the note and put it in my pocket. "Well that should be fun." I looked at Kate.

"What did it say, Sam?"

THE BINGO KILLER

"She'll be back on Monday morning with her attorney to clear her name," I said.

"Well at least she's willing to talk to us," Kate said.

"She's also threatening to sue the City of Bloomfield for violating her civil rights, Kate."

"Imagine that, Sam!" Kate said sarcastically.

I looked at Barker and then at Sgt. Pilgrim. "Great! Now I have the weekend to find another job." I said jokingly. I sighed.

Betsy Riddle came around the corner and noticed Kate and I talking to Sgt. Pilgrim. "Hello everybody," Riddle said in a soft voice.

"Hey Betsy!" I said.

"Goodnight, Sgt. Pilgrim. I'm done for the day."

"Thanks, Betsy!" Pilgrim replied. "Have a good night! See you Monday."

Betsy turned around. "Not if I see you first, sweetie!" Betsy made her way to the janitor's closet to get her things to leave.

"Let's go, Kate. I'll take you home."

Chapter 21

Monday, Sept. 22nd

8 a.m.

I walked into the pit, knowing today would be a day of reckoning, although to which degree I'd soon find out. *Shit, let's get it over with.*

Kate was on her way, or I assumed so. Say what you will about Kate but she's the kind of partner who gives me comfort weirdly enough.

Sgt. Whine brought the newspaper over to my desk and slammed it down in front of me. "We're in a world of shit, Sam, if this is true. Ain't nobody going to take us seriously," Whine said.

Next thing I saw were big bold letters in an embarrassing headline. "Yeah, no shit. That's all we need right now," I said as I looked out of the pit. My first instinct was to deflect any rumors to keep my secret safe, which sadly meant lying to my partner, other officers, Chief Williams and even my parents. The lesser of two evils, but which is which was the question. It often seemed like a revolving door at a fancy hotel. I absolutely hated being in this situation

THE BINGO KILLER

but a spy doesn't reveal his identity for a damn good reason. Call me a mind spy!

"I bet you $10 she went to the press and claimed this bullshit rumor. And they were dumb enough to print it. Just to get back at us and make us look like complete fools," I declared.

"Which one you talkin' about, Sam?" Whine said in a low, serious tone.

"Lisa Wilkins, the suspect I arrested at bingo at the Elks Lodge on Friday night. She thinks I'm some damn psychic or freak. She looks like the murder suspect from the security footage from Percy's we got last week."

"Well, are you?" Sgt. Whine asked curiously.

I shot Sgt. Whine a "get real" look as I rolled my eyes. "Yeah J.D., I'm about as psychic as Miss Cleo. Call me now and I tell you your fuckin' fortune," I said with all seriousness.

Whine let out a hearty laugh that echoed throughout the pit. "Shit, you know me. I'm just curious."

"You asked, JD. You asked," I said with a laugh. *Thanks for laughing it off as a joke,* I said to myself.

"I don't think it'll be that bad, Sam. I think the killer wants to see us in chaos and caught up in all this press bullshit. You're trying to do your job and put him behind bars. Besides, headlines don't catch criminals. We do!"

"Yeah, I know. I'm just trying not to fuck up too bad," I said as I looked at Sgt. Whine. "Sad thing is, the reporter who wrote that garbage is my ex-girlfriend. Now she's going to be up my ass about interviews. Seriously, is she doing her job now or is it revenge?"

Sgt. Whine nodded and picked up the newspaper. "They're always looking for a story to write their book or some shit. They're looking for a ticket to fame. One of the perks I guess," Whine said. "Don't let them get in your way now, Sam. Once you catch the killer, it's game over. All these rumors won't mean shit. You caught the big fish, man." Sgt. Whine headed back to his desk. "I'll see ya, Sam!"

"You're right! Thanks, JD!" I appreciated Whine's wise words. I felt a little better about how the day might go although I still was on my tippy toes.

Kate barreled around the corner with a box of Cheez-Its showing out of her big, brown purse. I swear she had half her apartment in that thing.

"Good morning, Ms. Barker. Nice to see you," Sgt. Whine said as they passed each other.

Kate gave Whine a big hug. "Good morning, JD."

"I'll see ya, baby!" Sgt. Whine crooned as he left the pit.

She settled into her desk and sat down. "Morning, Mr. Bingo," she said with a smile.

"Morning, Kate."

We both got to work processing our e-mail, paperwork and phone calls.

Chief came into the pit, about five minutes later, to talk to both of his detectives together.

"Good morning you two," Chief said.

THE BINGO KILLER

Here we go. Let it rain down on me, I thought to himself, as I gave my attention to our Chief.

Chief looked at Kate, then at me. "Both of you, get all your files, reports, codes and ciphers, everything you have on the double murders. Meet me in the conference room in five minutes. I'll see you there," Chief ordered as he exited the pit.

"Yes sir," I said. I looked over at Kate as she shrugged her shoulders at me.

Kate gathered up what she needed, grabbed her coffee and walked to the conference room.

I was about a minute behind my partner but still early to our impromptu meeting.

Chief walked into the room and sat at the head of the table with Kate on his left and me on his right. Chief paused a minute to let everyone settle in before he spoke.

"Sam, tell me about Friday night bingo and Lisa Wilkins."

"Well Chief, she came in with her mom, Jennifer, before the intermission between games. I told Kate that Lisa looked familiar with the woman on the security footage from Percy's. I walked over and asked Lisa to accompany me to a separate room for questioning. I told Lisa that she was a suspect in a double homicide. I asked her if she went shopping on August 27th at Percy's and if she ever heard Jill Sanders' music. She accused me of being a freak and a psychic of all things. Since she refused to answer my questions, I arrested her on suspicion of committing the double murders. That's when she lawyered up.

Officers Crisp and Harris arrived and brought her back here for further questioning. When Kate and I made it back here, Lisa was already gone. No bail or anything. She left a note for me saying she'd be here this morning with her attorney to clear her name," I explained.

"I want to see the footage right now. Go get the video right now, Sam," Chief ordered.

I returned two minutes later and gave the CD to the Chief. Chief popped the CD into his laptop and pushed play when the video player came up on screen. I sat back down.

"Sam, explain this to me. What am I looking at? I'm not psychic, like you are or Kate are, according to this morning's paper.

Chief looked at me as if he wanted an explanation for that piece of good and terrible news.

I ignored his comment and explained the footage. "This is footage of Oscar Tidwell shopping at Percy's Grocery Store," I explained.

Chief watched intently. "Okay. And the woman in black?"

I told the Chief the woman in black put a box of sugar packets into Tidwell's cart without him noticing and kept on shopping like nothing happened to avoid suspicion. She paid for a few items, left the store, walked around the back side of the store and got into a car without a license plate."

Chief watched all the footage and closed his laptop. "And you think it's Lisa Wilkins in the woman in black in this footage?" Chief looked at me with frustration.

"Yes I do, Chief," I said.

Chief shook his head. "Thanks for showing me that." Chief took off his glasses and rubbed his eyes and put his glasses back on. He let out a long sigh. "Kate, why weren't you in the room when Sam spoke to Wilkins? Aren't you supposed to be keeping an eye on him?"

"Yes, sir I am. I sat with Denise Riley while Sam talked with Lisa Wilkins."

"Playing bingo instead of doing your job?" Chief asked in a calm tone. "And you didn't think to join your partner?"

"No, I figured Sam could handle questioning one person. He's done it before as an officer."

Chief looked at Kate and I. "You two are partners, right? I assigned both of you to solve these homicides, did I not?"

"Yes sir, you did indeed," Kate said.

"START ACTING LIKE IT! Chief declared as he pointed fingers at Kate and I. "From now on, where one of you goes, the other goes if it relates to these murders, official police matters, interviewing witnesses, collecting evidence. All of it. Anything else outside of work, I don't care. Stick together so you don't make any mistakes or miss anything," Chief ordered. "Two people are dead and we're no closer to solving this case. It's slipping away from us." Chief told Kate that he was disappointed that she didn't take a bigger roll on Friday night.

Yeah, my mistake! Kate took a deep breath and looked down at her legal pad. "I'm sorry—"

"Save it, Kate," Chief snapped. He noticed Lisa Wilkins walking towards the conference room through the glass windows. "Follow my lead and speak when it's your turn. Sam, sit by Kate."

Sgt. Whine brought Lisa Wilkins and her attorney, Nancy Miller, into the conference room. "Thank you, Sgt. Whine!" Chief said.

"Alright, now!"

"Ladies, please have a seat."

Wilkins and Miller sat on the right side of the table.

Chief thanked the ladies for joining us that morning. He then introduced the ladies to Detective Barker and myself. "I asked you two here this morning so we can clear up this matter and have Detective Riley apologize to Lisa Wilkins," Chief stated.

I looked over at the chief with a confused look. "Apologize for doing my job?" I asked.

Miller reached into her briefcase and raised her arm to the table.

"*Psychic Detective Working Bingo Killer Case*," Miller said, as she opened Monday's Bloomfield Times. Big, bold, black letters, above the fold.

Silence filled the room.

"Everyone see that?" Miller asked as she moved it around the table in front of us all, like we were blind.

THE BINGO KILLER

"More like a psycho detective," Wilkins said, looking at me

I looked at Wilkins and shrugged my shoulders in confusion. *Someone's holding a grudge and doesn't mind letting everyone know.*

"Yes, apologize profusely, Detective Riley. Maybe grovel and beg Ms. Wilkins not to sue the shit out of you and this department? Which Ms. Wilkins will easily win by the way. Headlines like this don't do well in the court of law or public opinion. Very hard to get a fair and impartial jury. Then again, they might do very well for us," Miller said.

"Oh yeah, you're definitely her lawyer," I said. "I'm not apologizing for doing my job," I said. I looked over at Chief. "You want me to apologize to the Northside Burglar for chasing him down instead of power walking towards him, too?" I asked semi-sarcastically but kind of seriously.

"How do we know Ms. Wilkins didn't plant those rumors, over the weekend, in the press, to give herself cover for being a suspect? More leverage in today's therapy session? How do we know this whole thing isn't a setup? Did you give them that bullshit story to get back at me?"

Wilkins asked Miller if she could address me directly.

Miller nodded and pointed at me. "Go ahead Lisa. Give him a piece of your mind."

"You accused me of murdering Jill Sander and the other guy—what's his name?"

"Oscar Tidwell," Miller said.

KNIGHT

"Tidwell! After asking me if I listened to Jill's music. How the fuck did you even know that I listened to her music? Or even what music I listen to? I sure as hell didn't tell you that. Why would I? What does that have to do with anything? Furthermore, how the fuck is that proof I killer her? Lots of people listen to music they like everyday. Doesn't mean they want to murder them. As far as the rumors go of you being psychic, I didn't have a thing to do with that. But it makes me REALLY wonder if the rumors are true? Those psychic freaks do that shit," Wilkins said.

"Don't call them freaks. They're human just like me and you," I said with a serious, growlish tone.

"Tone it down, Sam,' Chief barked at me.

Wilkins laughed. "I rest my case." Wilkins looked at me. "I spent most of my weekend talking to Mrs. Miller so we could be here this morning."

"Thank you for that, by the way," Miller said sarcastically, as she looked at me. "I love giving up my weekends to advise clients who were arrested on some bullshit charge they had nothing to do with."

I leaned forward and looked Wilkins in the eye. "I also said you matched a suspect we've seen in security footage from Percy's. Or did you forget that part? You and your selective hearing."

"Show me the footage, right now, so I can tell you how you fucked up again, Mr. Riley." Wilkins declared.

THE BINGO KILLER

Chief and I obliged as Wilkins and Miller watched the video and made whispering comments to each other.

"Thanks for showing us that but it's a giant waste of time as I expected. That woman in black doesn't look anything like me. She's an older woman, probably in her 40's or 50's. I don't wear black clothes that often. She's a few inches shorter than I am. I'm almost 6 feet tall. That woman is barely over 5 feet. Needless to say, women notice these things about each other." Wilkins glanced and pointed at Kate. "I'm shocked this lady didn't know that. Could have saved a lot of time and embarrassment,"

"It's Detective Kate Barker, not "this lady," Kate responded. "I don't call you suspect, do I?"

Wilkins rolled her eyes.

Kate took a drink of her coffee.

I saw she was getting pretty annoyed herself.

"That's enough, you two." Chief pointed at Kate and I.

"We're dropping all charges due to lack of evidence. No evidence whatsoever, in fact," Chief declared.

"Thank you, Chief Williams," Wilkins said.

"What? Why?" I asked with a surprised tone.

"Hate to break it to you Sam, but Lisa Wilkins was not the woman in the video, nor a suspect in any murder," Chief said.

"How do you know for sure, Chief?"

"Go ahead, ask him," Wilkins said and smiled as she gestured to the Chief.

"You really want to know, Sam?"

"Yes, I absolutely do, Chief."

Chief smiled at Wilkins. "She's my niece, Sam. August 27th was on a Wednesday. She wasn't in Bloomfield during that week. She didn't get back in town until September 3rd," Chief explained.

"I was in Hawaii on a business trip and I stayed a few days for fun and sun," Wilkins explained.

"I drove her to the airport the Monday before," Chief said.

"Oh really? Well wouldn't that have been nice to hear a lot sooner. Why didn't you tell me that she's your niece?"

"I'll talk to you about that, in my office, after this meeting," Chief said.

Why would the Chief blindside me like this? "I get it. Make me squirm in my pants to teach me a lesson, huh? Fantastic job, you two!" *FUCKIN'—A!*

Wilkins smiled.

"So what do you want Ms. Wilkins?" I asked.

Wilkins said she wanted an apology from me.

I looked at Chief.

Chief nodded.

"Just get it over with, Sam," Kate said.

I hate this! Apologizing for doing my damn job! I took a deep breath. "I sincerely apologize for any inconvenience I may have caused you. I honestly had no idea you were Chief's niece, not that it mattered. I should have treated you with more respect and I am

THE BINGO KILLER

sorry," I said. *Happy now? Even though I meant it, it still took a lot out of my pride. Pride is a real bastard sometimes.*

Wilkins thanked me for my sincerity. "I accept your apology, Mr. Riley." Wilkins looked at Chief.

"Go ahead, Lisa." Chief pointed at me with eagerness.

"In exchange for my promise not to sue you or anyone, I have a proposal for you, Mr. Riley."

I shook my head in frustration. "What's that?"

"I want to write a book about these murders and Jill Sanders' life. I want access to all the files, reports and witness interviews. All of it, so I can write my book," Wilkins explained.

Oh, blackmail and bribery. How wonderful! "And if I don't?" I asked.

"We'll see your ass in court," Wilkins and Miller said at the same time.

"Oh, this just gets better and better." I sighed and shook my head. "I don't think it's a good idea, Ms. Wilkins. It opens us up to the possibility of not getting a conviction when we find the killer."

"No, not at all, Mr. Riley. I want to make you an instant, overnight celebrity with this book. Make you appear as God's gift to law enforcement," Lisa quipped sarcastically. "You're on top of your game and kickin' ass, man."

Kate laughed at Wilkins' sarcasm.

"I don't appreciate your sarcasm," I said. *I can't take her seriously not to write a shit-show of a book and get everything wrong, which is why I'm going to let her hang herself.*

KNIGHT

I sprung up with a sudden thought, like a lightning bolt in my ass.

"You know what, on second thought, Ms Wilkins. I think that's a great idea. But AFTER we find the killer. Your book won't be worth reading without interviews with the killer. I will gladly give you any records, notes and interviews you want. In fact, I know a great reporter who you can talk to. That's your first place to look for information about this case. She's lovely. You two will get along so great and she's your best shot at writing a great true crime story—No, THE next great true crime story," I said with a smile. I slid the newspaper over to Lisa. "Keep that! You'll need it for your story."

Kate turned her head and pretended to fake cough but smiled. "Excuse me!" She knew exactly what Sam was up to. "I agree, Sam. That's a great idea. I'll gladly give her everything I have too, AFTER we arrest this guy," Kate said. *Hell, I might even make up some shit to keep her staring at a brick wall. Diabolical move, Sam!*

See what I mean about my partner? She gets me in a weird way. We're good together, I thought to myself as I smiled.

"Great! I accept Mr. Riley. I'm glad we could come to a nice resolution to this injustice," Wilkins said. "See that wasn't too hard!"

"Are you sure this is what you want?" I asked assertively. "Because this is the deal—AFTER we catch the killer, however long that may be. There won't be any changes or demands or anything down

THE BINGO KILLER

the line. Only what we agreed to here today. You get access to us and the evidence and we stay out of civil court. Do you understand that?"

"Absolutely. I do. And thank you for agreeing to this deal," Wilkins said.

"Okay, just checking. Don't thank me just yet. We have to solve these murders and don't need you in our way," I said.

"Trust me, I won't be in your way," Wilkins promised.

"Good! I think you'll get more out of us if you let us give things to you as they happen."

"I understand and I'm okay with that," Wilkins said.

Chief looked surprised that both his detectives went along with their offer. "Well, that was easy."

I handed Wilkins a sheet of paper with Rose's number. "Savannah Rose is her name. I know her well. I'm sure you two will work beautifully together but don't let her push you around and hog all the credit and story. It's just as much yours as it is anyone else's."

"I'm easy to work with, Detective Riley."

I looked at Wilkins with shock. "Yes, Lisa you are." *As easy as working a rattlesnake not to bite you.* He gave her his business card and invited her to email him if she had any questions.

"Well our work here is done and both sides are in agreement. I'd call that a win," Miller said happily.

Yeah, I'd say so. The blood-sucking lawyer took a pay cut for once by staying out of a lawsuit, I thought to myself.

"Peachy," Kate sighed.

"Okay. Thank you ladies for coming by," Chief said.

Wilkins said goodbye and hugged her uncle. "Thanks, Uncle Mike."

"Keep your nose clean. I'm not going to always be here. Bye now, kiddo!"

Chief handed the footage CD back to me, grabbed his laptop and went back to his office.

I shook my head, stunned at the events that unfolded before my eyes. W*ell, I really had my ass handed to me this morning.*

Kate quickly turned to me. "Smooth move getting Rose and Wilkins to work together when this is all over."

"I thought you'd get a kick out of that. We're only giving Rose all our press releases and such so they have no choice but to work together. Let them fight it out. I may even convince Rose to write her own book. Create more tension between them, which has nothing to do with me."

"Diabolical, Sam!"

I shook my head with a smile. "Thanks. I do have a few good ideas from time to time," I said.

"Yeah, I'll give you that. But we have to be careful with your ideas, Sam."

"Now, all I have to do is convince Savannah to write her own book. But I need to chat with the Chief first. "Wish me luck, Kate."

Kate wished me good luck and went back to the pit.

I knocked on the Chief's wide open door. "May I come in for a minute, Chief?"

"Yeah, Sam, take a seat." Chief leaned back in his comfortable leather chair and pointed at the newspaper. "We have to talk about this headline. The damage is done I'm afraid. The mayor will probably jump my ass about this." Chief Williams rubbed his forehead. "That's the last thing I need. I don't think it's true for a second but I have to ask. I know Kate's not psychic. She couldn't keep a secret like that. The only thing Kate is guilty of is kissing ass here and there, over the years. Not a crime either. But don't tell her I said that either. So if there's something you want to explain to me, now is the time, Sam."

I looked at the newspaper for a second time and looked back at the Chief. "It's obviously sensational journalism. I honestly don't know who's ass they got such a stupid idea from," I explained. *That was the main question on my mind. Where did this headline come from if Wilkins didn't tell the Bloomfield Times?*

"Well they got it out of someone's ass. Didn't you mention something about a leak in the department, Sam?"

I told the Chief that I didn't know who could be the leak in our department. If it was anyone at all? "It's probably the newspaper folks making shit up to sell papers?"

Chief paused and thought for a moment. "Okay, let's tighten things up around here. You and Kate report to me and only me at certain times of the day. Hell, we'll all leave and meet somewhere else to talk about this case if we have to. You, me and Kate are the only three who have knowledge of the specific details of the case. Keep it that way, Sam. I'll talk to the forensics team and the coroner's office myself. Keep things private and make sure no one else hears you."

I agreed. I knew I wasn't the leak. I doubt Kate was and I never suspected the Chief. We didn't exactly have the time to spread false rumors among the officers to see who the leak was.

"As for the paper and the press, don't say a word to anyone without my approval. Everything we give them comes through me," the Chief demanded. "I know we just made a deal with Lisa earlier but we're going to keep that hush hush."

"They're just trying to sell papers. Nothing more, Chief."

"I'd say it's a lot more. Our community reads headlines. The Mayor reads headlines. The City Council reads headlines. I read headlines, Sam."

"I understand that, Chief! And I don't know how they justify this bullshit. It's no one's business anyway," I said, accidentally letting my secret slip out.

"What do you mean, no one's business? It's my business," Chief said, looking at me with knowing eyes. "So if you have something to tell me, now's the time, Sam," Chief demanded.

THE BINGO KILLER

I paused and closed the Chief's door. "Fine. I didn't want to say anything but yeah, it's true. I was going to tell you later on when I had things under control. I'm working on them though. It's not easy by any means," I explained.

"What are you talking about? What things?"

I sighed and sat down. "The headline is true. I do have psychic powers."

"I'm sorry. You what, Sam?"

"I have psychic powers, Chief!"

"You, of all people, have psychic powers?" Chief asked.

I looked at Chief. "Yeah, I do. I got them my first day as a detective. Could have been the night before. Some time around then," I said as I shook my head in confusion.

Chief leaned back in his chair and sighed. "I don't believe this. I should fire you for keeping it a secret from me. A little warning would have been nice so we could've gotten out ahead of this bullshit," Chief said as he pointed at the newspaper. "Have you used your psychic powers in this case?"

"Yeah, and she wants to write a book about it," I said.

"You mean to tell me everything Lisa said in there is true? You used your powers before arresting her?"

"Yeah, I did. I sensed her thoughts about Jill Sanders and her music."

"That's why you arrested her and nothing to do with the security footage?" Chief asked.

"Yes. I considered her a suspect at that point and she refused to answer my questions."

Chief lowered his head and spoke up with a soft and slow tone of voice. "Sam, Sam, Sam! I can't begin to tell you how many laws and ethics you broke by doing that without a warrant or evidence. Let alone zero probable cause. But what's done is done but here me, Sam, don't do anything like that when it comes to your job here. We can never tell Lisa that you really are psychic and can read minds or whatever it is you do. She'll want, and get, the farm. One more fuck up, Sam, and I'll have no choice than to put you back on patrol and give your badge to someone else."

"I understand, Chief! You're the first person in this department I've told, besides Dr. Kline. Kate doesn't even know, nor do my parents," I said.

"Who else have you told?"

"Besides you and Kline, Lydia Tate, who's also a fellow psychic," I answered.

"Too many people. I'll have to talk to Kline and get him on board," Chief said.

"I don't think Lydia will say anything," I said. "She's on my side."

"Okay, enough of the scolding like you're a teenager who broke curfew. Tell me exactly what you can do with these psychic powers?"

"Well I'll start from the beginning. I've been visited by and talked with three spirits since I became a detective."

"Spirits? You see and hear dead people?" Chief asked.

"Yeah, I've spoken to Jill Sanders ghost twice, Mystery twice, and a woman who didn't say anything when I was waiting for Lydia Tate at Candlewood Cemetery."

"Of course you have. Why am I not surprised? You haven't been using your powers in the Bingo case, have you?"

"Yes, I have. I went to Sanders' funeral to talk to her spirit and ask questions about her last few days before her passing," I explained. "She didn't give me anything though."

"Doesn't matter now, Sam. Nothing she said would be admissible in court. The judge would laugh you out of the courtroom. "

"Yes, Chief," I said.

"As long as you understand that. Don't do something stupid and let your psychic powers fuck up this investigation. This is a career-making case here, Sam."

"I totally understand, Chief. Believe it or not, I don't even want these powers. I'm giving myself a hard enough time with all this as it is." I sat in silence, debating if now was a good time to show the Chief what I could do. I looked to his left and back at Chief. "Chief, your mother, Delores, she's standing at the end of your desk."

Chief gave me an angry glance. "Christ, you're going to play the dead mother card on me?"

KNIGHT

"She's here with us in this room," I pointed and paused. "She said she's proud of you for having a great career as a police chief and all. She's proud of your kids - Duncan, Sarah and Emily also."

"How do I know you didn't make that up just now? I've said their names around here a lot over the years."

I looked at Delores and spoke. *Now he wants more proof. Would you believe that?*

Tell him what I'm wearing, young man!

"She's wearing a long black dress with a red belt. Left sleeve is white."

Chief sombered his tone as he looked at me. "That's the dress we buried her in. She loved that dress." Chief asked. "But anyone at her funeral could have known that."

I look like Cruella De Vil in this dress, Delores stated.

I blinked my eyes and focused again. "Chief, she forgives you for losing her mother's wedding ring before you joined the Navy. She found it a week later, hidden under the rug. She didn't want to tell you and get you distracted from being in the Navy."

Chief looked at me with curious intent. "How the hell did you know about that? I haven't told anyone that since I told my wife years ago. Did my wife tell you that by any chance?"

I shook my head and looked Chief dead in the eyes.

Say exactly what I say, young man! Delores said.

THE BINGO KILLER

Okay! Riley thought. "No, Skip. She didn't. I told this nice detective myself. Now sit up straight. You wanna turn out like your father? Chief Hunchback! That's what they'll call you one day. Chief Hunchback!"

Chief sat back in his chair and smiled. "You sounded like her just now. Skip, huh!"

Don't sass me, Skip! Delores said.

I shook my head and then looked left. "I can't say that to my boss."

Do it, young man!

I sighed. "What else do you want me to tell him?"

Easy for you to say, Mrs. Williams.

"God forgive me for what I'm about to say" I stated.

Fine, I'll tell him.

I worked up the courage to repeat what Delores said. "She said she caught you looking at you know what in the 8th grade. She came into your room to get your laundry. Is that good enough for you, or should she tell him some more? I can keep going."

Chief's eyes widened, as he threw his hands up. "No, Sam. You made your point. Sam, tell my mother that I love her and miss her."

I looked to the left side of Chief's desk and froze my gaze on the window. "Sorry, Chief, she's gone. I don't sense her energy anymore."

"Sam, I believe you have some kind of power but you have to get it under control," the Chief demanded.

I shook his head in agreement. "I will, Chief! I really don't like having this gift. I think it's a curse. Digging up wounds and secrets of the past, it's not my place. I don't want any part of it but I'm stuck with it. It's hard enough trying to figure this psychic shit out and not fuck up the investigation but I've managed to do that too."

"Follow the evidence, Sam. That's a proven approach. You know this more than anyone," Chief said.

I was afraid that the Chief would judge me negatively. "I'm afraid of a lot of things right now. I didn't ask for these gifts."

"Just remember what I told you, Sam. Know the lines YOU CAN'T cross. Know them well!!" Chief said.

"Yes Sir. I understand. I have too much riding on everything," I said.

"Good. Yes, you do. You're dismissed, Sam. Now go solve this case."

THE BINGO KILLER

Chapter 22

Monday, Oct. 6th

12:39 p.m.

Kate and I just ordered our combo plates at Chicken Canyon, a local soul food joint noted for their fried chicken dishes, topped with mashed potatoes and brown gravy. I had the chicken pot pie. Kate had the grilled chicken sandwich, topped with jalapeno peppers.

I felt my phone ring from my pocket. "I'm sorry the person you have dialed is not available—"

"Shush it, Sam," Chief blurted out.

"Afternoon, Chief!"

Chief informed me another body was found at 488 Maple Drive. "Get over there now. I'll meet you there."

"On our way, Chief. Good timing too. Kate just finished her second combo plate."

Kate let her napkin slip out of her hand as she shot me another go-to-hell look and a strong eye-roll.

"I don't think she likes my jokes, Chief!" I said, kind of afraid for my safety at that moment.

"No one does. That's why you're a cop and not a comic. And Kate's going to shoot you one day, Sam. I'm not going to say anything."

"Thanks, Chief! We're leaving now," I said as he hung up.

"You're a good partner, Sam, but sometimes, I just want to slap you," Kate said.

I smiled in agreement. "Let's go, Kate. There's been another body found over on Maple Drive."

"GREAT!" Kate said sarcastically. She grabbed her drink and we dashed to the car. A few minutes later, we pulled up in front of 488 Maple Drive—the home of George Nettles, a 48-year-old, local accountant with his own small, private firm. Small as in, his own office was in his house.

"We're here Chief," I said, as we entered the Nettles residence.

Chief stood in the middle of the living room, a few feet away from Nettles' body. Carlson also showed up and immediately got to work taking photos of Nettles body. "Be sure to take pictures of the whole house so we don't miss anything," Chief told Carlson.

"Yes, sir!" Carlson replied.

Chief motioned Kate and I over. "About time you two showed up. Tomorrow's Christmas!"

Kate pointed to me. "I wasn't the one driving, Chief. Grandpa here!"

I looked at Kate. "All those beans you ate, Kate. I wasn't taking any chances."

THE BINGO KILLER

Before Kate could respond, I approached Nettles' body on the floor between the couch and television. The shallow pool of blood on his body caught me off guard, although what I expected didn't matter. George Nettles was dead!

"We have to solve this case and find the killer. We're under the microscope and things aren't looking good, Sam. The clock is ticking!"

"We're trying, Chief," I replied.

Chief told Kate and I that he sent over Officer Harris to interview the neighbor who found Nettes body. "You can get his notes, Kate."

Kate stood near the couch, preoccupied with her notes in the binder she carried. "Thanks Chief. I'll do that here shortly."

"Have you found anything yet, Sam?" Chief asked.

"I'm looking high and low." I pondered around the room, using my gift like a weather radar as if it were some cheap, party trick. Aside from Nettles' body, the living room was clean.

Carlson went to the kitchen but didn't find any sugar in his pantry. All the sugar was in a sea of cold Mountain Dew cans lined up on the bottle shelf of his refrigerator.

I finessed my way through the rest of the house but didn't find anything out of the ordinary, until he walked into Nettles' home office. "Found it, finally! Chief, come take a look at this."

"Kate, can you go find out what the neighbor knows?"

KNIGHT

"Sure, Chief!" Kate asked Officer Harris about his interview with the neighbor.

"Alice Bradshaw is the neighbor. She came over to bring Nettles some more soft drinks but he didn't answer. She looked in his living room window and saw him on the floor. Dialed 911 and went home until we arrived. She came out and gave us her statement. That's about it. She didn't see any witnesses or unusual suspects around his house."

"Okay. We're chasing ghosts again. That's just great!" Kate said.

Officer Harris pointed across the street to the house Alice lived in.

Kate ventured to find out more about Mr. Nettles.

Officer Harris watched Detective Barker cross the street.

Chief's eyes centered on wall space about three foot by three foot, full of various newspaper articles of Nettles' own financial crimes trial, headlines relating to The Bingo Killer, as well as obituaries of Sanders and Tidwell. The articles had circles and scribblings all over it in red ink.

"What does this all mean?" I asked curiously. Only other time I ever saw such a thing is in those Serial killer/Zodiac-type movies. And now I'm looking right at one.

Chief looked closer at the wall, then around the empty room. "Let's not jump to any conclusions here, Sam but I think this is all staged. There's no other tack holes in any parts of the wall besides right here

THE BINGO KILLER

behind these articles." George's office was in another room next to the room Chief and I were in. We stood in front of the articles for a few seconds. "Nettles' acquitted of money laundering, embezzlement in a mistrial," Chief repeated. "Sam, look at this thoroughly. This doesn't look as it's presented. The devil is definitely in the details. There has to be clues in the fine print. All these circled words aren't for some art show," Chief said.

Kate walked back into the room and joined us at the wall. She noticed the date on the articles that captured her attention the most. Two articles faded to a light creme color over time. "October 6. October 8th....9th."

I mentioned the red circles in Sanders and Tidwell's obits. "Thirty! Sixty-seven! Their ages! How old is Geroge Nettles? I bet his age is important somehow."

"Why would their ages be circled? " Chief asked. "I don't think Nettles would add his own age to make himself look guilty."

"I doubt Nettles killed himself. Just didn't make sense."

"How so, Sam?" Chief asked.

"Probably someone trying to shift blame for the murders, that's how," I stated. "Someone trying to frame Nettles for the murders of Jill and her father." I noticed a corner of a sheet of white paper behind the articles. I raised the papers up and found a bingo card with their ages listed on the card, just as I had thought placed on the card.

"Surely it can't be true? It can't be that easy, after all the trouble the killer had gone through with the ciphers and cards?" Kate asked.

"Someone wants us to think Nettles' is The Bingo Killer. I guarantee it!"

"We have to assume he is and is not the killer. That's the safest way to play it," I explained. I saw the articles in front of me go blurry for a few seconds. Followed by a sudden and sharp pain radiating through my head and neck that lasted about thirty seconds. I scrunched up my face as I rubbed my head to take the focus of my pain.

"Are you okay, Sam? Talk to me!" Chief asked.

"Yeah, I'm okay. Just something that happens from time to time."

Kate looked at me with a slight concern in her eyes.

"Okay. Just checking. Good man!"

"I'll be okay," I said.

Chief pointed out the door and walked back into the living room.

Carlson looked inside his bedroom but saw nothing out of place. Nettles' bedroom was a bit dirty with laundry piled up in one corner. Mountain dew cans on the nightstand and in the small trash can between the bed and nightstand.

Ernie Smalls stood in the living room, filling out his required paperwork, when Chief, Kate and I walked back in the living room.

THE BINGO KILLER

"Ah, Mr. Smalls! There you are! You snuck in like the killer did, from the looks of things."

"I should have announced my presence but I didn't have a trumpet to play when I walked in," Smalls said.

Chief patted Smalls on the shoulder and smiled. "Just play the music on your phone. Much easier."

Smalls laughed. "I'll do that. Thanks!" Smalls said before turning his attention to Nettles.

"Smalls, how's it going?" I asked.

"Can't complain, Mr Riley. I'm alive."

I nodded.

Smalls wrote down more notes and focused on removing Nettles to the meat-mobile. "Victim has a black glove on his right hand. That's noteworthy since the other victims didn't have a glove on their hands." Smalls figured it best he left the glove on so Dr. Willow could examine it back at the morgue.

"We'll make a note of that," I said.

Smalls retreated to the van to get the gurney. He returned a few minutes later ready to move Nettles back to the morgue.

Kate looked around Nettles' house again. "Kara, can you bag up the newspaper articles in the empty room and bring them down to the station. I'd like for you and I to look at them again later this afternoon."

"Absolutely." Carlson excused herself to do as requested. Carlson grabbed some large, wide plastic bags and put the articles in them for safe keeping.

KNIGHT

Chief asked me to join him outside for a few minutes for some fresh air. "Okay, Sam, talk to me. What did you come up with?"

Before I could say anything, I noticed dark clouds approaching Bloomfield from the Southwest. My dream sprang into my mind like a kangaroo hopping around the zoo. I didn't tell the Chief the truth inside the office. I didn't want Kate to jump to conclusions about me.

"I didn't sense anything in there right now. It doesn't work on a schedule. It happens when it happens. I'll stick around for a while and see if I can pick up anything."

"Good. I think you two have this covered. Call me if you need me. I'll see you back at the station," Chief said.

"Thanks, Chief. Later," I said as I walked back inside.

Smalls needed my help to put Nettles' body on the stretcher. I obliged before Smalls draped the white sheet over Nettles' and buckled him in for his last ride to the morgue.

Kate looked under the couch for any evidence, now that Nettles was gone but no luck. "Whoever did this was very careful and meticulous. Didn't leave anything behind, except the clippings in the office. Maybe this was staged?" Kate took another look around the kitchen.

I sensed Nettles' spirit looking at a bookshelf by a window with white curtains. Nettles sprang to life and

THE BINGO KILLER

faced me when he heard my voice. I took a moment and nodded and pointed at Nettles. I casually looked around the room to make sure Kate didn't see me talking to Nettles. I needed a distraction to keep my partner away for another minute or two.

"Hey Chief, how are you doing?"

"Are you talking to me?" Nettles asked.

I shook my head while holding my phone. "Yes, Chief!"

"Oh, you're pretending—that's smart, man!" Nettles said as he walked towards me.

"Yeah, there's been a change of plans, Chief!"

"Wait, are you guys cops? What is going on here?"

"Yeah, Chief. Detective Barker and I are going to the morgue to see Nettles body after we leave. I'm curious to see why he was wearing a glove on his right hand?"

"Nettles? I'm Nettles? Morgue? Am I dead? That was my body? I thought it was a dream. Oh, man. No, no, no. It wasn't my time." Nettles slumped to his knees. He noticed Kate in the kitchen looking around. "Hey, what is she doing in my kitchen?"

"No Chief, Detective Barker is still looking for evidence in the kitchen. That's why I'm talking to you in private. I don't want to freak her out," I said softly.

"This whole thing is freaking me out!" Nettles' said.

"Yeah, no shit," I said, looking at Nettles.

Nettles looked around the room.

KNIGHT

"No, Chief. We're not done here. I'm not sure why the newspaper articles were found in Nettles' office," I stated as he walked to the office.

"What articles?"

I stopped in the office doorway to check on Carlson.

Nettles darted through me into his office as I stopped in the doorway. "Whoa…shit, what was that? Did I just run through you, man?"

"Yeah, Chief. You did."

A light, slow gust of wind startled Carlson as she took one out of several clippings, down. She looked around the room. "Whoa, that was weird." She looked at me. "Did you feel that?"

I didn't tell her about Nettles. "Feel what?"

"That gust of wind?" Carlson said.

"The front door is still open to let the blood smell out. Probably the wind!" I declared.

"Must have been strong wind." She nodded and continued working.

Nettles' jaw dropped when he saw Carlson securing the clips into a big Ziploc bag. "Where did these come from?" Nettles asked. "I've never seen these. There was nothing on this wall. No art. Nothing! Who the fuck puts up old newspapers? What is going on here?"

"I don't think Nettles put these articles up on his wall and then killed himself. Doesn't make sense. Surely, he'd want to get credit for the murders but not his own," I said. "That's not typical serial killer

THE BINGO KILLER

behavior. They want the big show. Not crumbled ink on rotting paper."

"I don't know where these came from. I didn't put them there. Take a look around the room. They don't belong here," Nettles cried out.

"Bye, Chief!"

I wasn't sure I had enough evidence to believe Nettles wasn't the killer but I still kept an eye on him.

Kate waited for me back in the living room. "Did you find anything back there?"

"No, not really. I didn't check the master bedroom," I said.

"Let's go check it just to make sure," Kate suggested.

"Lead the way, partner."

Kate checked the nightstand but found a small pharmacy of anxiety and high blood pressure meds. "Looks like this guy had more health issues than legal troubles."

"Guess I won't need those anymore," Nettles quipped. "I won't need any of this any more. Spent my whole life buying this house and paying off school loan debts. I had a year left of house payments. Home free. Now, someone else gets it. It's not fair."

I didn't respond to Nettles' rants about how unfair things were.

I noticed the finer quality furniture in Nettles' bedroom. "This guy had it made. Six-figure salary. His own business. I bet he had a good life insurance policy. At least half a million dollars and a fat will. I'm not sure how useful his will is with no family. He's not married and has no family."

"You're somewhat right, friend," Nettles said. "You could say I had an excellent retirement fund."

"It's our job to find his Killer. No matter the cost or salary, for that matter. Justice shouldn't come at a cost. Some people can afford private investigators or offer expensive rewards and get nothing for years. But on the other scale, guilty criminals get off because of their wealthy parents giving donations to judges and prosecutors. A slap on the wrist for some punk ass, spoiled rich kid killing a family of four while driving drunk. But I'm a detective, not a judge. I just call it like I see it," Kate declared.

I nodded. "We can only do so much with what we are given. It's not a perfect world by means. That's why I fought hard for this job."

"Sorry to break up your Shakespearean moment but I deserve justice as much as the dead body you find at your next crime scene," Nettles declared.

"Well, I think we have what we came for, Kate. Let's get to the morgue to talk to Dr. Willow."

"Might as well, Sam." Kate walked back to the living room.

Nettles' thought openly bribing a cop would be a winning move. "Wait, wait, hear me out, man! Find my killer! I got you covered. Look behind the painting."

I looked in the direction of the painting. "What about the painting?"

THE BINGO KILLER

"Look behind the painting."

I took down the painting of a sailboat in front of an island.

"There's $100,000 dollars in there. Take every penny! I'm dead now. What do I need it for?" Nettles said with a sense of anxious urgency. "Find my killer!"

I looked at Nettles and shook my head.

"Are you out of your mind, Nettles?" I asked as I walked back to the living room. As I made the corner into the hallway, Mystery suddenly appeared.

I stopped in my tracks. *God, now what do you want?*

"Yo, man, don't you take that man's money. That's drug or blood money. Just because those Benjamins' are bad doesn't mean you gotta be too."

Nettles' marched over and stepped in between Mystery and I. "Who the ever-loving fuck is this guy? Get your own justice, buddy!"

"Don't do that, little man. I'm a lot more ghostlier than you are."

"I don't give a shit what you are. My justice is worth a lot more than yours," Nettles declared.

"Arrogant prick," Mystery exclaimed.

I didn't have the time or energy to endure a ghost fight. *Goodbye, gentleman*, I said as I rolled my eyes and walked to the living room.

"Are you ready, Kate?"

"Yeap. Let's go see Dr. Willow."

Twenty minutes later, Kate and I walked into the autopsy room as Dr. Willow played Operation on a guy who looked like the guy on the actual game board.

KNIGHT

"Hello, Dr. Willow," Kate said.

"Oh, hello, Kate!"

"Mr. Riley," Dr. Willow crooned.

As expected, I cringed at the site of Nettles' open ribcage and his skin pulled back. "I can't go any further. I'm glad we had lunch already and I take back the second combo plate comment, Kate!"

"Wimp!" Kate walked right up to Nettles body, like it was second nature to her. Oddly, morgue visits didn't bother her. It's even safe to say, she might have become a medical examiner herself if she hadn't gone into law enforcement. And she would have been a great medical examiner doctor.

"I know we're early Doctor but we're working hard to solve these murders. Detective Riley's actually sweating like a whore in church," Kate said, looking back at me.

I stepped towards Nettles' body but kept my distance. "Uh, God, how can you do this every day, doc?"

"I'm not going to ask about Mr. Riley. I've all but given up trying to figure him out."

"Welcome to my world," Kate said as she winked at Dr. Willow.

Dr. Willow winked at Kate.

What are they up to, I thought to myself.

Kate looked at me and peaked inside Nettles. "You're right, Sam. It is a good thing we had lunch already," she said as she pointed at Nettles' chest.

THE BINGO KILLER

"The veins look like spaghetti noodles. Intestines look like uncooked sausages."

"Shut the fuck up, Kate!" I said as I looked away and took a few steps away from the autopsy table. "If you don't stop, I swear I'm going to vomit all over this floor."

Dr. Willow and Kate both laughed.

"Dammit, it's not funny," I said as I felt my stomach rumble with nausea.

"Okay, I'll make this as quick as I can. Mr. Riley, your eyes need to see this."

I told Dr. Willow I could see just fine from three feet away. "What! What do I need to see?"

"My thumb!!!! Because it's missing. EEEHEHEHE!!!!!!" Dr. Willow screamed, as he held up and shook Nettles right hand.

I didn't see Nettles' thumb. All I saw was Nettles head as it lifted up and stared at me as Dr. Willow did what he did. I then quickly bolted away to the trash can like I was about to blow chunks. And I very well was close to doing just that.

"Got him, Dr. Willow!" Kate said merrily. Kate laughed and high-fived Dr. Willow. "That was a good one, Dr. I like your style."

Dr. Willow put the hand down and high-fived Kate "Thanks. I can only do it once with Mr. Riley. Once is enough though!"

Once is all you get. Next time, I arrest you for abusing a corpse, Dr. Willow. "You guys are the fucking worst!" I said. "Okay, so his thumb is missing. What the hell do you want me to do about it?"

KNIGHT

"Nothing you can do, my boy! It'll turn up eventually," Dr. Willow declared. "Unfortunately, that's all I can give you at the moment. I won't have the toxicology report ready for a few days. It looks like the lacerations all over his chest, arms and legs were done with a thin blade. Perhaps a box cutter or utility knife? It's often used in stabbings or to inflict more damage quickly. Aside from knives and swords."

I nodded her head. "I see. Will you let me know as soon as you know?"

"Absolutely. I always do."

"Thank you, Dr. Willow. Always a pleasure. I'm hungry, Sam. Let's go get some pasta." Kate smiled as she walked past me.

I took a few deep breaths and held a handkerchief over his mouth. "Fuck your pasta," I murmured as I staggered out behind her.

Dr. Willow pulled the sheet back over Nettles. "I love how they fight like a married couple."

I breathed in fresh air once I saw daylight outside the morgue. "AIR!!!" I yelled.

Kate laughed all the way to the truck.

I was too busy trying to erase the last five minutes from my memory forever. "What was that, Kate?" I asked as I opened my door.

"Oh, now you want to know what that was?" Kate asked as she got into the truck. "Start talking, Sam. You tell me yours, I'll tell you mine." Kate smiled her cute smile.

THE BINGO KILLER

I shook my head and drove back to the station. *Fuck, she's good!*

Chapter 23

Sunday, Oct. 12

6:09 a.m.

I found myself walking down a wide, gray sidewalk on Erie Ridge Drive, on a sunny afternoon. The newer houses, with bright shutters lining the neighborhood, had well maintained yards and sidewalks about two feet from the street curb. Some weird feeling drew me to this run down, gray-colored house, omitting an ominous vibe from the windows and front door. My white, cotton T-shirt waved in the whirlwind around me as the sky turned into a raging, pitch black thunderstorm, inducive of a tornado dropping out of the clouds. I looked around the neighborhood in a panic and thought to myself, *Am I the only one seeing this?*

A woman's deathly scream coming from inside the house caught my attention.

I trotted towards the front door. "What the hell is going on in there?" I muttered, gazing inside the house intently.

She screamed again. "No! Please! NO!!!"

THE BINGO KILLER

The wind picked up loose grass and pieces of trash all around me. I was never the kind of guy who let my fear get the best of me and this moment was no different. I ignored the voice in my head telling me to stay away from this house and the woman's screams were none of my business. I banged on the door. "Hello, is everything okay? This is Officer Riley. Does anybody need help?"

A loud commotion crashed down, followed by the scuffling of feet from inside the house. I quickly side stepped past the big hedge bush, over to a broken window.

Peeking inside just enough not to be seen, I noticed a tall, dark-clothed figure standing with its back towards me in the living room. This intruder is up to something and I was curious. The figure stood still, looking at the floor in front of him.

I ran back to the old, decrepit door and battered it with my shoulder until it burst wide open, crashing into a nearby wall. Walking across the wooden floor in the foyer, my footsteps crackled across the debris swirling and landing inside from the storm. *What have I gotten myself into? Good idea, Sam!*

Reaching for my waist, I felt an empty space where my firearm should have been. My adrenaline shot through the roof at this point. Seemed like the higher my adrenaline rose, the worse the situation grew. I walked towards the black and white striped couch in the middle of the living room.

The intruder knelt down in front of the couch, as the woman screamed again. "Your turn to die," he said in a crackly, rough tone, similar to a smokers' voice.

"Don't kill me, please! I want to see my kids grow up," the woman whimpered, tears flowing from her eyes. Sweat fell from her face onto her white dress with different-sized black lines in a square pattern.

With silent steps, I crept up to the intruder and kicked him in the stomach but my leg went right through him and hit the coffee table. "Dammit! My foot," I belted out. I grabbed his clothing but my hands went through his black coat. *Shit! Nothing I'm doing is stopping this guy.*

He ignored me—which pissed me off even more—and grabbed a six-inch steel knife from his trench coat pocket and held the knife up. He wore a black mask with no eye covers.

He's going to kill her!! "Put the knife down and put your hands up," I shouted. "Who are you? What's your name?"

He knelt down next to the woman and stabbed her four times in between her breasts and waist.

The sound of each stab pierced my ears, leaving me with a haunting and helpless feeling.

She screamed in pain as drops of blood flew off the knife blade and landed on the carpet and floor behind Bullseye.

"Bullseye strikes again," he said, laughing hysterically. His laugh raised the hairs on my arm as I felt a cold rush rippling across my skin.

THE BINGO KILLER

"Bullseye, put the knife down and step away from her," I repeated to no avail. I paused for him to do as ordered but he stood over the woman, admiring his handy work. "Such beautiful body art," Bullseye whispered.

Barely conscious, she laid on the floor where the rug and the wooden floor meet. The left side of her body laid on the wooden floor and her right side laid on a white rug with black lines running parallel with each other. Her dress and the rug looked like one big labyrinth of light and dark with splashes of blood. Her breathing slowed down and softened and she eventually stopped moving. She kept her eyes open, despite her tremendous pain.

Bullseye stood up and wiped the knife off before putting the knife away. "My work is done and so is she."

I looked around the room to find anything to use to stop him "Guess I'm improvising!" I said to myself. I grabbed a cheap, five-foot tall, brass lamp in the corner and swung it at Bullseye's head, causing me to fall on the couch.

"You missed me," Bullseye belted out with an evil laugh.

"Dammit!"

She jolted awake when the lamp landed next to her body. The woman looked at me and said, "Well, would you look at that? He's going to kill me with his knife. I blame you, Officer Riley," the woman said. "I'll see you in the afterlife!"

KNIGHT

Frozen with fear and shock when I heard her gargled words, I couldn't move my body long enough to stop Bullseye from finishing his macabre job. Fixated on the terror in her wide eyes, Bullsyee raised his knife and stabbed her four more times in the chest. "NO!!" I shouted, reaching for the knife Bullseye wielded. The knife went through my hands. I'm lucky I didn't cut myself good.

Her screams turned into gargles as blood bubbled and squirted out of her mouth, down the side of her cheeks, down her neck, resting in a pool on the floor. Her head flopped to its final resting place, eyes pointed at the coffee table.

Bullseye looked at me with soul-piercing eyes. Dark energy radiated from his eyes.

Holy shit! Bullseye isn't human

Bullseye raised up the knife and wiped off the blood in between its pointer and middle fingers. Blood oozed down his black gloves. The two colors blended together with a slow, doomy flow down to his wrist. Bullseye gently rubbed her blood on his skin. "Wanna be my next victim?" He said, gazing in my direction.

Regaining control of my fear, I broke away from the trance-like stare just long enough to declare, "Don't move. You're under arrest!"

"Maybe in your next dream, Sam." Bullseye bolted to the exit.

I checked the woman's pulse on the side of her neck. "Shit, she's dead," I said, overcome with anger. I

THE BINGO KILLER

stepped back a few feet as she stood up, in a pool of her own blood, looking at me. Blood seeped down her chin. Her dress looked like a canvas full of red paint.

"I'm so sorry this happened. I did all I could," I said.

"My name is—" She looked at me with confusion. "Well, don't just stand there. Go after my killer! Unless you're too chickenshit." Rachel raised her arm and pointed towards the direction Bullseye ran.

"Unless I'm too chickenshit?" I took a few steps back, looking in the direction she pointed. *Right! Go after the killer, chickenshit!!*

Bullseye slammed a barstool into the sliding glass door in the kitchen, leading out to the backyard. Glass shattered into thousands of pieces all over the kitchen floor and patio. He darted across the backyard and towards the back alley gate. Bullseye stopped and pulled a crossbow out of thin air, waiting for me.

I ran through the kitchen, across the glass pieces, and out onto the patio. I saw the crossbow aimed at me but kept running towards Bullseye.

Bullseye shot two arrows at me as I ran towards him. One arrow hit the house and another hit the wooden fence a few yards away.

I didn't think about the arrows being shot at me. I was too focused on catching him. I sprinted across the St. Augustine grass yard, into the alley where Bullseye ran ahead a few yards down the side road. *Shit, he's fast!*

KNIGHT

With my adrenaline flowing like a raging river, I chased Bullseye through the alley until I tried to tackle Bullseye forcefully. I landed near a mud puddle in front of a dumpster.

"STOP!!! You're going to jail for murder," I said, jumping back up on my feet, covered in mud and dirt. Rain fell around us.

Bullseye stood in front of me, sizing me up. He took a big swing at me as I stepped back. I returned the favor and kicked him in the chest. I swung a right hook back but he pulled out a 10-inch, Damascus steel knife with a wide handle for a better grip. I stepped back before he swung low and stabbed my left leg. Blood trickled down over my kneecap.

Bullseye kicked my legs out from under me. I landed in a big puddle of muddy water hard enough to knock the wind out of my lungs. I leaned on my right side and took deep breaths. Despite the pain radiating through my chest, I coughed loudly and quickly got back on my feet. "You fucked up, pal," I yelled as I tightened my fists.

"Are we having fun yet?" Bullseye laughed. He pranced around, jokingly, taunting me to make my next move.

"The fun's just begun, asshole."

Bullseye stopped moving and faced me head on. "Any day, please!"

We stood in front of each other, not moving a muscle. Looking at each other with God's fury. I hoped Bullseye felt my dark energy as much as I did

THE BINGO KILLER

his. I slowly walked over to him and swung with all my might, knocking him to his feet.

"Let's see who you really are." I grabbed his mask right off his head.

Bullseye had no facial features. Nothing! Just a gray, blank face. I dangled the mask in front of the figure's face, with my right hand. "What are you? What the hell is going on?" I stood still as he slowly moved closer to me.

Two eye sockets quickly emerged from beneath Bullseye's stretched skin. His black, square, soul-piercing eyes opened with an intensity that rivaled demons' eyes. He shook his head back and forth violently, thrashing right and left at a rapid speed, like he was having a seizure or severe muscle convulsions.

Water seeped into my right sock and shoe as I stepped into a mud puddle backing away from him.

Bullseye suddenly stopped thrashing its head and stood still. He spoke in a dark, monotone, scratchy voice that raised the hairs on my arms and neck. "You can't stop it. There will be more death to come, so prepare yourself, Sam Riley. Get your game face on. Save your spirits. X doesn't always mark the spot."

"What's coming? Prepare myself for what?"

"You may have won this round but don't get too cocky. You might not be so lucky next time," he said, shattering into small cubes that fell to the ground. The sound of breaking glass echoed out against the sound of rain falling around us. The small cubes

KNIGHT

bounced all around my feet and slowly melted into rain drops.

The sky above me immediately turned back into sunshine. I felt the sunshine hit my shoulders but I was far from calm or happy. I couldn't help but hang my head in shame and defeat as I staggered my way back down the alley. *She's dead because of me.*

I heard a strange whistling noise that stopped me in my tracks as it got louder and closer.

"Who's there? Show yourself! Don't think I'm scared!"

I looked around the alley, over the fences on both sides of the alley road, but saw no one whistling. I ignored the whistling and walked slowly back up the alleyway. Several giant, white, plastic balls, the size of minivans, with black numbers in a circle, fell all around me. *Shit, I can't catch a break, can I?*

I looked down and saw vibrations rippling across the puddles around me. I quickly dodged and ducked the bouncing balls as the balls rolled towards me like boulders sliding down a steep mountain. I hauled ass back to the white gate before the B-5 ball squashed me, only to trip over the gate. I fell to the ground just inside the gate as the giant ball rolled over me. My vision went black as I screamed, "NOOOO!!!!!"

I woke up, covered in sweat. I wiped off the sweat from my forehead as I tried to catch my breath. *It's just a dream. Just a—she looked a lot like Kate. Was Kate in my dream?* I didn't know if the dream I woke up from was only a dream or a warning of things to come.

THE BINGO KILLER

Either way, it stuck with me and wasn't going anywhere, being the second time I had this same dream. *Maybe it was a warning after all?*

Chapter 24

Tuesday, Oct. 14.

9:30 a.m.

Betsy Riddle wandered into the pit to take out the trash, dust the blinds and mop the areas she could. "Morning, detectives. Don't mind me. I'll just be here for a few minutes."

"It's fine. We're too busy to notice anyway," Kate said.

"Morning Betsy," I said.

"Morning, Mr. Riley," Betsy said.

Betsy finished up and moved on to clean another part of the building. Say what you want about Betsy's social skills and slight awkwardness but Betsy was a great janitor.

Sgt. Whine entered the pit and brought two letters for Kate. One for a gym membership special and a letter from her parents in Florida. She told them she would get the letters quicker, with the post office being two blocks from the police station. Our mail was brought to the right department, junkmail included, after the morning mail ran at its usual time around 9:30 a.m. Almost a month had gone by since

THE BINGO KILLER

the second cipher, despite three murders. I expected the third cipher any day now. Preparing for it in fact.

"What do you two have going on this morning?" Sgt. Whine asked enthusiastically.

"Trying to survive another day," Kate said.

"Solving these murders," I said.

"I hear that. Let me know if I can ever be of assistance to you or Sammie."

"Thanks so much, JD. If I had to work with anyone on this case, I'd choose you in a second, but I'm stuck with the rookie," Kate said as she extended her left arm, pointed at me and looked at Sgt. Whine.

"Eat your Cheez-Its, Kate!"

Kate went back to her paperwork.

Sgt. Whine laughed as he handed me a letter.

I opened the letter but wasn't surprised to see a third cipher. "Oh look, another cipher. Right on time. Why am I not surprised? Let's see what this one says."

Sgt. Whine noticed the look on my eyes all too well as he walked by. "Sam looks really frustrated and upset by these ciphers."

"Yeah, I don't blame him. I just try to help him out the best I can, when I can," Barker said.

"If you need me, you know where I'll be," Sgt. Whine.

"Thanks, JD."

"Here it is," I said to my partner, before leaving the pit to make copies.

I took a copy to Chief Williams.

Chief waved me in his office.

"Another cipher came this morning, Chief."

KNIGHT

I handed it to him but he refused to touch the envelope.

"Imagine that. You know what to do, Sam," Chief said. "Let me know what it says."

"Yes sir." I went back to my desk and texted Kara Carlson to come retrieve and examine the original copy for prints.

Carlson showed up a few minutes later. "Good morning, Detective Barker," Carlson said.

"Morning Kara," Kate said.

Carlson turned to me. "Yes, Detective Riley?"

"We got another cipher today. Our third one. Here's the original, so do your thing, if you will. My prints are on it," I said. "So are Sgt. Whines' prints."

"I see. Thanks for telling me." Carlson put on a pair of gloves and took the cipher. "Give me a little time, as usual."

Carlson disappeared around the corner out of the pit.

"This one is longer. Two pages. Must have a special message today," I said. I made two copies of the cipher before Carlson took it away. I matched dice to letters and within five minutes, I decoded the message. "Kate, come take a look at this."

Kate slid her chair over and read the cipher message. "Go show Chief this right now, Sam."

"I will in a minute."

Kate sat beside my desk for a moment.

I looked at the bingo card that came with the cipher. The N free space was circled with a red

THE BINGO KILLER

marker on a blank card. *I guess I fill this blank card in with a number under each letter. What numbers? Guess I'll start with the victims. Maybe there's something there?* I looked over the case files and wrote down certain numbers for each victim. *What about their ages? Jill was 30. I-30. Oscar was 67. O-67. Nettles was 48. G-48. I-N-G-O!*

I wrote each number in the corresponding letter columns. B was the only letter without a known number. *B must have something to do with the next victim since it's unknown right now. Could it be a letter in the victims' name or a relevant number from a victim? Maybe the next victim? It has to be the next victim.* I sat back and thought about the conclusion I just came to. I stared out over the pit, lost in deep thought. But for good reason. *That makes sense. At least I think it does. The killer wants me to solve these damn things. Well maybe I'm wrong, but this is what I got and I'm going with it. I can't stand by while someone else dies. This isn't cat and mouse anymore. It's a chess game played in Clue. What's my next move? We don't have much evidence. But then again, we're way past evidence. We don't need much to bring the killer out anyway. They always slip up. They always do. Their ego gets the best of them.*

I looked over at my partner and in that moment, it became crystal clear how much I cared for and enjoyed working with her. Maybe I didn't know it or wasn't paying attention enough? Who could blame me, with all these murders and codes to crack like I'm the Einstein of law enforcement? *That's what I'll do—go fishing and I have the perfect bait.*

KNIGHT

I quietly got up and looked at Kate, nodded and smiled.

"Why are you looking at me like that, Sam? It's kind of weird."

"Kate, no matter what happens. Let me say it's been great working with you on this case. I couldn't have asked for a better partner."

"Okay, thanks, Sam, I guess," Kate said. "What makes you say that?"

I looked a bit perplexed at Kate's response.

"I mean, absolutely Sam. I AM the best partner you could ask for and the best you'll ever have the honor of, indeed, working with," Kate said. "But right now, I'm busy."

"Duly noted, Kate." I paused for a minute and looked out over the pit in wonderment.

Mystery stood in front of the pit, looking at me. "You got that crazy look in your eye, Mister. What are you up to?"

"Fishing for a killer," I replied.

"It won't work, man. I'm telling you."

Yes, it will. Don't follow me! I walked to the Chief's office to talk to him about the cipher and bingo card.

"NO, IT WONT!" Mystery yelled out.

Yes it most certainly will, I thought to myself, as I rounded the corner.

Chief stood at the big whiteboard behind his desk.

"Chief, I solved the cipher and bingo card."

THE BINGO KILLER

"Come in, Sam. I've been waiting for my star detective, in fact. And now you're here, the universe is in harmony again."

"Yeah, hold that thought Chief. Here me out first."

Chief suggested we go to the conference room. "Get Kate in here. She needs to hear this also."

I went back to the pit long enough to grab my partner and head to the conference room.

"On my way, Sam."

We both sat down on different sides of the table near where the Chief sat.

"Morning, Children," Chief Williams said. "Go ahead, Sam. Enlighten us, Einstein."

I showed the Chief the cipher with the new message on it.

"Play my game or I will kill again. My name is a secret. I'm The Bingo Killer," Chief said. "Quite the poet isn't he? Yeah, it's a game alright."

I then showed Chief the blank bingo card.

"What about these numbers? Are they relevant to this case?' Chief asked.

"I used the victims' ages as numbers on the blank bingo card. The B is still blank. The I, N, G and O are all filled in. I-30 for Sanders. N has free space. G-48 for Nettles and O-67 for Tidwell," I explained.

"Okay, and what if you're wrong, Sam?" Chief asked.

"I don't think I am Chief. I am going strictly by the ciphers' messages and it's only logical that the victims have a place on the bingo card. I'm following the card we found at Nettles' house," I said. "They're winning moves. Like trophies."

"As much as I hate to admit it, you might be right. Sanders, Tidwell and Nettles were expendable. Until we know otherwise," Chief stated. "Go on, Sam." Kate and the Chief eagerly listened to my plan of action. "Like I said, the B is still unknown. Let's use that to our advantage. We don't know who the next victim is but our collective guess is that it's someone with a B name," I said.

"What did you have in mind, Sam?" Chief asked. "Just drop it on us."

I got up, took a deep breath and walked to the front of the room away from my partner and my Chief. "Okay, Bingo has been taunting and toying with us since the first cipher. The headlines, the rumors, all of it has been to throw us off our game one way or the other. And I'm sure the killer was sitting somewhere and laughing at us, while planning another murder."

"Yeah, what's your point, Sam?" Kate said.

"Instead of being reactive, let's be proactive. Let's get out in front of this thing. Take the fight to him. Call his bluff. Dare him to make a move."

Chief looked at Kate and back at me.

"And how do you plan to do that, Sam?" Kate asked.

"It's not a bad idea but how do we get out in front of it without looking like fools," Chief asked.

THE BINGO KILLER

"What if Kate is the killers' next victim? She's the perfect target and it makes sense that the winning move for the killer is to kill a cop, right?"

"The killer hasn't gotten to our officers but then again, most wouldn't hesitate to kill a cop," Chief explained.

"You think I'm the next target?" Kate asked. She obviously thought I was terribly wrong and didn't have much faith in me at all. "Enlighten me, Sam."

"Yeah, you could be, Kate. But let's not wait around to find out. I want to catch this asshole. But the way I see it, given the circumstances, we have two options."

"God, this ought to be good," Kate replied.

I motioned to Kate to pause for a second. "One, we fake Kate's death. We emphasize the B in Barker as the last victim. We make up a fake cipher, get it in the press. Wait for the killer to take credit and toss him in a five by ten cell for life. Or the second option is we commit Kate to the psych ward for being the mole, the leak inside the department. Say she's the one who planted the headlines and sent the ciphers. Basically, take credit for the murders and steal his thunder. What do you think, Kate? Chief?"

Kate was shooting daggers at me at this point. I could tell without using my psychic powers that she was highly pissed at such a suggestion. In my defense, I didn't mean any disrespect to my partner. Hell, if I had a name that started with B, I'd fake my own death instead of Kate's. But the alphabet is the alphabet.

KNIGHT

As much as Chief sensed Kate's rage and discomfort, he thought I had a good idea. "I actually like those options, considering our circumstances."

And the shit show just keeps getting shittier! Kate thought to herself. "Hell no, Sam. I'm not doing it. I don't care how well thought out or revolutionary you think your plan is. I will not be the bait in your stupid plan. Why would you think I'd be okay with this? Let alone go along with it," Kate said. "Fake my death? Are you insane?"

"Well aside from a few big boxes of regular sized Cheez-Its that I always get you, because you're such an amazing partner, you'll have a week or two vacation. You'd still be working but away somewhere local," I explained with a charming smile. *Please let it work!*

"Don't butter me up Sam or try to weasel your way out of this," Kate said.

"And I'm not using you specifically as bait. I'm not that cruel. I'm using your fake death or trip to the looney bin as bait. Either way, we show the killer he won the game, basically." I asserted. "Show him we couldn't compete in his game and that he is getting away with it."

"I'm afraid those are your two options, Kate," Chief said.

Kate rolled her eyes at the Chief and I. "Where would I be staying while I'm pretending to be dead for a while?" Kate asked angrily.

THE BINGO KILLER

I suggested she could and should spend the time at my parents' house. "That's the best place that's safe for you. Besides, my mother would love to have you help make dinner for me and dad every night."

Kate looked at me in confusion.

"Yeah, you'll be like the daughter they never had," I said. "I mean, YAY, I have a sister for two weeks." *That's all I can handle to be honest.*

Chief laughed. "Mrs. Riley did make some good meals when I ate at their house over the years. You'll learn from the best."

Well kiss my ass. This isn't going to work and I'm going to be miserable the entire time. But it's by far the craziest thing I've done while having this job. I'm definitely telling Wilkins all of this for her book. "Fine. I'll be your little guinea pig test subject," Kate stated. "Let me say for the record, I don't think it's going to work. It's a terrible idea."

"Duly noted, Kate," I said.

"So which one, Kate?" Chief asked.

Kate looked at the Chief. "Why are you even considering this, Chief?"

"Do you have any better ideas, Kate?"

Kate sighed and shook her head.

"Fake my death, of course. Much easier to do that than go to the goddamn psych ward," Kate said. *Fuck this asinine plan!*

I casually hit the table with my right hand in excitement. "Good choice, Kate. That's what I would do if I had to choose," I said.

"Oh really? You'd go to the psych ward? Psych Ward Sam!!!" Kate said as she threw her hands up and shook them briefly. "That explains a lot. Might even do you some good."

"You two act like a married couple," Chief said. "That's not a complement either."

"Thanks, Chief," Kate said sarcastically.

"You're welcome, Kate.

"What tipped you off, Chief?" Kate asked.

Chief smiled at Kate. "He's trying to kill you, by the way. Let that sink in."

Kate rolled her eyes again and leaned back in her chair. *Why do I even bother with this shit?*

Chief asked me how exactly we would fake Kate's death. "That's a lot of work, Sam."

"Yes, I know and I have a plan. It'll work, Chief. Let's meet back here at 2:30 p.m. I'll call in the only people we need to be a part of our plan and explain their roles. Also, we need to meet with the media tomorrow to give them a statement saying Kate was killed and the suspect was captured. He surrendered peacefully after the shooting," I suggested.

Chief couldn't help but ask how I came up with my plan all of the sudden. "Have you been watching too many cop shows or Dirty Harry? It's okay if you have. I just didn't think they would manifest into actual real police work."

"Play two moves behind but think five moves ahead, Chief! You were in Navy intelligence, right?" I stated.

THE BINGO KILLER

"I was indeed, which is why I'm curious to hear your plan. But remember Sam, I have the final say if this plan goes forward."

"Yes sir, I do and it'll be a good plan. I promise," I said.

"Anything you want to add, Kate?"

Kiss my ass, Sam! "I should've gone to medical school when my dad asked me to," Kate said freely. "I'll say that for the record."

"Good to know, Kate," I said. "You would've been a fine medical examiner."

"Okay. Dismissed until 2:30." Chief declared.

Chapter 25

2:30 p.m.

The secret seven crucial to my plan, gathered in the conference room. I spent a few minutes earlier calling and texting the right people I needed to make this plan work.

"Okay, Sam. I assume we're all here for the same thing. If not, back to work," Chief said.

I looked at the group and took a deep breath. I was fairly confident but not overly confident I could make my plan a reality, perhaps with a few promises down the road. Lunches on me type of thing. "Alright everyone, as you know, we're trying to catch the Bingo Killer. No leads yet and the bodies are piling up, which has kept Mister Smalls here quite busy the past few weeks for all the wrong reasons."

I paused for a second while I looked around to make sure I had everyone's attention.

"Yes, it has. It's been sad too. When I picked up Sanders body, I said a prayer for her soul, before I removed her from her bed. She's the only person I've said a prayer for since my first day as a coroner," Smalls said. "So I'm here to help in any way I can."

THE BINGO KILLER

"I'm all in also. Anything to help," Carlson said.

"Glad you called me, Sam. Now I know this plan will work," Sloan said jokingly. "How many times have I bailed you out when we were on patrol all those years?" Sloan leaned back and rubbed his beard. "Why stop now?"

I wasn't even insulted by my best friend's sarcasm. It was refreshing to be honest. Something I really needed at that moment.

Chief Williams laughed. "That's right, Sloan. Wait until you hear his plan!"

"I'm not sure why I'm here but I'll do my best to help," Dr. Willow stated. "I'm afraid I can only give you one thumb up, Mr. Riley."

"So we're all in agreement. We're going to fake Detective Barker's death to try to lure the killer out." I pushed the card into the center of the table so everyone could have a look.

Kate sat quietly and shook her head as I explained my plan.

"As you can see, the B is still empty. Presumably, it's the last victim whose name starts with B. That being said, we're going to have Kate pretend to be the B. We get out ahead and just wait for the killer to slip up and we nail him."

"Wow, I wasn't expecting to fake someone's death but it might just work. And not in Hollywood either. Small Town America," Sloan said. "Not my approach but at least we're trying something."

"You're probably wondering how exactly we fake Kate's death?" I asked.

KNIGHT

Kate rolled her eyes and mumbled, "God, here we go. If this doesn't work, I'll show you, Sam, how much of a B I can be."

Everyone in the room smiled and laughed softly.

"Love your enthusiasm, Kate. It's easy! We use the parking lot as the place where she's shot, exiting her vehicle, on our home turf. This would be preferable to the killer to send a message and end his game. I fire my gun in the air from the back entrance so no one sees me but the sound is loud enough for her to fall down and wait. I've got three or four shells already in a plastic bag for you, Kara Carlson. I'll give you those after the meeting. I went to the shooting range last week after work. So just set those aside and give us a fake forensic report or something," I explained.

"I can do that," Carlson said.

Sloan and I are going to run out to the parking lot, check on Kate and secure the crime scene.

"Mr. Smalls, all we need from you is to quietly put her body on the gurney, load her up and take her to Dr. Willow."

"Absolutely. Consider it done," Smalls said eagerly. Smalls looked at Kate. "Don't worry Detective Barker, I'll go easy on you and keep you as safe as I can."

"Great! So happy to hear that," Kate said with a fake, two-second smile.

"Dr. Willow?" I said.

"How may I be of service, Mr. Riley?"

THE BINGO KILLER

"Dr. Willow, I need you to make her autopsy a quick but secret one. Make up something but make it professional. And give it to me or Chief as soon as you can. Put a body in storage for a week at least and say it's her," I said.

"Sure, Mr. Riley. I was wrong about you, if I may be so blunt. I didn't think you had a sense of humor but this is beyond what I expected from you. I have a male and female mannequin in storage down at the morgue that I use for teaching purposes. I can use the female one for Detective Barker."

"That's great and a little weird, Dr. Willow. Let's just leave it at that. I trust you know what you're doing." I told Kate I would inform her later on of what she's to do after she arrives at the morgue. "Only me, Chief, Kate herself, and Dr. Willow, will know that part of the plan. I want to keep that a secret for obvious reasons."

I told Sloan I'll need him at the station all tomorrow afternoon. "Let's keep this off the radios and scanners across town. I don't want the entire cavalry coming with guns blazing. Only me and you, Sloan. Keep it tight," I declared. "Anything that gets out is a training exercise."

"Yeah Sam, sure. I'll be here," Sloan said. "Only way this plan will work."

"Chief, you and I can handle the media and press aftermath of Kate's death. We'll just give them the basics."

"We can talk about that after this meeting. But let me say this for everybody to hear. What Sam and I say to the press is our official statement. Stick with it and don't say anything else. In fact, if anyone asks, tell them you don't know what's going on. I'll tell everyone in the department and the Mayor's office not to speak to the press for the next week," Chief declared.

"Everybody else knows their roles tomorrow?" I asked as heads around the table nodded in agreement. "Good. I trust you all will make this plan go over as smoothly as it can. Tomorrow afternoon. Be on top of your game," I said.

"Thanks for coming on such short notice, folks. We appreciate your participation and confidence in us at this time. Good luck to you all," Chief said.

The four participants all left the conference room and went back to their workplaces to prepare for tomorrow. Sloan went back out on patrol. Kate and the Chief stayed behind to talk to me.

"That's not all, Chief. That's just the first part of the plan," I said.

Chief Williams looked at Riley. "I had a feeling, Sam."

"We schedule a press conference to announce her death and announce we have a suspect who surrendered peacefully minutes later. We have to do both at the same time for this to work. I think this will drive the killer over the edge. He can't stand to see someone else get credit for his work. They want to be media-famous. Just like the Zodiac."

THE BINGO KILLER

Chief said he was impressed with my plan. In the back of his mind, Chief still had his doubts. "I gotta hand it to you Sam. I wasn't expecting any of this at all. It's far-fetched but well thought out."

Kate asked how long she would have to stay at my parents house.

"As long as it takes but hopefully a few days," I said.

Kate sighed. "You'll have to bring me my work so I can finish it there. I'll pack a small suitcase tonight and put it in your truck in the morning, Sam. You can bring it to your parent's house."

"Absolutely, Kate."

"I'll give it two weeks and then I'll pull the plug on this whole thing and have Kate back in here, on the 29th. Regardless of whether or not we found our killer. Are we clear, Sam?"

"Crystal clear, Chief!" I said. "I'll talk to Savannah Rose myself and give her an exclusive interview so we get what we need out there in the press to really get this guys' attention. I'm not going to hold much back." I told the Chief he would have to call his niece, Lisa, to explain what's happening. "We need her silence on this for the sake of our deal and chances of catching this guy."

"I'll take care of it, Sam. Good luck tomorrow, you two."

"Tell her my idea should make her book more interesting. She'll love me for it," I said.

"I'll tell her but she won't love you, Sam."

Chapter 26

Wednesday, Oct. 15th.

9 a.m.

I sat at my desk, both anxious and excited for this plan to happen. I had a few calls to make to put the last few pieces in place. My dad being the first on my list.

"What's going on, Sam?"

"Dad, I need you to listen very carefully. We have a lot of shit about to happen but everything will be ok," I said. "It's all for a reason."

"Hope you have plenty of ass paper, Sam."

"What?" I asked, caught off guard.

"You told me a lot of shit's about to happen. Grab your toilet paper, son."

It's too early for his jokes. "Good one, Dad! That's not what I meant."

"Okay, if you say so. I suspect it involves me, otherwise you wouldn't be calling so early?" Dad inquired.

"It does. We have a plan to catch the Bingo Killer and it involves faking Kate's death."

THE BINGO KILLER

"Wait, what? You're going to fake Kate's death?" Dad asked.

"Yes. I know it sounds weird but I solved the ciphers and put the victims ages on the blank bingo card. The B square is the only one still blank. So I believe she's the killers' next target. We fake Kate's death to draw out the killer."

"Ahhh, the fish trap move I told you about years ago. That's smart, Sam. I was wondering when you would use it. The only thing I would do differently is use someone else instead of Kate. She seems like too lovely a girl to use like this," Dad stated.

"I'll tell her you said that but hold that thought dad. I need to stash her at your house for 2 weeks, until the 29th."

"She's staying at our house for 2 weeks?" Dad asked.

"Yes. She'll have my old room and she'll be working also. But no one must know she's there. She can't go outside or leave," I requested. "But she'll gladly help around the house. Maybe mom can teach her how to cook or something. I don't know."

My dad laughed at my plan. "Yeah, sure Sam. She can stay for a while. I'm sure your mom would love to have her for a while. She's always thought highly of Kate. Things would be a lot more lively around the house."

"Good, thanks Dad. This is such a big help to us. I need you to be at the back entrance of the morgue between 2:30 to 3 p.m., this afternoon, to pick her up.

She can't be seen either. She has to lay down in the back seat."

"Not my first time doing this, Sam. I know how these things usually work. She's in good hands," Dad said. "You know you can count on me."

"I know. I know. I'm just a bit on edge until this afternoon. I've got too much riding on this for one detective to handle. I feel like this is my last shot, last move to catch this freakin' psycho," I declared.

"I know it seems like a lot but it's worth trying. I'm sure Chief Williams is beyond thrilled with your plan and I mean that sarcastically, Sam!"

"Chief actually liked my plan, to my surprise. Everyone knows their part. It should go smoothly," I said.

"I'll pick Kate up and call you when we arrive at the house," Dad said.

"Thanks, Dad. I'll come by when I can to give Kate her suitcase and her work files."

"Okay. See you later, Sam!"

I hung up the phone and looked at my partner. "Kate, you should probably call your parents to let them know about this afternoon, in case it makes the national news," I said.

Kate glanced up at me. "I told them last night, Sam, and they think your plan is ridiculously stupid. But that's not the worst thing about it." Kate focused on her paperwork.

I wasn't ready for what Kate told me but hearing her out was the least I could do.

THE BINGO KILLER

"What's worse is they blame me for letting you do this to me. Nothing like your parents laughing at you and your career choices to help with your confidence and self-esteem. Especially when you're faking your death for some stupid plan."

"I'm sorry they feel that way but I don't know of any other way, short of interrogating everyone in Bloomfield," I said. "I appreciate you doing this Kate. Maybe one day they'll thank me for keeping their daughter safe."

Kate looked up at me and said what she had been holding in for a day or two. "Excuse me? You're keeping me safe? You have a funny way of showing it, Sam!"

"What do you propose we do? What's Kate's big plan? I don't know about you but I'm tired of sitting around and watching people die while we solve goddamn puzzles. Would you rather me fake my death and stay at your place?" She had her truth and I had mine.

"You don't get it and I don't think you ever will," Kate said, as she shook her head and went back to her work.

I understood my partner loathed my plan but I would've kindly gone along with any other plans we had. I was prepared for a total failure of my plan to fail but I also expected it to work. Maybe with a rain drop of luck somewhere in the known universe, it all might work out and end the way we all hoped it would.

I noticed Sgt. Whine roaming the halls, delivering mail and running errands. I caught up with him near the break room, so we stepped inside to talk. "Hey Sgt. Whine, I don't know if you heard about this afternoon?"

"Naw, not really. What's going down, Sam?"

"Well, I convinced Chief Williams to let us fake Detective Barker's death this afternoon. Right outside in the parking lot. Our home turf. We've got it all figured out and everyone knows what to do. We tell the press she's the Bingo Killers' last victim. Hopefully this asshole slips up and we catch him for good. Kate's going to a safe place for two weeks. I wanted you to know so we're all on the same page," I explained.

"That's stone cold bold, Sam. You're playing chess with blow torches instead of matches. I like it. I dig it, man. I appreciate you telling me this. I got a text from Chief Williams about some afternoon training exercise and I guess that's it. Well, if you need me, I'll be around, Sam."

"Thanks, JD. I couldn't do this without you all." I said.

Sgt. Whine and I shook hands and parted ways for a few hours.

Chief Williams, on the other hand, called his niece, Lisa Wilkins, and told her what was happening.

"Hey girl, how ya doing?"

"Okay, Uncle Mike. Working on this book or trying to at least."

THE BINGO KILLER

"I had a feeling you'd be doing such a thing. Look Lisa, we have something going on this afternoon. It's okay. It's a training exercise only. No one will be hurt so don't believe what you hear on the news starting this afternoon," Chief Williams said.

"Well, that's unexpected but I trust you Uncle Mike."

"Thanks. It's nothing bad. It's Detective Riley's idea and he told me to tell you that."

"Oh gawd, are you serious? Tell me you're okay during whatever this is?"

"I'll be fine, Lisa. I approved his plan but if I didn't think it was worth a damn, we wouldn't be having this conversation."

"Fair point. Well, tell him I'll do more than sue him if anything happens to you, Uncle Mike."

"I will when I see him," Chief said with a laugh. "Let's keep this quiet for now, Lisa."

"I will. Thanks for telling me, Uncle Mike."

"Bye, my favorite niece," Chief said before he hung up.

Chief sent out a department wide text message to inform his officers of a training exercise happening at 2:30 p.m., and everything is under control. The Chief ordered the officers to stay out on patrol. Keeping her crime scene low key was a high priority. Less chance for anyone to ruin it or call it a hoax. Her death in the media's eyes was a priority and needed to be spoon-fed to them as much as they wanted.

The Chief even met briefly with Mayor Dexter Gibbles to inform him of the plan. Fear and panic were looming over the community like an eclipse. Gibbles was a bit intrigued but obviously wanted these murders to stop. Gibbles supported the plan, although he had his doubts.

3:30 p.m.

The press statement had already been written hours ago. I figured the press conference would last about fifteen minutes.

Savannah Rose was set up in the conference room, as well as one or two news stations.

I sat beside Rose and quietly told her to stick around after Chief's statement for an exclusive interview. "This will be so good for your career," I mumbled.

Rose agreed.

The Chief came into the conference room and began with his opening statement. "A short time ago, Detective Kate Barker was shot and killed in the parking lot outside the Bloomington Police Department around 2:10 p.m., by a suspect who pulled up next to her vehicle and opened fire through the driver's side window. Officers heard the gunshots from inside our building and immediately ran outside to find Detective Barker lying on the ground beside her vehicle. She was shot four times—and died where she fell, near her car. Detective Barker was an 11-year

THE BINGO KILLER

veteran of the BPD and one of the best detectives we've ever had. The main thing I want to let the citizens of Bloomfield know is that her killer has been caught and can rest easy knowing this individual is behind bars. Detective Barker's killer also confessed to being the Bingo Killer. He is one in the same and we are charging this person with four counts of murder for the deaths of Jill Sanders, Oscar Tidwell, George Nettles and now, the late-Detective Barker, who was working this case. We'll release more details as they become available. I'll now turn it over to Detective Riley, who was also working this case, for further comment."

Before I stepped forward and gave my part of the official statement, It finally hit me what Kate meant to me. I started to realize what she tried to tell me only hours before. "Thank you, Chief Williams. We are mourning the loss of our colleague, Detective Katherine Isabelle Barker, and I am mourning my partner, Kate Barker. We do have a suspect in custody who admitted to being the Bingo Killer. We believe the late-Detective Barker was the killers' last victim. The fact she was killed in our parking lot made it very clear. This individual will be interrogated and charged with four felony counts of murder and held in our jail under heavy guard until the first court appearance next week sometime. That's all the details we are prepared to give at this time. If we have any further developments, we will let the press, the media know immediately. We will not be taking any questions at this time. Thank you all for coming," I stated.

KNIGHT

Reporters left our building and went back to file Kate's death as the top story for the evening news tonight. Rose stayed behind in the conference room for the exclusive interview with me. A single chair separated her from me.

"You have a few minutes to ask me about this case. Some things I will answer and some I can't but it'll get you on the front page, no less," I informed Ms. Rose. "Go!"

"Let me just say I am incredibly sorry for your loss," Rose said.

"Thank you, Savannah. I appreciate that very much," I said.

"Are you okay, Sam? I know it's incredibly hard to lose someone you worked with and admired."

I shook my head, popped my middle finger over my upper lip and grabbed my chin.

"Why did you think Detective Barker was the Bingo Killers' next target?" Rose asked.

"This guy really thought he was on the same level as the Zodiac and sent us these bullshit ciphers. When in reality, he was nowhere near the Zodiac's level. He wasn't that smart. We were able to quickly solve them. Maybe that was on purpose? To appear unbreakable but quite easy to solve. I plugged in the victim's ages in the bingo card we received. Detective Barker was obviously the last letter to be filled in on the card. This guy wasn't brave and man enough to face us in person. Instead, this maniac wanted to play these childish games, hide behind a damn bingo card and

THE BINGO KILLER

we lost a damn fine cop this afternoon," I explained. "Kate Barker was one of the most honorable and bravest officers I've ever served with."

Rose asked me if there was any idea when we might reveal the identity of the Bingo Killer.

I sighed and glanced at the windows. "My best guess is next week in court. We're keeping that information private for now. We have to notify the victims' families, including Detective Barkers'. We don't want a panic or mob coming after the suspect either," I said. "We have to let our team do their job, gather evidence and interrogate the suspect. But the main thing we're doing is mourning the loss of Detective Kate Barker."

Rose pointed out some people would jump to the conclusion that Detective Barker being the killers' last victim is nothing but a coincidence. What do you say to that?"

"It's not a coincidence my partner is still dead, is it? How much more proof do they need? More dead law enforcement officers or innocent people?" I said. "Thank you for your time today, Ms. Rose. Good luck with your article."

Savannah stopped writing and looked at me.

"We're now off the record for a few seconds, Savannah. Listen to me here! What I'm about to tell you—don't take it personally as it has little to do with you and everything to do with the killer—but I want you to put it in your article. I want the public to know what I'm about to say."

"Okay, Sam."

KNIGHT

"Are you ready, Rose?"

Rose grabbed her pen and eagerly awaited my words.

I told Rose we're back on the record again. "First off, a word of advice, don't believe your sources. They're lying to you with their bullshit rumors about us being psychic. "That's beyond absurd and makes us question your credibility, Savannah," I said. "We had a good laugh with those headlines."

"I completely understand. And I am sorry for your loss but my job is to find the truth and bring it to the public. I will continue to do that," Rose stated.

"That's why I'm giving you an exclusive here no one else has regarding today's sad events," I said. "Here's your chance to set things right with this article for tomorrow. Please don't disrespect Detective Barker's memory either. I will never forgive you if you do." I declared.

"You have nothing to worry about, Sam. I'll do my best to write the best article I can and respect Detective Barker at the same time. It was never my intention to do anything else," Rose explained.

"Back off the record," I stated. "Savannah, there's one more thing. A case like this, with these murders, the ciphers, only comes around once in a few generations. My point is that you should follow this case to the end. Get everything you need and write your book. I'll give you more detailed insight as you go along. Until we meet again, Savannah." I patted

THE BINGO KILLER

her shoulder twice. "Think about the book offer." I walked back to the Chief's office.

Rose sat for about a minute, thinking about the conversation she just had with me. She eventually left the building and went back to write her career-making story for Thursday's edition.

I spoke briefly with Chief Williams about the press conference and the plan.

Chief Williams was laying on the blue-cushioned futon in his office when I walked in.

"God, what have we done, Sam?"

"Well, that was fun." I said. "We're okay. It's not as bad. Now we just wait."

"Yeah, that's the hardest part. Shit, I hope this works. We got a lot riding on this and I can't say what will happen if we don't follow through and catch this asshole," Chief said.

"I know, Chief. I'm well aware of the consequences."

"Are you, Sam? You have two weeks and if we don't make an arrest, we admit to the press this was a hoax to catch that psycho and we don't know our ass from a hole in the ground. Kate comes back to work and we find your replacement. That's it, Sam."

Needless to say, I got the hint my Chief was dead serious about my two week deadline. I quietly left the Chiefs' office and went back to the pit. The rest of the afternoon seemed like time stopped for me in the pit. Eventually, I stopped by my parents' house around 6:30 p.m. I walked through the door as I rang the doorbell. "Knock, knock!" I said as I opened the door and came into the living room as my dad got up and walked to the front door.

"Well come right in, why don't you?" Dad asked. "You got a warrant?"

"No, I don't, old man," I said as I sat Kate's suitcase and her work files against the living room wall.

"You better get one before I show you how old I am." Dad said. "How was it?"

Kate and my mother walked into the living room.

"How did it go, Sam?" Mom eagerly asked.

"It went exactly as I hoped it would. But no one else can know anything about today beyond the 10 o'clock news and tomorrow's paper. I'm serious, Mom. Keep it quiet," I demanded.

My mom didn't hesitate to give me a sarcastic salute. "Yes sir," she said with a smile.

"Now you see what I go through, Mrs. Riley," Kate said. "This wasn't even my idea."

"Yes I do, dear. But to his credit, you're staying with us now while he's at work. The best thing is he doesn't live here anymore. He did you a favor, Kate."

"Yeah, mom. She's your problem for the next two weeks," I declared.

"I think he did," Kate said as she looked at Denise. "I look forward to hearing all the stories about Sam growing up. I'm eager to have some embarrassing dirt on him."

"I've got so many things that will turn his cheeks as red as a baboons' ass," Mom said.

THE BINGO KILLER

"I'm just here to check on Kate and make sure everything is good. Your stuff is over there, Kate."

"We're fine, Sam. Kate's got plenty of Cheez-Its. Your mom has someone else to pester, errr.....talk to," Dad said.

"What, Gerald? Sounded like you said something?" Mom said.

"I said I missed the attention you're giving Kate, forcing me to watch television in peace."

"I am the peace, you fart knocker!" Mom said to Dad.

Silence sat it for a few seconds.

"Good. Okay then. If you need anything from work, Kate, I'll have to bring it back tomorrow."

"No, I'm good for now," Kate said.

"Alright. I have dinner plans so everyone have a good—"

"Dinner plans?" Kate inquired. "You had me fake my death today and you have dinner plans out on the town?"

"Yeah, that's how this works." I asked with a smile. "What's your point?"

Kate shook her head. "Nothing, Sam. You enjoy yourself. You have the best night of your life tonight." Kate abruptly left me in the living room and went to the kitchen to help my mom with dinner.

"Thanks, I will." I sat down on the couch next to his dad's chair. "What was that about?"

Dad sat down in his chair and looked at the kitchen and back at me. He muted the TV. "Boy, you're playing with fire with that one. You better recognize the danger you're in. I understand you're doing your job by having her here and I'm totally fine with that. We love having Kate here. But you missed what Kate was trying to say, Sam, without telling you directly," Dad said in a low tone of voice so he couldn't be heard in the kitchen.

Dad casually hit me on the shoulder and pointed towards the kitchen. "Now she's talking to your mom about it and I'll have to hear about it. I think Kate's a great detective. I just want you two to trust each other and know you can depend on one another."

"I know what you're saying, Dad. But She didn't exactly have a plan in mind to catch the killer. I was the only one doing something. I know she didn't like my plan but what else were we supposed to do?"

Dad sighed and looked at his son. "Did you even hear what I said just now?"

"Yeah and I'm telling you she—," I stated, as I raised my shoulders.

"No, Sam," Dad whispered as he peaked around the corner. "She wanted you to show her some appreciation and offer to bring her some dessert perhaps?" Dad explained. "She thinks all you see her as is someone who doesnt matter."

"She said that? How could you tell?"

Dad rolled his eyes. "It was so obvious Sam, if it were a snake, it would have bitten you on the ass cheek."

I glanced into the kitchen at Kate standing by the dining room table. "Yeah, maybe I could work on my communication a little bit. We've always kept it professional and nothing more than that."

"Why do you think you two were paired up for this case?" Dad said.

"Are you suggesting or thinking what I think you are, Dad?"

Dad leaned back and crossed his hands on his stomach. He cocked his head to the left side, shrugged his shoulders and looked in my eyes. "The other day, your mom said she hopes she's a grandma one day. That's all I'm saying."

I shook my head and felt defeated. "Okay, Dad. Now is not the time to even think about anything like that, for both of us. I'm hellbent on finding the real killer. But I will say that I'm glad she's here where she's safe. I'll say that."

Dad focused back on the television.

I walked to the kitchen and said goodbye to mom and Kate. They were too busy cooking to acknowledge me.

"See you later dad."

"Remember what I said," my dad said loudly. I didn't give it much thought but I later realized it was entirely by fate that Kate and I were chosen to work together to catch our killer.

Chapter 27

Saturday, Oct. 18th

7 p.m.

I looked at the text messages from Tess before I dared knocking on her door.

Tess opened the door quietly. "Hi, handsome, how are you? Please come inside, Sam."

"I'm sorry for the passing of your partner. My heart goes out to you and her family."

Tess embraced me with a comforting vigor that made me feel wanted and loved.

"Thank you, Tess. It's been a rough few days for sure. I just need a great dinner with amazing company. Get my mind off of work for a few hours."

"Absolutely. I'm almost ready. Let me get my purse and turn out the lights."

I smiled as I put my hands in my pockets and waited by the door.

Tess locked her door and grabbed my arm as we walked to my truck. "So where are we going to have dinner tonight?"

"I haven't given it much thought to be honest. The last few days I've been on autopilot. We might

THE BINGO KILLER

just drive around until we find some place that sounds good. Unless you have a good suggestion."

"You know what? I'm in the mood for Sushi. I've heard good things about a new place here in town." Tess suggested we try Sushi-ya, a swanky place next to an Italian dessert shop, *Dolce's*.

Sushi? In Bloomfield? When did this happen?

"Yeah! Sounds good, Tess. I'm sure I'll find something on the menu that I can stomach," I said.

"I just figured you deserved a nice place where we can have an intimate dinner and great conversation," Tess said with a smile.

"You know what Tess, you are absolutely right. I do need this. We need this."

Tess smiled and settled into her seat.

We made it to Sushi-ya and requested a table for two away from the other diners. We were seated right away and I ordered my usual sweet tea and Tess ordered Sprite. The waitress brought our drinks over and took our orders. Sushi wasn't my forte so I was a little apprehensive about ordering. "Tess, what's good here? I'm not too sure about this but I'll trust your selection."

Tess looked at the menu and told Cindy, the waitress, our picks. "Two steak teriyaki bowls with a side of teriyaki sauce and two sides of cheddar cheese, please."

"Coming right up." Cindy took our menus and placed our orders.

"Wow, I'm impressed. You're two-for-two, Tess."

KNIGHT

Tess smiled and raised a toast. "To us. May our friendship grow through amazing food, company and conversations."

"Can't go wrong with any of that," I boasted.

"Sam, I just have to ask and forgive me for prying, but if you want to talk about Detective Barker's passing, you know you can talk to me. You don't have to but I'm here to listen if you want me to."

"Thank you, Tess, but I don't want to ruin our good time. I'll grieve in my own way so please don't take it personally." I put my right hand over her left hand and squeezed it gently.

"Sure, Sam. I completely understand. I'm just glad I could be here for you."

I nodded. "Yeah, me too."

Tess squeezed my hand again.

"How's your week been?" I asked.

"Oh, you know. Same old shit, different day."

"That sounds great, compared to my wheelhouse," I said.

We carried on with small talk, which led to deeper talk for ten more minutes until Cindy brought out our steak bowls, sides and a few fortune cookies.

"Oh, Cindy, do you guys have those sugar biscuits here? I had some at a Chinese buffet place a few years ago and I was just wondering if you served those here," I asked.

THE BINGO KILLER

Cindy looked at Tess and back at me. "I'm sorry sir, we don't have anything like that here. We just have Japanese desserts."

"Ahh okay. Didn't think so," I said as he looked down at my teriyaki bowl. "This is fine, Thanks Cindy!"

"Great! Please let me know if there's anything else I can get you," Cindy asked.

"How about a couple more fortune cookies?" I asked.

"Sure."

"I like to find one that fits my mood and makes for a good story," I explained.

Tess smiled at my genuineness, which she found absolutely adorable. "Is that so? How's your mood now, Mr. Riley?"

"Wonderful, Tess," I said before taking a bite of steak. "Sorry I just had to ask about those sugar biscuits but we might as well stock up on those cookies."

Tess laughed.

"You have a pretty smile when you laugh, Tess."

"Thank you, Sam."

We enjoyed our food and our conversation.

I placed the four fortune cookies side by side in the middle of the table.

"What are you doing?" Tess asked softly.

"Close your eyes, Tess."

I guided her hands to the middle of the table. "Pick two for yourself and the other two are mine."

KNIGHT

Tess opened her eyes and brought her hand back with her two cookies.

I opened the first fortune cookie and read it out loud. "A dream you have will come true." I looked up and stared at Tess. "I sure hope not," I said with a smile. "That would be weird."

"Are you okay, Sam?"

"Yeah, I'm fine. That cookie caught me off guard. What does yours say, Tess?"

"You will marry your lover." Tess had a confused look on her face as she looked at me. "I'll just throw that one away and look at the second one."

"Good idea."

As much as I enjoyed my time with Tess, I couldn't get Kate out of his mind. I thought about her more than I thought I would this evening. I realized I wasn't doing the right thing by having the date with Tess instead of Kate. *Perhaps my plan to fake her death meant more to me than I thought? I swear to God, I better not be falling in love with Kate Barker. No, no, no!!!*

I nodded. "You know what Tess," I said as I grabbed the last two cookies. "Let's just save these two for tomorrow. I'm ready to get out of here. Let's get some real dessert from next door."

"Of course, Sam. It's getting late anyway. We should probably head home."

I put $50 in the black ticket book and we walked over to Dulce's next door for dessert.

THE BINGO KILLER

"They have a better selection there. How else am I going to get you in bed tonight?" I said playfully. "Maybe those last two cookies say otherwise?"

Tess smiled and blushed. "You hush now."

I laughed as we walked over to *Dulce's*. I ordered a dozen chocolate covered strawberries for Tess to enjoy in my absence. A parting souvenir. The clerk handed me my order as I paid and we walked back to my truck.

Once back at Tess' apartment, I turned the truck off and put my hands on the steering wheel. "I'm sorry I wasn't the best company tonight. I tried to be but those fortune cookies kind of ruined things."

Tess scooted her way closer to me and leaned her head on his right shoulder. "You didn't ruin anything. You made my evening ten times better. Seriously, Sam. I hope I added more to your evening."

She did for sure but my mind was elsewhere. I smiled and looked at Tess. "Are you kidding, Tess. I've been looking forward to this. But the truth is Tess, I'm swamped at work and finding the—." I hated using my work as an excuse here but if that made me the bad guy, I'd happily live with that.

"Finding what, Sam?"

"Finding justice, Tess. Wherever that may take me, however long it takes."

"I know, Sam. I know. It's not easy being a cop. I can't imagine what you went through losing Detective Barker. I don't imagine there's anything I can say to take your hurt and pain away but I am truly sorry."

KNIGHT

I smiled. "Thanks for understanding, Tess. Come on, I'll make sure you get inside safely."

Tess nodded her head and grabbed onto my arm as we walked to her front door.

I paused and gave Tess a hug.

Tess opened her door, quietly walked inside and locked her door. Tess looked out the peephole and saw me standing outside her door. She leaned against the door and placed her hand on the door, as mine was on the other side.

I casually walked back to my truck and I noticed Tess forgot the box of strawberries in my truck when she got out. Her simple mistake became my gain. I already said goodbye. I couldn't undo that for a box of strawberries. I drove to my parents house to give the strawberries to Kate. *I hope I'm not making another mistake by choosing Kate over Tess. I know I could have Tess but I don't think she's the one I want. Would Kate even go for a guy like me? What if she says no? Then there's always going to be this thing between us like an empty void between planets.*

I knocked on my parents door this time before my mom opened the door.

"Come in, Sam. Kate's in the kitchen putting up the food and dishes."

"Thanks. I brought her something to show my appreciation."

"Good. I raised you right," my mom said to me, closing the door.

THE BINGO KILLER

I walked into the living room and saw my dad passed out from dinner. I grabbed his leg really fast and said, "Go to bed."

Dad jolted up out of his snooze coma. He looked around feverishly. "Dammit, Sam!" Dad yelled as he rose to his feet and trotted off to use the bathroom.

"Still got it." I laughed and turned to the kitchen.

"Sam, don't do things like that to him. Leave your father alone."

"Okay, okay." I saw Kate wiping down the table as I looked around the room. *Maybe she does belong with me? Maybe the universe is telling me something?*

"Kate, I got you these chocolate covered strawberries."

Kate looked at me and took the box of strawberries. "Thanks, Sam!" She smiled briefly and put the last plate in the dishwasher.

"Are you okay, Kate?" I asked.

Kate turned around and with a tear in her eye and whispered, "I'm fine, Sam!"

I took a few steps towards Kate and hugged her. She resisted and tried to pull away from a hug.

I wasn't letting her go so easily. I held on to her with his arms around her. "Kate, I'm sorry for how I treated you and I want to show you how much I appreciate you."

Kate held onto me tight for a good, solid minute. She looked up at me and rested her head on my chest. "The next time you want to fake someone's death, it BETTER not be mine. I'm not doing this again. Are we clear?"

KNIGHT

"Yes, Kate. I'll fake mine next time."

Kate grabbed the box of strawberries. "Goodnight, Sam!" She headed to my old room for the night.

I stood there between the refrigerator and sink. I sighed and shook my head.

My mom walked into the kitchen to grab a soda. "What's wrong, Sam?"

"Nothing, Mom. I don't think Kate likes me very much for faking her death this week."

Mom gave me a confused look. "What woman would?"

"Yeah," I said as I leaned back on the counter in front of the sink.

"I know you're doing your best, Sam, but just because you have an idea doesn't always mean it will work. Sometimes it does. Sometimes not. Kate's a real woman with real feelings."

"I know, mom."

Dad came back into the kitchen to also get a soda. "Denise, let's watch our show."

"Be right there!" Mom hugged me on her way out to the living room. "Sleep on it and we'll talk about it in the morning."

I walked back to my room to tell Barker goodnight.

"Come in!"

I walked in and my first instinct was to make a dumb joke. "Finally got a hot woman in my bed and I live a few miles away."

THE BINGO KILLER

Kate rolled her eyes, which I couldn't blame her.

I looked at my partner as she laid quietly. "I'm sorry Kate. I should have chosen someone else."

"It's okay, Sam. Let's drop it before I get really pissed." Kate was on her fourth or fifth strawberry. I was glad she didn't let them go to waste.

"Right," I said as he made his way to the door. "Goodnight, Kate."

"What made you show your appreciation now instead of a few days ago?" Kate softly asked.

I paused before I turned the door knob. "I couldn't stop thinking about you this evening. Honest truth." I looked over my right shoulder back at her. "Goodnight, Kate."

Kate waved at me and grabbed another strawberry.

I told my parents goodnight as I walked into the living room.

"Goodnight, Sam," Mom yelled. "Gerald, lock the door behind the straggler."

Dad ushered me out and locked the door behind me.

Chapter 28

Sunday, Oct. 19th.

8:47 a.m.

Kate noticed the headline in the Sunday Edition of the Bloomfield Times, while she drank her coffee. She called me as quickly as she could tap her phone.

"Hello?"

"Sam, you're not going to believe today's headline."

"Oh yeah, what now?" I inquired.

"I don't want to say over the phone but I think you should get over to your parent's house as soon as possible."

"Yeah, sure thing, Kate! Anything you want while I'm in town?"

"Caramel latte and a bacon and egg sandwich."

"On my way," I said before I hung up. *What's in the paper now? Bigfoot named suspect in Bingo Killer case? Psychic detective solves case with decoder toy from cereal box? Same bullshit, different day.* I threw on my jeans and a blue fleece sweater and arrived at his parent's house some twenty minutes later, carrying our breakfast.

"Good morning, Kate."

THE BINGO KILLER

"Morning, Sam," she said, looking up at me and smiling.

I handed Kate her food and latte before setting my food in front of my chair. Kate had the newspaper folded over on the left side of her as she worked the Sunday crossword and drank her coffee, in her robe—part of her Sunday morning ritual, dead or alive.

I got some silverware and grabbed the orange juice jug. "Dammit, there's only a swallow of juice left in the jug. This has to be dad's doing."

"No, that was me. I haven't given your parents money for a shopping list yet."

I threw the jug in the trash can. "So what's so important that you had me——HOLY SHIT!!!!" I yelled as Kate held up the Sunday paper.

Local Detective Fakes Death In Hoax To Catch The Bingo Killer.

"AHHH....NOOO!!!" I cringed and sulked as I stared at the front page. *Well kiss my ass! I can't believe this is actually in the Sunday paper. Well, the shit just hit the fan for sure now. Mayor's going to see this. City council members. Chief Williams. Bring it all down on me. What the fuck can I do?*

"Yeah, what are you going to do, Sammy boy?" Mystery asked. "Good morning by the way."

I glanced over my shoulder at the kitchen. *Ahh fuck, not you again. I can't deal with you today. You gotta go, Mystery. Seriously, just leave.*

"Fine. I'll go but you don't get to hear what I have to say."

KNIGHT

I honestly don't give a shit right now. I'm done speaking with you, Mystery. You haven't said or done one useful thing since you introduced yourself to me over a month ago.

"What is it, Sam? You okay?"

Don't give yourself away. Now is not the time. Play it cool, Sam. "Nothing, Kate. I thought I heard something."

Dad came around the corner into the kitchen. "Nope, it's just the old man."

"Kate, good morning. Sam, why are you in my house this morning, without breakfast?" Dad asked.

I grabbed the paper from Kate and held up the Sunday newspaper. "That's why?"

"Oh, shit! There's something you do see everyday," Dad quipped.

I slammed the paper down and dug into my biscuits and gravy.

Mom shot a weird look at the newspaper as she rounded the corner.

"What does this mean Sam? Are you going to get fired?" Mom asked.

"No, mom. I'm not going to get fired or anything like that."

"What's for breakfast, Denise?" Dad asked as he sat down.

"Whatever's on the list I send you to get, dear!" Mom said as hugged me.

Kate smiled at me. "Your mom's so sweet. We could be friends."

THE BINGO KILLER

"We are friends, Kate. You stay here for two weeks and learn all my recipes. We're friends," Mom said.

"Yeah, I'm the one with his ass in a sling with these headlines and she's making you and dad pancakes." I pointed at Kate.

"Relax, Sam. It's not the end of the world," Dad said.

"Easy for you to say, Detective Riley."

"It is easy for me to say Detective Riley, Junior!!" Dad quipped. "Junior!!!!"

Kate laughed at the synchronistic moment she just witnessed.

Right on cue, my phone buzzed alive. "Oh look, it's Chief Williams calling to burn my biscuits." I took another drink of milk before answering. I didn't know where the whiskey was.

"Good morning, Chie—."

"Why the hell is this headline in today's paper? You better have a good explanation, Sam?" Chief asked.

I sighed and sat my phone in the middle of the table and pushed the speakerphone button. "Wow, Chief. We all heard you."

"Who's we? Are you at your parents house or has your lady friend left already?"

I shook my head at everybody in the room. "Uh, it's me, Kate and my parents."

"Hi, Chief, how are you?" Dad said.

"Sam doesn't share his breakfast with anyone, including his lady friends," Kate said.

"I know. He's so rude," Chief said.

I put my head down on the table. "I can't win for shit this morning."

"Sam, I'm still waiting for an explanation," Chief demanded.

I stared at the paper for a few seconds. "Chief, remember when I said we have a leak in the department? Now do you believe me?" I shrugged my shoulders at my dad.

"Assuming you're right for a moment, who do you think the leak is?" Chief asked.

"I'm not sure. I'll have to press Savannah Rose about her sources, again," I said.

"Better you call her than me, Sam."

Not really but if you say so, Chief. "I was expecting this to be honest. It means we're getting to them. I think it's the killer trying to throw us off his trail. Cover his tracks. Besides, it doesn't change anything about Kate.

"Breakfast is ready," Mom said, as she filled plates with eggs, sausage and pancakes.

Finally some good news.

Mom brought dad his plate before she sat down to have her own breakfast.

"What do you think Gerald?" Chief asked.

"I agree with Sam. There's a leak in the department. It wasn't Kate, I assure you. She wouldn't do that. I don't know why anyone in the department would purposely sabotage this investigation. Nothing to gain."

THE BINGO KILLER

"That doesn't help me," Chief said.

"Hang on a second, Mike." Dad took my phone and walked out into the backyard to speak privately with his old Chief.

I ate my breakfast as Kate watched and guessed what they spoke about outside.

"Any new information, Kate?"

"Yeah, Dr. Willow called yesterday and told me that Nettles' toxicology report came back negative. No traces of high amounts of caffeine, well nothing more than soda drinkers. I think Nettles was more about sending a message. Completely different crime scenes and MO. But connected with the articles found in Nettles' house."

"I think so too, Kate. The headline means we're getting to them. The killer is trying to throw a monkey wrench into the cogs and wheels of our investigation," I said.

"Hey mom, you and I should go shopping later. Leave Kate here to do the dishes."

I agreed. "Yes, you should go with your mom shopping again, Sam."

"Again? What do you mean, Kate? Me and Sam haven't been shopping together in years," Mom stated.

"Oh really?" Kate said, glancing at me. "Sam, should take this one."

Mom gawked my way.

"I should explain but I have dishes to do. Rules of the house!" I said as I gathered up my plate, silverware and cup.

KNIGHT

Mom smiled at Kate. "I'll take it."

Kate smiled back and gave my mom a high five. "You're now my second mom."

Mom smiled and patted Kate's right arm. "Kate, I've loved having you the past few days. You're a wonderful guest, dear."

"Thanks, Denise. I've enjoyed it even more. I can't thank you enough," Kate replied.

"What is going on here? I feel like I've been replaced," I asked.

"Maybe," my mom said as she pointed at the dishwasher. "Wash, Sam, Wash!"

Kate and my mom bursted out laughing.

Dad came inside and gave me my phone. "You're safe for now, Sam. You're welcome!"

"Thanks, Dad!"

Dad sat down to have his breakfast.

I pulled out the second fortune cookie from last night and opened it. *Keep your eye out for someone special.*

Mom asked me where the fortune cookie came from.

"Sushi-ya. I wanted something different for dinner," I said.

"What's it say?" Dad asked, taking a bite of bacon.

I handed dad the little slip of paper.

Kate pointed at Kate. "She's right there. Remember what I told you last night, Sam!"

I looked at Kate and decided I had to tell them all my party tricks. I couldn't keep them in the dark. Besides, I owed Kate an explanation, among many

THE BINGO KILLER

things. She deserved an explanation but over a great dinner.

Chapter 29

Monday, Oct. 20th

9 a.m.

I called the Bloomfield Times, right at the start of business hours and asked for Ms. Rose.

"Savannah Rose, speaking."

"Well, well, well, the traitor has done it again," I said with a laugh.

"Good morning to you too, Sam."

"Listen, I'm not calling to bust your chops and give you shit. We caught The Bingo Killer, who also killed the late-Detective Barker."

"Really? You're not mad or disappointed?" Rose asked.

"I wasn't mad when I saw the paper yesterday. Surprised, yes but not mad. But a lot of people were, Savannah. Chief Williams. Mayor Gibbles. The City Council. Not to mention your readers."

"I see. You're not going to ask for my sources like Detective Barker did?" Rose asked.

I paused and my answer surprised Rose. "No, I don't think I will. Doesn't matter anyway. The headlines are complete lies and it's your credibility, not ours. We found our killer. We've done our job. That's what matters. You can tell me if you want but I'm not going to ask. That's beneath my pay grade."

"Will the suspect be arraigned this week?" Rose asked.

"We're not sharing that information yet. The investigation is on-going," I said.

"I'll keep my sources to myself to play it safe," Rose declared.

"Very well, Savvy Rose," I said.

"Savvy? That's a new one, Sam."

"Just go with it. It's alright."

"If you say so," Rose said. "Anything else, Sam?"

"Any more thoughts on writing your own book of the murders?" I asked.

"I'm thinking about it. The more stories I write, the easier my decision becomes, if that makes sense, Sam."

"Absolutely. I'm glad to hear that. I know you would do a great job with your book."

"Thank you, Sam."

"Alright, Savy. We've got work to do. We'll talk soon.

"We will. Bye, Sam!"

6:30 p.m.

KNIGHT

The phone rang until it was answered, seven rings later.

"Speak, my child," said the slow, low and ominous-toned voice.

"My work is done here. They're all dead as requested. I still serve The Master. Time to start phase two," said the caller.

"Yes, it is so ordered," said The Master.

"Faith in The Master!" said the caller.

"Faith in The Master!" said The Master.

"Faith in The Master!" They both said together.

They both hung up at the same time.

Tuesday, Oct. 21st

6:24 a.m.

A white, four-door van pulled up at the end of the red carpet, under a blue, sunny sky, that stretched to the entrance to the Mackaby Maximum Penitentiary. Two guards dressed in gingerbread men costumes got out and got the prisoner out so he could walk the red carpet up to the main doors. Shackles and chains clinked and clanged back and forth as he stepped out, wearing a bright orange jumpsuit. He stood at the front of the red carpet, to the left of the press and took in all the fame—a relished end to his crime spree. To be the name on everyone's tongue soothed a deep

THE BINGO KILLER

burning desire in his soul for the spotlight. He smiled and laughed like a kid opening presents on Christmas morning.

The guards escorted the prisoner. "Move forward now, maggot," said one guard. He took a step forward and waved both his raised hands as he walked up the red carpet. The reporters and press were behind the velvet rope. He walked close enough to the rope to get the good pictures from the photographers, flashing their lights with a single button. He waved at every person behind the rope, answering the reporters' questions, one by one. The guards actually took the time to let him answer the reporters' questions. It didn't matter if they were ordered to do so or not. He was doing it.

"Why did you commit these murders?" asked one reporter.

He spoke his words but his voice was silent, even though his lips were moving. Oddly enough, the reporter knew exactly what he said and wrote down his answer.

"The Master commanded me to murder them. I didn't want to but I was ordered to. Anything for the Master," the reporter repeated, as she wrote down his answer. He then smiled and laughed.

She continued the interview as she normally would with a follow-up question before he walked away. "Do you feel any remorse for your actions?"

He didn't realize, nor did it bother him, that his voice was silent, when he spoke again. In his mind, he

KNIGHT

genuinely thought he spoke normally and wasn't missing a beat.

"No. I trust The Master with my life and whatever his word is, I accept and believe it. He is my God," he said again, verbatim.

"Come on, dammit! We don't have all day," another guard said sternly.

"Relax dude! I'm working the rope line for my fans," he said.

He walked down the line a few feet until another reporter stopped him.

"What was your motive? Money? Sex? Greed?" asked another reporter.

"The Master said I was settling scores of revenge for him," said the reporter. "There's no higher honor than settling scores for The Master."

He kept moving down the rope line, answering reporters' questions until he answered them all silently, yet loud and clear. He signed autographs, shook hands and posed for pictures all the way down the red carpet. He eventually made it to the front steps where he turned around and waved back at the crowd. "I love you all, my children. Thank you for believing in me. I am the Bingo Killer. It was my great pleasure to put on a show for you all," he said, as tears of happiness fell down his cheek. He blew a kiss to the press as the ginger-guards took him inside to be processed into the jail.

The alarm clock went off.

"That was a great dream. It's good to be alive."

THE BINGO KILLER

Hysterical laughter filled the room.
A minute later—silence.
"Time for work!

Chapter 30

Wednesday, Oct. 22nd

10 a.m.

A well-dressed middle-aged man, wearing a dark suit with short, black hair walked into the BPD. The front-desk receptionist pointed the man to Maureen Downs' desk. The man walked over to Maureen Downs' desk.

"Good morning, I'm Agent Al Dockson with the FBI. I'm here to speak with Chief Williams."

Downs stood up. "Just one moment, please."

Dockson nodded. "Yes ma'am!"

She knocked on the Chief's open door.

Chief Williams waved her in his office.

"Chief, FBI Agent Al Dockson is here to see you."

"Oh, okay," Chief said, perplexed. "That's weird. I wasn't expecting anyone from the FBI." Chief greeted Agent Dockson near Downs' desk with a handshake.

Dockson showed his credentials to the chief.

"Agent Dockson, how can I help you this morning?"

THE BINGO KILLER

"Thanks for meeting me on such short notice, Chief. I wouldn't be here if it wasn't important, as you can imagine" Dockson said.

"Sure, absolutely. Let's go into my office so we can chat."

Agent Dockson nodded and followed Chief to his office and took a seat. "Chief, I'll get right to it. I'm here to pick up one of our witnesses assigned to the witness protection program, Betsy Riddle. She's working here as a janitor," Dockson said.

"Yeah, she's been here for about three years now. I'd hate to lose her. Say what you want about her but she's done a hell of a job here. Great work ethic," Chief said.

"That's good to know. I'll include that in my report."

"Agent Dockson, if I may ask, why are you here to get Betsy? I don't mean to intrude but I'm just curious. For my report anyways!"

"We believe all the media attention and TV cameras that are covering the bingo murders will expose her identity. We're trying to get ahead of all that and get her out safely," Agent Dockson said. "I'm just here following orders."

"I see. That's as good a reason as any. Good timing too, I guess, before the circus comes to town. And there will be a lot of clowns."

"There always are. Yes, sir," Agent Dockson said.

Chief stood up and walked to the door. "Alright, let me go find her right quick."

KNIGHT

"Sure thing, Chief!" Agent Dockson waited for Chief to return.

Chief went to the janitor's closet but didn't see Betsy there. He checked the bathrooms but didn't see her there either. He checked the briefing room and found her cleaning the tables off. He popped in and asked her to be in his office in five minutes.

"Am I in trouble? Did I forget to do something?" Betsy asked.

"No, not at all. Unless you want to be?" Chief laughed and shook his head.

"Yes, sir! I'll be right there," Betsy said.

"Thank you, Betsy!"

Chief went back to his office.

Betsy put her cleaning supply cart back in the janitor's closet. She came into the Chief's office and noticed Agent Dockson sitting in front of the desk.

"Betsy, have a seat for a minute, please."

"Am I in trouble, Chief?" She asked as she slowly sat down.

"No, ma'am. But there will be if we don't get you out of here."

Betsy looked confused in her sudden predicament.

"Betsy, this is Agent Al Dockson. I'll let him explain why he's here," Chief said, as he pointed at Dockson.

"Hi, Ms. Riddle. Like the Chief said, I'm Agent Dockson. I'm here to transfer you to another secure location. We've been monitoring the press from this

THE BINGO KILLER

Bingo Killer case and we feel it's best that we get you out of here before your identity is compromised," Agent Dockson explained.

"You think they'll come for me?" Betsy asked.

"I do. And it won't be pretty this time," Agent Dockson declared.

Betsy looked at Dockson with confusion. "I don't understand. We just up and leave? What about my things? I need to go pack everything up before I leave," she asked.

"We can make a pit stop right quick and let you grab essential items but it has to be quick," Agent Dockson said. "In and out!"

"I'll make it quick. I have things ready to go if I ever had to leave suddenly. I just didn't think it would be this soon. I love it here in Bloomfield." Betsy motioned at the Chief. "Working with you, Chief Williams, was amazing. You were always kind and nice to me. You made this job 10 times better," Betsy declared.

"Well thank you, Betsy. I appreciate that. I'm sorry we have to lose you so soon. You've done one hell of a job for us the past few years. We're going to miss you around here," Chief said.

Agent Dockson looked at Betsy. "The sooner we move, the safer you are, Ms. Riddle"

"I'll go get my stuff and get the keys."

Chief looked at Dockson with curiosity. "If I may ask, Agent Dockson, where are you guys going next?"

Dockson leaned forward. "Well Chief, you know I can't tell you that. It's all classified. I don't even know for sure. I'm just here to take Betsy to our office in St. Louis. That's all I was told to do."

"I see. Well, that's okay. I just wanted to know she'll be just as safe wherever she's going as she was here."

"She will be, Chief. She's in safe hands."

Betsy came into the Chief's office three minutes later and set her keys on his desk. "Here you go, Chief!"

Dockson stood up and shook the Chief's hand. "Ready, Betsy?"

"Agent Dockson, can I say goodbye to some of my friends?" Betsy asked.

"Afraid not. They'll have to wait. We have to make this quick. We can't afford to lose you for obvious reasons, Ms. Riddle."

Chief gave Betsy a hug before she left.

"Thanks for everything, Chief. I really enjoyed my time here, and you as well."

"Likewise. Be good wherever you end up, Betsy."

Chief sat at his desk for a few minutes thinking about all the great conversations he and Betsy had over the years. He eventually emailed the mayor about hiring a new janitor as soon as possible. He didn't give the reason why, except Betsy up and quit without any notice.

Agent Dockson and Betsy got in the car and looked at each other.

Chapter 31

Tuesday, Oct. 28th

5 p.m.

I sat behind my desk all afternoon, finishing reports and other paperwork. The sunshine came through the open blinds and lit up the pit with an orange glow as the sun set. My elbows propped up my weary head and stress-laden shoulders. *Shit, Sam. Tomorrow's the day this whole thing comes undone. A little luck would be nice right now!*

I shuffled papers to one side of my desk when I was done filling them out. *Two weeks and not a damn thing. No better off now than we were before Kate's fake death. That's just great.*

An older gentleman suddenly appeared a few feet away from my desk and walked quietly towards me. "Hello, I'm sorry to bother you," the man asked calmly but with a hint of frustration.

I looked up from my paperwork and saw the man standing beside my desk. *Oscar Tidwell!!!*

Tidwell wore a white dress shirt, unbuttoned three from the top, under a tan, corduroy jacket and black khakis with shiny dress shoes. His hair was combed back.

"Maybe you can help me, young man. Can I talk to you?"

This was not the break I asked for but it'll do I guess.

"Uh...yeah, sure. Have a seat, please," I said.

"Thank you so much. I'm Oscar Tidwell." Tidwell let out a big sigh of relief as he sat down. "I've been walking for hours, trying to get someone to talk to me and you're the first person that even paid me any attention. I need to catch my breath."

"Absolutely. Take your time, Mr. Tidwell," I advised him. "You know this is a police station, right?"

"Oh yes, I know. If anyone could tell me anything, it would be someone here," Tidwell said with a hearty laugh.

"And you made your way back here to me. Well, how can I help you, Mr. Tidwell?" I offered my hand to Oscar and we shook hands. "Nice to meet you, Mr. Tidwell! I'm Detective Sam Riley."

"Likewise. I just want to know what's going on, detective. No one can give me a straight answer," Tidwell explained.

"Well, Mr. Tidwell, I have some news that might be difficult to hear and even understand."

"Just tell me, detective. I've waited long enough," Tidwell asked.

THE BINGO KILLER

"Mr. Tidwell, you passed away a few weeks ago from ingesting a high concentration of caffeine disguised as sugar and or tea," I explained.

Tidwell paused to wrap his head around my explanation. He looked around the room and felt his head. "That's why they ignored me. But you, Mr. Riley, can see me and hear me."

I looked at Tidwell. "Yes, Mr. Tidwell, I can. You're a ghost now, I'm sorry to say."

Tidwell slapped his hands on both his knees in disbelief. "I've led a good life, son. I'm 67 years old and for the first time in my life, I don't have a plan or anything to keep me here," Tidwell said.

"I'm glad to hear that Mr. Tidwell. That's all that matters I guess. Whether or not you are satisfied with how things turned out, that is."

"I am, for the most part," Tidwell said, nodding his head.

I saw Jill Sanders walk into the pit and sneak up behind her father. "Any regrets, Mr. Tidwell?"

"Yeah, one. That I wasn't a good of a father to Jill. That would have made my life better instead of just good, you know? Knowing I raised a great woman. But at least I got to tell her I'm sorry and that I loved her before she passed."

"I'm so sorry for your loss, Mr. Tidwell. I truly am."

Tears fell from Tidwell's eyes, as he sat in silence for a few moments. "Excuse me, detective."

I gave him a tissue but the tears kept coming. He threw the tissue in the trash can next to Kate's desk.

KNIGHT

"Forgive me!"

"It's going to be okay, Mr. Tidwell," I said with a smile.

"You often smile at an old man's pain and misery?" Tidwell asked softly.

"Today I do," I declared with a smile.

Tidwell felt a calm embrace on his left shoulder as Jill made her way around to present herself.

"Hi, dad," Jill said, as she leaned down to look at him with a smile.

"JILL!!" Tidwell said with glee as he lit up. "JILL!"

"Stand up and give your only daughter a hug, old man!"

Tidwell leaped out of the chair. "I'm so happy to see you, Jill!"

"Mr. Riley, my daughter, Jill." Tidwell pointed with gusto.

"We've met before," Jill said. "I met Mr. Riley in the morgue."

"I see." Tidwell's smile vanished as he held back tears once again. "I'm sorry, Jill, that I wasn't there to protect you. I feel this is all my fault," Tidwell said.

I told Tidwell none of this was his fault, nor Jill's fault.

Tidwell looked at Jill as he held her hand.

"Dad, I don't blame you for anything. None of this is your fault. I want you to know that."

Tidwell squeezed Jill's hands tighter and nodded. "Okay, Jill." His guilt never moved an inch.

THE BINGO KILLER

"Why don't I give you two some privacy? Take my seat for a minute or two, Jill," I said as I went to the bathroom and got a drink from the vending machine.

Jill sat down close to her father. "Can I tell you something, dad, and please let me finish before you say anything? This is important to me."

"Speak your heart and truth, Jill. Dad's listening."

Jill smiled and took a deep breath. "One of the hardest things I've had to do is try and make peace with my death. And I don't think anyone can truly be at peace with their death. But I have made peace with what happened between you and mom over the years and the resentment and hostility I had towards you and mom." Jill teared up as she thought of her mother. "It kills me to no end to know my mother is all alone in this world without me and you. I'll never make peace with that."

"I'm so glad you were able to work through all that, Jill. That means so much to me, you telling me that. I hated living with that guilt all these years."

"I'm so sorry I didn't tell you this earlier, dad!"

"It's okay, Jill. I never wanted you to get caught up in things between me and Connie."

"Making peace with everything gave me courage to sing and be on stage and make music a big part of my world. I know you're proud of me, dad!"

"Since the day you were born. The best thing that ever happened to me was being your father, Jill. I mean that with all sincerity."

"You were an amazing father and I'm truly lucky and blessed to call you dad!"

Tidwell teared up again.

"Everything's going to be okay. We have each other. That's all I need. Mr. Riley will deliver our justice. I have faith in him," Jill said.

"How's it going in here," I blurted out as I sat back down at my desk.

"Peaceful, Mr. Riley," Jill said.

"Do you have any children, Mr. Riley?" Tidwell asked.

"No, not yet. Maybe someday. Haven't met the right woman yet."

"I pray you have a daughter one day that is as smart and wonderful as my daughter, Jill Sanders," Tidwell said.

"That's what I pray for too," I said.

"I also pray you never feel the anger and pain of having to bury your daughter," Tidwell said.

"Oscar, were you planning to investigate Jill's murder before you passed away, Mr. Tidwell?" I asked.

"No. I couldn't investigate her death. I couldn't even if I tried. I didn't have the energy or will." Tidwell breathed a sigh of relief and smiled. "My headache is gone. So is my chest pain. Imagine that!"

"Good. Glad to hear that Mr. Tidwell."

"It's Oscar now. Mr. Tidwell sounds like my dad."

"Oscar. That's a good name I must say," I said. "Good name for a boy. If I ever have a son, Oscar is in the mix of names for him. Jill for a girl."

THE BINGO KILLER

"Thank you," Tidwell said, as he paused for a moment. "I guess I better get to spooking some people then, shouldn't I? Perhaps an old acquaintance? Who said being a ghost can't be any fun?"

I laughed. "That's up to you, sir! But good luck!"

"Thank you, Mr. Riley." Tidwell said. "I have faith in you."

I nodded. "Thank you!" *I need it more than you know.*

"Let's get out of here, dad! We can go find a better place to spend our time."

"Bye, Jill. Oscar!" I said.

Tidwell stood up and held Jill's hand, as they walked a few steps away from my desk and disappeared.

I composed myself and got back to work for half an hour until it was time to leave for the day. *At least dinner with Kate should be fun.*

Chapter 32

6 p.m.

I drove to my parents house to talk with my parents and check on Kate. I came inside and saw them sitting at the kitchen table. "Hey, you two. How's it going?"

"Hey Sam. We were just talking about what to make for dinner," mom said.

"I've enjoyed cooking with your mom, Sam. She's taught me a lot I'll be using from now on."

"That's great, Kate. See, my plan worked and was in no way a ploy to get you to cook for me one day."

My mom laughed.

"What? Sam Riley, you didn't just say what I think you just said?" Kate asked.

"Don't worry. Everything goes back to normal tomorrow and we get back to work. So tonight, I thought I'd take you out to a nice dinner."

"I don't think that's a good idea," Kate declared.

"I'm going to take a quick shower so be ready in 30 minutes. You like Italian right, Kate?" I headed for the shower before Kate could answer. "Sure you do." I pointed. "That's on the menu tonight."

"Better get ready, dear," my mom suggested.

THE BINGO KILLER

Kate waited in the kitchen until I came back from showering.

Dad returned from the store with a few ingredients for dinner.

"About time you got out of the shower, Sam. I thought I was going to have to go take a leak outside," dad declared in front of everybody.

"You have another bathroom, Dad."

"I have two bathrooms and I use my bathroom."

Mom and Kate smiled.

"Whatever, Dad. Are you ready to go, Kate?"

"You guys aren't staying for dinner. I bought this stuff."

"No, Sam's taking me out somewhere."

"No, Mr. Two toilets. Have a good evening my lovely parents," I said. "You guys gonna be okay for dinner on your own?"

"Absolutely. Your dad is cooking tonight."

"Right! Well you know how to call 911, Mom," I said.

Dad plopped down in his chair. "We'll go out to eat."

"Speaking of which, our table awaits, Kate." I drove us to the east side of town, to Gino's Italian Restaurant.

"You said you know fine dining so prove it, Kate."

"Ahh Gino's. Great choice, Sam."

"It's the least I could do to show you my appreciation for being such a good sport the past two weeks." I wanted to tell my partner my news, regardless if it affected our professional, working relationship. I parked near the front entrance and opened the door for Kate.

"Welcome to Gino's," said Rick, the evening host, as we made our way inside.

"Table for two, please?" Kate said as we approached the podium.

"Absolutely. Right this way." Rick led us to a table in the middle of the restaurant.

"Excuse me, Rick, do you have something a little more intimate? We need to quietly discuss a private matter," I asked eagerly.

"Absolutely. Please follow me," Rick said.

"Thank you!"

"Nina will be your server this evening. Here she comes now," Rick said, before walking back to the podium.

The tables were laminated with a blue, starry night, glossy finish that complimented the ambiance of the restaurant. We sat down at our secluded, low-lit table by the window, next to the back wall. I couldn't help staring at Kate in our moment to memorize her face into my memories. *Damn, she's beautiful!* I looked around the restaurant. "Nice place here. I've been here once before. I hardly ever eat Italian food, nor Mexican food. Too spicy for me."

"I've been coming here for years. Surprised they haven't named a dish after me or asked me if I wanted something on the menu. Maybe one day," Kate said.

THE BINGO KILLER

"Oh yeah, like what? Barker Bread? Bread with an attitude," I said with a laugh.

"Fuck you," Kate said with a smile and a laugh.

I let out a hearty, genuine laugh. "Don't mind me giving you jabs every now and then. Just means I like you as a person."

"Good to know. I'll have to do the same."

I looked at the menu. "What's good here, Kate?"

"I always get the Spaghetti with sliced grilled chicken on top with a garlic bread basket."

"Hello, I'm Nina. I will be your server tonight. Can I start you off with something to drink?

I ordered a sweet tea with lemon and Kate ordered a glass of Chardonnay.

"Sounds good. I'll bring those right out," Nina said, before leaving the table.

Kate told me she learned so much about me as a kid while staying with my parents.

"Of course they told you about me as a kid," I said. "I can't trust them any more than I trust wild hogs."

"We're working a very dangerous job and trust is important, Sam."

"I totally agree. Trust is absolutely important," I said.

Nina returned with the drinks and placed them on the table. "Have you decided what you want to order?"

"I'll have my usual spaghetti with sliced grilled chicken on top with the garlic bread basket," Kate said.

"Lasagna, I guess. Topped with the powdered cheese stuff."

"Parmesan cheese," Nina and Kate both said simultaneously.

"Yeah, that. Sprinkle it on top, please."

"I'll have those out as soon as I can. Let me know if I can get you anything else," Nina said. Nina took the menus before putting their orders into the kitchen.

"Thank you, Nina!" Kate said.

"She's good. I'll be sure to give her a great tip later on," I said.

"Yeah, she's always been great when she was my server," Kate said.

"I wanted to order before we got down to business," I said.

"Business? What business?" Kate said in wonderment.

"I'll just get right to it. I never answered your questions of what's been going on since we became partners."

"No, you haven't, which I'm very curious to hear by the way." Kate looked at me with curious eyes as she grabbed my hand on the table. "Just tell me. You have nothing to fear. Trust, remember?"

I tapped my leg on the floor out of sheer nervousness before I looked at my partner with my undivided attention. "Okay, here it goes," I said. *Don't lose it now, Sam. Just say it! Say it!* "The psychic rumors about us—well me–are absolutely true. I've had

THE BINGO KILLER

psychic visions since the day we became partners." *There I said it. Secret's out. She's going to think I'm a freak, turn my ass into the Chief for incompetence and never speak to me again.* I looked at her with a serious look. Those few seconds seemed like a month.

Kate was more curious than she was disgusted or disappointed. "What do you mean you're psychic? Are you saying the rumors in the newspaper are true and we knowingly lied to the press? Explain it to me, Sam."

"Yes, the rumors are true. I am a psychic. We lied to the press," I said.

"Good. I didn't care about whether we lied to the press. I care more about you lying to me."

"Me neither and I'm sorry for lying to you, Kate. I have visions of the past. I read people's energies and their memories. And the worst of all, I see, hear and talk to dead people. Ghosts, Kate! I see them and hear them when I shouldn't. When no one else does. They can show up anytime without warning or just walk up to me like someone I know," I explained. I continued with my rundown of everything that happened to me since my powers awoke.

Kate's response really surprised me. "I wouldn't say I'm freaked out, Sam, if that's what you're thinking. I'm concerned about your new ability, believe it or not. Truth is, I am open-minded to the paranormal. I can't say I believe for sure but I can't say I don't either." Kate took another sip of wine. "Tell me what really happened at the morgue," Kate asked.

KNIGHT

"When you walked in and asked who I was talking to, I was talking to Jill Sanders' ghost. She suddenly appeared behind me, said "Boo" over my shoulder, which scared the ever-loving fuck out of me."

Nina walked back to their table. "How are you doing over here? Good, yes?"

My eyes widened and hoped she didn't hear our conversation.

"We're good, Nina. Thank you," Kate said.

"Your food should be out any minute now." Nina said as she walked back towards the kitchen.

"Can't wait, Nina!" I said, taking another drink of his tea. "Damn, this tea is good."

"You were saying?" Kate said.

"Sanders was about to tell me something when you asked me who I was talking with. I looked at you and then back at her but she was gone."

"Sorry I interrupted. Maybe you can ask her the next time you see her," Kate said.

Nina brought their plates and placed each one down in front of them. "Here you go. Those plates are hot so be careful, please."

"Looks delicious. Thank you Nina," I said.

Kate grabbed her fork. "Thank you, Nina."

"You're most welcome. I'll check on you in a few minutes." Nina went to clear a neary table.

"What about when we were standing in Tidwell's closet?" Kate asked.

THE BINGO KILLER

"Oh, that!" I shrugged. "You showed up at the right moment to get my attention, Kate. Mystery is its name. That's all Mystery wants to be called."

"I see. Sam, I have something to tell you as well," Kate said.

"Okay, by all means, please do."

"I saw you on the security cameras in the autopsy room at the morgue the day we went to get Sanders' autopsy results. I saw you moving around like someone scared you and I saw you talking to someone. But I didn't see anyone else there on the screen, besides you."

I looked at Kate with a surprised look. "You saw that?"

Kate put her fork down and leaned back in her chair. "Yeah, I passed the security guard desk in the back and saw you on the screen. I stopped to watch what you were doing. Luckily, I walked back to check on you and Willow caught up with me."

"Did Dr. Willow see it too?" I asked.

"No, I was the only one who saw it."

"Glad he didn't see it. That would have been a problem," I said.

"Yeah, you wouldn't be my partner anymore. You'd be back in a patrol car or working security at the mall. Don't get me wrong, you don't owe me any favors or anything like that. I don't like owing anyone any favors or anyone having something to guilt trip me with," Kate said.

I took a few bites of lasagna as Kate took a sip of Chardonnay. "That's a fair request. I don't like favors either. And thank you for giving me the benefit of the doubt."

"Damn right it is! Honestly, Sam, I think you're a good detective, from what I've seen so far. I know you've worked your ass off to get to sit beside me. I don't want to see you derailed by your sixth sense or whatever you call it and lose everything," Kate said. "That's not a good enough excuse for me to justify sabotaging you. That's not what good partners do for each other."

"I appreciate that. I really do. I'm glad we are partners. For what it's worth, I don't have any hard feelings four years ago when they chose you over me," I said.

"Thank you, Sam. I didn't think there were any hard feelings."

"None," I said as I pointed at her.

We raised our glasses and toasted each other working together.

"Yo man, listen up," Mystery said suddenly, popping up out of thin air next to their table.

I spat my tea out over the floor. "Wow, that's got a kick."

"The powers that be have decided your fate, Sam. Open yourself up to it."

What do you mean, open myself up to it? I looked around the restaurant to admire the decor.

"A fight is coming your way. Be prepared, Mr. Riley."

THE BINGO KILLER

We'll see about that Mystery. Now excuse us, we're in the middle of dinner.

Mystery vanished as quick as he arrived.

"Are you okay, Sam?" Kate asked.

"Fine! Perfectly fine! Thanks for asking." I played Mystery's sudden intrusion off as best I could.

We finished up our food and called Nina over to our table. "That was the best lasagna I've had in a long while, besides my mom's of course," I said.

"The spaghetti here always hits the spot. I try to come once a week so I don't get tired of it."

"I'll take these plates away. How about refills on the tea and Chardonnay?" Nina asked.

"One more glass, please," Kate said.

"Of course!" Nina brought back over a refill of Chardonnay. "Here you go!"

"Thank you," Kate said.

"Can we get the check also," I asked.

"Absolutely."

"Thank you, Nina."

"Maybe we should set some ground rules for when we're together and you see a spirit. Maybe we should have a signal or code word or something, so that I know we're not alone," Kate suggested.

"Casper sounds good."

Kate nodded. "Casper, it is."

Nina brought the check to the table.

"Thank you, Nina. Here's my card, if you will," I said.

"Be right back, Mr. Riley."

"A quick toast to us, Sam," Kate insisted.

"To us, our friendship and partnership!"

Nina came back a minute later.

"Saved by the bill, Kate." I said. "A thirty-dollar tip for Nina. My John Hancock." I looked at my partner. "And we are done here because the night is just beginning." I slid the black check book to the middle of the table. "Alright, let's get out of here."

I paused for a second to look in Kate's eyes once we made it outside Gino's.

"Get in, Kate. I'll drive us home."

"A girl should be so lucky." She said as I opened my truck door. Kate didn't hesitate to do as she was told to do, despite the irony of a veteran detective with years of experience taking orders from a rookie partner with only a few weeks experience.

"Good girl," I said, as I looked into her eyes.

Kate smiled.

8:30 p.m.

"Thank you for dinner, Mr. Riley."

"You're most welcome, Ms. Barker," I said as I pulled out of Gino's parking lot.

"I do have something to say about us and tonight. And this is a rule I never break. During working hours, we keep things professional—no flirting, no kissing, no holding hands, no inappropriate texting. Department's rules. Not mine. Those rules we must follow while on duty. Last thing we need are violations for affection with a co-worker on our records," Kate said.

"I'll follow your rules if you follow mine."

"I'm serious, Sam!" She said sternly.

I smirked and glanced at Kate but was interrupted when I saw a patrol car in my rearview mirror. "Get down now, please,"

"What?"

"Quick, Kate. Duck down in your seat. There's another patrol car behind us. I don't want them to see us together and we get in trouble."

Kate leaned forward in her seat as far as she could.

I pulled up to the light just as it turned red. A few seconds later, a patrol car pulled up beside them, in the turning lane. I looked over, smiled and waved as I rolled down my window. Luckily, the officers in the car couldn't see Kate.

"Evening Detective Riley. That's going to take some getting used to," Officer Wheeler said.

"Evening Wheeler. How are you fellas doing tonight?" I asked.

"Good and you?" asked Officer Sweeney.

"Meanie Sweeney! It's been a great evening so far but I have to get home and do some maintenance work."

"Been slow since shift change but we might get a speeder or two tonight," Sweeney said.

"I hear that. I've had plenty of those nights, believe me. I'm glad for those slow nights.

KNIGHT

"My condolences to you for Detective Barker's tragic passing last week. She was a great member of our department. Damn fine detective!" said Wheeler.

"Yeah, she'll be missed. She was a great partner. Every time I see Cheez-Its, I'll think of her and buy a few boxes. Cheesy Kate!" I said.

What did he just say? Kate quietly unbuckled my seat belt, retracting over to my left side, with a loud thud.

Kate smiled.

"Whoa, shit!! Would you look at that! Damn seat belt came undone on me." I plugged the seatbelt back in. "Safety first. I'll have to get this fixed tomorrow."

The light turned green.

"See you boys later. Have a good night. Stay safe!" I turned right and kept on going towards my home.

Wheeler looked at Sweeney eagerly. "You think he knows we saw her duck down before we stopped?" Sweeney asked.

"No. Not a chance," Wheeler said, shaking his head.

"Let's not say anything. Let them have their fun," Sweeney said.

Barker sat back up. "You unbuckled my seatbelt!"

"Yeah, what are you gonna do about it?" Kate asked.

"I don't know. Haven't decided yet but I better because I'm almost home."

"Oh really?" She smiled and laughed.

THE BINGO KILLER

I pulled into my garage a few minutes later. "Come inside, Kate. Make yourself at home."

Kate walked into the kitchen through the garage door.

I could tell she was surprised when she saw my house. "This is my place. It's not much but it works for me." My shelves full of Ghostbusters toys, memorabilia and other toys from different movies caught her eye more than anything, as she walked into the living room. A row of bookcases lined the walls near the television. Books from all kinds of subjects on my shelves, as well as one tall bookcase next to it that held his massive DVD collection. I set up a few tables in one of the spare bedrooms that had all of my other toys he collected over the years, including vintage signs and lego sets. One big nerd cave, basically.

"Let me show you my toy room," I said, as I led Kate down the hallway. I opened the door, flipped on the light and walked inside. "What do you think?"

Kate peaked her head inside before moving in for a closer look. "Wow, you're a bigger nerd than I thought, Sam. This explains so much."

"Yeah, well nerds do it better. We take our time and get it right the first time. Details matter. I'm paraphrasing Louis Skulnick, from "Revenge of the Nerds," of course. Our King!"

Kate laughed so hard she had tears in her eyes. "I'm going to wet myself. Holy Shit, that was too funny."

KNIGHT

"What? You better be careful, you're in danger of sleeping on the couch."

"Ohh, poor baby!" Kate said with a pout, as she looked at me.

"You know what. Couch! That's my rule," I said with a smile.

I took her hand, turned off the light and led her back to the living room.

"Oh, your rule, huh? I get it. You want some alone time with your ghost friends. Well, don't let me stop you. Besides, I don't want to sleep on Minecraft or Star Wars bed sheets anyway. The couch will do just fine."

"Guess so. The Force will be with me, in my bed."

Kate smiled and laughed. "Good, then the Force can keep you warm."

"Funny, Kate," I said. I pointed towards the hallway. "Bathroom is down the hallway there. My bedroom is past it, on the right." I walked to my bedroom and got a blanket off the chair and a pillow from my bed. "Here. This should suffice for tonight."

"Oh, you weren't kidding, Sam. Thanks!" Kate said, a bit disappointed.

"Sorry, I don't have a set of pajamas or a change of clothes. Well, I do but you won't want them. You can sleep in one of my cotton shirts if you dare."

"That might work. I'll take it," she said.

I walked to the laundry room and got one of my nerd-shirts for Kate. "Star Wars, Star Trek, Super Mario Brothers, Ghostbusters? Take your pick, Kate."

THE BINGO KILLER

"Are you serious? That's all you have?"

"I don't wear women's clothes, Kate."

Kate stared back at me with knowing eyes.

"Fine!" I handed her a Star Wars shirt. "Here you go. Sweet dreams, Kate. May the—"

"No, Sam! Goodnight." Kate said.

"I'll shower in the morning before I take you home to change work clothes. Or you can drop me off at the station, go home, change and come back. However you want to do it," I said.

"Okay, we'll figure it out I'm sure," Kate said.

"Goodnight, Kate," I said as I staggered off to my room.

"Goodnight, Sam."

I showered and got ready for bed but I had trouble falling right asleep. I couldn't stop thinking about our evening. *Dinner was nice. Sweet of him to pay. The flirting was wonderful. Definitely a turn on. I felt like a lady for the first time in years. I wasn't lonely for the first time in years. I felt seen and heard. Like I was special and mattered to someone. It's always been work, work, work for years to get where I'm at in my career.* I sighed as I rubbed my forehead. *I said I wouldn't break my rule of dating anyone in law enforcement, much less a detective I'm working with. Too much to risk without a guaranteed return on my investment. I can't throw everything away for him or anyone. What if it doesn't work out? What if it does? I hate this. It's not fair. If those other women can have a family and a job, I should be free to have a career with absolutely no regrets.*

I rejoiced in knowing Sam cared about me enough to see I had a warm and comfortable place to stay the night. I'm grateful for him. I turned on my right side and faced the television and coffee table. I eventually fell asleep as it had been a long day.

******

I didn't close my bedroom door all the way, in case Kate needed something and found herself in my bed by accident when I woke up, although I wasn't too worried about her crawling into my bed. We both made our rules crystal clear. Kate on the couch and me in my blue, silky sheets. I thought about her lying on the couch alone instead of the other way around. *Was it rude of me to not offer her my bed? But it is my bed and my rule is that no one I work with sleeps in my bed with me. The question is, is she worth breaking that rule for? It shouldn't be this tough, let alone me, and her, even being in this position.*

I thought about whether I should tap into her energy and sense what she's thinking about me at that very moment, out there on that couch, alone. Normally, I wouldn't hesitate but I was really torn with this one. *No, I respect her too much and it sets me on a dangerous path between us. Our working relationship would fall apart so quickly if I did. She wouldn't trust me anymore. Probably have me reassigned or transferred to another department somewhere, if I mind-spied on her. She means too much to me. But I can't stop my feelings. I feel how I feel and*

THE BINGO KILLER

deserve to be happy. Then again, I just made detective, which is a blessing in itself. I can't throw that away for a one night stand with my partner. I'll never get a chance and I'll lose any chance I have with her. It's a huge gamble though if it doesn't work out between us. We become strangers that work together. Is she even into me? What if I make a move and she shoots me down? What if she doesn't? Maybe I'm overthinking this and should let things play out naturally without using my powers to sway things this way or that way. I checked my email, played around on Facebook. Nothing too social. If I wanted to be social, I'd be social with my house guest. I fell asleep around 9:30 and slept for a few hours at least.

Chapter 33

Wednesday, Oct. 29

I dreamed of a beautiful woman on stage, under the spotlight. She sang and looked right at me as I was the only person in the audience. No music or instruments. Just her heavenly voice—calm, warm and inviting. I felt the soul in her voice and never felt more at peace when I heard her voice, in that dream, than anything I ever heard. She sang the entire song for me. I didn't know the song but was mesmerized by her voice nonetheless. Her lyrics resonated with my soul, as chills rose up my back. Suddenly, the lights turned off and she disappeared right in front of his eyes. The doors to the club opened and suddenly, I was whisked away outside to the front of the club where I saw a row of Marquee signs with her name on them. Jill Sanders: One Night Only!

Around 3:17 a.m. in the morning, I awoke from this dream, in a sweat. I forgot to turn on the fan beside my bed. I looked around the room and saw a glowing white light through the blinds of the bedroom window.

THE BINGO KILLER

What the hell is going on out there? They better not be messing up my backyard. I turned my head back and saw Jill Sanders, standing in the doorway.

"Oh shit, Jill? What are you doing in my house? How do you know where I live?"

She didn't say anything. She turned and slowly walked through the house.

I got my shoes on and followed her through the house. "Jill, where are you? Where did you go, girl?" I whispered quietly. I saw Jill standing by the back patio door.

"Come with me, Sam," she said as she walked through the sliding glass door and into the backyard.

I left the patio door open, not wanting to wake Kate up.

She stopped just short of the fence, a few feet, and turned around. Not even the last shades of moonlight, before the storm clouds rolled in, could illuminate her soul at that moment. The air was still and calm. Peaceful.

I felt exactly how I did in my dream, which seemed a bit too real for me. "Jill, what are you doing? What's going on?" I took a step towards her and she took one step towards me.

Suddenly, she was on a well-lit dance floor outside. Strings of lights hung from tall wooden poles around the dance floor, like an outdoor dance at night. The sudden vision all aglow left me mesmerized once again. That calm and peaceful feeling washed over me again.

KNIGHT

"Come here, Sam. I have a few things to share with you." She said as she walked towards the old-timey microphone in the center of the floor. Seeing Jill behind the microphone reminded me of a young Marilyn Monroe-type on stage.

I walked closer to her as the microphone disappeared into thin air. She walked closer to me also. "What can I do for you, Jill Sanders?"

"Dance with me, Detective. Time's almost up!"

I took her hand and she followed my lead. She sighed in happiness and she pulled me closer, as we danced to soft, jazzy piano music. "Don't be spooked, Detective. Call it intuition but I had a feeling you were dreaming of me and here I am. I don't know how it works exactly but I'm glad I'm here with you," Jill said.

"I was hoping I would see you again, even if it's for the last time. You're the first ghost I saw and spoke with. I'll never forgive you. I'll keep a picture of you on my desk as a reminder to never let Jill Sanders down," I said.

Jill looked up at me and smiled, as we continued to dance silently around the dancefloor. "Why couldn't I have found this when I was alive? Why now, when I'm dead? Doesn't seem fair at all."

"I wish I could give you an honest answer, Jill, but nothing I say will ever make sense. Best I can do is say this is one of the happiest moments of my life so far."

"That's more than enough for me, Mr. Riley. More than enough!"

THE BINGO KILLER

A tear fell from my eye at the joy she found with me. I put my arms around her and drew her in closer. She felt a tear on her arm as she danced with me. "That felt magical. Who knew a single tear could change someone so profoundly?" Jill asked.

"I try not to question matters of the heart. Just let fate have its way. Experience them as they come. The good and the bad. That's what life is about, I think."

We continued to dance, like star-crossed lovers, meeting for the first time by time travel.

"Can I ask you something, Jill? I never had the chance, nor had the nerve too, out of respect but please don't think bad of me. Do you forgive your killer?"

"You know, I've been trying to make peace with my death, ever since that day we first met in the morgue, but it's not easy. Did I have something to do with it? Could I have done more? Should I have paid more attention? That's what will haunt me in my thoughts forever."

"No, Jill! None of this is your fault. Not at all. You didn't ask for your life to end."

"You know, Mr. Riley, I had a dream once where I died on stage after finishing my last song of my last performance. Just dropped dead on the stage. Before I died, I felt the happiest I had ever felt in my life. My life began on stage with my first performance and ended on stage with my last. And to be honest, I would have preferred that when I'm 70, not 30." Jill looked out at the yard. "But no, I don't forgive my killer. How can I? He took my life. I had so much music left to give the world. It's almost like a curse, you know."

I felt an extreme sadness for Jill and the unique talent she possessed. I truly realized the importance and the impact of my work. *She deserved much better and I'm going to find her killer.*

"Your way of thinking about life, your life, definitely changes after death. What you should have done? Regrets? How precious every second is. How it's our responsibility to make the most of it. All of that. We take time for granted, that's for sure."

"I agree, Jill."

"Damn, I never thought I'd get used to a man saying my name the way you did just now. Why couldn't I have met you when I was alive?" She laughed and looked away from me. "I can't believe I just said that."

"Good question to ask Ms. Sanders. I wish I could have seen you perform on stage just one time. You looked like an angel on that stage in my dream," I said.

"Well, I hope singing was all I was doing in your dream," she said with a laugh.

I laughed too. "I promise you it's just a dance. Best way to remember you, Jill."

"I agree, Detective Riley. Have you found my killer yet?"

"Not yet, but we're really close. We solved the ciphers we got from the killer. Didn't tell us much. Just chasing a ghost, with all due respect, Jill. Maybe

THE BINGO KILLER

that's what the killer wanted all along—for us to chase ghosts."

"I won't lie. I honestly thought my killer would be behind bars by now. But I do have faith in you and the other detective."

"Well thank you. And you mean Kate Barker?" I said.

"Well sure, if that's her name! She likes you, ya know!" Jill said.

"No she doesn't." I skipped telling Jill that I faked Kate's death to catch her killer.

"Oh yes, she does. Then again, maybe she doesn't. You're the detective. You know best. I'm sure your people and observation skills are top notch, Mr. Holmes," Jill said with a smile.

"Yeah, I'm not her type."

"How do you know that? Is she your type?" Jill asked.

"Well....."

"Are you saying that because she's your partner and you're trying to keep things professional? Or are you genuinely curious now?"

I smiled from embarrassment but looked at Jill, "I—"

"Exactly. Remember, I'm a ghost. A good ghost but still a ghost. I, too, can play detective, even better than you, in fact. I'm invisible. I am the fly on the wall, Mr. Riley."

"Again, fair point. Which is what exactly?"

"She likes you, Mr. Riley."

"She's glad you're her partner in trying to solve my murder. Dinner at your parents house was the most fun she had in a long while."

"Yeah, that was a good night and I enjoyed her company. She's easy to talk to."

"I got the sense she felt like she belonged there like she was a family member. I wish I could have tasted those pork chops."

"She said that?"

"She doesn't have to. I see what you don't see. During working hours. She's wearing a different perfume. Smiles at you, laughs at your jokes. She asks your opinion on stuff. She asks if you've eaten."

"Oh. I thought she was being nice. Shows what I know, not that I was looking for anything beyond a working relationship." I said as I twirled her around.

"Not much, Mr. Riley."

I shrugged my shoulders in agreement. "Guess not!"

"So what are you going to do?"

"About what? Kate? The Bingo Killer?"

"Your partner, Kate, Mr. Riley. Don't pass up an opportunity of having a good woman in your life. And yes, there are good women out there. Not all of us are bad."

"I don't know why you're telling me this but I'm focusing on my career and balancing this new gift I have that I didn't ask for, by the way."

THE BINGO KILLER

"Oh, you definitely have a gift, Mr. Riley. A few if you ask me. Use them wisely and don't let your talents spoil like milk."

"True enough I guess."

"You don't have the luxury of guessing or coincidences, Mr. Riley."

More tears fell from her eyes and onto my arms as I held her as close to me as I could. "My one regret, Mr. Riley, is not knowing a man's love, if even for a second. I was always too busy in the spotlight. That's where I truly felt like I belonged. I felt safe there. I was home on that stage. At peace, even. That's all that mattered. I figured I had plenty of time to settle down in my 30's." More tears fell from her eyes.

"I'm truly and terribly sorry for what happened to you. The world is a bit darker without your light in it," I said.

"Now, I guess I'll be a singer in God's choir, if he'll have me."

"Why would you think he wouldn't?"

"I'm humbled by your faith in the universe, Sam."

"Well, I'm sure he has a special place for you to sing, next to all the other angels. Or maybe he'll send your spirit back to Earth one day and grace us again with your voice and music."

"The world should be so lucky, Mr. Riley."

"God's miracle, Ms. Sanders."

"Ever feel like you don't fit in anywhere or with anyone? Ever feel like you are born to stand out, Mr. Riley?"

"No, never gave it much thought. I just went with the flow and did my own thing. I never got caught up in finding the right crowd or clicks or any of that mess."

"Well, aren't you a rebel, Mr. Riley? Tell me dear, what's your first name?"

"How about you call me Rebel Riley?"

"Come now, Mr. Riley, you wouldn't deprive a charming, Southern woman the pleasure of knowing your real name in the afterlife forever? There is no greater injustice, besides my murder of course."

"Samuel Eugene Riley. Sam for short."

She looked up into my brown eyes as I looked into her baby blue eyes. "Samuel Riley," Jill said. "What a beautiful name for such a good and noble man."

A moment of silence passed as I smiled.

"Your momma named you just right. And I shall miss mine very much. No parent should outlive their child. Detective Riley, promise me something. Find my mother, Connie Sanders, and tell her one thing for me, will you, please Sir?"

"I promise I'll tell her anything and everything you want me to, Jill."

"Tell her to take care of the cardinals. She gets lonely at times. She knows what it means."

"Consider it done," I said. "What's the story of the red bird, if I may ask?"

"You don't know about the cardinal and its meaning, do you Mr. Riley?

THE BINGO KILLER

"No, I don't."

"Cardinals are said to be the spirits of loved ones, who have passed on, coming to check on those who they loved in life. Sometimes they land and stay on fences or in birdhouses near those loved ones. Maybe I'll learn to fly myself."

"That sounds wonderful," I said.

We smiled at each other. A white light shined down behind us as a warm, calm sensation flowed over the both of us. Jill looked back at the light for a few seconds and then back at me. "Time for me to go now, Mr. Riley. It's been a pleasure of a lifetime, dancing and talking with you one last time. One that I shall always remember."

"That it has, Ms. Sanders. There's no way you could forget me."

Jill held my hand for a split second, smiled and walked away just as quickly. She walked a few feet away, almost into the light but stopped and turned around to have one good look at me. "Goodbye, Sam! Be sure to find my mother and tell her what I said. Until we meet again," Jill said calmly. She turned around confidently and disappeared into the light.

"Goodbye, Jill!" The stage and lights suddenly disappeared and everything turned back into the darkness of the night, although the same calm and peaceful mood stayed with me. I looked down for a moment in temporary sadness when it hit me that Jill Sanders was gone forever.

Chapter 34

8:30 a.m.

"Sam, wake up. Wake up," Kate said, jostling me about my bed. "Sam, time to go to work." Kate shook me again.

I finally opened my eyes and looked around.

Kate stood next to my bed. "Sam, get your ass up!"

"I'm up! I'm up." I threw the covers over me and out of bed and stretched.

"Oh, while I'm thinking about it, what were you doing in the backyard in the middle of the night? Sleepwalking?"

"I'll tell you in the car."

Kate nodded. "Okay!"

I went to the hall closet and got a towel. After my shower, I got dressed in my favorite, comfortable Khakis and a short sleeved, light blue, button-up shirt. I grabbed my blue blazer and headed into the living room. Kate waited for me on the couch.

"Alright Kate. You turn. You'll have to shower and wear the same clothes from yesterday or shower

THE BINGO KILLER

and wear my bathrobe & shoes to your place to change. Just give me my robe back. I like it."

"I'll be quick, I promise. We'll go by my place afterwards."

"Okay." Ten minutes later, she came back into the living room with my Star Wars robe on. She looked at me in disappointment. "Really? Star Wars? You don't have a regular looking robe like most men your age?"

I won't lie. Kate looked great with my robe on. "May the Force be with you, Kate."

She rolled her eyes and sighed. "Nerd!!"

"Always!"

"Nice place, by the way. Cleaner than I imagined it would be. I figured you were more on the nerd, cosplayer side," Kate said.

"Thanks. I love my nerd palace."

She smiled at me. "We better get to work." She grabbed her clothes and wadded them into a ball.

"Kate, you drive. I don't know the way to your house," I said as I handed her my keys.

I closed the garage door as she backed down the driveway to my mailbox. I hadn't checked my mail in a few days, which was normal for me. I grabbed the mail and looked through it all one by one. "Water bill, auto insurance statement, coupons, junk mail, unknown small package. Same old shit, different day." I carefully opened the package and read the letter. "Dear Mr. Riley, if you're reading this, there's a good chance you and your partner either caught me or I escaped scott free. Either way, you, Detective Riley, you've been a formidable opponent in this game of chance, logic and luck but you were too predictable. Maybe you've watched too much television of wishful thinking and looking for a lucky break? I applaud your efforts to put the cuffs on me. It was fun. Now let's take this show on the road. Catch me if I let you? Better luck this next time. Signed, The Bingo Killer." *This guy's definitely taunting me. It's personal, now.*

I sat in silence, stunned I would get such a letter. I was more concerned with the fact the killer sent a letter to my home, rather than what was actually in the letter. My anger built into a rage that I didn't catch the Bingo Killer. *He's playing with us. Son of a bitch got away with it.* I noticed a small box with something rattling around inside it.

I opened it, "Oh shit, it's Nettles' thumb. That asshole sent me George's thumb. HOLY SHIT!!"

Kate stopped at a red light and glanced over at me holding the small box. "That's creepy. Something out of a Hannibal Lecter movie. It's a cat and mouse game with this guy now that he has your address," Kate said.

"Yeah, tell me about it. Why send it to me at home and not here at the station?"

We both endured the silence for a minute or two as the heaviness of the letter and impact on their investigation became very clear. Reading the letter no doubt stung me to my core. Kate was more focused on catching the killer instead of dwelling on personal vendettas and sentimental feelings, like I was. I wasn't sure if I should be glad we covered both emotion and logic and in reverse, no less.

"Chief's gonna shit a brick when he sees this letter," Kate declared.

"Let's not tell him just yet. We can still catch this guy, Kate," I stated.

"How, Sam? We have no leads. No clear evidence. Three deceased victims. A bunch of riddles from a Zodiac wannabe that's gotten us nowhere. More questions than answers," Kate said.

"I know. But now, it's time to do things my way. Dig a little deeper. The answers are always there if we know how and where to look," I said.

"What exactly do you mean by doing things your way?" Kate asked.

"Let's just get back to the station and I'll talk to the Chief. Maybe I can convince him to take the gloves off."

"No, Sam. I want to know. I need to know what the hell you mean by that?"

"All I'm saying is I'll have to mind-dive into the evidence a little. Read them with my energy. Maybe get some hidden clues and get results to lock them away."

""Mind-dive?" Have you ever done that with anyone?"

"The Chief but he was chewing my ass out about a bad headline and he needed convincing I really had my gift. Nothing like what we did. Hell, his mother was in the room also."

"No shit!! You don't say." Kate stated. *Glad I wasn't there*.

"Nope!"

"Anyway, it's one thing to mind-dive into someone's energy to find information relevant to our police work but anything else is a violation of the right to privacy. We're talking about a person's free will here. Wouldn't hold up in court no matter how you spin it. No lawyer would be dumb enough to take it before the judge and a jury."

"You know, you're the third person that's told me that," I said.

"Maybe you ought to listen instead of being all John Wayne about it all. I know you want to solve the case but do it legally." *Can't believe we're even having this conversation right now.*

Because you care about me! You like having me as a partner. I said to Kate in a whimsical voice.

She swerved the truck into the other lane but quickly jerked us back into our lane. "STOP SAM!!!" She yelled out. "Almost made me wreck your truck."

I laughed. "Easy, Kate. Just because I have insurance doesn't mean I want to use it. Besides, you're wearing your seatbelt."

Kate looked at me angrily.

I laughed at how cute she was when she was mad. "Gotcha, Kate!"

"Okay, new rule. No reading my thoughts unless I give you permission. Understand me?"

THE BINGO KILLER

"Oh come on, you're taking all the fun away," I declared.

"I'm serious, Sam! You haven't seen me mad but you will," Kate asserted.

"Okay, fine. Let's just get to your place so you can change and we can get to the pit."

"Almost there, Sam!" Kate drove up to her duplex and parked out front.

"I'll be right back." She got her clothes and purse from the backseat and headed inside to change.

I sat in the truck and read the letter a few times. I focused my energy on the letter to see if I could get a reading on or any visions of the letter. *Come on, show me something. I need this to prove everyone wrong.* As much as I tried, I couldn't get anything of evidentiary value.

"Nothing!!" I angrily put the letter back in the envelope. I rubbed my forehead, then my beard in confusion. I sighed and looked out the window.

Kate finally came out in black pants and a white shirt, with blue stripes. Hair in a ponytail. Firearm on her right side and badge on the left side of her belt. *Damn, she's fucking hot the way she walked out here. Woman on a mission.*

Ten minutes later, we walked through the front door and towards the pit.

I threw the letter on my desk, put a rubber band around my other mail and stashed it in a side drawer for later.

Kate sat down and opened up a box of Cheez-Its on the side of her desk. We both had L-shaped desks for more space and work efficiency.

KNIGHT

I got all the ciphers, the bingo card and looked at this final letter. I tried to get a reading on every single cipher and the bingo card but again, came up short. *Fuck, that's not good. Can't catch a break. Maybe I can't read objects and things. Only people.* "Nothing on this other evidence, Kate."

"That doesn't surprise me. Whoever this guy is, he covered his tracks very well."

"Yes he did. Too well, I'm fact. Very meticulous and methodical. The dice ciphers alone are a new one for me. He made it weird but easy enough. Just had to take the time to solve it," I said.

"Yeah. With all this technology at our disposal, we still come up short. He kept it simple. Pen and paper. He could have bought those anywhere, any time. Waste of our time to track down paper and pen leads," Kate stated.

We continued going through all the evidence for the next hour. Talking them all over. Piece by piece. Trying to find a hidden connection or clue. I took the letter and thumb box to the Chief's office. I handed him the letter. "Chief, I got this in the mail this morning when I checked my mailbox before coming into work. The killer sent it, postmarked Little Rock. He must be heading west."

"Alright, I'll take a look." Chief read the letter and agreed that it was a thanks-for-playing letter. "The killer is taunting you, Sam. All condescension. No substance."

"That's not all Chief."

THE BINGO KILLER

"Inside that box is George Nettles' thumb."

Chief looked at me with a shocked face.

"He sent me his thumb, Chief!" I asserted. "I don't know if it's a souvenir, a warning or an invitation. I'll have to give it to Kara Carlson to run forensics on it."

"Do that Sam. Let me know."

"Sure thing, Chief!" I paid Cara Karlson a visit.

FBI Agent Perry Gillham walked into the Bloomfield Police Department and went straight to Chief Williams office to retrieve his assignment. Chief sat in his chair, turned sideways, looking out at the officers doing their work and the conference room.

Gillham knocked on the Chief's door. "Chief Williams, Agent Gillham, FBI."

"Yes, Agent Gilbert."

"It's Gillham. Agent Gillham."

"My mistake. Hearing has been a little off lately." Chief got up and shook Gillham's hand. "How can I help you, Agent Gillham?"

Gillham presented his badge and credentials. "I'm here under orders from Washington to retain custody of Betsy Riddle. I understand she was working undercover here as a janitor, as part of the witness relocation program."

Chief looked over at Gillham with a confused and shocked look on his face. "You must be bullshittin' me. One of your people came here and picked her up a week ago today."

Silence between the Chief and Gillham was deafening as the two men stared at each other, waiting for the other to blink.

To Be Continued…

Milton Keynes UK
Ingram Content Group UK Ltd.
UKHW021014061024
449204UK00011B/599